MARY BARTON:

MARY BARTON:

A TALE OF MANCHESTER LIFE.

BY

MRS. GASKELL

GYAN

Published by

Gyan Publishing House
5, Ansari Road
Daryaganj, New Delhi-110002
Phone: 011-47034999, 9811692060
E-mail: books@gyanbooks.com

Distribution Network
gyanbooks.com
India, USA, Canada, UK, Australia

ISBN: 978-81-212-8446-2 (HB)
First Published, 1848

2nd Impression 2024

Printed at: Gyan Press, Delhi.

MARY BARTON
Author: MRS. GASKELL

MARY BARTON

A

TALE OF MANCHESTER LIFE.

LEIPZIG

BERNH. TAUCHNITZ JUN.

1849.

" 'How knowest thou,' may the distressed Novel-wright exclaim, 'that I, here where I sit, am the Foolishest of existing mortals; that this my Long-ear of a fictitious Biography shall not find one and the other, into whose still longer ears it may be the means, under Providence, of instilling somewhat?' We answer, 'None knows, none can certainly know: therefore, write on, worthy Brother, even as thou canst, even as it is given thee.' "

CARLYLE.

„Nimm nur, Fährmann, nimm die Miethe,
Die ich gerne dreifach biete!
Zween, die mit mir überfuhren,
Waren geistige Naturen.“

PREFACE.

THREE years ago I became anxious (from circumstances that need not be more fully alluded to) to employ myself in writing a work of fiction. Living in Manchester, but with a deep relish and fond admiration for the country, my first thought was to find a frame-work for my story in some rural scene; and I had already made a little progress in a tale, the period of which was more than a century ago, and the place on the borders of Yorkshire, when I bethought me how deep might be the romance in the lives of some of those who elbowed me daily in the busy streets of the town in which I resided. I had always felt a deep sympathy with the care-worn men, who looked as if doomed to struggle through their lives in strange alternations between work and want; tossed to and fro by circumstances, apparently in even a greater degree than other men. A little manifestation of this sympathy, and a little attention to the expression of feelings on the part of some of the work-people with whom I was acquainted, had laid open to me the hearts of one or two of the more thoughtful among them; I saw that they were sore and irritable against the rich, the even tenor of whose seeming happy lives appeared to increase the anguish caused by the lottery-like nature of their own. Whether the bitter complaints made by them, of the neglect which they experienced from the prosperous — especially from the masters whose fortunes they had helped to build up — were well-founded or no, it is not for me to judge. It is enough to say, that this belief of the injustice and unkindness which they endure from their fellow-creatures, taints what might be resignation to God's will, and turns it to revenge in too many of the poor uneducated factory-workers of Manchester.

The more I reflected on this unhappy state of things between those so bound to each other by common interests, as the employers and the employed must ever be, the more anxious I became to give some utterance to the agony which, from time to time, convulses this dumb people; the agony of suffering without the sympathy of the happy, or of erroneously believing that such is the case. If it be an error, that the woes, which come with ever-returning tide-like flood to overwhelm the workmen in our manufacturing towns, pass unregarded by all but the sufferers, it is at any rate an error so bitter in its consequences to all parties, that whatever public effort can do in the way of legislation, or private effort in the way of merciful deeds, or helpless love in the way of "widow's mites," should be done, and that speedily, to disabuse the work-people of so miserable a misapprehension. At present they seem to me to be left in a state, wherein lamentations and tears are thrown aside as useless, but in which the lips are compressed for curses, and the hands clenched and ready to smite.

I know nothing of Political Economy, or the theories of trade. I have tried to write truthfully; and if my accounts agree or clash with any system, the agreement or disagreement is unintentional.

To myself the idea which I have formed of the state of feeling among too many of the factory-people in Manchester, and which I endeavoured to represent in this tale (completed above a year ago), has received some confirmation from the events which have so recently occurred among a similar class on the Continent.

OCTOBER, 1848.

MARY BARTON:

A TALE OF MANCHESTER LIFE.

CHAPTER I.

"Oh! 't is hard, 't is hard to be working
The whole of the live-long day,
When all the neighbours about one
Are off to their jaunts and play.

There's Richard he carries his baby,
And Mary takes little Jane,
And lovingly they 'll be wandering
Through field and briery lane."

MANCHESTER SONG.

There are some fields near Manchester, well known to the inhabitants as "Freen Heys Fields," through which runs a public footpath to a little village about two miles distant. In spite of these fields being flat, and low, nay, in spite of the want of wood (the great and usual recommendation of level tracts of land), there is a charm about them which strikes even the inhabitant of a mountainous district, who sees and feels the effect of contrast in these common-place but thoroughly rural fields, with the busy, bustling manufacturing town, he left but half an hour ago. Here and there an old black and white farm-house, with its rambling outbuildings, speaks of other times and other occupations than those which now absorb the population of the neighbourhood. Here in their seasons may be seen the country business of hay-making, ploughing, &c., which are such pleasant mysteries for towns-people to watch; and here the artisan, deafened with noise of tongues and engines, may come to listen awhile to the delicious sounds of rural life: the lowing of cattle, the milk-maid's call, the clatter and cackle of poultry in the old farm-yards. You cannot wonder, then, that these fields are popular places of resort at every holiday time; and you would not wonder, if you could see, or I properly describe, the charm of one particular style, that it should be, on such occasions, a crowded halting-place. Close by it is a deep, clear pond, reflecting in its dark green depths the shadowy trees that bend over it to exclude the sun. The only place where its banks are shelving is on the side next to a rambling farm-yard, belonging to one of those old-world, gabled, black and white houses I named above, overlooking the field through which the public footpath leads. The porch of this farm-house is covered by a rose-tree; and the little garden surrounding it is crowded with a medley of old-fashioned herbs and flowers, planted long ago, when the garden was the only druggist's shop within reach, and allowed to grow in scrambling and wild luxuriance — roses, lavender, sage, balm (for tea), rosemary, pinks and wall-flowers, onions and jessamine, in most republican and indiscriminate order. This farm-house and garden are within a hundred yards of the stile of which I spoke, leading from the large pasture field into a smaller one, divided by a hedge of hawthorn and black-thorn; and near this stile, on the further side, there runs a tale that primoses may often be found, and occasionally the blue sweet violet on the grassy hedge bank.

I do not know whether it was on a holiday granted by the masters, or a holiday seized in right of nature and her beautiful spring time by the workmen, but one afternoon (now ten or a dozen years ago) these fields were much thronged. It was an early May evening — the April of the poets; for heavy showers had fallen all the morning, and the round, soft, white clouds which were blown by a west wind over the dark blue sky, were sometimes varied by one blacker and more threatening. The softness of the day tempted forth the young green leaves, which almost visibly fluttered into life; and the willows, which that morning had had only a brown reflection in the water below, were now of that tender gray-green which blends so delicately with the spring harmony of colours.

Groups of merry and somewhat loud-talking girls, whose ages might range from twelve to twenty, came by with a buoyant step. They were most of them factory girls, and wore the usual out-of-doors dress of that particular class of maidens; namely, a shawl, which at mid-day or in fine weather was allowed to be merely a shawl, but towards evening, or if the day were chilly, became a sort of Spanish mantilla or Scotch plaid, and was brought over the head and hung loosely down, or was pinned under the chin in no unpicturesque fashion.

Their faces were not remarkable for beauty; indeed, they were below the average, with one or two exceptions; they had dark hair, neatly and classically arranged, dark eyes, but sallow complexions and irregular features. The only thing to strike a passer-by was an acuteness and intelligence of countenance, which has often been noticed in a manufacturing population.

There were also numbers of boys, of rather young men, rambling among these fields, ready to bandy jokes with any one, and particularly ready to enter into conversation with the girls, who, however, held themselves aloof, not in a shy, but rather in an independent way, assuming an indifferent manner to the noisy wit or obstreperous compliments of the lads. Here and there came a sober quiet couple, either whispering lovers, or husband and wife, as the case might be; and if the latter, they were seldom unencumbered by an infant, carried for the most part by the father, while occasionally even three or four little toddlers had been carried or dragged thus far, in order that the whole family might enjoy the delicious May afternoon together.

Some time in the course of that afternoon, two working men met with friendly greeting at the stile so often named. One was a thorough specimen of a Manchester man; born of factory workers, and himself bred up in youth, and living in manhood, among the mills. He was below the middle size and slightly made; there was almost a stunted look about him; and his wan, colourless face, gave you the idea, that in his childhood he had suffered from the scanty living consequent upon bad times, and improvident habits. His features were strongly marked, though not irregular, and their expression was extreme earnestness; resolute either for good or evil, a sort of latent, stern enthusiasm. At the time of which I write, the good predominated over the bad in the countenance, and he was one from whom a stranger would have asked a favour with tolerable faith that it would be granted. He was accompanied by his wife, who might, without exaggeration, have been called a lovely woman, although now her face was swollen with crying, and often hidden behind her apron. She had the fresh beauty of the agricultural districts; and somewhat of the deficiency of sense in her countenance, which is likewise characteristic of the rural inhabitants in comparison with the natives of the manufacturing towns. She was far advanced in pregnancy, which perhaps occasioned the overpowering and hysterical nature of her grief. The friend whom they met was more handsome and less sensible-looking than the man I have just described; he seemed hearty and hopeful, and although his age was greater, yet there was far more of youth's buoyancy in his appearance. He was tenderly carrying a baby in arms, while his wife, a delicate fragile-looking woman, limping in her gait, bore another of the same age; little, feeble twins, inheriting the frail appearance of their mother.

The last-mentioned man was the first to speak, while a sudden look of sympathy dimmed his gladsome face. "Well, John, how goes it with you?" and, in a lower voice, he added, "any news of Esther, yet?" Meanwhile the wives greeted each other like old friends, the soft and plaintive voice of the mother of the twins seeming to call forth only fresh sobs from Mrs. Barton.

"Come women," said John Barton, "you 've both walked far enough. My Mary expects to have her bed in three weeks; and as for you, Mrs. Wilson, you know you are but a cranky sort of a body at the best of times." This was said so kindly, that no offence could be taken. "Sit you down here; the grass is well nigh dry by this time; and you 're neither of you nesh* folk about taking cold. Stay," he added, with some tenderness, "here 's my pocket-handkerchief to spread under you to save the gowns, women always think so much on; and now, Mrs. Wilson, give me the baby, I may as well carry him, while you talk and comfort my wife; poor thing, she takes on sadly about Esther."

These arrangements were soon completed: the two women sat down on the blue cotton handkerchiefs of their husbands, and the latter, each carrying a baby, set off for a further walk; but as soon as Barton had turned his back upon his wife, his countenance fell back into an expression of gloom.

"Then you 've heard nothing of Esther, poor lass?" asked Wilson.

"No, nor shan't, as I take it. My mind is, she 's gone off with somebody. My wife frets, and thinks she 's drowned herself, but I tell her, folks don't care to put on their best clothes to drown themselves; and Mrs. Bradshaw (where she lodged, you know), says the last time she set eyes on her was last Tuesday, when she came down stairs, dressed in her Sunday gown, and with a new ribbon in her bonnet, and gloves on her hands, like the lady she was so fond of thinking herself."

"She was as pretty a creature as ever the sun shone on."

"Ay, she was a farrantly** lass; more's the pity now," added Barton, with a sigh. "You see them Buckinghamshire people as comes to work here has quite a different look with them to us Manchester folk. You 'll not see among the Manchester wenches such fresh rosy cheeks, or such black lashes to gray eyes (making them look like black), as my wife and Esther had. I never seed two such pretty women for

* "Nesh;" Anglo-Saxon, nesc, tender.

"It semeth for love his herte is tendre and neshe."

CHAUCER — "*Court of Love.*"

** "Farrantly," comely, pleasant-looking.

sisters; never. Not but what beauty is a sad snare. Here was Esther so puffed up, that there was no holding her in. Her spirit was always up, if I spoke ever so little in the way of advice to her; my wife spoiled her, it is true, for you see she was so much older than Esther she was more like a mother to her, doing every thing for her."

"I wonder she ever left you," observed his friend.

"That 's the worst of factory work for girls. They can earn so much when work is plenty, that they can maintain themselves any how. My Mary shall never work in a factory, that I 'm determined on. You see Esther spent her money in dress, thinking to set off her pretty face; and got to come home so late at night, that at last I told her my mind: my missis thinks I spoke crossly, but I meant right, for I loved Esther, if it was only for Mary's sake. Says I, 'Esther, I see what yo 'll end at with your artificials, and your fly-away veils, and stopping out when honest women are in their beds; you 'll be a street-walker Esther, and then, don't you go to think I 'll have you darken my door, though my wife is your sister.' So says she, 'Don't trouble yourself, John. I 'll pack up and be off now, for I 'll never stay to hear myself called as you call me.' She flushed up like a turkey-cock, and I thought fire would come out of her eyes; but when she saw Mary cry (for Mary can't abide words in a house), she went and kissed her, and said she was not so bad as I thought her. So we talked more friendly, for, as I said, I liked the lass well enough, and her pretty looks, and her cheery ways. But she said (and at that time I thought there was sense in what she said) we should be much better friends if she went into lodgings, and only came to see us now and then."

"Then you still were friendly. Folks said you 'd cast her off, and said you 'd never speak to her again."

"Folks always make one a deal worse than one is," said John Barton, testily. "She came many a time to our house after she left off living with us. Last Sunday se'nnight — no! it was this very last Sunday, she came to drink a cup of tea with Mary; and that was the last time we set eyes on her."

"Was she any ways different in her manner?" asked Wilson.

"Well, I don't know. I have thought several times since, that she was a bit quieter, and more womanly-like; more gentle, and more blushing, and not so riotous and noisy. She comes in towards four o'clock, when afternoon church was loosing, and she goes and hangs her bonnet up on the old nail we used to call hers, while she lived with us. I remember thinking what a pretty lass she was, as she sat on a low stool by Mary, who was rocking herself, and in rather a poor way. She laughed and cried by turns, but all so softly and gently, like a child, that I couldn't find in my heart to scold her, especially as Mary was fretting already. One thing I do remember I did say, and pretty sharply too. She took our little Mary by the waist, and —"

"Thou must leave off calling her 'little' Mary, she's growing up into as fine a lass as one can see on a summer's day; more of her mother's stock than thine," interrupted Wilson.

"Well, well, I call her 'little,' because her mother's name is Mary. But, as I was saying, she takes Mary in a coaxing sort of way, and 'Mary,' says she, 'what should you think if I sent for you some day and made a lady of you.' So I could not stand such talk as that to my girl, and I said, 'Thou'd best not put that nonsense i' th' girl's head I can tell thee; I'd rather see her earning her bread by the sweat of her brow, as the Bible tells her she should do, ay, though she never got butter to her bread, than be like a do-nothing lady, worrying shopmen all morning, and screeching at her pianny all afternoon, and going to bed without having done a good turn to any one of God's creatures but herself.'"

"Thou never could abide the gentlefolk," said Wilson, half amused at his friend's vehemence.

"And what good have they ever done me that I should like them?" asked Barton, the latent fire lighting up his eye: and bursting forth, he continued, "If I am sick, do they come and nurse me? If my child lies dying (as poor Tom lay, with his white wan lips quivering, for want of better food than I could give him), does the rich man bring the wine or broth that might save his life? If I am out of work for weeks in the bad times, and winter comes, with black frost, and keen east wind, and there is no coal for the grate, and no clothes for the bed, and the thin bones are seen through the ragged clothes, does the rich man share his plenty with me, as he ought to do, if his religion wasn't a humbug? When I lie on my death-bed, and Mary (bless her) stands fretting, as I know she will fret," and here his voice faltered a little, "will a rich lady come and take her to her own home if need be, till she can look round, and see what best to do? No, I tell you, it's the poor, and the poor only, as does such things for the poor. Don't think to come over me with th' old tale, that the rich know nothing of the trials of the poor, I say, if they don't know, they ought to know. We're their slaves as long as we can work; we pile up their fortunes with the sweat of our brows; and yet we are to live as separate as if we were in two worlds; ay, as separate as Dives and Lazarus, with a great gulf betwixt us: but I know who was best off then," and he wound up his speech with a low chuckle that had no mirth in it.

"Well neighbour," said Wilson, "all that may be very true, but what I want to know now is about Esther — when did you last hear of her?"

"Why, she took leave of us that Sunday night in a very loving way, kissing both wife Mary, and daughter Mary (if I must not call her little), and shaking hands with me; but all in a cheerful sort of manner, so we thought nothing about her kisses and skakes. But on Wednesday night comes Mrs. Bradshaw's son with Esther's box, and presently Mrs. Bradshaw follows with the key; and when we began to talk, we found Esther told her she was coming back to live with us, and would pay her week's money for not giving notice; and on Tuesday night she carried off a little bundle (her best clothes were on her back, as I said before) and told Mrs. Bradshaw not to hurry herself about the big box, but bring it when she had time. So of course she thought she should find Esther with us; and when she told her story, my missis set up such a screech, and fell down in a dead swoon. Mary ran up with water for her mother, and I thought so much about my wife, I did not seem to care at all for Esther. But the next day I asked all the neighbours (both our own and Bradshaw's) and they'd none of 'em heard or seen nothing of her. I even went to a policeman, a good enough sort of man, but a fellow I'd never spoken to before because of his livery, and I asks him if his 'cuteness could find any thing out for us. So I believe he asks other policemen; and one on 'em had seen a wench, like our Esther, walking very quickly, with a bundle under her arm, on Tuesday night, toward eight o'clock, and get into a hackney coach, near Hulme Church, and we don't know th' number, and can't trace it no further. I'm sorry enough for the girl, for bad 's come over her, one way or another, but I'm sorrier for my wife. She loved her next to me, and Mary, and she 's never been the same body since poor Tom's death. However let 's go back to them; your old woman may have done her good."

As they walked homewards with a brisker pace, Wilson expressed a wish that they still were the near neighbours they once had been.

"Still our Alice lives in the cellar under No. 14, in Barber Street, and if you 'd only speak the word she'd be with you in five minutes to keep your wife company when she 's lonesome. Though I'm Alice's brother, and perhaps ought not to say it, I will say there 's none more ready to help with heart or hand than she is. Though she may have done a hard day's wash, there's not a child ill within the street but Alice goes to offer to sit up, and does sit up too, though may be she 's to be at her work by six next morning."

"She's a poor woman, and can feel for the poor, Wilson," was Barton's reply; and then he added, "Thank you kindly for your offer, and mayhap I may trouble her to be a bit with my wife, for while I'm at work, and Mary 's at school, I know she frets above a bit. See, there 's Mary!" and the father's eye brightened, as in the distance, among a group of girls, he spied his only daughter, a bonny lass of thirteen or so, who came bounding along to meet and to greet her father, in a manner that showed that the stern-looking man had a tender nature within. The two men had crossed the last stile, while Mary loitered behind to gather some buds of the coming hawthorn, when an overgrown lad came past her, and snatched a kiss, exclaiming, "For old acquaintance sake, Mary."

"Take that for old acquaintance sake, then," said the girl, blushing rosy red, more with anger than shame, as she slapped his face. The tones of her voice called back her father and his friend, and the aggressor proved to be the eldest son of the latter, the senior by eighteen years of his little brothers.

"Here, children, instead o' kissing and quarrelling, do ye each take a baby, for if Wilson's arms be like mine they are heartily tired."

Mary sprang forward to take her father's charge, with a girl's fondness for infants, and with some little foresight of the event soon to happen at home; while young Wilson seemed to lose his rough, cubbish nature as he crowed and cooed to his little brother.

"Twins is a great trial to a poor man, bless 'em," said the half-proud, half-weary father, as he bestowed a smacking kiss on the babe ere he parted with it.

CHAPTER II.

Polly, put the kettle on,
  And let's have tea!
Polly, put the kettle on,
  And we 'll all have tea.

"Here we are, wife; didst thou think thou'd lost us?" quoth hearty-voiced Wilson, as the two women rose and shook themselves in preparation for their homeward walk. Mrs. Barton was evidently soothed, if not cheered, by the unburdening of her fears and thoughts to her friend; and her approving look went far to second her husband's invitation that the whole party should adjourn from Green Heys Fields to tea, at the Bartons' house. The only faint opposition was raised by Mrs. Wilson, on account of the lateness of the hour at which they would probably return, which she feared on her babies' account.

"Now, hold your tongue, Missis, will you?" said her husband, good-temperedly. "Don't you know them brats never goes to sleep till long past ten? and haven't you a shawl, under which you can tuck one lad's head, as safe as a bird's under its wing? And as for t'other one, I'll put it in my pocket rather than not stay, now we are this far away from Ancoats.'

"Or I can lend you another shawl," suggested Mrs. Barton.

"Ay, any thing rather than not stay."

The matter being decided, the party proceeded home, through many half-finished streets, all so like one another that you might have easily been bewildered and lost your way. Not a step, however, did our friends lose; down this entry, cutting off that corner, until they turned out of one of these innumerable streets into a little paved court, having the backs of houses at the end opposite to the opening, and a gutter running through the middle to carry off household slops, washing suds, &c. The women who lived in the court were busy taking in strings of caps, frocks, and various articles of linen, which hung from side to side, dangling so low, that if our friends had been a few minutes sooner, they would have had to stoop very much, or else the half-wet clothes would have flapped in their faces: but although the evening seemed yet early when they were in the open fields — among the pent-up houses, night, with its mists, and its darkness, had already begun to fall.

Many greetings were given and exchanged between the Wilsons and these women, for not along ago they had also dwelt in this court.

Two rude lads, standing at a disorderly looking house-door, exclaimed, as Mary Barton (the daughter) passed, "Eh, look! Polly Barton 's getten* a sweet-heart."

* "For he had *geten* him yet no benefice."
Prologue to Canterbury Tales.

Of course this referred to young Wilson, who stole a look to see how Mary took the idea. He saw her assume the air of a young fury, and to his next speech she answered not a word.

Mrs. Barton produced the key of the door from her pocket; and on entering the house-place it seemed as if they were in total darkness, except one bright spot, which might be a cat's eye, or might be, what it was, a red-hot fire, smouldering under a large piece of coal, which John Barton immediately applied himself to break up, and the effect instantly produced was warm and glowing light in every corner of the room. To add to this (although the coarse yellow glare seemed lost in the ruddy glow from the fire), Mrs. Barton lighted a dip by sticking it in the fire, and having placed it satisfactorily in a tin candlestick, began to look further about her, on hospitable thoughts intent. The room was tolerably large, and possessed many conveniences. On the right of the door, as you entered, was a longish window, with a broad ledge. On each side of this, hung blue-and-white check curtains, which were now drawn, to shut in the friends met to enjoy themselves. Two geraniums, unpruned and leafy, which stood on the sill, formed a further defence from outdoor pryers. In the corner between the window and the fireside was a cupboard, apparently full of plates and dishes, cups and saucers, and some more nondescript articles, for which one would have fancied their possessors could find no use — such as triangular pieces of glass to save carving knives and forks from dirtying table-cloths. However, it was evident Mrs. Barton was proud of her crockery and glass, for she left her cupboard door open, with a glance round of satisfaction and pleasure. On the opposite side to the door and window was the staircase, and two doors; one of which (the nearest to the fire), led into a sort of little back kitchen, where dirty work, such as washing up dishes, might be done, and whose shelves served as larder, and pantry, and storeroom, and all. The other door, which was considerably lower, opened into the coal-hole — the slanting closet under the stairs; from which, to the fire-place, there was a gay-coloured piece of oil-cloth laid. The place seemed almost crammed with furniture (sure sign of good times among the mills). Beneath the window was a dresser, with three deep drawers. Opposite the fire-place was a table, which I should call a Pembroke, only that it was made of deal, and I cannot tell how far such a name may be applied to such humble material. On it, resting against the wall, was a bright green japanned tea-tray, having a couple of scarlet lovers embracing in the middle. The fire-light danced merrily on this, and really (setting all taste but that of a child's aside) it gave a richness of colouring to that side of the room. It was in some measure propped up by a crimson tea-caddy, also of japan ware. A round table on one branching leg really for use, stood in the corresponding corner to the cupboard; and, if you can picture all this, with a washy, but clean stencilled pattern on the walls you can form some idea of John Barton's home.

The tray was soon hoisted down, and before the merry clatter of cups and saucers began, the women disburdened themselves of their out-of-door things, and sent Mary up stairs with them. Then came a long whispering, and chinking of money, to which Mr. and Mrs. Wilson were too polite to attend; knowing, as they did full well, that it all related to the preparations for hospitality; hospitality that, in their turn, they should have such pleasure in offering. So they tried to be busily occupied with the children, and not to hear Mrs. Barton's directions to Mary.

"Run, Mary dear, just round the corner, and get some fresh eggs at Tipping's (you may get one a-piece, that will be five-pence), and see if he has any nice ham cut, that he would let us have a pound of."

"Say two pounds, Missis, and don't be stingy," chimed in the husband.

"Well, a pound and a half, Mary. And get it Cumberland ham, for Wilson comes from there-away, and it will have a sort of relish of home with it he 'll like, — and Mary" (seeing the lassie fain to be off), "you must get a pennyworth of milk and a loaf of bread — mind you get it fresh and new — and, and — that 's all, Mary."

"No, it 's not all," said her husband. "Thou must get sixpennyworth of rum, to warm the tea; thou 'll get it at the 'Grapes.' And thou just go to Alice Wilson; he says she lives just right round the corner, under 14, Barber street" (this was addressed to his wife), "and tell her to come and take her tea with us; she 'll like to see her brother, I 'll be bound, let alone Jane and the twins."

"If she comes she must bring a tea-cup and saucer, for we have but half-a-dozen, and here 's six of us," said Mrs. Barton.

"Pooh! pooh! Jem and Mary can drink out of one, surely."

But Mary secretly determined to take care that Alice brought her tea-cup and saucer, if the alternative was to be her sharing any thing with Jem.

Alice Wilson had but just come in. She had been out all day in the fields, gathering wild herbs for drinks and medicine, for in addition to her invaluable qualities as a sick nurse and her worldly occupations as a washer-woman, she added a considerable knowledge of hedge and field simples; and on fine days, when no more profitable occupation offered itself, she used to ramble off into the lanes and meadows as far as her legs could carry her. This evening she had returned loaded with nettles, and her first object was to light a candle and see to hang them up in bunches in every available place in her cellar room. It was the perfection of cleanliness; in one corner stood the modest looking bed, with a check curtain at the head, the whitewashed wall filling up the place where the corresponding one should have been. The floor was bricked, and scrupulously clean, although so damp that it seemed as if the last washing would never dry up. As the cellar window looked into an area in the street, down which boys might throw stones, it was protected by an outside shutter, and was oddly festooned with all manner of hedge row, ditch, and field plants, which we are accustomed to call valueless, but which have a powerful effect either for good or for evil, and are consequently much used among the poor. The room was strewed, hung, and darkened with these bunches, which emitted no very fragrant odour in their process of drying. In one corner was a sort of broad hanging shelf, made of old planks, where some old hoards of Alice's were kept. Her little bit of crockery ware was ranged on the mantelpiece, where also stood her candlestick and box of matches. A small cupboard contained at the bottom coals, and at the top her bread and basin of oatmeal, her frying pan, tea-pot, and a small tin saucepan, which served as a kettle, as well as for cooking the delicate little messes of broth which Alice was sometimes able to manufacture for a sick neighbour.

After her walk she felt chilly and weary, and was busy trying to light her fire with the damp coals, and half-green sticks, when Mary knocked.

"Come in," said Alice, remembering, however, that she had barred the door for the night, and hastening to make it possible for any one to come in.

"Is that you, Mary Barton?" exclaimed she, as the light from the candle streamed on the girl's face. "How you are grown since I used to see you at my brother's! Come in, lass, come in."

"Please," said Mary, almost breathless, "mother says you 're to come to tea, and bring your cup and saucer, for George and Jane Wilson is with us, and the twins, and Jem. And you 're to make haste, please."

"I 'm sure it 's very neighbourly and kind in your mother, and I 'll come, with many thanks. Stay, Mary, has your mother got any nettles for spring drink? If she hasn't I 'll take her some."

"No, I don't think she has."

Mary ran off like a hare to fulfil what, to a girl of thirteen, fond of power, was the more interesting part of her errand — the money-spending part. And well and ably did she perform her business, returning home with a little bottle of rum, and the eggs in one hand, while her other was filled with some excellent red-and-white, smoke-flavoured, Cumberland ham, wrapped up in paper.

She was at home, and frying ham, before Alice had chosen her nettles, put out her candle, locked her door, and walked in a very foot-sore manner as far as John Barton's. What an aspect of comfort did his houseplace present, after her humble cellar. She did not think of comparing; but for all that she felt the delicious glow of the fire, the bright light that revelled in every corner of the room, the savoury smells, the comfortable sounds of a boiling kettle, and the hissing, frizzling ham. With a little old-fashioned curtsey she shut the door, and replied with a loving heart to the boisterous and surprised greeting of her brother.

And now all preparations being made, the party sat down. Mrs. Wilson in the post of honour, the rocking chair on the right hand side of the fire, nursing her baby, while its father, in an opposite arm-chair tried vainly to quieten the other with bread soaked in milk.

Mrs. Barton knew manners too well, to do any thing but sit at the tea-table and make tea, though in her heart she longed to be able to superintend the frying of the ham, and cast many an anxious look at Mary as she broke the eggs and turned the ham, with a very comfortable portion of confidence in her own culinary powers. Jem stood awkwardly leaning against the dresser, replying rather gruffly to his aunt's speeches, which gave him, he thought, the air of being a little boy; whereas he considered himself as a young man, and not so very young neither, as in two months he would be eighteen. Barton vibrated between the fire and the tea-table, his only draw-back being a fancy that every now and then his wife's face flushed and contracted as if in pain.

At length the business actually began. Knives and forks, cups and saucers made a noise, but human voices were still, for human beings were hungry and had no time to speak. Alice first broke silence; holding her tea-cup with the manner of one proposing a toast, she said, "Here's to absent friends. Friends may meet, but mountains never."

It was an unlucky toast or sentiment, as she instantly felt. Every one thought of Esther, the absent Esther; and Mrs. Barton put down her food, and could not hide the fast dropping tears. Alice could have bitten her tongue out.

It was a wet blanket to the evening; for though all had been said and suggested in the fields that could be said or suggested, every one had a wish to say something in the way of comfort to poor Mrs. Barton, and a dislike to talk about any thing else while her tears fell fast and scalding. So George Wilson, his wife, and children set off early home, not before (in spite of *mal-à-propos* speeches) they had expressed a wish that such meetings might often take place, and not before John Barton had given his hearty consent; and declared that as soon as ever his wife was well again they would have just such another evening.

"I will take care not to come and spoil it," thought poor Alice, and going up to Mrs. Barton, she took her hand almost humbly, and said, "You don't know how sorry I am I said it."

To her surprise, a surprise that brought tears of joy into her eyes, Mary Barton put her arms round her neck, and kissed the self-reproaching Alice. "You didn't mean any harm, and it was me as was so foolish; only this work about Esther, and not knowing where she is, lies so heavy on my heart. Good night, and never think no more about it. God bless you, Alice."

Many and many a time, as Alice reviewed that evening in her after life, did she bless Mary Barton for these kind and thoughtful words. But just then all she could say was, "Good night, Mary, and may God bless *you*."

CHAPTER III.

"But when the morn came dim and sad,
And chill with early showers,
Her quiet eyelids closed — she had
Another morn than ours." HOOD.

In the middle of that same night a neighbour of the Bartons was roused from her sound, well-earned sleep, by a knocking, which had at first made part of her dream; but starting up, as soon as she became convinced of its reality, she opened the window, and asked who was there?

"Me — John Barton," answered he in a voice tremulous with agitation. "My missis is in labour, and, for the love of God, step in while I run for th' doctor, for she 's fearful bad."

While the woman hastily dressed herself, leaving the window still open, she heard the cries of agony, which resounded in the little court in the stillness of the night. In less than five minutes she was standing by Mrs. Barton's bed-side, relieving the terrified Mary, who went about, where she was told, like an automaton; her eyes tearless, her face calm, though deadly pale, and uttering no sound, except when her teeth chattered for very nervousness.

The cries grew worse.

The doctor was very long in hearing the repeated rings at his night-bell, and still longer in understanding who it was that made this sudden call upon his services; and then he begged Barton just to wait while he dressed himself, in order that no time might be lost in finding the court and house. Barton absolutely stamped with impatience, outside the doctor's door, before he came down; and walked so fast homewards, that the medical man several times asked him to go slower.

"Is she so very bad?" asked he.

"Worse, much worser than I ever saw her before," replied John.

No! she was not — she was at peace. The cries were still for ever. John had no time for listening. He opened the latched door, stayed not to light a candle for the mere ceremony of showing his companion up the stairs, so well known to himself; but, in two minutes was in the room, where lay the dead wife, whom he had loved with all the power of his strong heart. The doctor stumbled up-stairs by the fire-light, and met the awe-struck look of the neighbour, which at once told him the state of things. The room was till, as he, with habitual tip-toe step, approached the poor frail body, whom nothing now could more disturb. Her daughter knelt by the bed-side, her face buried in the clothes, which were almost crammed into her mouth, to keep down the choking sobs. The husband stood like one stupified. The doctor questioned the neighbour in whispers, and then approaching Barton, said, "You must go down stairs. This is a great shock, but bear it like a man. Go down."

He went mechanically and sat down on the first chair. He had no hope. The look of death was too clear upon her face. Still, when he heard one or two unusual noises, the thought burst on him that it might only be a trance, a fit, a — he did not well know what, — but not death! Oh, not death! And he was starting up to go up-stairs again, when the doctor's heavy cautious creaking footstep was heard on the stairs. Then he knew what it really was in the chamber above.

"Nothing could have saved her — there has been some shock to the system —" and so he went on; but, to unheeding ears, which yet retained his words to ponder on; words not for immediate use in conveying sense, but to be laid by, in the store-house of memory, for a more convenient season. The doctor seeing the state of the case, grieved for the man; and, very sleepy, thought it best to go, and accordingly wished him good-night — but there was no answer, so he let himself out; and Barton sat on, like a stock or a stone, so rigid, so still. He heard the sounds above too, and knew what they meant. He heard the stiff unseasoned drawer, in which his wife kept her clothes, pulled open. He saw the neighbour come down, and blunder about in search of soap and water. He knew well what she wanted, and *why* she wanted them', but he did not speak, nor offer to help. At last she went, with some kindly-meant words (a text of comfort, which fell upon a deafened ear, and something about "Mary," but which Mary, in his bewildered state, he could not tell).

He tried to realise it — to think it possible. And then his mind wandered off to other days, to far different times. He thought of their courtship; of his first seeing her, an awkward beautiful rustic, far too shiftless for the delicate factory work to which she was apprenticed; of his first gift to her, a bead necklace, which had long ago been put by, in one of the deep drawers of the dressers, to be kept for Mary. He wondered if it was there yet, and with a strange curiosity he got up to feel for it; for the fire by this time was well-nigh out, and candle he had none. His groping hand fell on the piled-up tea things, which at his desire she had left unwashed till morning — they were all so tired. He was reminded of one of the daily little actions, which acquire such power when they have been performed for the last time by one we love. He began to think over his wife's daily round of duties: and something in the remembrance that these would never more be done by her, touched the source of tears, and he cried aloud. Poor Mary, meanwhile, had mechanically helped the neighbour in all the last attentions to the dead; and when she was kissed, and spoken to soothingly, tears stole quietly down her cheeks: but she reserved the luxury of a full burst of grief till she should be alone. She shut the chamber-door softly, after the neighbour was gone, and then shook the bed by which she knelt with her agony of sorrow. She repeated, over and over again, the same words; the same vain, unanswered address to her who was no more. "Oh, mother! mother, are you really dead! Oh, mother, mother!"

At last she stopped, because it flashed across her mind that her violence of grief might disturb her father. All was still below. She looked on the face so changed, and yet so strangely like. She bent down to kiss it. The cold, unyielding flesh, struck a shudder to her heart, and hastily obeying her impulse, she grasped the candle, and opened the door. Then she heard the sobs of her father's griefs; and quickly, quietly, stealing down the steps, she knelt by him, and kissed his hand. He took no notice at first, for his burst of grief would not be controlled. But when her shriller sobs, her terrified cries (which she could not repress), rose upon his ear, he checked himself.

"Child, we must be all to one another, now *she* is gone," whispered he.

"Oh, father, what can I dor for you? Do tell me! I'll do any thing."

"I know thou wilt. Thou must not fret thyself ill, that's the first thing I ask. Thou must leave me, and go to bed now, like a good girl as thou art."

"Leave you, father! oh, don't say so."

"Ay, but thou must! thou must go to bed, and try and sleep; thou'lt have enough to do and to bear, poor wench, to-morrow."

Mary got up, kissed her father, and sadly went up stairs to the little closet, where she slept. She thought it was of no use undressing, for that she could never, never sleep, so threw herself on her bed in her clothes, and before ten minutes had passed away, the passionate grief of youth had subsided into sleep.

Barton had been roused by his daughter's entrance; both from his stupor and from his incontrollable sorrow. He could think on what was to be done, could plan for the funeral, could calculate the necessity of soon returning to his work, as the extravagance of the past night would leave them short of money, if he long remained away from the mill. He was in a club, so that money was provided for the burial. These things settled in his own mind, he recalled the doctor's words, and bitterly thought of the shock his poor wife had so recently had, in the mysterious disappearance of her cherished sister. His feelings towards Esther almost amounted to curses. It was she who had brought on all this sorrow. Her giddiness, her lightness of conduct, had wrought this woe. His previous thoughts about her had been tinged with wonder and pity, but now he hardened his heart against her for ever.

One of the good influences over John Barton's life had departed that night. One of the ties which bound him down to the gentle humanities of earth was loosened, and henceforward the neighbours all remarked he was a changed man. His gloom and his sternness became habitual instead of occasional. He was more obstinate. But never to Mary. Between the father and the daughter there existed in full force that mysterious bond which unites those who have been loved by one who is now dead and gone. While he was harsh and silent to others, he humoured Mary with tender love; she had more of her own way than is common in any rank with girls of her age. Part of this was the necessity of the case; for, of course, all the money went through her hands, and the household arrangements were guided by her will and pleasure. But part was her father's indulgence, for he left her, with full trust in her unusual sense and spirit, to choose her own associates, and her own times for seeing her associates.

With all this, Mary had not her father's confidence in the matters which now began to occupy him, heart and soul; she was aware that he had joined clubs, and become an active member of the Trades' Union, but it was hardly likely that a girl of Mary's age (even when two or three years had elapsed since her mother's death) should care much for the differences between the employers and the employed, — an eternal subject for agitation in the manufacturing districts, which, however it may be lulled for a time, is sure to break forth again with fresh violence at any depression of trade, showing that in its apparent quiet, the ashes had still smouldered in the breasts of a few.

Among these few was John Barton. At all times it is a bewildering thing to the poor weaver to see his employer removing from house to house, each one grander than the last, till he ends in building one more magnificent than all, or withdraws his money from the concern, or sells his mill, to buy an estate in the country, while all the time the weaver, who thinks he and his fellows are the real makers of this wealth, is struggling on for bread for his children, through the vicissitudes of lowered wages, short hours, fewer hands employed, &c. And when he knows trade is bad, and could understand (at least partially) that there are not buyers enough in the market to purchase the goods already made, and consequently that there is no demand for more; when he would bear and endure much without complaining, could he also see that his employers were bearing their share; he is, I say, bewildered and (to use his own word) "aggravated" to see that all goes on just as usual with the mill-owners. Large houses are still occupied, while spinners' and weavers' cottages stand empty, because the families that once filled them are obliged to live in rooms or cellars. Carriages still roll along the streets, concerts are still crowded by subscribers, the shops for expensive luxuries still find daily customers, while the workman loiters away his unemployed time in watching these things, and thinking of the pale, uncomplaining wife at home, and the wailing children asking in vain for enough of food, of the sinking health, of the dying life of those near and dear to him. The contrast is too great. Why should he alone suffer from bad times?

I know that this is not really the case; and I know what is the truth in such matters: but what I wish to impress is what the workman feels and thinks. True, that with child-like improvidence, good times will often dissipate his grumbling, and make him forget all prudence and foresight.

But there are earnest men among these people, men who have endured wrongs without complaining, but without ever forgetting or forgiving those whom (they believe) have caused all this woe.

Among these was John Barton. His parents had suffered, his mother had died from absolute want of the necessaries of life. He himself was a good, steady workman, and, as such, pretty certain of steady employment. But he spent all he got with the confidence (you may also call it improvidence) of one who was willing, and believed himself able, to supply all his wants by his own exertions. And when his master suddenly failed, and all hands in the mill were turned back, one Tuesday morning, with the news that Mr. Hunter had stopped, Barton had only a few shillings to rely on; but he had good heart of being employed at some other mill, and accordingly, before returning home, he spent some hours in going from factory to factory, asking for work. But at every mill was some sign of depression of trade! some were working short hours, some were turning off hands, and for weeks Barton was out of work, living on credit. It was during this time that his little son, the apple of his eye, the cynosure of all his strong power of love, fell ill of the scarlet fever. They dragged him through the crisis, but his life hung on a gossamer thread. Every thing, the doctor said, depended on good nourishment, on generous living, to keep up the little fellow's strength, in the prostration in which the fever had left him. Mocking words! when the commonest food in the house would not furnish one little meal. Barton tried credit; but it was worn out at the little provision shops which were now suffering in their turn. He thought it would be no sin to steal, and would have stolen; but he could not get the opportunity in the few days the child lingered. Hungry himself, almost to an animal pitch of ravenousness, but with the bodily pain swallowed up in anxiety for his little sinking lad, he stood at one of the shop windows where all edible luxuries are displayed; haunches of venison, Stilton cheeses, moulds of jelly — all appetising sights to the common passer-by. And out of this shop came Mrs. Hunter! She crossed to her carriage, followed by the shopman loaded with purchases for a party. The door was quickly slammed to, and she drove away; and Barton returned home with a bitter spirit of wrath in his heart, to see his only boy a corpse!

You can fancy, now, the hoards of vengeance in his heart against the employers. For there are never wanting those who, either in speech or in print, find it their interest to cherish such feelings in the working classes; who know how and when to rouse the dangerous power at their command;

and who use their knowledge with unrelenting purpose to either party.

So while Mary took her own way, growing more spirited every day, and growing in her beauty too, her father was chairman at many a Trades' Union meeting; a friend of delegates, and ambitious of being a delegate himself; a Chartist, and ready to do any thing for his order.

But now times were good; and all these feelings were theoretical, not practical. His most practical thought was getting Mary apprenticed to a dressmaker; for he had never left off disliking a factory life for a girl, on more accounts than one.

Mary must do something. The factories being, as I said, out of the question, there were two things open — going out to service, and the dressmaking business; and against the first of these, Mary set herself with all the force of her strong will. What that will might have been able to achieve had her father been against her, I cannot tell; but he disliked the idea of parting with her, who was the light of his hearth; the voice of his otherwise silent home. Besides, with his ideas and feelings towards the higher classes, he considered domestic servitude as a species of slavery; a pampering of artificial wants on the one side, a giving-up of every right of leisure by day and quiet rest by night on the other. How far his strong exaggerated feelings had any foundation in truth, it is for you to judge. I am afraid that Mary's determination not to go to service arose from far less sensible thoughts on the subject than her father's. Three years of independence of action (since her mother's death such a time had now elapsed) had little inclined her to submit to rules as to hours and associates, to regulate her dress by a mistress's ideas of propriety, to lose the dear feminine priviliges of gossiping with a merry neighbour, and working night and day to help one who was sorrowful. Besides all this, the sayings of her absent, her mysterious aunt, Esther, had an unacknowledged influence over Mary. She knew she was very pretty; the factory people as they poured from the mills, and in their freedom told the truth (whatever it might be) to every passer-by, had early let Mary into the secret of her beauty. If their remarks had fallen on an unheeding ear, there were always young men enough, in a different rank from her own, who were willing to compliment the pretty weaver's daughter as they met her in the streets. Besides, trust a girl of sixteen for knowing it well if she is pretty; concerning her plainness she may be ignorant. So with this consciousness she had early determined that her beauty should make her a lady; the rank she coveted the more for her father's abuse; the rank to which she firmly believed her lost Aunt Esther had arrived. Now, while a servant must often drudge and be dirty, must be known as her servant by all who visited at her master's house, a dressmaker's apprentice must (or so Mary thought) be always dressed with a certain regard to appearance; must never soil her hands, and need never redden or dirty her face with hard labour. Before my telling you so truly what folly Mary felt or thought, injures her without redemption in your opinion, think what are the silly fancies of sixteen years of age in every class, and under all circumstances. The end of all the thoughts of father and daughter was, as I said before, Mary was to be a dressmaker; and her ambition prompted her unwilling father to apply at all the first establishments, to know on what terms of painstaking and zeal his daughter might be admitted into ever so humble a workwoman's situation. But high premiums were asked at all; poor man! he might have known that without giving up a day's work to ascertain the fact. He would have been indignant, indeed, had he known that if Mary had accompanied him, the case might have been rather different, as her beauty would have made her desirable as a show-woman. Then he tried second-rate places; at all the payment of a sum of money was necessary, and money he had none. Disheartened and angry he went home at night, declaring it was time lost; that dressmaking was at all events a toilsome business, and not worth learning. Mary saw that the grapes were sour, and the next day she set out herself, as her father could not afford to lose another day's work; and before night (as yesterday's experience had considerably lowered her ideas) she had engaged herself as apprentice (so called, though there were no deeds or indentures to the bond) to a certain Miss Simmonds, milliner and dressmaker, in a respectable little street leading off Ardwick Green, where her business was duly announced in gold letters on a black ground, enclosed in a bird's-eye maple frame, and stuck in the front parlour window; where the workwomen were called "her young ladies;" and where Mary was to work for two years without any remuneration, on consideration of being taught the business; and where afterwards she was to dine and have tea, with a small quarterly salary (paid quarterly because so much more genteel than by week), a *very* small one, divisible into a minute weekly pittance. In summer she was to be there by six, bringing her day's meals during the first two years; in winter she was not to come till after breakfast. Her time for returning home at night must always depend upon the quantity of work Miss Simmonds had to do.

And Mary was satisfied; and seeing this, her father was contented too, although his words were grumbling and morose; but Mary knew his ways, and coaxed and planned for the future so cheerily, that both went to bed with easy if not happy hearts.

CHAPTER IV.

"To envy nought beneath the ample sky;
To mourn no mournful deed, no hour mis-spent;
And, like a living violet, silently
Return in sweets to Heaven what goodness lent,
Then bend beneath the chastening shower content." ELLIOTT.

ANOTHER year passed on. The waves of time seemed long since to have swept away all trace of poor Mary Barton. But her husband still thought of her, although with a calm and quiet grief, in the silent watches of the night: and Mary would start from her hard-earned sleep, and think in her half-dreamy, half-awakened state, she saw her mother stand by her bed-side, as she used to do "in the days of long ago;" with a shaded candle and an expression of ineffable tenderness, while she looked on her sleeping child. But Mary rubbed her eyes and sank back on her pillow, awake, and knowing it was a dream; and still, in all her troubles and perplexities, her heart called on her mother for aid, and she thought, "If mother had but lived, she would have helped me." Forgetting that the woman's sorrows are far more difficult to mitigate than a child's, even by the mighty power of a mother's love; and unconscious of the fact, that she was far superior in sense and spirit to the mother she mourned. Aunt Esther was still mysteriously absent, and people had grown weary of wondering and began to forget. Barton still attended his club, and was an active member of a Trades' Union; indeed, more frequently than ever, since the time of Mary's return in the evening was so uncertain; and, as she occasionally, in very busy times, remained all night. His chiefest friend was still George Wilson, although he had no great sympathy on the questions that agitated Barton's mind. Still their hearts were bound by old ties to one another, and the remembrance of former things gave an unspoken charm to their meetings. Our old friend, the cub-like lad, Jem Wilson, had shot up into the powerful, well-made young man, with a sensible face enough; nay a face that might have been handsome, had it not been here and there marked by the small-pox. He worked with one of the great firms of engineers, who send from out their towns of workshops, engines and machinery to the dominions of the Czar and the Sultan. His father and mother were never weary of praising Jem, at all which commendation pretty Mary Barton wonld toss her head, seeing clearly enough that they wished her to understand what a good husband he would make, and to favour his love, about which he never dared to speak, whatever eyes and looks revealed.

One day, in the early winter time, when people were provided with warm substantial gowns, not likely soon to wear out, and when, accordingly, business was rather slack at Miss Simmond's, Mary met Alice Wilson, coming home from her half-day's work at some tradesman's house. Mary and Alice had always liked each other; indeed, Alice looked with particular interest on the motherless girl, the daughter of her whose forgiving kiss had comforted her in many sleepless hours. So there was a warm greeting between the tidy old woman and the blooming young work-girl; and then Alice ventured to ask if she would come in and take her tea with her that very evening.

"You 'll think it dull enough to come just to sit with an old woman like me, but there 's a tidy young lass as lives in the floor above, who does plain work, and now and then a bit in your own line, Mary; she 's grand-daughter to old Job Legh, a spinner, and a good girl she is. Do come, Mary, I've a terrible wish to make you known to each other. She 's a genteel-looking lass, too."

At the beginning of this speech Mary had feared the intended visitor was to be no other than Alice's nephew; but Alice was too delicate-minded to plan a meeting, even for her dear Jem, when one would have been an unwilling party; and Mary, relieved from her apprehension by the conclusion, gladly agreed to come. How busy Alice felt! it was not often she had any one to tea; and now her sense of the duties of a hostess were almost too much for her. She made haste home, and lighted the unwilling fire, borrowing a pair of bellows to make it burn the faster. For herself she was always patient, she let the coals take their time. Then she put on her pattens, and went to fill her kettle at the pump in the next court, and on her way she borrowed a cup; of odd saucers she had plenty, serving as plates when occasion required. Half an ounce of tea and a quarter of a pound of butter went far to absorb her moning's wages; but this was an unusual occasion. In general, she used herb-tea for herself, when at home, unless some thoughtful mistress made a present of tea-leaves from her more abundant household. The two chairs drawn out for visitors, and duly swept and dusted; an old board arranged with some skill upon two old candle-boxes set on end (rather rickety to be sure, but she knew the seat of old, and when to sit lightly; indeed the whole affair was more for apparent dignity of position than for any real ease); a little, very little round table, put just before the fire, which by this time was blazing merrily; her unlackered, ancient, third-hand tea-tray arranged with a black tea-pot, two cups with a red and white pattern, and one with the old friendly willow pattern, and saucers, not to match (on one of the extra supply, the lump of butter flourished away); all these preparations complete, Alice began to look about her with satisfaction, and a sort of wonder what more could be done to add to the comfort of the evening. She took one of the chairs away from its appropriate place by the table, and putting it close to the broad large hanging shelf I told you about when I first described her cellar-dwelling, and mounting on it, she pulled towards her an old deal box, and took thence a quantity of the oat bread of the north, the "clap-bread" of Cumberland and Westmoreland, and descending carefully with the thin cakes threatening to break to pieces in her hand, she placed them on the bare table, with the belief that her visitors would have an unusual treat in eating the bread of her childhood. She brought out a good piece of a four-pound loaf of common household bread as well, and then sat down to rest, really to rest, and not to pretend, on one of the rush-bottomed chairs. The candle was ready to be lighted, the kettle boiled, the tea was awaiting its doom in its paper parcel; all was ready.

A knock at the door! It was Margaret, the young work-woman who lived in the rooms above, who having heard the bustle, and the subsequent quiet, began to think it was time to pay her visit below. She was a sallow, unhealthy, sweet-looking young woman, with a careworn look; her dress was humble and very simple, consisting of some kind of dark stuff gown, her neck being covered by a drab shawl or large hand-kerchief, pinned down behind and at the sides in front. The old woman gave her a hearty greeting, and made her sit down on the chair she had just left, while she balanced herself on the board seat, in order that Margaret might think it was quite her free and independent choice to sit there.

"I cannot think what keeps Mary Barton. She's quite grand with her late hours," said Alice, as Mary still delayed.

The truth was, Mary was dressing herself; yes, to come to poor old Alice's — she thought it worth while to consider what gown she should put on. It was not for Alice, however, you may be pretty sure; no, they knew each other too well. But Mary liked making an impression, and in this it must be owned she was pretty often gratified — and there was this strange girl to consider just now. So she put on her pretty new blue merino, made tight to her throat, her little linen collar and linen cuffs, and sallied forth to impress poor gentle Margaret. She certainly succeeded. Alice, who never thought much about beauty, had never told Margaret how pretty Mary was; and, as she came in half-blushing at her own self-consciousness, Margaret could hardly take her eyes off her, and Mary put down her long black lashes with a sort of dislike of the very observation she had taken such pains to secure. Can you fancy the bustle of Alice to make the tea, to pour it out, and sweeten it to their liking, to help and help again to clap-bread and bread-and-butter? Can you fancy the delight with which she watched her piled-up clap-bread disappear before the hungry girls, and listened to the praises of her home-remembered dainty?

"My mother used to send me some clap-bread by any north-country person — bless her! She knew how good such things taste when far away from home. Not, but what every one likes it. When I was in service my fellow-servants were always glad to share with me. Eh, it's a long time ago, yon."

"Do tell us about it, Alice," said Margaret.

"Why, lass, there's nothing to tell. There was more mouths at home than could be fed. Tom, that 's Will's father (you don't know Will, but he's a sailor to foreign parts), had come to Manchester, and sent word what terrible lots of work was to be had, both for lads and lasses. So father sent George first (you know George, well enough, Mary), and then work was scarce out toward Burton, where we lived, and father said I maun try and get a place. And George wrote as how wages were far higher in Manchester than Milnthorpe or Lancaster; and, lasses, I was young and thoughtless, and thought it was a fine thing to go so far from home. So, one day, th' butcher he brings us a letter fra George, to say he'd heard on a place — and I was all agog to go, and father was pleased like; but mother said little, and that little was very quiet. I've often thought she was a bit hurt to see me so ready to go — God forgive me! But she packed up my clothes, and some of the better end of her own as would fit me, in yon little paper box up there — it's good for nought now, but I would liefer live without fire than break it up to be burnt; and yet it's going on for eighty years old, for she had it when she was a girl, and brought all her clothes in it to father's when they were married. But, as I was saying, she did not cry, though the tears was often in her eyes; and I seen her looking after me down the lane as I were in sight, with her hand shading her eyes — and that were the last look I ever had on her."

Alice knew that before long she should go to that mother; and, besides, the griefs and bitter woes of youth have worn themselves out before we grow old; but she looked so sorrowful that the girls caught her sadness, and mourned for the poor woman who had been dead and gone so many years ago.

"Did you never see her again, Alice? Did you never go home while she was alive?" asked Mary.

"No, nor since. Many a time and oft have I planned to go. I plan it yet, and hope to go home again before it please God to take me. I used to try and save money enough to go for a week when I was in service; but first one thing came, and then another. First, missis's children fell ill of the measles, just when the week I'd asked for came, and I couldn't leave them, for one and all cried for me to nurse them. Then missis herself fell sick, and I could go less than ever. For, you see, they kept a little shop, and he drank, and missis and me was all there was to mind children, and shop, and all, and cook and wash besides."

Mary was glad she had not gone into service, and said so.

"Eh, lass! thou little knows the pleasure o' helping others; I was as happy there as could be; almost as happy as I was at home. Well, but next year I thought I could go at a leisure time, and missis telled me I should have a fortnight then, and I use to sit up all that winter working hard at patchwork, to have a quilt of my own making to take to my mother. But master died, and missis went away fra Manchester, and I'd to look out for a place again."

"Well, but," interrupted Mary, "I should have thought that was the best time to go home."

"No, I thought not. You see it was a different thing going home for a week on a visit, may be with money in my pocket to give father a lift, to going home to be a burden to him. Besides, how could I hear o' a place there? Anyways I thought it best to stay, though perhaps it might have been better to ha' gone, for then I should ha' seen mother again;" and the poor old woman looked puzzled.

"I'm sure you did what you thought right," said Margaret, gently.

"Ay, lass, that's it," said Alice, raising her head and speaking more cheerfully. "That's the thing, and then let the Lord send what he sees fit; not but that I grieved sore, oh, sore and sad, when toward spring next year, when my quilt were all done to th' lining, George came in one evening to tell me mother was dead. I cried many a night at after;* I'd no time for crying by day, for that missis was terrible strict; she would not hearken to my going to th' funeral; and indeed I would have been too late, for George set off that very night by th' coach, and the letter had been kept or summut (posts were not like th' posts now-a-days), and he found the burial all over and father talking o' flitting; for he couldn't abide the cottage after mother was gone."

"Was it a pretty place?" asked Mary.

"Pretty, lass! I never seed such a bonny bit anywhere. You see there are hills there as seem to go up into th' skies, not near may be, but that makes them all the bonnier. I used

* A common Lancashire phrase.

to think they were the golden hills of heaven, about which my mother sang when I was a child,

'Yon are the golden hills o' heaven,
Where ye sall never win.'

Something about a ship and a lover that should hae been na lover, the ballad was. Well, and near our cottage were rocks. Eh, lasses! ye don't know what rocks are in Manchester! Gray pieces o' stone as large as a house, all covered over wi' mosses of different colours, some yellow, some brown; and the ground beneath them knee deep in purple heather, smelling sae sweet and fragrant, and the low music of the humming-bee for ever sounding among it. Mother used to send Sally and me out to gather ling and heather for besoms, and it was such pleasant work! We used to come home of an evening loaded so as you could not see us, for all that it was so light to carry. And then mother would make us sit down under the old hawthorn tree (where we used to make our house among the great roots as stood above th' ground), to pick and tie up the heather. It seems all like yesterday, and yet it's a long long time agone. Poor sister Sally has been in her grave this forty year and more. But I often wonder if the hawthorn is standing yet, and if the lasses still go to gather heather, as we did many and many a year past and gone. I sicken at heart to see the old spot once again. May be next summer I may set off, if God spares me to see next summer."

"Why have you never been in all these many years?" asked Mary.

"Why lass! first one wanted me and then another; and I couldn't go without money either, and Igot very poor at times. Tom was a scapegrace, poor fellow, and always wanted help of one kind or another; and his wife (for I think scapegraces are always married long before steady-folk) was but a helpless kind of body. She were always ailing, and he were always in trouble; so I had enough to do with my hands and my money too, for that matter. They died within twelvemonth of each other, leaving one lad (they had had seven, but the Lord had taken six to himself), Will, as I was telling you on:

and I took him myself, and left service to make a bit on a home-place for him, and a fine lad he was, the very spit of his father as to looks, only steadier. For he was steady, although nought would serve him but going to sea. I tried all I could to set him again a sailor's life. Says I, 'Folks is as sick as dogs all the time they 're at sea. Your own mother telled me (for she came from foreign parts, being a Manx woman) that she'd ha' thanked any one for throwing her into the water.' Nay, I sent him a' the way to Runcorn by th' Duke's canal, that he might know what th' sea were;' and I looked to see him come back as white as a sheet wi' vomiting. But the lad went on to Liverpool and saw real ships, and came back more set than ever on being a sailor, and he said as how he had never been sick at all, and thought he could stand the sea pretty well. So I told him he mun do as he liked; and he thanked me and kissed me, for all I was very frabbit* with him; and now he's gone to South America, at t'other side of the sun, they tell me."

Mary stole a glance at Margaret to see what she thought of Alice's geography; but Margaret looked so quiet and demure, that Mary was in doubt if she were not really ignorant. Not that Mary's knowledge was very profound, but she had seen a terrestrial globe, and knew where to find France and the continents on a map.

After this long talking Alice seemed lost for a time in reverie; and the girls respecting her thoughts, which they suspected had wandered to the home and scenes of her childhood, were silent. All at once she recalled her duties as hostess, and by an effort brought back her mind to the present time.

"Margaret, thou must let Mary hear thee sing. I don't know about fine music myself, but folks say Margar't is a rare singer, and I know she can make me cry at any time by singing 'Th' Owdham Weaver.' Do sing that Margaret, there's a good lass."

* "Frabbit," peevish.

With a faint smile, as if amused at Alice's choice of a song, Margaret began.

Do you know "The Oldham Weaver?" Not unless you are Lancashire born and bred, for it is a complete Lancashire ditty. I will copy it for you.

THE OLDHAM WEAVER.

I.

Oi'm a poor cotton-weyver, as mony a one knoowas,
Oi've nowt for t' yeat, an' oi've worn eawt my cloas,
Yo'ad hardly gi' tuppence for aw as oi 've on,
My clogs are both brosten, an' stuckings oi've none,
Yo 'd think it wur hard,
To be browt into th' warld,
To be — clemmed,* an' do th' best as yo con.

II.

Owd Dicky o'Billy's kept telling me lung,
Wee s'd ha' better toimes if I 'd but howd my tung.
Oi've howden my tung, till oi've near stopped my breath,
Oi think i' my heeart oi'se soon clem to deeath,
Owd Dicky's weel crammed,
He never wur clemmed,
An' he ne'er picked ower i' his loife.**

III.

We tow'rt on six week — thinking aitch day wur the last,
We shifted, an' shifted, till neaw we 're quoite fast;
We lived upo' nettles, whoile nettles wur good,
An' Waterloo porridge the best o' eawr food,
Oi'm tellin' yo' true,
Oi can find folk enow,
As wur livin' na better nor me.

IV.

Owd Billy o' Dans sent th' baileys one day,
Fur a shop deebt oi eawd him, as oi could na pay,
But he wur too lat, fur owd Billy o' th' Bent,
Had sowd th' tit an' cart, an' ta'en goods for th' rent,
We 'd neawt left bo' th' owd stoo',
That wur seeats fur two,
An' on it ceawred Marget an' me.

* "Clem," to starve with hunger. "Hard is the choice, when the valiant must eat their arms or *clem*." — *Ben Jonson.*

** To "pick ower," means to throw the shuttle in hand-loom weaving.

V.

Then t' baileys leuked reawnd as sloy as a meawse,
When they seed as aw t' goods were ta'en eawt o' t' heawse,
Says one chap to th' tother, "Aws gone, theaw may see;"
Says oi, "Ne'er freet, mon, yeaur welcome ta me."
They made no moor ado
But whopped up th' eawd stoo,'
An' we booath leet, whack — upo' t' flags!

VI.

Then oi said to eawr Marget, as we lay upo' t' floor,
"We 's never be lower i' this warld, oi'm sure,
If ever things awtern, oi'm sure they mun mend,
For oi think i' my heart were booath at t' far eend;
For meeat we ha' none;
Nor looms t'weyve on, —
Edad! they 're as good lost as fund."

VII.

Eawr Marget declares bad hoo cloo'as to put on,
Hoo'd goo up to Lunnon an' talk to th' greet mon;
An' if things were na awtered when there hoo had been,
Hoo's fully resolved t' sew up meawth an' eend;
Hoo's neawt to say again t' king,
But hoo loikes a fair thing,
An' hoo says hoo can tell when hoo's hurt.

The air to which this is sung is a kind of droning recitative, depending much on expression and feeling. To read it, it may, perhaps, seem humorous; but it is that humour which is near akin to pathos, and to those who have seen the distress it describes, it is a powerfully pathetic song. Margaret had both witnessed the destitution, and had the heart to feel it; and withal, her voice was of that rich and rare order, which does not require any great compass of notes to make itself appreciated. Alice had her quiet enjoyment of tears. But Margaret, with fixed eye, and earnest, dreamy look, seemed to become more and more absorbed in realising to herself the woe she had been describing, and which she felt might at that very moment be suffering and hopeless within a short distance of their comparative comfort.

Suddenly she burst forth with all the power of her magnificent voice, as if a prayer from her very heart for all who were in distress, in the grand supplication, "Lord remember

David." Mary held her breath, unwilling to lose a note, it was so clear, so perfect, so imploring. A far more correct musician than Mary might have paused with equal admiration of the really scientific knowledge, with which the poor depressed-looking young needle-woman used her superb and flexile voice. Deborah Travis herself (once an Oldham factory girl, and afterwards the darling of fashionable crowds as Mrs. Knyvett), might have owned a sister in her art.

She stopped; and with tears of holy sympathy in her eyes, Alice thanked the songstress, who resumed her calm, demure manner, much to Mary's wonder, for she looked at her unweariedly, as if surprised that the hidden power should not be perceived in the outward appearance.

When Alice's little speech of thanks was over, there was quiet enough to hear a fine, though rather quavering, male voice, going over again one or two strains of Margaret's song.

"That 's grandfather!" exclaimed she. "I must be going, for he said he should not be at home till past nine."

"Well, I 'll not say nay, for I have to be up by four for a very heavy wash at Mrs. Simpson's; but I shall be terrible glad to see you again at any time, lasses; and I hope you 'll take to one another."

As the girls ran up the cellar steps together, Margaret said: "Just step in, and see grandfather. I should like him to see you."

And Mary consented.

CHAPTER V.

> "Learned he was; nor bird, nor insect flew,
> But he its leafy home and history knew:
> Nor wild-flower decked the rock, nor moss the well,
> But he its name and qualities could tell." ELLIOTT.

THERE is a class of men in Manchester, unknown even to many of the inhabitants, and whose existence will probably be doubted by many, who yet may claim kindred with all the noble names that science recognises. I said in "Manchester," but they are scattered all over the manufacturing districts of Lancashire. In the neighbourhood of Oldham there are weavers, common hand-loom weavers, who throw the shuttle with unceasing sound, though Newton's "Principia" lie open on the loom, to be snatched at in work hours, but revelled over in meal times, or at night. Mathematical problems are received with interest, and studied with absorbing attention by many a broad-spoken, common-looking factory-hand. It is perhaps less astonishing that the more popularly interesting branches of natural history have their warm and devoted followers among this class. There are botanists among them, equally familiar with either the Linnæan or the Natural system, who know the name and habitat of every plant within a day's walk from their dwellings; who steal the holiday of a day or two when any particular plant should be in flower, and tying up their simple food in their pocket-handkerchiefs, set off with single purpose to fetch home the humble-looking weed. There are entomologists, who may be seen with a rude-looking net, ready to catch any winged insect, or a kind of dredge, with which they rake the green and slimy pools; practical, shrewd, hard-working men, who pore over every new specimen with real scientific delight. Nor is it the common and more obvious divisions of Entomology and Botany that alone attract these earnest seekers after knowledge. Perhaps it may be owing to the great annual town-holiday of Whitsun-week so often falling in May or June, that the two great beautiful families of Ephemeridæ and Phryganidæ have been so much and so closely studied by Manchester workmen, while they have in a great measure escaped general observation. If you will refer to the preface to Sir J. E. Smith's Life (I have it not by me, or I would copy you the exact passage), you will find that he names a little circumstance corroborative of what I have said. Being on a visit to Roscoe, of Liverpool, he made some inquiries from him as to the habitat of a very rare plant, said to be found in certain places in Lancashire. Mr. Roscoe knew nothing of the plant; but stated, that if any one could give him the desired information, it would be a hand-loom weaver in Manchester, whom he named. Sir J. E. Smith proceeded by boat to Manchester, and on arriving at that town, he inquired of the porter who was carrying his luggage if he could direct him to So and So.

"Oh, yes," replied the man. "He does a bit in my way;" and, on further investigation, it turned out, that both the porter, and his friend the weaver, were skilful botanists; and able to give Sir J. E. Smith the very information which he wanted.

Such are the tastes and pursuits of some of the thoughtful, little understood, working men of Manchester.

And Margaret's grandfather was one of these. He was a little wiry-looking old man, who moved with a jerking motion, as if his limbs were worked by a string like a child's toy, with dun-coloured hair lying thin and soft at the back and sides of his head; his forehead was so large it seemed to overbalance the rest of his face, which had, indeed, lost its natural contour by the absence of all the teeth. The eyes absolutely gleamed with intelligence; so keen, so observant, you felt as if they were almost wizard-like. Indeed, the whole room looked not unlike a wizard's dwelling. Instead of pictures were hung rude wooden frames of impaled insects; the little table was covered with cabalistic books; and beside them lay a case of mysterious instruments, one of which Job Legh was using when his granddaughter entered.

On her appearance he pushed his spectacles up so as to rest midway on his forehead, and gave Mary a short, kind welcome. But Margaret he caressed as a mother caresses her first born; stroking her with tenderness, and almost altering his voice as he spoke to her.

Mary looked round on the odd, strange things she had never seen at home, and which seemed to her to have a very uncanny look.

"Is your grandfather a fortune-teller?" whispered she to her new friend.

"No," replied Margaret, in the same voice; "but you 're

not the first as has taken him for such. He is only fond of such things as most folks know nothing about."

"And do you know aught about them too?"

"I know a bit about some of the things grandfather is fond on; just because he 's fond on 'em, I tried to learn about them."

"What things are these?" said Mary, struck with the weird-looking creatures that sprawled around the room in their roughly-made glass cases.

But she was not prepared for the technical names which Job Legh pattered down on her ear, on which they fell like hail on a skylight; and the strange language only bewildered her more than ever. Margaret saw the state of the case, and came to the rescue.

"Look, Mary, at this horrid scorpion. He gave me such a fright: I am all of a twitter yet when I think of it. Grandfather went to Liverpool one Whitsun-week to go strolling about the docks and pick up what he could from the sailors, who often bring some queer thing or another from the hot countries they go to; and so he sees a chap with a bottle in his hand, like a druggist's physic-bottle; and says grandfather, 'What have ye gotten there?' So the sailor holds it up, and grandfather knew it was a rare kind o' scorpion, not common even in the East Indies where the man came from; and says he, 'How did you catch this fine fellow, for he wouldn't be taken for nothing I 'm thinking?' And the man said as how when they were unloading the ship he 'd found him lying behind a bag of rice, and he thought the cold had killed him, for he was not squashed nor injured a bit. He did not like to part with any of the spirit out of his grog to put the scorpion in, but slipped him into the bottle, knowing there were folks enow who would give him something for him. So grandfather gives him a shilling."

"Two shillings," interrupted Job Legh, "and a good bargain it was."

"Well! grandfather came home as proud as Punch, and pulled the bottle out of his pocket. But you see th' scorpion were doubled up, and grandfather thought I couldn't fairly see how big he was. So he shakes him out right before the fire; and a good warm one it was, for I was ironing, I remember. I left off ironing and stooped down over him, to look at him better, and grandfather got a book, and began to read how this very kind were the most poisonous and vicious species, how their bite were often fatal, and then went on to read how people who were bitten got swelled, and screamed with pain. I was listening hard, but as it fell out, I never took my eyes off the creature, though I could not ha' told I was watching it. Suddenly it seemed to give a jerk, and before I could speak it gave another, and in a minute it was as wild as it could be, running at me just like a mad dog."

"What did you do?" asked Mary.

"Me! why, I jumped first on a chair, and then on all the things I 'd been ironing on the dresser, and I screamed for grandfather to come up by me, but he did not hearken to me."

"Why, if I 'd come up by thee, who 'd ha' caught the creature, I should like to know?"

"Well, I begged grandfather to crush it, and I had the iron right over it once, ready to drop, but grandfather begged me not to hurt it in that way. So I couldn't think what he 'd have, for he hopped round the room as if he were sore afraid, for all he begged me not to injure it. At last he goes to th' kettle, and lifts up the lid, and peeps in. What on earth is he doing that for, thinks I; he 'll never drink his tea with a scorpion running free and easy about the room. Then he takes the tongs, and he settles his spectacles on his nose, and in a minute he had lifted the creature up by th' leg, and dropped him into the boiling water."

"And did that kill him?" said Mary.

"Ay, sure enough; he boiled for longer time than grandfather liked though. But I was so afeard of his coming round again. I ran to the public-house for some gin, and grandfather filled the bottle, and then we poured off the water, and picked him out of the kettle, and dropped him into the bottle, and he were there above a twelvemonth."

"What brought him to life at first?" asked Mary.

"Why, you see, he were never really dead, only torpid — that is, dead asleep with the cold, and our good fire brought him round."

"I 'm glad father does not care for such things," said Mary.

"Are you! Well, I 'm often downright glad grandfather is so fond of his books, and his creatures, and his plants. It does my heart good to see him so happy, sorting them all at home, and so ready to go in search of more, whenever he 's a spare day. Look at him now! he 's gone back to his books, and he 'll be as happy as a king, working away till I make him go to bed. It keeps him silent, to be sure; but so long as I see him earnest, and pleased, and eager, what does that matter? Then, when he has his talking bouts, you can't think how much he has to say. Dear grandfather! you don't know how happy we are!"

Mary wondered if the dear grandfather heard all this, for Margaret did not speak in an under tone; but no! he was far too deep and eager in solving a problem. He did not even notice Mary's leave-taking, and she went home with the feeling that she had that night made the acquaintance of two of the strangest people she ever saw in her life. Margaret, so quiet, so common-place, until her singing powers were called forth; so silent from home, so cheerful and agreeable at home; and her grandfather so very different to any one Mary had ever seen. Margaret had said he was not a fortune-teller, but she did not know whether to believe her.

To resolve her doubts, she told the history of the evening to her father, who was interested by her account, and curious to see and judge for himself. Opportunities are not often wanting where inclination goes before, and ere the end of that winter Mary looked upon Margaret almost as an old friend. The latter would bring her work when Mary was likely to be at home in the evenings and sit with her; and Job

Legh would put a book and his pipe in his pocket and just step round the corner to fetch his grand-child, ready for a talk if he found Barton in; ready to pull out pipe and book if the girls wanted him to wait, and John was still at his club. In short, ready to do whatever would give pleasure to his darling Margaret.

I do not know what points of resemblance or dissimilitude (for the one joins people as often as that), attracted the two girls to each other. Margaret had the great charm of possessing good strong common sense, and do you not perceive how involuntarily this is valued? It is so pleasant to have a friend who possesses the power of setting a difficult question in a clear light; whose judgment can tell what is best to be done; and who is so convinced of what is "wisest, best," that in consideration of the end, all difficulties in the way diminish, People admire talent, and talk about their admiration. But they value common sense without talking about it, and often without knowing it.

So Mary and Margaret grew in love one toward the other; and Mary told many of her feelings in a way she had never done before to any one. Most of her foibles also were made known to Margaret, but not all. There was one cherished weakness still concealed from every one. It concerned a lover, not beloved, but favoured by fancy. A gallant, handsome young man; but — not beloved. Yet Mary hoped to meet him every day in her walks, blushed when she heard his name, and tried to think of him as her future husband, and above all, tried to think of herself as his future wife. Alas! poor Mary! Bitter woe did thy weakness work thee.

She had other lovers. One or two would gladly have kept her company, but she held herself too high, they said. Jem Wilson said nothing, but loved on and on, ever more fondly; he hoped against hope; he would not give it up, for it seemed like giving up life to give up thought of Mary. He did not dare to look to any end of all this; the present, so that he saw her, touched the hem of her garment, was enough. Surely, in time, such deep love would beget love.

He would not relinquish hope, and yet her coldness of manner was enough to daunt any man; and it made Jem more despairing than he would acknowledge for a long time even to himself.

But one evening he came round by Barton's house, a willing messenger for his father, and opening the door saw Margaret sitting asleep before the fire. She had come in to speak to Mary; and worn out by a long working, watching night, she fell asleep in the genial warmth.

An old-fashioned saying about a pair of gloves came into Jem's mind, and stepping gently up, he kissed Margaret with a friendly kiss.

She awoke, and perfectly understanding the thing, she said, "For shame of yourself, Jem. What would Mary say?"

Lightly said, lightly answered.

"She'd nobbut* say, practice makes perfect." And they both laughed. But the words Margaret had said rankled in Jem's mind. Would Mary care? Would she care in the very least? They seemed to call for an answer by night, and by day; and Jem felt that his heart told him Mary was quite indifferent to any action of his. Still he loved on, and on, ever more fondly.

Mary's father was well aware of the nature of Jem Wilson's feelings for his daughter, but he took no notice of them to any one, thinking Mary full young yet for the cares of married life, and unwilling, too, to entertain the idea of parting with her at any time, however distant. But he welcomed Jem at his house, as he would have done his father's son, whatever were his motives for coming; and now and then admitted the thought, that Mary might do worse when her time came, than marry Jem Wilson, a steady workman at a good trade, a good son to his parents, and a fine manly spirited chap — at least when Mary was not by; for when she was present he watched her too closely, and too anxiously, to have much of what John Barton called "spunk" in him.

* "Nobbut," none but, only. "No man sigh evere God *no but* the oon bigitun sone." — *Wiclif's Version.*

It was towards the end of February, in that year, and a bitter black frost had lasted for many weeks. The keen east wind had long since swept the streets clean, though on a gusty day the dust would rise like pounded ice, and make people's faces quite smart with the cold force with which it blew against them. Houses, sky, people, and every thing looked as if a gigantic brush had washed them all over with a dark shade of Indian ink. There was some reason for this grimy appearance on human beings, whatever there might be for the dun looks of the landscape; for soft water had become an article not even to be purchased; and the poor washerwomen might be seen vainly trying to procure a little by breaking the thick gray ice that coated the ditches and ponds in the neighbourhood. People prophesied a long continuance to this already lengthened frost; said the spring would be very late; no spring fashions required; no summer clothing purchased for a short uncertain summer. Indeed there was no end to the evil prophesied during the continuance of that bleak east wind.

Mary hurried home one evening, just as daylight was fading, from Miss Simmonds', with her shawl held up to her mouth, and her head bent as if in deprecation of the meeting wind. So she did not perceive Margaret till she was close upon her at the very turning into the court.

"Bless me Margaret! is that you? Where are you bound to?"

"To nowhere but your own house (that is, if you'll take me in). I've a job of work to finish to-night; mourning, as must be in time for the funeral to-morrow; and grandfather has been out moss-hunting, and will not be home till late."

"Oh, how charming it will be. I'll help you if you're backward. Have you much to do?"

"Yes, I only get the order yesterday at noon; and there's three girls beside the mother; and what with trying on and matching the stuff (for there was not enough in the piece they chose first), I'm above a bit behindhand. I've the skirts all to make; I kept that work till candlelight; and the sleeves, to say nothing of little bits to the bodies; for the missis is very particular, and I could scarce keep from smiling while they were crying so, really taking on sadly I 'm sure, to hear first one and then t'other clear up to notice the sit of her gown. They weren't to be misfits I promise you, though they were in such trouble."

"Well, Margaret, you're right welcome, as you know, and I 'll sit down and help you with pleasure, though I was tired enough of sewing to-night at Miss Simmonds'."

By this time Mary had broken up the raking coal, and lighted her candle; and Margaret settled herself to her work on one side of the table, while her friend hurried over her tea at the other. The things were then lifted *en masse* to the dresser; and dusting her side of the table with the apron she always wore at home, Mary took up some breadths and began to run them together.

"Who 's it all for, for if you told me I 've forgotten?"

"Why for Mrs. Ogden as keeps the greengrocer's shop in Oxford Road. Her husband drank himself to death, and though she cried over him and his ways all the time he was alive, she 's fretted sadly for him now he 's dead."

"Has he left her much to go upon?" asked Mary, examining the texture of the dress. "This is beautifully fine soft bombazine."

"No, I'm much afeard there 's but little, and there's several young children, besides the three Miss Ogdens."

"I should have thought girls like them would ha' made their own gowns," observed Mary.

"So I dare say they do, many a one, but now they seem all so busy getting ready for the funeral; for it 's to be quite a grand affair, well-nigh twenty people to breakfast, as one of the little ones told me; the little thing seemed to like the fuss, and I do believe it comforted poor Mrs. Ogden to make all the piece o' work. Such a smell of ham boiling and fowls roasting while I waited in the kitchen; it seemed more like a wedding nor* a funeral. They said she'd spend a matter o' sixty pound on th' burial."

* "Nor," generally used in Lancashire for "than."
"They had lever sleep *nor* be in laundery." — *Dunbar.*

"I thought you said she was but badly off," said Mary.

"Ay, I know she's asked for credit at several places, saying her husband laid hands on every farthing he could get for drink. But th' undertakers urge her on you see, and tell her this thing 's usual, and that thing 's only a common mark of respect, and that every body has t'other thing, till the poor woman has no will o' her own. I dare say, too, her heart strikes her (it always does when a person 's gone) for many a word and many a slighting deed to him, who 's stiff and cold; and she thinks to make up matters, as it were, by a grand funeral, though she and all her children, too, may have to pinch many a year to pay the expenses, if ever they pay them at all."

"This mourning, too, will cost a pretty penny," said Mary. "I often wonder why folks wear mourning; it 's not pretty or becoming; and it costs a deal of money just when people can spare it least; and if what the Bible tells us be true, we ought not to be sorry when a friend, who's been good, goes to his rest; and as for a bad man, one 's glad enough to get shut* on him. I cannot see what good comes o' wearing mourning."

"I 'll tell you what I think th' fancy was sent for (Old Alice calls every thing 'sent for,' and I believe she 's right). It does do good, thought not as much as it costs, that I do believe, in setting people (as is cast down by sorrow and feels themselves unable to settle to anything but crying) something to do. Why now I told you how they were grieving; for, perhaps, he was a kind husband and father, in his thoughtless way, when he wasn't in liquor. But they cheered up wonderful while I was there, and I asked 'em for more directions than usual, that they might have something to talk over and fix about; and I left 'em my fashion-book (though it were two months old) just a purpose."

"I don't think every one would grieve a that way. Old Alice wouldn't."

"Old Alice is one in a thousand. I doubt, too, if she would fret much, however sorry she might be. She would say it were

* "Shut," quit.

sent, and fall to trying to find out what good it were to do. Every sorrow in her mind is sent for good. Did I ever tell you, Mary, what she said one day when she found me taking on about something?"

"No, do tell me. What were you fretting about, first place?"

"I can't tell you just now; perhaps I may sometime."

"When?"

"Perhaps this very evening, if it rises in my heart; perhaps never. It's a fear that sometimes I can't abide to think about, and sometimes I don't like to think on any thing else. Well, I was fretting about this fear, and Alice comes in for something, and finds me crying. I would not tell her no more than I would you, Mary; so she says, 'Well, dear, you must mind this, when you're going to fret and be low about anything. 'An anxious mind is never a holy mind.' Oh, Mary, I have so often checked my grumbling sin'* she said that."

The weary sound of stitching was the only sound heard for a little while, till Mary inquired,

"Do you expect to get paid for this mourning?"

"Why I do not much think I shall. I've thought it over once or twice, and I mean to bring myself to think I shan't, and to like to do it as my bit towards comforting them. I don't think they can pay, and yet they're just the sort of folk to have their minds easier for wearing mourning. There's only one thing I dislike making black for, it does so hurt the eyes."

Margaret put down her work with a sigh, and shaded her eyes. Then she assumed a cheerful tone, and said,

"You'll not have to wait long, Mary, for my secret's on the tip of my tongue. Mary! do you know I sometimes think I'm growing a little blind, and then what would become of grandfather and me? Oh, God help me, Lord help me!"

She fell into an agony of tears, while Mary knelt by her,

* "Sin'," since.

"*Sin* that his lord was twenty yere of age."

Prologue to Canterbury Tales.

striving to soothe and to comfort her; but, like an inexperienced person, striving rather to deny the correctness of Margaret's fear, than helping her to meet and overcome the evil.

"No," said Margaret, quietly fixing her tearful eyes on Mary; "I know I'm not mistaken. I have felt one going some time, long before I ever thought what it would lead to; and last autumn I went to a doctor; and he did not mince the matter, but said unless I sat in a darkened room, with my hands before me, my sight would not last me many years longer. But how could I do that, Mary? For one thing, grandfather would have known there was somewhat the matter; and, oh! it will grieve him sore whenever he 's told, so the later the better; and besides, Mary, we've sometimes little enough to go upon, and what I earn is a great help. For grandfather takes a day here, and a day there, for botanising or going after insects, and he'll think little enough of four or five shillings for a specimen; dear grandfather! and I 'm so loath to think he should be stinted of what gives him such pleasure. So I went to another doctor to try and get him to say something different, and he said, 'Oh, it was only weakness,' and gived me a bottle of lotion; but I 've used three bottles (and each of 'em cost two shillings), and my eye is so much worse, not hurting so much, but I can't see a bit with it. There now, Mary," continued she, shutting one eye, "now you only look like a great black shadow, with the edges dancing and sparkling."

"And can you see pretty well with th' other?"

"Yes, pretty near as well as ever. Th' only difference is, that if I sew a long time together, a bright spot like th' sun comes right where I'm looking; all the rest is quite clear but just where I want to see. I 've been to both doctors again, and now they 're both o' the same story; and I suppose I 'm going dark as fast as may be. Plain work pays so bad, and mourning has been so plentiful this winter, that I were tempted to take in any black work I could; and now I 'm suffering from it."

"And yet, Margaret, you're going on taking it in; that's what you'd call foolish in another."

"It is Mary! and yet what can I do? Folk mun live; and I think I should go blind any way, and I darn't tell grandfather else I would leave it off, but he will so fret."

Margaret rocked herself backward and forward to still her emotion.

"Oh Mary!" she said, "I try to get his face off by heart, and I stare at him so when he's not looking, and then shut my eyes to see if I can remember his dear face. There's one thing, Mary, that serves a bit to comfort me. You'll have heard of old Jacob Butterworth, the singing weaver? Well, I know'd him a bit, so I went to him, and said how I wished he'd teach me the right way o' singing; and he says I've a rare fine voice, and I go once a week, and take a lesson fra' him. He's been a grand singer in his day. He led the chorusses at the Festivals, and got thanked many a time by London folk; and one foreign singer, Madame Catalani, turned round and shook him by th' hand before the Oud Church* full o' people. He says I may gain ever so much money by singing; but I don't know. Any rate, it's sad work, being blind."

She took up her sewing, saying her eyes were rested now, and for some time they sewed on in silence.

Suddenly there were steps heard in the little paved court; person after person ran past the curtained window.

"Something's up," said Mary. She went to the door, and stopping the first person she saw, inquired the cause of the commotion.

"Eh, wench! donna ye see the fire-light? Carsons' mill is blazing away like fun;" and away her informant ran.

"Come, Margaret, on wi' your bonnet, and let's go to see Carsons' mill; it's afire, and they say a burning mill is such a grand sight. I never saw one."

"Well, I think it's a fearful sight. Besides, I've all this work to do."

* "Old Church;" now the Cathedral of Manchester.

But Mary coaxed in her sweet manner, and with her gentle caresses, promising to help with the gowns all night long if necessary, nay, saying she should quite enjoy it.

The truth was, Margaret's secret weighed heavily and painfully on her mind, and she felt her inability to comfort; besides, she wanted to change the current of Margaret's thoughts; and in addition to these unselfish feelings, came the desire she had honestly expressed, of seeing a factory on fire.

So in two minutes they were ready. At the threshold of the house they met John Barton, to whom they told their errand.

"Carsons' mill! Ay, there is a mill on fire somewhere, sure enough, by the light, and it will be a rare blaze, for there's not a drop o' water to be got. And much Carsons will care, for they 're well insured, and the machines are a' th' oud-fashioned kind. See if they don't think it a fine thing for themselves. They 'll not thank them as tries to put it out."

He gave way for the impatient girls to pass. Guided by the ruddy light more than by any exact knowledge of the streets that led to the mill, they scampered along with bent heads, facing the terrible east wind as best they might.

Carsons' mill ran lengthways from east to west. Along it went one of the oldest thoroughfares in Manchester. Indeed, all that part of the town was comparatively old; it was there that the first cotton mills were built, and the crowded alleys and back streets of the neighbourhood made a fire there particularly to be dreaded. The staircase of the mill ascended from the entrance at the western end, which faced into a wide, dingy-looking street, consisting principally of public-houses, pawnbrokers' shops, rag and bone warehouses, and dirty provision shops. The other, the east end of the factory, fronted into a very narrow back street, not twenty feet wide, and miserably lighted and paved. Right against this end of the factory were the gable ends of the last house in the principal street — a house which from its size, its handsome stone facings, and the attempt at ornament in the front, had probably been once a gentleman's house; but now the light which streamed from its enlarged front windows, made clear the interior of the splendidly fitted up room, with its painted walls, its pillared recesses, its gilded and gorgeous fittings up, its miserable, squalid inmates. It was a gin palace.

Mary almost wished herself away, so fearful (as Margaret had said) was the sight when they joined the crowd assembled to witness the fire. There was a murmur of many voices whenever the roaring of the flames ceased for an instant. It was easy to perceive the mass were deeply interested.

"What do they say?" asked Margaret, of a neighbour in the crowd, as she caught a few words, clear and distinct from the general murmur.

"There never is any one in the mill, surely!" exclaimed Mary, as the sea of upward-turned faces moved with one accord to the eastern end, looking into Dunham Street, the narrow back lane already mentioned.

The western end of the mill, whither the raging flames were driven by the wind, was crowned and turreted with triumphant fire. It sent forth its infernal tongues from every window hole, licking the black walls with amorous fierceness; it was swayed or fell before the mighty gale, only to rise higher and yet higher, to ravage and roar yet more wildly. This part of the roof fell in with an astounding crash, while the crowd struggled more and more to press into Dunham Street, for what were magnificent terrible flames, what were falling timbers or tottering walls, in comparison with human life?

There, where the devouring flames had been repelled by the yet more powerful wind, but where yet black smoke gushed out from every aperture — there, at one of the windows on the fourth story, or rather a doorway where a crane was fixed to hoist up goods, might occasionally be seen, when the thick gusts of smoke cleared partially away for an instant, the imploring figures of two men. They had remained after the rest of the workmen for some reason or other, and, owing to the wind having driven the fire in the opposite direction, had perceived no sight or sound of alarm, till long after (if any thing could be called long in that throng of terrors which passed by in less time than half an hour) the fire had consumed the old wooden staircase at the other end of the building. I am not sure whether it was not the first sound of the rushing crowd below that made them fully aware of their awful position.

"Where are the engines?" asked Margaret of her neighbour.

"They 're coming, no doubt; but bless you, I think it 's bare ten minutes since we first found out th' fire; it rages so wi' this wind, and all so dry-like."

"Is no one gone for a ladder?" gasped Mary, as the men were imperceptibly, though not audibly, praying the great multitude below for help.

"Ay, Wilson's son and another man were off like a shot, well nigh five minute ago. But th' masons, and slaters, and such like, have left their work, and locked up the yards.

Wilson! then, was that man whose figure loomed out against the ever increasing dull hot light behind, whenever the smoke was clear, — was that George Wilson? Mary sickened with terror. She knew he worked for Carsons; but at first she had had no idea that any lives were in danger; and since she had become aware of this, the heated air, the roaring flames, the dizzy light, and the agitated and murmuring crowd, had bewildered her thoughts.

"Oh! let us go home, Margaret, I cannot stay."

"We cannot go! See how we are wedged in by folks. Poor Mary! ye won't hanker after a fire again. Hark! listen!"

For through the hushed crowd, pressing round the angle of the mill, and filling up Dunham Street, might be heard the rattle of the engine, the heavy, quick tread of loaded horses.

"Thank God!" said Margaret's neighbour, "the engine 's come."

Another pause; the plugs were stiff, and water could not be got.

Then there was a pressure through the crowd, the front rows bearing back on those behind, till the girls were sick with the close ramming confinement. Then a relaxation, and a breathing freely once more.

"'T was young Wilson and a fireman wi' a ladder," said Margaret's neighbour, a tall man who could overlook the crowd.

"Oh, tell us what you see?" begged Mary.

"They 've getten it fixed against the gin-shop wall. One o' the men i' the factory has fell back; dazed wi' the smoke, I 'll warrant. The floor 's not given way there. God!" said he, bringing his eye lower down, "the ladder 's too short! It's a' over wi' them, poor chaps. Th' fire 's coming slow and sure to that end, and afore they 've either gotten water, or another ladder, they 'll be dead out and out. Lord have mercy on them!"

A sob, as if of excited women, was heard in the hush of the crowd. Another pressure like the former! Mary clung to Margaret's arm with a pinching grasp, and longed to faint, and be insensible, to escape from the oppressing misery of her sensations. A minute or two.

"They 've taken th' ladder into th' Temple of Apollor. Can't press back with it to the yard it came from."

A mighty shout arose; a sound to wake the dead. Up on high, quivering in the air, was seen the end of the ladder, protruding out of a garret window, in the gable end of the gin palace, nearly opposite to the doorway where the men had been seen. Those in the crowd nearest the factory, and consequently best able to see up to the garret window, said that several men were holding one end, and guiding by their weight its passage to the doorway. The garret window-frame had been taken out before the crowd below were aware of the attempt.

At length — for it seemed long, measured by beating hearts, though scarce two minutes had elapsed — the ladder was fixed, an aërial bridge at a dizzy height, across the narrow street.

Every eye was fixed in unwinking anxiety, and people's very breathing seemed stilled in suspense. The men were nowhere to be seen, but the wind appeared, for the moment, higher than ever, and drove back the invading flames to the other end.

Mary and Margaret could see now; right above them danced the ladder in the wind. The crowd pressed back from under; firemen's helmets appeared at the window, holding the ladder firm, when a man, with quick, steady tread, and unmoving head, passed from one side to the other. The multitude did not even whisper while he crossed the perilous bridge, which quivered under him; but when he was across, safe comparatively in the factory, a cheer arose for an instant, checked, however, almost immediately, by the uncertainty of the result, and the desire not in any way to shake the nerves of the brave fellow who had cast his life on such a die.

"There he is again!" sprung to the lips of many, as they saw him at the doorway, standing as if for an instant to breathe a mouthful of the fresher air, before he trusted himself to cross. On his shoulders he bore an insensible body.

"It 's Jem Wilson and his father," whispered Margaret; but Mary knew it before.

The people were sick with anxious terror. He could no longer balance himself with his arms; every thing must depend on nerve and eye. They saw the latter was fixed, by the position of the head, which never wavered; the ladder shook under the double weight; but still he never moved his head — he dared not look below. It seemed an age before the crossing was accomplished. At last the window was gained; the bearer relieved from his burden; both had disappeared.

Then the multitude might shout; and above the roaring flames, louder than the blowing of the mighty wind, arose that tremendous burst of applause at the success of the daring enterprise. Then a shrill cry was heard, asking,

"Is the oud man alive, and likely to do?"

"Ay," answered one of the firemen to the hushed crowd below. "He 's coming round finely, now he 's had a dash of cowd water."

He drew back his head; and the eager inquiries, the shouts, the sea-like murmurs of the moving rolling mass began again to be heard — but only for an instant. In far less time than even that in which I have endeavoured briefly to describe the pause of events, the same bold hero stepped again upon the ladder, with evident purpose to rescue the man yet remaining in the burning mill.

He went across in the same quick steady manner as before, and the people below, made less acutely anxious by his previous success, were talking to each other, shouting out intelligence of the progress of the fire at the other end of the factory, telling of the endeavours of the firemen at that part to obtain water, while the closely packed body of men heaved and rolled from side to side. It was different from the former silent breathless hush. I do not know if it were from this cause, or from the recollection of peril past, or that he looked below, in the breathing moment before returning with the remaining person (a slight little man), slung across his shoulders, but Jem Wilson's step was less steady, his tread more uncertain; he seemed to feel with his foot for the next round of the ladder, to waver, and finally to stop half-way. By this time the crowd was still enough; in the awful instant that intervened no one durst speak, even to encourage. Many turned sick with terror, and shut their eyes to avoid seeing the catastrophe they dreaded. It came. The brave man swayel from side to side, at first as slightly as if only balancing himself; but he was evidently losing nerve, and even sense; it was only wonderful how the animal instinct of self-preservation did not overcome every generous feeling, and impel him at once to drop the helpless, inanimate body he carried; perhaps the same instinct told him, that the sudden loss of so heavy a weight would of itself be a great and imminent danger.

"Help me! she 's fainted," cried Margaret. But no one heeded. All eyes were directed upwards. At this point of time a rope, with a running noose, was dexterously thrown by one of the firemen, after the manner of a lasso, over the head and round the bodies of the two men. True, it was with rude and slight adjustment: but, slight as it was, it served as a steadying guide; it encouraged the sinking heart, the dizzy head. Once more Jem stepped onwards. He was not hurried by any jerk or pull. Slowly and gradually the rope was hauled in, slowly and gradually did he make the four or five paces between him and safety. The window was gained, and all were saved. The multitude in the street absolutely danced with triumph, and huzzaed and yelled till you would have fancied their very throats would crack; and then, with all the fickleness of interest characteristic of a large body of people, pressed and stumbled, and cursed and swore, in the hurry to get out of Dunham Street, and back to the immediate scene of the fire, the mighty diapason of whose roaring flames formed an awful accompaniment to the screams, and yells, and imprecations, of the struggling crowd.

As they pressed away, Margaret was left, pale and almost sinking under the weight of Mary's body, which she had preserved in an upright position by keeping her arms tight round Mary's waist, dreading, with reason, the trampling of unheeding feet.

Now, however, she gently let her down on the cold clean pavement; and the change of posture, and the difference in temperature, now that the people had withdrawn from their close neighbourhood, speedily restored her to consciousness.

Her first glance was bewildered and uncertain. She had forgotten where she was. Her cold, hard bed felt strange; the murky glare in the sky affrighted her. She shut her eyes to think, to recollect.

Her next look was upwards. The fearful bridge had been withdrawn; the window was unoccupied.

"They are safe," said Margaret.

"All? Are all safe, Margaret?" asked Mary.

"Ask yon fireman, and he 'll tell you more about it than I can. But I know they 're all safe."

The fireman hastily corroborated Margaret's words.

"Why did you let Jem Wilson go twice?" asked Margaret?

"Let? — why we could not hinder him. As soon as ever he 'd heard his father speak (which he was na long a doing), Jem were off like a shot; only saying he knowed better nor us where to find t' other man. We 'd all ha' gone, if he had na been in such a hurry, for no one can say as Manchester firemen is ever backward when there 's danger."

So saying, he ran off; and the two girls, without remark or discussion, turned homewards. They were overtaken by the elder Wilson, pale, grimy, and blear-eyed, but apparently as strong and well as ever. He loitered a minute or two alongside of them, giving an account of his detention in the mill; he then hastily wished goodnight, saying he must go home and tell his missis he was all safe and well: but after he had gone a few steps, he turned back, came on Mary's side of the pavement, and in an earnest whisper, which Margaret could not avoid hearing, he said,

"Mary, if my boy comes across you to-night, give him a kind word or two for my sake. Do! bless you, there 's a good wench."

Mary hung her head and answered not a word, and in an instant he was gone.

When they arrived at home, they found John Barton smoking his pipe, unwilling to question; yet very willing to hear all the details they could give him. Margaret went over the whole story, and it was amusing to watch his gradually increasing interest and excitement. First, the regular puffing abated, then ceased. Then the pipe was fairly taken out of his mouth, and held suspended. Then he rose, and at every further point he came a step nearer to the narrator.

When it was ended he swore (an unusual thing for him) that if Jem Wilson wanted Mary he should have her to-morrow, if he had not a penny to keep her.

Margaret laughed, but Mary, who was now recovered from her agitation, pouted and looked angry.

The work which they had left was resumed: but with full hearts, fingers never go very quickly; and I am sorry to say, that owing to the fire, the two younger Miss Ogdens were in such grief for the loss of their excellent father, that they were unable to appear before the little circle of sympathising friends gathered together to comfort the widow, and see the funeral set off.

CHAPTER VI.

"How little can the rich man know
  Of what the poor man feels,
When Want, like some dark demon foe,
  Nearer and nearer steals!

He never tramp'd the weary round,
  A stroke of work to gain,
And sicken'd at the dreaded sound
  Telling him 't was in vain.

Foot-sore, heart-sore, *he* never came
  Back through the winter's wind,
To a dank cellar, there no flame,
  No light, no food, to find.

He never saw his darlings lie
  Shivering, the flags their bed;
He never heard that maddening cry,
  'Daddy, a bit of bread!'" MANCHESTER SONG.

JOHN BARTON was not far wrong in his idea that the Messrs. Carsons would not be over-much grieved for the consequences of the fire in their mill. They were well insured; the machinery lacked the improvements of late years, and worked but poorly in comparison with that which might now be procured. Above all, trade was very slack; cottons could find no market, and goods lay packed and piled in many a warehouse. The mills were merely worked to keep the machinery, human and metal, in some kind of order and readiness for better times. So this was an excellent opportunity, Messrs. Carsons thought, for refitting their factory with first-rate improvements, for which the insurance money would amply pay. They were in no hurry about the business, however. The weekly drain of wages given for labour, useless in the present state of the market, was stopped. The partners had more leisure than they had known for years; and promised wives and daughters all manner of pleasant excursions, as soon as the weather should become more genial. It was a pleasant thing to be able to lounge over breakfast with a review or newspaper in hand; to have time for becoming acquainted with agreeable and accomplished daughters, on whose education no money had been spared, but whose fathers, shut up during a long day with calicoes and accounts, had so seldom had leisure to enjoy their daughters' talents. There were happy family evenings, now that the men of business had time for domestic enjoyments. There is another side to the picture. There were homes over which Carsons' fire threw a deep, terrible gloom; the homes of those who would fain work, and no man gave unto them — the homes of those to whom leisure was a curse. There, the family music was hungry wails, when week after week passed by, and there was no work to be had, and consequently no wages to pay for the bread the children cried aloud for in their young impatience of suffering. There was no breakfast to lounge over; their lounge was taken in bed, to try and keep warmth in them that bitter March weather, and, by being quiet, to deaden the gnawing wolf within. Many a penny that would have gone little way enough in oatmeal or potatoes, bought opium to still the hungry little ones, and make them forget their uneasiness in heavy troubled sleep. It was mother's mercy. The evil and the good of our nature came out strongly then. There were desperate fathers; there were bitter-tongued mothers (Oh God! what wonder!); there were reckless children; the very closest bonds of nature were snapt in that time of trial and distress. There was Faith such as the rich can never imagine on earth; there was "Love strong as death;" and self-denial, among rude, coarse men, akin to that of Sir Philip Sidney's most glorious deed. The vices of the poor sometimes astound us *here;* but when the secrets of all hearts shall be made known, their virtues will astound us in far greater degree. Of this I am certain.

As the cold, bleak spring came on (spring, in name alone), and consequently as trade continued dead, other mills shortened hours, turned off hands, and finally stopped work altogether.

Barton worked short hours; Wilson, of course, being a hand in Carsons' factory, had no work at all. But his son, working at an engineer's, and a steady man, obtained wages enough to maintain all the family in a careful way. Still it preyed on Wilson's mind to be so long indebted to his son. He was out of spirits and depressed. Barton was morose, and soured towards mankind as a body, and the rich in particular. One evening, when the clear light at six o'clock contrasted strangely with the Christmas cold, and when the bitter wind piped down every entry, and through every cranny, Barton sat brooding over his stinted fire, and listening for Mary's step, in unacknowledged trust that her presence would cheer him. The door was opened, and Wilson came breathless in.

"You 've not got a bit o' money by you, Barton?" asked he.

"Not I; who has now, I 'd like to know. Whatten you want it for?"

"I donnot* want it for mysel' tho' we 've none to spare. But don ye know Ben Davenport as worked at Carsons'? He 's down wi' the fever, and ne'er a stick o' fire nor a cowd** potatoe in the house."

"I han got no money, I tell ye," said Barton. Wilson looked disappointed. Barton tried not to be interested, but

* "Don" is constantly used in Lancashire for "do;" as it was by our older writers. "And that may non Hors *don.*" — *Sir J. Mandeville.* "But for th'entent to *don* this sinne." — *Chaucer.*

** "Cowd," cold. Teut. *kaud.* Dutch, *koud.*

he could not help it in spite of his gruffness. He rose, and went to the cupboard (his wife's pride long ago). There lay the remains of his dinner, hastily put by ready for supper. Bread, and a slice of cold fat boiled bacon. He wrapped them in his handkerchief, put them in the crown of his hat, and said — "Come, let us be going."

"Going — art thou going to work this time o' day."

"No, stupid, to be sure not. Going to see the chap thou spoke on." So they put on their hats and set out. On the way Wilson said Davenport was a good fellow, though too much of the Methodee; that his children were too young to work, but not too young to be cold and hnngry; that they had sunk lo wer and lower, and pawned thing after thing, and that they now lived in a cellar in Berry Street, off Store Street. Barton growled inarticulate words of no benevolent import to a large class of mankind, and so they went along till they arrived in Berry Street. It was unpaved: and down the middle a gutter forced its way, every now and then forming pools in the holes with which the street abounded. Never was the old Edinburgh cry of "Gardez l'eau," more necessary than in this street. As they passed, women from their doors tossed household slops of *every* description into the gutter; they ran into the next pool, which overflowed and stagnated. Heaps of ashes were the stepping-stones, on which the passer-by, who cared in the least for cleanliness, took care not to put his foot. Our friends were not dainty, but even they picked their way till they got to some steps leading down to a small area, where a person standing would have his head about one foot below the level of the street, and might at the same time, without the least motion of his body, touch the window of the cellar and the damp muddy wall right opposite. You went down one step even from the foul area into the cellar in which a family of human beings lived. It was very dark inside. The window panes of many of them were broken and stuffed with rags, which was reason enough for the dusky light that pervaded the place even at mid-day. After the account I have given of the state of the street, no one can be surprised that on going into the cellar inhabited by Davenport, the smell was so fœtid as almost to knock the two men down. Quickly recovering themselves, as those innured to such things do, they began to penetrate the thick darkness of the place, and to see three or four little children rolling on the damp, nay wet brick floor, through which the stagnant, filthy moisture of the street oozed up; the fire-place was empty and black; the wife sat on her husband's lair, and cried in the dark loneliness.

"See, missis, I'm back again. — Hold your noise, children, and don't mither* your mammy for bread, 'here 's a chap as has got some for you."

In that dim light, which was darkness to strangers, they clustered round Barton, and tore from him the food he had brought with him. It was a large hunch of bread, but it vanished in an instant.

"We mun do summut for 'em," said he to Wilson. "Ye stop here, and I 'll be back in half-an-hour."

So he strode, and ran, and hurried home. He emptied into the ever-useful pocket handkerchief the little meal remaining in the mug. Mary would have her tea at Miss Simmonds'; her food for the day was safe. Then he went upstairs for his better coat, and his one, gay red-and-yellow silk pocket-handkerchief — his jewels, his plate, his valuables, these were. He went to the pawnshop; he pawned them for five shillings; he stopped not, nor stayed, till he was once more in London Road, within five minutes' walk of Berry Street — then he loitered in his gait, in order to discover the shops he wanted. He bought meat, and a loaf of bread, candles, chips, and from a little retail yard he purchased a couple of hundred-weights of coal. Some money still remained — all destined for them, but he did not yet know how best to spend it. Food, light, and warmth, he had instantly seen were necessary; for luxuries he would wait. Wilson's eyes filled with tears when he saw Barton enter with his purchases. He understood it all, and longed to be once more in work that he might help

* "Mither," to trouble, and perplex. "I 'm welly mithered" — I 'm well nigh crazed.

in some of these material ways, without feeling that he was using his son's money. But though "silver and gold he had none," he gave heart-service, and loveworks of far more value. Nor was John Barton behind in these. "The fever" was (as it usually is in Manchester), of a low, putrid, typhoid kind; brought on by miserable living, filthy neighbourhood, and great depression of mind and body. It is virulent, malignant, and highly infectious. But the poor are fatalists with regard to infection; and well for them it is so, for in their crowded dwellings no invalid can be isolated. Wilson asked Barton if he thought he should catch it, and was laughed at for his idea.

The two men, rough, tender nurses as they were, lighted the fire, which smoked and puffed into the room as if it did not know the way up the damp, unused chimney. The very smoke seemed purifying and healthy in the thick clammy air. The children clamoured again for bread; but this time Barton took a piece first to the poor, helpless, hopeless woman, who still sat by the side of her husband, listening to his anxious miserable mutterings. She took the bread, when it was put into her hand, and broke a bit, but could not eat. She was past hunger. She fell down on the floor with a heavy unresisting bang. The men looked puzzled. "She 's well-nigh clemmed," said Barton. "Folk do say one mustn't give clemmed people much to eat; but, bless us, she 'll eat naught."

"I 'll tell yo what I 'll do," said Wilson. "I 'll take these two big lads, as does nought but fight, home to my missis for to-night, and I 'll get a jug o' tea. Them women always does best with tea and such like slop."

So Barton was now left alone with a little child, crying (when it had done eating) for mammy; with a fainting, dead-like woman; and with the sick man, whose mutterings were rising up to screams and shrieks of agonized anxiety. He carried the woman to the fire, and chafed her hands. He looked around for something to raise her head. There was literally nothing but some loose bricks. However, those he got; and taking off his coat he covered them with it as well as he could. He pulled her feet to the fire, which now began to emit some faint heat. He looked round for water, but the poor woman had been too weak to drag herself out to the distant pump, and water there was none. He snatched the child, and ran up the area-steps to the room above, and borrowed their only saucepan with some water in it. Then he began, with the useful skill of a working-man, to make some gruel; and when it was hastily made, he seized a battered iron table-spoon (kept when many other little things had been sold in a lot), in order to feed baby, and with it he forced one or two drops between her clenched teeth. The mouth opened mechanically to receive more, and gradually she revived. She sat up and looked round; and recollecting all, fell down again in weak and passive despair. Her little child crawled to her, and wiped with its fingers the thick-coming tears which she now had strength to weep. It was now high time to attend to the man. He lay on straw, so damp and mouldy, no dog would have chosen it in preference to flags; over it was a piece of sacking, coming next to his worn skeleton of a body; above him was mustered every article of clothing that could be spared by mother or children this bitter weather; and in addition to his own, these might have given as much warmth as one blanket, could they have been kept on him; but as he restlessly tossed to and fro, they fell off and left him shivering in spite of the burning heat of his skin. Every now and then he started up in his naked madness, looking like the prophet of woe in the fearful plague-picture; but he soon fell again in exhaustion, and Barton found he must be closely watched, lest in these falls he should injure himself against the hard brick floor. He was thankful when Wilson reappeared, carrying in both hands a jug of steaming tea, intended for the poor wife; but when the delirious husband saw drink, he snatched at it with animal instinct, with a selfishness he had never shown in health.

Then the two men consulted together. It seemed decided without a word being spoken on the subject, that both should spend the night with the forlorn couple; that was settled. But could no doctor be had? In all probability no; the next day an infirmary order must be begged, but meanwhile the only medical advice they could have must be from a druggist's. So Barton (being the moneyed man) set out to find a shop in London Road.

It is a pretty sight to walk through a street with lighted shops; the gas is so brilliant, the display of goods so much more vividly shown than by day, and of all shops a druggist's looks the most like the tales of our childhood, from Aladdin's garden of enchanted fruits to the charming Rosamond with her purple jar. No such associations had Barton; yet he felt the contrast between the well-filled, well-lighted shops and the dim gloomy cellar, and it made him moody that such contrasts should exist. They are the mysterious problem of life to more than him. He wondered if any in all the hurrying crowd, had come from such a house of mourning. He thought they all looked joyous, and he was angry with them. But he could not, you cannot, read the lot of those who daily pass you by in the street. How do you know the wild romances of their lives; the trials, the temptations they are even now enduring, resisting, sinking under? You may be elbowed one instant by the girl desperate in her abandonment, laughing in mad merriment with her outward gesture, while her soul is longing for the rest of the dead, and bringing itself to think of the cold-flowing river as the only mercy of God remaining to her here. You may pass the criminal, meditating crimes at which you will to-morrow shudder with horror as you read them. You may push against one, humble and unnoticed, the last upon eerth, who in Heaven will for ever be in the immediate light of God's countenance. Errands of mercy — errands of sin — did you ever think where all the thousands of people you daily meet are bound? Barton's was an errand of mercy; but the thoughts of his heart were touched by sin, by bitter hatred of the happy whom he, for the time, confounded with the selfish.

He reached a druggist's shop, and entered. The druggist

(whose smooth manners seemed to have been salved over with his own spermaceti) listened attentively to Barton's description of Davenport's illness; concluded it was typhus fever, very prevalent in that neighbourhood; and proceeded to make up a bottle of medicine, sweet spirits of nitre, or some such innocent potion, very good for slight colds, but utterly powerless to stop, for an instant, the raging fever of the poor man it was intended to relieve. He recommended the same course they had previously determined to adopt, applying the next morning for an Infirmary order; and Barton left the shop with comfortable faith in the physic given him; for men of his class, if they believe in physic at all, believe that every description is equally effiacious.

Meanwhile, Wilson had done what he could at Davenport's home. He had soothed, and covered the man many a time; he had fed and hushed the little child, and spoken tenderly to the woman, who lay still in her weakness and her weariness. He had opened a door, but only for an instant; it led into a back cellar, with a grating instead of a window, down which dropped the moisture from pigstyes, and worse abominations. It was not paved; the floor was one mass of bad smelling mud. It had never been used, for there was not an article of furniture in it; nor could a human being, much less a pig, have lived there many days. Yet the "back apartment" made a difference in the rent. The Davenports paid threepence more for having two rooms. When he turned round again, he saw the woman suckling the child from her dry, withered breast.

"Surely the lad is weaned!" exclaimed he, in surprise. "Why, how old is he?"

"Going on two year," she faintly answered. "But, oh! it keeps him quiet when I've nought else to gi' him, and he'll get a bit of sleep lying there, if he's getten nought beside. We han done our best to gi' the childer* food, howe'er we pinche ourselves."

"Han** ye had no money fra th' town?"

* Wickliffe uses "*childre*" in his Apology, page 26.

** "What concord *han* light and dark." — *Spenser*.

"No; my master is Buckhinghamshire born; and he 's feared the town would send him back to his parish, if he went to th' board; so we've just borne on in hope o' better times. But I think they 'll never come in my day;" and the poor woman began her weak high-pitched cry again.

"Here, sup* this drop o' gruel, and then try and get a bit o' sleep. John and I will watch by your master to-night."

"God's blessing be on you."

She finished the gruel, and fell into a dead sleep. Wilson covered her with his coat as well as he could, and tried to move lightly for fear of disturbing her; but there need have been no such dread, for her sleep was profound and heavy with exhaustion. Once only she roused to pull the coat round her little child.

And now Wilson's care, and Barton's to boot, was wanted to restrain the wild mad agony of the fevered man. He started up, he yelled, he seemed infuriated by overwhelming anxiety. He cursed and swore, which surprised Wilson, who knew his piety in health, and who did not know the unbridled tongue of delirium. At length he seemed exhausted, and fell asleep; and Barton and Wilson drew near the fire, and talked together in whispers. They sat on the floor, for chairs there were none; the sole table was an old tub turned upside-down. They put out the candle and conversed by the flickering fire-light.

"Han yo known this chap long?" asked Barton.

"Better nor three year. He's worked wi' Carsons that long, and were always a steady, civil-spoken fellow, though, as I said afore, somewhat of a Methodee. I wish I'd getten a letter he'd sent his missis, a week or two agone, when he were on tramp for work. It did my heart good to read it; for, yo see, I were a bit grumbling mysel; it seemed hard to be spunging on Jem, and taking a' his flesh-meat money to buy bread for me and them as I ought to be keeping. But, yo know, though I can earn nought, I mun eat summit. Well, as I telled ye, I were grumbling, when she (indicating the

* "And thay *soupe* the brothe thereof." — *Sir J. Mandeville.*

sleeping woman by a nod) brought me Ben's letter, for she could na' read hersel. It were as good as Bible-words; ne'er a word o' repining; a' about God being our father, and that we mun bear patiently whate'er he sends."

"Don ye think he's th' masters' father, too? I'd be loth to have 'em for brothers."

"Eh, John! donna talk so; sure there's many and many a master as good or better nor us."

"If you think so, tell me this. How comes it they're rich, and we're poor? I'd like to know that. Han they done as they'd be done for by us?"

But Wilson was no arguer; no speechifier, as he would have called it. So Barton, seeing he was likely to have it his own way, went on.

"You'll say (at least many a one does), they'n* getten capital an' we'n getten none. I say, our labour's our capital and we ought to draw interest on that. They get interest on their capital somehow a' this time, while ourn is lying idle, else how could they all live as they do? Besides, there's many on 'em has had nought to begin wi'; there's Carsons, and Duncombes, and Mengies, and many another, as comed into Manchester with clothes to their back, and that were all, and now they're worth their tens of thousands, a' getten out of our labour; why the very land as fetched but sixty pound twenty year agone is now worth six hundred, and that, too, is owing to our labour: but look at yo, and see me, and poor Davenport yonder; whatten better are we? They'n screwed us down to th' lowest peg, in order to make their great big fortunes, and build their great big houses, and we, why we're just clemming, many and many of us. Can you say there's nought wrong in this?"

"Well, Barton, I'll not gainsay ye. But Mr. Carsons spoke to me after th' fire, and says he, 'I shall ha' to retrench, and be very careful in my expenditure during these bad times, I assure ye;' so yo see th' masters suffer too."

* "They'n," contraction of "they han," they have.

"Han they ever seen a child o' their'n die for want o' food?" asked Barton, in a low, deep voice.

"I donnot mean," continued he, "to say as I'm so badly off. I'd scorn to speak for mysel; but when I see much men as Davenport there dying away, for very clemming, I cannot stand it. I 've but gotten Mary, and she keeps hersel pretty much. I think we 'll ha' to give up house-keeping; but that I donnot mind."

And in this kind of talk the night, the long heavy night of watching, wore away. As far as they could judge, Davenport continued in the same state, although the symptoms varied occasionally. The wife slept on, only roused by the cry of her child now and then, which seemed to have power over her, when far louder noises failed to disturb her. The watchers agreed, that as soon as it was likely Mr. Carsons would be up and visible, Wilson should go to his house, and beg for an Infirmary order. At length the gray dawn penetrated even into the dark cellar; Davenport slept, and Barton was to remain there until Wilson's return; so, stepping out into the fresh air, brisk and reviving, even in that street of abominations, Wilson took his way to Mr. Carsons'.

Wilson had about two miles to walk before he reached Mr. Carsons' house, which was almost in the country. The streets were not yet bustling and busy. The shopmen were lazily taking down the shutters, although it was near eight o'clock; for the day was long enough for the purchases people made in that quarter of the town, while trade was so flat. One or two miserable-looking women were setting off on their day's begging expedition. But there were few people abroad. Mr. Carsons' was a good house, and furnished with disregard to expense. But, in addition to lavish expenditure, there was much taste shown, and many articles chosen for their beauty and elegance adorned his rooms. As Wilson passed a window which a housemaid had thrown open, he saw pictures and gilding, at which he was tempted to stop and look; but then he thought it would not be respectful. So he hastened on to the kitchen door. The servants seemed very busy with preparations for breakfast; but good-naturedly, though hastily, told him to step in, and they could soon let Mr. Carsons know he was there. So he was ushered into a kitchen hung round with glittering tins, where a roaring fire burnt merrily, and where numbers of utensils hung round, at whose nature and use Wilson amused himself by guessing. Meanwhile, the servants bustled to and fro; an out-door man-servant came in for orders, and sat down near Wilson. The cook broiled steaks, and the kitchen-maid toasted bread, and boiled eggs.

The coffee steamed upon the fire, and altogether the odours were so mixed and appetizing, that Wilson began to yearn for food to break his fast, which had lasted since dinner the day before. If the servants had known this, they would have willingly given him meat and bread in abundance; but they were like the rest of us, and not feeling hunger themselves, forgot it was possible another might. So Wilson's craving turned to sickness, while they chatted on, making the kitchen's free and keen remarks upon the parlour.

"How late you were last night, Thomas?"

"Yes, I was right weary of waiting; they told me to be at the rooms by twelve; and there I was. But it was two o'clock before they called me."

"And did you wait all that time in the street?" asked the housemaid, who had done her work for the present, and come into the kitchen for a bit of gossip.

"My eye as like! you don't think I'm such a fool as to catch my death of cold, and let the horses catch their death too, as we should ha' done if we'd stopped there. No! I put th' horses up in th' stables at th' Spread Eagle, and went mysel', and got a glass or two by th' fire. They 're driving a good custom, them, wi' coachmen. There were five on us, and we'd many a quart o' ale, and gin wi' it, to keep out cold."

"Mercy on us, Thomas; you'll get a drunkard at last!"

"If I do, I know whose blame it will be. It will be missis's, and not mine. Flesh and blood can't sit to be starved to death on a coach-box, waiting for folks as don't know their own mind."

A servant, semi-upper-housemaid, semi-lady's-maid, now came down with orders from her mistress.

"Thomas, you must ride to the fishmonger's, and say missis can't give above half-a-crown a pound for salmon for Tuesday; she 's grumbling because trade 's so bad. And she'll want the carriage at three to go to the lecture, Thomas; at the Royal Execution, you know."

"Ay, ay, I know."

"And you 'd better all of you mind your P's and Q's, for she 's very black this morning. She 's got a bad headache."

"It 's a pity Miss Jenkins is not here to match her. Lord! how she and missis did quarrel which had got the worst headaches, it was that Miss Jenkins left for; she would not give up having bad heachaches, and missis could not abide any one to have 'em but herself."

"Missis will have her breakfast up-stairs, cook, and the cold partridge as was left yesterday, and put plenty of cream in her coffee, and she thinks there 's a roll left, and she would like it well buttered."

So saying, the maid left the kitchen to be ready to attend to the young ladies' bell when they chose to ring, after their late assembly the night before.

In the luxurious library, at the well-spread breakfast-table, sat the two Mr. Carsons, father and son. Both were reading —the father a newspaper, the son a review—while they lazily enjoyed their nicely prepared food. The father was a prepossessing-looking old man; perhaps self-indulgent you might guess. The son was strikingly handsome, and knew it. His dress was neat and well appointed, and his manners far more gentlemanly than his father's. He was the only son, and his sisters were proud of him; his father and mother were proud of him: he could not set up his judgment againt theirs; he was proud of himself.

The door opened and in bounded Amy, the sweet youngest

daughter of the house, a lovely girl of sixteen, fresh and glowing, and bright as a rosebud. She was too young to go to assemblies, at which her father rejoiced, for he had little Amy with her pretty jokes, and her bird-like songs, and her playful caresses all the evening to amuse him in his loneliness; and she was not too much tired, like Sophy and Helen, to give him her sweet company at breakfast the next morning.

He submitted willingly while she blinded him with her hands, and kissed his rough red face all over. She took his newspaper away after a little pretended resistance, and would not allow her brother Harry to go on with his review.

"I 'm the only lady this morning, papa, so you know you must make a great deal of me."

"My darling, I think you have your own way always, whether you 're the only lady or not."

"Yes, papa, you 're pretty good and obedient, I must say that; but I 'm sorry to say Harry is very naughty, and does not do what I tell him; do you, Harry?"

"I 'm sure I don't know what you mean to accuse me of, Amy; I expected praise and not blame; for did not I get you that eau de Portugal from town, that you could not meet with at Hughes', you little ungrateful puss?"

"Did you? Oh, sweet Harry; you 're as sweet as eau de Portugal yourself; you 're almost as good as papa; but still you know you did go and forget to ask Bigland for that rose, that new rose they say he has got."

"No, Amy, I did not forget. I asked him, and he has got the Rose, *sans reproche;* but do you know, little Miss Extravagance, a very small one is half a guinea?"

"Oh, I don't mind. Papa will give it me, won't you, dear father? He knows his little daughter can't live without flowers and scents."

Mr. Carsons tried to refuse his darling, but she coaxed him into acquiescence, saying she must have it, it was one of her necessaries. Life was not worth having without flowers.

"Then, Amy," said her brother, try and be content with peonies and dandelions."

"Oh you wretch! I don't call them flowers. Besides, you 're every bit as extravagant. Who gave half-a-crown for a bunch of lilies of the valley at Yates', a month ago, and then would not let his poor little sister have them, though she went on her knees to beg them? Answer me that, Master Hal."

"Not on compulsion," replied her brother, smiling with his mouth, while his eyes had an irritated expression, and he went first red, then pale, with vexed embarrassment.

"If you please, Sir," said a servant, entering the room, "here 's one of the mill people wanting to see you; his name is Wilson, he says."

"I 'll come to him directly; stay, tell him to come in here."

Amy danced off into the conservatory which opened out of the room, before the gaunt, pale, unwashed, unshaven weaver was ushered in. There he stood at the door, sleeking his hair with old country habit, and every now and then stealing a glance round at the splendour of the apartment.

"Well, Wilson, and what do you want to-day, man?"

"Please, Sir, Davenport 's ill of the fever, and I 'm come to know if you 've got an Infirmary order for him?"

"Davenport — Davenport; who is the fellow? I don't know the name."

"He 's worked in your factory better nor three years, Sir."

"Very likely, I don't pretend to know the names of the men I employ; that I leave to the overlooker. So he 's ill, eh?"

"Ay, Sir, he 's very bad; we want to get him in at the Fever Wards."

"I doubt if I 've an in-patient's order to spare at present; but I 'll give you an out-patient's, and welcome."

So saying, he rose up, unlocked a drawer, pondered a minute, and then gave Wilson an out-patient's order.

Meanwhile, the younger Mr. Carsons had ended his review, and began to listen to what was going on. He finished his breakfast, got up, and pulled five shillings out of his pocket, which he gave to Wilson as he passed him, for the "poor fellow." He went past quickly, and calling for his horse, mounted gaily, and rode away. He was anxious to be in time to have a look and a smile from lovely Mary Barton, as she went to Miss Simmonds'. But to-day he was to be disappointed. Wilson left the house, not knowing whether to be pleased or grieved. They had all spoken kindly to him, and who could tell if they might not inquire into Davenport's case, and do something for him and his family. Besides, the cook, who, when she had had time to think, after breakfast was sent in, had noticed his paleness, had had meat and bread ready to put in his hand when he came out of the parlour; and a full stomach makes every one of us more hopeful.

When he reached Berry Street, he had persuaded himself he bore good news, and felt almost elated in his heart. But it fell when he opened the cellar-door, and saw Barton and the wife both bending over the sick man's couch with awe-struck, saddened look.

"Come here," said Barton. "There 's a change comed over him sin' yo left, is there not?"

Wilson looked. The flesh was sunk, the features prominent, bony, and rigid. The fearful clay-colour of death was over all. But the eyes were open and sensitive, though the films of the grave were setting upon them.

"He wakened fra his sleep, as yo left him in, and began to mutter and moan; but he soon went off again, and we never knew he were awake till he called his wife, but now she 's here he 's gotten nought to say to her."

Most probably, as they all felt, he could not speak, for his strength was fast ebbing. They stood round him still and silent; even the wife checked her sobs, though her heart was like to break. She held her child to her breast, to try and keep him quiet. Their eyes were all fixed on the yet living one, whose moments of life were passing so rapidly away. At length he brought (with jerking convulsive effort) his two hands into the attitude of prayer. They saw his lips move, and bent to catch the words, which came in gasps, and not in tones.

"Oh Lord God! I thank thee, that the hard sruggle of living is over."

"Oh, Ben! Ben!" wailed forth his wife, "have you no thought for me? Oh, Ben! Ben! do say one word to help me through life."

He could not speak again. The trump of the archangel would set his tongue free; but not a word more would it utter till then. Yet he heard, he understood, and though sight failed, he moved his hand gropingly over the covering. They knew what he meant, and guided it to her head, bowed and hidden in her hands, when she had sunk in her woe. It rested there with a feeble pressure of endearment. The face grew beautiful, as the soul neared God. A peace beyond understanding came over it. The hand was a heavy stiff weight on the wife's head. No more grief or sorrow for him. They reverently laid out the corpse — Wilson fetching his only spare shirt to array it in. The wife still lay hidden in the clothes, in a stupor of agony.

There was a knock at the door, and Barton went to open it. It was Mary, who had received a message from her father, through a neighbour, telling her where he was; and she had set out early to come and have a word with him before her day's work; but some errands she had to do for Miss Simmonds had detained her until now.

"Come in, wench!" said her father. "Try if thou canst comfort yon poor, poor woman, kneeling down there. God help her." Mary did not know what to say, or how to comfort; but she knelt down by her, and put her arm round her neck, and in a little while fell to crying herself so bitterly that the source of tears was opened by sympathy in the widow, and her full heart, was, for a time, relieved.

And Mary forgot all purposed meeting with her gay lover, Harry Carsons; forgot Miss Simmonds' errands, and her anger, in the anxious desire to comfort the poor lone woman. Never had her sweet face looked more angelic, never had her gentle voice seemed so musical as when she murmured her broken sentences of comfort.

"Oh, don't cry so, dear Mrs. Davenport, pray don't take on so. Sure he 's gone where he 'll never know care again. Yes, I know how lonesome you must feel; but think of your children. Oh! we 'll all help to earn food for 'em. Think how sorry *he 'd* be, if he sees you fretting so. Don't cry so, please don't."

And she ended by crying herself as passionately as the poor widow.

It was agreed the town must bury him; he had paid to a burial club as long as he could, but by a few weeks' omission, he had forfeited his claim to a sum of money now. Would Mrs. Davenport and the little child go home with Mary? The latter brightened up as she urged this plan; but no! where the poor, fondly loved remains were, there would the mourner be; and all that they could do was to make her as comfortable as their funds would allow, and to beg a neighbour to look in and say a word at times. So she was left alone with her dead, and they went to work that had work, and he who had none, took upon him the arrangements for the funeral.

Mary had many a scolding from Miss Simmonds that day for her absence of mind. To be sure Miss Simmonds was much put out by Mary's non-appearance in the morning with certain bits of muslin, and shades of silk which were wanted to complete a dress to be worn that night; but it was true enough that Mary did not mind what she was about; she was too busy planning how her old black gown (her best when her mother died) might be spunged, and turned, and lengthened into something like decent mourning for the widow. And when she went home at night (though it was very late, as a sort of retribution for her morning's negligence), she set to work at once, and was so busy and so glad over her task, that she had, every now and then, to check herself in singing merry ditties, that she felt little accorded with the sewing on which she was engaged.

So when the funeral day came, Mrs. Davenport was neatly arrayed in black, a satisfaction to her poor heart in the midst of her sorrow. Barton and Wilson both accompanied her, as she led her two elder boys, and followed the coffin. It was a simple walking funeral, with nothing to grate on the feelings of any; far more in accordance with its purpose, to my mind, than the gorgeous hearses, and nodding plumes, which form the grotesque funeral pomp of respectable people. There was no "rattling the bones over the stones," of the pauper's funeral. Decently and quietly was he followed to the grave by one determined to endure her woe meekly for his sake. The only mark of pauperism attendant on the burial concerned the living and joyous, far more than the dead, or the sorrowful. When they arrived in the churchyard, they halted before a raised and handsome tombstone; in reality a wooden mockery of stone respectabilities which adorned the burial-ground. It was easily raised in a very few minutes, and below was the grave in which pauper bodies were piled until within a foot or two of the surface; when the soil was shovelled over, and stamped down, and the wooden cover went to do temporary duty over another hole.* But little they recked of this who now gave up their dead.

CHAPTER VII.

"How infinite the wealth of love and hope
Garnered in these same tiny treasure-houses!
And oh! what bankrupts in the world we feel,
When Death, like some remorseless creditor,
Seizes on all we fondly thought our own." 'THE TWINS.'

THE ghoul-like fever was not to be braved with impunity, and baulked of its prey. The widow had reclaimed her children; her neighbours, in the good Samaritan sense of the word, had paid her little arrears of rent, and made her a few

* The case to my certain knowledge, in one churchyard in Manchester. There may be more.

shillings beforehand with the world. She determined to flit from that cellar to another less full of painful associations, less haunted by mournful memories. The board, not so formidable as she had imagined, had inquired into her case; and, instead of sending her to Stoke Claypole, her husband's Buckinghamshire parish, as she had dreaded, had agreed to pay her rent. So food for four months was all she was now required to find; only for three she would have said; for herself, and the unweaned child were but reckoned as one in her calculation.

She had a strong heart, now her bodily strength had been recruited by a week or two of food, and she would not despair. So she took in some little children to nurse, who brought their daily food with them, which she cooked for them, without wronging their helplessness of a crumb; and when she had restored them to their mother's at night, she set to work at plain sewing, "seam, and gusset, and band," and sat thinking how she might best cheat the factory inspector, and persuade him that her strong, big, hungry Ben, was above thirteen. Her plan of living was so far arranged, when she heard, with keen sorrow, that Wilson's twin lads were ill of the fever.

They had never been strong. They were like many a pair of twins, and seemed to have but one life divided between them. One life, one strength, and in this instance, I might almost say, one brain; for they were helpless, gentle, silly children, but not the less dear to their parents and to their strong, active, manly, elder brother. They were late on their feet, late in talking, late every way; had to be nursed and cared for when other lads of their age were tumbling about in the street, and losing themselves, and being taken to the police-office miles away from home.

Still want had never yet come in at the door to make love, for these innocents fly out of the window. Nor was this the case even now, when Jem Wilson's earnings, and his mother's occasional charrings were barely sufficient to give all the family their fill of food.

But when the twins, after ailing many days, and caring little for their meat, fell sick on the same afternoon, with the same heavy stupor of suffering, the three hearts that loved them so, each felt, though none acknowledged to the other, that they had little chance for life. It was nearly a week before the tale of their illness spread as far as the court where the Wilsons had once dwelt, and the Bartons yet lived.

Alice had heard of the sickness of her little nephews several days before, and had locked her cellar door, and gone off straight to her brother's house, in Ancoats; but she was often absent for days, sent for, as her neighbours knew, to help in some sudden emergency of illness or distress, so that occasioned no surprise.

Margaret met Jem Wilson several days after his brothers were seriously ill, and heard from him the state of things at his home. She told Mary of it as she entered the court late that evening; and Mary listened with saddened heart to the strange contrast which such woeful tidings presented to the gay and loving words she had been hearing on her walk home. She blamed herself for being so much taken up with visions of the golden future, that she had lately gone but seldom on Sunday afternoons, or other leisure time, to see Mrs. Wilson, her mother's friend; and with hasty purpose of amendment she only stayed to leave a message for her father with the next-door neighbour, and then went off at a brisk pace on her way to the house of mourning.

She stopped with her hand on the latch of the Wilsons' door, to still her beating heart, and listened to the hushed quiet within. She opened the door softly: there sat Mrs. Wilson in the old rocking-chair, with one sick, death-like boy lying on her knee, crying without let or pause, but softly, gently, as fearing to disturb the troubled gasping child; while behind her, old Alice let her fast-dropping tears fall down on the dead body of the other twin, which she was laying out on a board, placed on a sort of sofa-settee in a corner of the room. Over the child, which yet breathed, the father bent, watching anxiously for some ground of hope, where hope there was none. Mary stepped slowly and lightly across to Alice.

"Ay, poor lad! God has taken him early, Mary."

Mary could not speak; she did not know what to say; it was so much worse than she had expected. At last she ventured to whisper,

"Is there any chance for the other one, think you?"

Alice shook her head, and told with a look that she believed there was none. She next endeavoured to lift the little body, and carry it to its old-accustomed bed in its parent's room. But earnest as the father was in watching the yet-living, he had eyes and ears for all that concerned the dead, and sprang gently up, and took his dead son on his hard couch in his arms with tender strength, and carried him upstairs as if afraid o' wakening him.

The other child gasped longer, louder, with more of effort.

"We mun get him away from his mother. He cannot die while she's wishing him."

"Wishing him?" said Mary, in a tone of inquiry.

"Ay; donno' ye know what wishing mean? There 's none can die in the arms of those who are wishing them sore to stay on earth. The soul o' them as holds them won't let the dying soul go free; so it has a hard struggle for the quiet of death. We mun get him away fra' his mother, or he'll have a hard death, poor lile* fellow."

So without circumlocution she went and offered to take the sinking child. But the mother would not let him go, and looking in Alice's face with brimming and imploring eyes, declared in earnest whispers, that she was not wishing him, that she would fain have him released from his suffering. Alice and Mary stood by with eyes fixed on the poor child, whose struggles seemed to increase, till at last his mother said with a choking voice,

* "Lile," a north-country word for "little."
"Wit *leil* labour to live." — *Piers Ploughman.*

"May happen* yo'd better take him, Alice; I believe my heart 's wishing him a' this while, for I cannot, no, I cannot bring mysel to let my two childer go in one day; I cannot help longing to keep him, and yet he sha'n't suffer longer for me."

She bent down, and fondly, oh! with what passionate fondness, kissed her child, and then gave him up to Alice, who took him with tender care. Nature's struggles were soon exhausted, and he breathed his little life away in peace.

Then the mother lifted up her voice and wept. Her cries brought her husband down to try with his aching heart to comfort her's. Again Alice laid out the dead, Mary helping with reverent fear. The father and mother carried him up-stairs to the bed, where his little brother lay in calm repose.

Mary and Alice drew near the fire, and stood in quiet sorrow for some time. Then Alice broke the silence by saying,

"It will be bad news for Jem, poor fellow, when he comes home."

"Where is he?" asked Mary.

"Working over-hours at th' shop. They'n getten a large order fra' forrin parts; and yo' know, Jem mun work, though his heart 's well-nigh breaking for these poor laddies."

Again they were silent in thought, and again Alice spoke first.

"I sometimes think the Lord is against planning. Whene'er I plan over-much, He is sure to send and mar all my plans, as if He would ha' me put the future into His hands. Afore Christmas-time I was as full as full could be, of going home for good and all; yo' han heard how I 've wished it this terrible long time. And a young lass from behind Burton came into place in Manchester last Martinmas; so after awhile, she had a Sunday out, and she comes to me, and tells me some cousins o' mine bid her find me out, and say how glad they should be to ha' me to bide wi' 'em, and look after th' childer, for they'n getten a big farm, and she 's a deal to do among th'

* "May happen," perhaps.

cows. So many a winter's night did I lie awake and think, that please God, come summer, I'd bid George and his wife good bye, and go home at last. Little did I think how God Almighty would baulk me, for not leaving my days in His hands, who had led me through the wilderness hitherto. Here 's George out of work, and more cast down than ever I seed him; wanting every chip o' comfort he can get, e'en afore this last heavy stroke; and now I'm thinking the Lord's finger points very clear to my fit abiding place; and I'm sure if George and Jane can say 'His will be done,' it 's no more than what I'm beholden to do."

So saying, she fell to tidying the room, removing as much as she could every vestige of sickness; making up the fire, and setting on the kettle for a cup of tea for her sister-in-law, whose low moans and sobs were occasionally heard in the room below.

Mary helped her in all these little offices. They were busy in this way when the door was softly opened, and Jem came in, all grimed and dirty from his nightwork, his soiled apron wrapped round his middle, in guise and apparel in which he would have been sorry at another time to have been seen by Mary. But just now he hardly saw her; he went straight up to Alice, and asked how the little chaps were. They had been a shade better at dinner-time, and he had been working away through the long afternoon, and far into the night, in the belief that they had taken the turn. He had stolen out during the half-hour allowed at the works for tea, to buy them an orange or two, which now puffed out his jacket-pocket.

He would make his aunt speak: he would not understand her shake of the head and fast coursing tears.

"They 're both gone," said she.

"Dead!"

"Ay! poor fellows. They took worse about two o'clock. Joe went first, as easy as a lamb, and Will died harder like."

"Both!"

"Ay, lad! both. The Lord has ta'en them from some evil to come, or He would na ha' made choice o' them. Ye may rest sure o' that."

Jem went to the cupboard, and quietly extricated from his pocket the oranges he had bought. But he stayed long there, and at last his sturdy frame shook with his strong agony. The two women were frightened, as women always are, on witnessing a man's overpowering grief. They cried afresh in company. Mary's heart melted within her as she witnessed Jem's sorrow, and she stepped gently up to the corner where he stood, with his back turned to them, and putting her hand softly on his arm, said,

"Oh, Jem, don't give way so; I cannot bear to see you."

Jem felt a strange leap of joy in his heart, and knew the power she had of comforting him. He did not speak, as though fearing to destroy by sound or motion the happiness of that moment, when her soft hand's touch thrilled through his frame, and her silvery voice was whispering tenderness in his ear. Yes! it might be very wrong; he could almost hate himself for it; with death and woe so surrounding him, it yet was happiness, was bliss, to be so spoken to by Mary.

"Don't, Jem, please don't," whispered she again, believing that his silence was only another form of grief.

He could not contain himself. He took her hand in his firm yet trembling grasp, and said, in tones that instantly produced a revulsion in her mood,

"Mary, I almost loathe myself when I feel I would not give up this minute, when my brothers lie dead, and father and mother are in such trouble, for all my life that 's past and gone. And, Mary (as she tried to release her hand), you know what makes me feel so blessed."

She did know — he was right there. But as he turned to catch a look at her sweet face, he saw that it expressed unfeigned distress, almost amounting to vexation; a dread of him, that he thought was almost repugnance.

He let her hand go, and she quickly went away to Alice's side.

"Fool that I was — nay, wretch that I was — to let myself take this time of trouble to tell her how I loved her; no wonder that she turns away from such a selfish beast."

Partly to relieve her from his presence, and partly from natural desire, and partly, perhaps, from a penitent wish to share to the utmost his parents' sorrow, he soon went up-stairs to the chamber of death.

Mary mechanically helped Alice in all the duties she performed through the remainder of that long night, but she did not see Jem again. He remained up-stairs until after the early dawn showed Mary that she need have no fear of going home through the deserted and quiet streets, to try and get a little sleep before work-hour. So leaving kind messages to George and Jane Wilson, and hesitating whether she might dare to send a few kind words to Jem, and deciding that she had better not, she stepped out into the bright morning light, so fresh a contrast to the darkened room where death had been.

"They had
Another morn than ours."

Mary lay down on her bed in her clothes; and whether it was this, or the broad daylight that poured in through the sky window, or whether it was over-excitement, it was long before she could catch a wink of sleep. Her thoughts ran on Jem's manner and words; not but what she had known the tale they told for many a day; but still she wished he had not put it so plainly.

"Oh dear," said she to herself, "I wish he would not mistake me so; I never dare to speak a common word o' kindness, but his eye brightens and his cheek flushes. It 's very hard on me; for father and George Wilson are old friends; and Jem and I ha' known each other since we were quite children. I cannot think what possesses me, that I must always be wanting to comfort him when he 's downcast, and that I must go meddling wi' him to-night, when sure enough it was his aunt's place to speak to him. I don't care for him, and yet, unless I'm always watching myself, I'm speaking to him in a loving voice. I think I cannot go right, for I either check myself till I'm downright cross to him, or else I speak just natural, and that's too kind and tender by half. And I'm as good as engaged to be married to another; and another far handsomer than Jem; only I think I like Jem's face best for all that; liking's liking, and there's no help for it. Well, when I'm Mrs. Harry Carsons, may happen I can put some good fortune in Jem's way. But will he thank me for it? He's rather savage at times, that I can see, and perhaps kindness from me, when I'm another's, will only go against the grain. I'll not plague myself wi' thinking any more about him, that I won't."

So she turned on her pillow, and fell asleep, and dreamt of what was often in her waking thoughts; of the day when she should ride from church in her carriage, with wedding-bells ringing, and take up her astonished father, and drive away from the old dim work-a-day court for ever, to live in a grand house, where her father should have newspapers, and pamphlets, and pipes, and meat dinners, every day,—and all day long if he liked.

Such thoughts mingled in her predilection for the handsome young Mr. Carsons, who, unfettered by work-hours, let scarcely a day pass without contriving a meeting with the beautiful little milliner he had first seen while lounging in a shop where his sisters were making some purchases, and afterwards never rested till he had freely, though respectfully, made her acquaintance in her daily walks. He was, to use his own expression to himself, quite infatuated by her, and was restless each day till the time came when he had a chance, and, of late, more than a chance of meeting her. There was something of keen practical shrewdness about her, which contrasted very bewitchingly with the simple, foolish, unworldly ideas she had picked up from the romances which Miss Simmonds' young ladies were in the habit of recommending to each other.

Yes! Mary was ambitious, and did not favour Mr. Carsons the less because he was rich and a gentleman. The old leaven, infused, years ago by her aunt Esther, fermented in her little bosom, and perhaps all the more for her father's aversion to the rich and the gentle. Such is the contrariness of the human heart, from Eve downwards, that we all, in our old Adam state, fancy things forbidden sweetest. So Mary dwelt upon and enjoyed the idea of some day becoming a lady, and doing all the elegant nothings appertaining to ladyhood. It was a comfort to her, when scolded by Miss Simmonds, to think of the day when she would drive up to the door in her own carriage, to order her gowns from the hasty-tempered yet kind dressmaker. It was a pleasure to her to hear the general admiration of the two elder Miss Carsons, acknowledged beauties in ball-room and street, on horseback and on foot, and to think of the time when she should ride and walk with them in loving sisterhood. But the best of her plans, the holiest, that which in some measure redeemed the vanity of the rest, were those relating to her father; her dear father, now oppressed with care, and always a disheartened, gloomy person. How she would surround him with every comfort she could devise (of course, he was to live with them); till he should acknowledge riches to be very pleasant things, and bless his lady-daughter! Every one who had shown her kindness in her low estate should then be repaid a hundred-fold.

Such were the castles in the air, the Alnaschar-visions in which Mary indulged, and which she was doomed in after days to expiate with many tears.

Meanwhile, her words—or, even more, her tones—would maintain their hold on Jem Wilson's memory. A thrill would yet come over him when he remembered how her hand had rested on his arm. The thought of her mingled with all his grief, and it was profound, for the loss of his brothers.

CHAPTER VIII.

"Deal gently, with them, they have much endured,
Scoff not at their fond hopes and earnest plans,
Though they may seem to thee wild dreams and fancies.
Perchance, in the rough school of stern experience,
They 've something learned which Theory does not teach;
Or if they greatly err, deal gently still,
And let their error but the stronger plead
'Give us the light and guidance that we need!'"

'Love Thoughts.'

One Sunday afternoon, about three weeks after that mournful night, Jem Wilson set out with the ostensible purpose of calling on John Barton. He was dressed in his best, his Sunday suit of course; while his face glittered with the scrubbing he had bestowed on it. His dark black hair had been arranged and re-arranged before the household looking-glass, and in his button-hole he stuck a narcissus (a sweet Nancy is its pretty Lancashire name), hoping it would attract Mary's notice, so that he might have the delight of giving it her.

It was a bad beginning of his visit of happiness that Mary saw him some minutes before he came into her father's house. She was sitting at the end of the dresser, with the little window-blind drawn on one side, in order that she might see the passers-by, in the intervals of reading her Bible, which lay open before her. So she watched all the greeting a friend gave Jem; she saw the face of condolence, the sympathetic shake of the hand, and had time to arrange her own face and manner before Jem came in, which he did, as if he had eyes for no one but her father, who sat smoking his pipe by the fire, while he read an old "Nothern Star," borrowed from a neighbouring public-house.

Then he turned to Mary, who, he felt by the sure instinct of love, by which almost his body thought, was present. Her hands were busy adjusting her dress; a forced and unnecessary movement Jem could not help thinking. Her accost was quiet and friendly, if grave; she felt that she reddened like a rose, and wished she could prevent it, while Jem wondered if her blushes arose from fear, or anger, or love.

She was very cunning, I am afraid. She pretended to read diligently, and not to listen to a word that was said, while in fact she heard all sounds, even to Jem's long, deep sighs, which wrung her heart. At last she took up her Bible, and as if their conversation disturbed her, went up-stairs to her little room. And she had scarcely spoken a word to Jem; scarcely looked at him; never noticed his beautiful sweet Nancy, which only awaited her least word of praise to be hers! He did not know—that pang was spared—that in her little dingy bed-room, stood a white jug, filled with a luxuriant bunch of early spring roses, making the whole room fragrant and bright. They were the gift of her richer lover. So Jem had to go on sitting with John Barton, fairly caught in his own trap, and had to listen to his talk, and answer him as best he might.

"There 's the right stuff in this here 'Star,' and no mistake. Such a right-down piece for short hours."

"At the same rate of wages as now?" asked Jem.

"Ay, ay! else where 's the use? It 's only taking out o' the master's pocket what they can well afford. Did I ever tell yo what th' Infirmary chap let me into, many a year agone?"

"No," said Jem, listlessly.

"Well! yo must know I were in th' Infirmary for a fever, and times were rare and bad, and there be good chaps there to a man, while he 's wick,* whate'er they may be about cutting him up at after.** So when I were better o' th' fever, but weak as water, they says to me, says they, 'If yo' can write, you may stay in a week longer, and help our surgeon wi' sorting his papers; and we'll take care yo 've your belly fully of meat and drink. Yo 'll be twice as strong in a week.' So there wanted but one word to that bargain. So I were set to writing and copying; th' writing I could do well enough, but they 'd such

* "Wick," alive. Anglo-Saxon, cwic. "The *quick* and the dead." —*Book of Common Prayer.*

** "At after."

"*At after* souper goth this noble king."

Chaucer; 'The Squire's Tale.'

queer ways o' spelling that I 'd ne'er been used to, that I 'd to look first at th' copy and then at my letters, for all the world like a cock picking up grains o' corn. But one thing startled me e'en then, and I thought I 'd make bold to ask the surgeon the meaning o't. I 've gotten no head for numbers, but this I know, that by *far th' greater part o' the accidents as comed in, happened in th' last two hours o' work* when folk getten tired and careless. Th' surgeon said it were all true, and that he were going to bring that fact to light."

Jem was pondering Mary's conduct; but the pause made him aware he ought to utter some civil listening noise; so he said

"Very true."

"Ay, it 's true enough, my lad, that we 're sadly overborne, and worse will come of it afore long. Block-printers is going to strike; they 'n getten a bang-up union, as won't let 'em be put upon. But there 's many a thing will happen afore long, as folk don't expect. Yo may take my word for that, Jem."

Jem was very willing to take it, but did not express the curiosity he should have done. So John Barton thought he 'd try another hint or two.

"Working folk won't be ground to the dust much longer. We 'n a' had as much to bear as human nature can bear. So, if th' masters can't do us no good, and they say they can't, we mun try higher folk."

Still Jem was not curious. He gave up hope of seeing Mary again by her own good free will; and the next best thing would be, to be alone to think of her. So muttering something which he meant to serve as an excuse for his sudden departure, he hastily wished John good afternoon, and left him to resume his pipe and politics.

For three years past, trade had been getting worse and worse, and the price of provisions higher and higher. This disparity between the amount of the earnings of the working classes and the price of their food, occasioned in more cases than could well be imagined, disease and death. Whole families went through a gradual starvation. They only wanted a Dante to record their sufferings. And yet even his words would fall short of the awful truth; they could only present an outline of the tremendous facts of the destitution that surrounded thousands upon thousands in the terrible years 1839, 1840, and 1841. Even philanthropists who had studied the subject were forced to own themselves perplexed in the endeavour to ascertain the real causes of the misery; the whole matter was of so complicated a nature, that it became next to impossible to understand it thoroughly. It need excite no surprise then to learn that a bad feeling between working-men and the upper classes became very strong in this season of privation. The indigence and sufferings of the operatives induced a suspicion in the minds of many of them, that their legislators, their magistrates, their employers, and even the ministers of religion, were, in general, their oppressors and enemies; and were, in league for their prostration and enthralment. The most deplorable and enduring evil that arose out of the period of commercial depression to which I refer, was this feeling of alienation between the different classes of society. It is so impossible to describe, or even faintly to picture, the state of distress which prevailed in the town at that time, that I will not attempt it; and yet I think again that surely, in a Christian land, it was not known even so feebly as words could tell it, or the more happy and fortunate would have thronged with their sympathy and their aid. In many instances the sufferers wept first, and then they cursed. Their vindictive feelings exhibited themselves in rabid politics. And when I hear, as I have heard, of the sufferings and privations of the poor, of provision-shops where ha'porths of tea, sugar, butter, and even flour, were sold to accommodate the indigent, — of parents sitting in their clothes by the fire-side during the whole night for seven weeks together, in order that their only bed and bedding might be reserved for the use of their large family, — of others sleeping upon the cold hearth-stone for weeks in succession, without adequate means of providing themselves with food or fuel (and this in the depth of winter), — of others being compelled to fast for days together, uncheered by any hope of better fortune, living, moreover, or rather starving, in a crowded garret, or damp cellar, and gradually sinking under the pressure of want and despair into a premature grave; and when this has been confirmed by the evidence of their care-worn looks, their excited feelings, and their desolate homes, — can I wonder that many of them, in such times of misery and destitution, spoke and acted with ferocious precipitation?

An idea was now springing up among the operatives, that originated with the Chartists, but which came at last to be cherished as a darling child by many and many a one.* They could not believe that government knew of their misery: they rather chose to think it possible that men could voluntarily assume the office of legislators for a nation ignorant of its real state; as who should make domestic rules for the pretty behaviour of children without caring to know that those children had been kept for days without food. Besides, the starving multitudes had heard, that the very existence of their distress had been denied in Parliament; and though they felt this strange and inexplicable, yet the idea that their misery had still to be revealed in all its depths, and that then some remedy would be found, soothed their aching hearts, and kept down their rising fury.

So a petition was framed, and signed by thousands in the bright spring days of 1839, imploring Parliament to hear witnesses who could testify to the unparalleled destitution of the manufacturing districts. Nottingham, Sheffield, Glasgow, Manchester, and many other towns, were busy appointing delegates to convey this petition, who might speak, not merely of what they had seen, and had heard, but from what they had borne and suffered. Life-worn, gaunt, anxious, hunger-stamped men, were those delegates.

One of them was John Barton. He would have been ashamed to own the flutter of spirits his appointment gave him. There was the childish delight of seeing London — that went a little way, and but a little way. There was the vain idea of speaking out his notions before so many grand folk —

that went a little further; and last, there was the really pure gladness of heart arising from the idea that he was one of those chosen to be instruments in making known the distresses of the people, and consequently in procuring them some grand relief, by means of which they should never suffer want or care any more. He hoped largely, but vaguely, of the results of his expedition. An argosy of the precious hopes of many otherwise despairing creatures, was that petition to be heard concerning their sufferings.

The night before the morning on which the Manchester delegates were to leave for London, Barton might be said to hold a levée, so many neighbours came dropping in. Job Legh had early established himself and his pipe by John Barton's fire, not saying much, but puffing away, and imagining himself of use in adjusting the smoothing-irons that hung before the fire, ready for Mary when she should want them. As for Mary, her employment was the same as that of Beau Tibbs' wife, "Just washing her father's two shirts," in the pantry back-kitchen; for she was anxious about his appearance in London. (The coat had been redeemed, though the silk handkerchief was forfeited.) The door stood open, as usual, between the houseplace and back-kitchen, so she gave her greeting to their friends as they entered.

"So, John, yo 're bound for London, are yo?" said one.

"Ay, I suppose I mun go," answered John, yielding to necessity as it were.

"Well, there 's many a thing I 'd like yo to speak on to the parliament people. Thou 'lt not spare 'em, John, I hope. Tell 'em our minds; how we 're thinking we 've been clemmed long enough, and we donnot see whatten good they 'n been doing, if they can't give us what we 're all crying for sin' the day we were born."

"Ay, ay! I 'll tell 'em that, and much more to it, when it gets to my turn; but thou knows there 's many will have their word afore me."

"Well, thou 'lt speak at last. Bless thee, lad, do ask 'em

to make th' masters to break th' machines. There 's never been good times sin' spinning-jennies came up."

"Machines is th' ruin of poor folk," chimed in several voices.

"For my part," said a shivering, half-clad man, who crept near the fire, as if ague-stricken, "I would like thee to tell 'em to pass th' short-hours' bill. Flesh and blood gets wearied wi' so much work; why should factory hands work so much longer nor other trades? Just ask 'em that, Barton, will ye?"

Barton was saved the necessity of answering, by the entrance of Mrs. Davenport, the poor widow he had been so kind to; she looked half-fed, and eager, but was decently clad. In her hand she brought a little newspaper parcel, which she took to Mary, who opened it, and then called out, dangling a shirt collar from her soapy fingers:

"See, father, what a dandy you 'll be in London! Mrs. Davenport has brought you this; made new cut, all after the fashion. — Thank you for thinking on him."

"Eh, Mary!" said Mrs. Davenport, in a low voice. "Whatten 's all I can do, to what he 's done for me and mine? But, Mary, sure I can help ye, for you 'll be busy wi' this journey."

"Just help me wring these out, and then I 'll take 'em to th' mangle."

So Mrs. Davenport became a listener to the conversation; and after a while joined in.

"I 'm sure, John Barton, if yo are taking messages to the parliament folk, yo 'll not object to telling 'em what a sore trial it is, this law o' theirs, keeping childer fra' factory work, whether they be weakly or strong. There 's our Ben; why, porridge seems to go no way wi' him, he eats so much; and I han gotten no money to send him t' school, as I would like; and there he is, rampaging about the streets a' day, getting hungrier and hungrier, and picking up a' manner o' bad ways; and th' inspector won't let him in to work in th' factory, because he 's not right age; though he 's twice as strong as

Sankey's little rittling* of a lad, as works till he cries for his legs aching so, though he is right age, and better."

"I 've one plan I wish to tell John Barton," said a pompous, careful-speaking man, "and I should like him for to lay it afore the honourable house. My mother comed out o' Oxfordshire, and were under-laundry-maid in Sir Francis Dashwood's family; and when we were little ones, she 'd tell us stories of their grandeur: and one thing she named were, that Sir Francis wore two shirts a day. Now he were all as one as a parliament man; and many on 'em, I han no doubt, are like extravagant. Just tell 'em John, do, that they 'd be doing the Lancashire weavers a great kindness, if they 'd ha' their shirts a' made o' calico; 't would make trade brisk, that would, wi' the power o' shirts they wear."

Job Legh now put in his word. Taking the pipe out of his mouth, and addressing the last speaker, he said:

"I 'll tell ye what, Bill, and no offence mind ye; there 's but hundreds of them parliament folk as wear so many shirts to their back; but there 's thousands and thousands o' poor weavers as han only gotten one shirt i' th' world; ay, and don't know where t' get another when that rag 's done, though they 're turning out miles o' calico every day; and many o' mile o't is lying in warehouses, stopping up trade for want o' purchasers. Yo take my advice, John Barton, and ask parliament to set trade free, so as workmen can earn a decent wage, and buy their two, ay and three, shirts a-year; that would make weaving brisk."

He put his pipe in his mouth again, and redoubled his puffing to make up for lost time.

"I'm afeard, neighbours," said John Barton, "I've not much chance o' telling 'em all yo say; what I think on, is just speaking out about the distress, that they say is nought. When they hear o' children born on wet flags, without a rag t' cover 'em, or a bit o' food for th' mother; when they hear of folk lying down to die i' th' streets, or hiding their want i' some

* "Ritling," probably a corruption of "ricketling," a child that suffers from the rickets — a weakling.

hole o' a cellar till death come to set 'em free; and when they hear o' all this plague, pestilence, and famine, they 'll surely do somewhat wiser for us than we can guess at now. Howe'er, I han no objection, if so be there 's an opening to speak up for what yo say; anyhow, I 'll do my best, and yo see now, if better times don't come after Parliament knows all."

Some shook their heads, but more looked cheery: and then one by one dropped off, leaving John and his daughter alone.

"Didst thou mark how poorly Jane Wilson looked?" asked he, as they wound up their hard day's work by a supper eaten over the fire, which glowed and glimmered through the room, and formed their only light.

"No, I can't say as I did. But she 's never rightly held up her head since the twins died; and all along she has never been a strong woman."

"Never sin her accident. Afore that I mind her looking as fresh and likely a girl as e'er a one in Manchester."

"What accident, father?"

"She cotched * her side again a wheel. It were afore wheels were boxed up. It were just when she were to have been married, and many a one thought George would ha' been off his bargain; but I knew he wern't the chap for that trick. Pretty near the first place she went to when she were able to go about again, was th' Oud Church; poor wench, all pale and limping she went up the aisle, George holding her up as tender as a mother, and walking as slow as e'er he could, not to hurry her, though there were plenty enow of rude lads to cast their jests at him and her. Her face were white like a sheet when she came in church, but afore she got to th' altar she were all on flush. But for a' that it 's been a happy marriage, and George has stuck by me through life like a brother. He 'll never hold up his head again if he loses Jane. I didn't like her looks to-night."

And so he went to bed, the fear of forthcoming sorrow to his friend mingling with his thoughts of to-morrow, and his

* "Cotched," caught.

hopes for the future. Mary watched him set off, with her hands over her eyes to shade them from the bright slanting rays of the morning sun, and then she turned into the house to arrange its disorder before going to her work. She wondered if she should like or dislike the evening and morning solitude; for several hours when the clock struck she thought of her father, and wondered where he was; she made good resolutions according to her lights; and by-and-bye came the distractions and events of the broad full day to occupy her with the present, and to deaden the memory of the absent.

One of Mary's resolutions was, that she would not be persuaded or induced to see Mr. Harry Carsons during her father's absence. There was something crooked in her conscience after all; for this very resolution seemed an acknowledgment that it was wrong to meet him at any time; and yet she had brought herself to think her conduct quite innocent and proper, for although unknown to her father, and certain, even did he know it, to fail of obtaining his sanction, she esteemed her love-meetings with Mr. Carsons as sure to end in her father's good and happiness. But now that he was away, she would do nothing that he would disapprove of; no, not even though it was for his own good in the end.

Now, amongst Miss Simmonds' young ladies was one, who had been from the beginning a confidante in Mary's love affair, made so by Mr. Carsons himself. He had felt the necessity of some third person to carry letters and messages, and to plead his case when he was absent. In a girl named Sally Leadbitter he had found a willing advocate. She would have been willing to have embarked in a love-affair herself (especially a clandestine one), for the mere excitement of the thing; but her willingness was strengthened by sundry half-sovereigns, which from time to time Mr. Carsons bestowed upon her.

Sally Leadbitter was vulgar-minded to the last degree; never easy unless her talk was of love and lovers; in her eyes it was an honour to have had a long list of wooers. So constituted, it was a pity that Sally herself was but a plain, red-haired, freckled, girl; never likely, one would have thought, to become a heroine on her own account. But what she lacked in beauty she tried to make up for by a kind of witty boldness, which gave her what her betters would have called piquancy. Considerations of modesty or propriety never checked her utterance of a good thing. She had just talent enough to corrupt others. Her very good nature was an evil influence. They could not hate one who was so kind; they could not avoid one who was so willing to shield them from scrapes by any exertion of her own; whose ready fingers would at any time make up for their deficiencies, and whose still more convenient tongue would at any time invent for them. The Jews, or Mohammedans (I forget which), believe that there is one little bone of our body, one of the vertebræ, if I remember rightly, which will never decay and turn to dust, but will lie incorrupt and indestructible in the ground until the Last Day: this is the Seed of the Soul. The most depraved have also their Seed of the Holiness that shall one day overcome their evil. Their one good quality, lurking hidden, but safe, among all the corrupt and bad.

Sally's seed of the future soul was her love for her mother, an aged bed-ridden woman. For her she had self-denial; for her, her good-nature rose into tenderness; to cheer her lonely bed, her spirits, in the evenings, when her body was often woefully tired, never flagged, but were ready to recount the events of the day, to turn them into ridicule, and to mimic, with admirable fidelity, any person gifted with an absurdity who had fallen under her keen eye. But the mother was lightly principled like Sally herself; nor was there need to conceal from her the reason why Mr. Carsons gave her so much money. She chuckled with pleasure, and only hoped that the wooing would be long a-doing.

Still neither she, nor her daughter, nor Harry Carsons liked this resolution of Mary, not to see him during her father's absence.

One evening (and the early summer evenings were long and bright now), Sally met Mr. Carsons by appointment, to be charged with a letter for Mary, imploring her to see him.

which Sally was to back with all her powers of persuasion. After parting from him she determined, as it was not so very late, to go at once to Mary's, and deliver the message and letter.

She found Mary in great sorrow. She had just heard of George Wilson's sudden death: her old friend, her father's friend, Jem's father — all his claims came rushing upon her. Though not guarded from unnecessary sight or sound of death, as the children of the rich are, yet it had so often been brought home to her this last three or four months. It was so terrible thus to see friend after friend depart. Her father, too, who had dreaded Jane Wilson's death the evening before he set off. And she, the weakly, was left behind while the strong man was taken. At any rate the sorrow her father had so feared for him was spared. Such were the thoughts which came over her.

She could not go to comfort the bereaved, even if comfort were in her power to give; for she had resolved to avoid Jem; and she felt that this of all others was not the occasion on which she could keep up a studiously cold manner.

And in this shock of grief, Sally Leadbitter was the last person she wished to see. However, she rose to welcome her, betraying her tear-swollen face.

"Well, I shall tell Mr. Carsons to-morrow how you 're fretting for him; it 's no more nor he 's doing for you, I can tell you."

"For him, indeed!" said Mary, with a toss of her pretty head.

"Ay, Miss, for him! You 've been sighing as if your heart would break now for several days, over your work; now, arn't you a little goose not to go and see one who I am sure loves you as his life, and whom you love; 'How much, Mary?' 'This much,' as the children say' (opening her arms very wide).

"Nonsense," said Mary, pouting; "I often think I don't love him at all."

"And I 'm to tell him that, am I, next time I see him?" asked Sally.

"If you like," replied Mary. "I 'm sure I don't care for that or anything else now;" weeping afresh.

But Sally did not like to be the bearer of any such news. She saw she had gone on the wrong tack, and that Mary's heart was too full to value either message or letter as she ought. So she wisely paused in their delivery, and said, in a more sympathetic tone than she had hitherto used,

"Do tell me, Mary, what 's fretting you so? You know I never could abide to see you cry."

"George Wilson 's dropped down dead this afternoon," said Mary, fixing her eyes for one minute on Sally, and the next hiding her face in her apron as she sobbed anew.

"Dear, dear! All flesh is grass; here to-day and gone to-morrow, as the Bible says. Still he was an old man, and not good for much; there 's better folk than him left behind. Is th' canting old maid as was his sister alive yet?"

"I don't know who you mean," said Mary, sharply; for she did know, and did not like to have her dear, simple Alice so spoken of.

"Come, Mary, don't be so innocent. Is Miss Alice Wilson alive, then; will that please you? I haven't seen her hereabouts lately."

"No, she 's left living here. When the twins died, she thought she could, may be, be of use to her sister, who was sadly cast down, and Alice thought she could cheer her up; at any rate she could listen to her when her heart grew over-burdened; so she gave up her cellar and went to live with them."

"Well, good go with her. I 'd no fancy for her, and I 'd no fancy for her making my pretty Mary into a Methodee."

"She wasn't a Methodee, she was Church o' England."

"Well, well, Mary, you 're very particular. You know what I meant. Look, who is this letter from?" holding up Henry Carsons' letter.

"I don't know, and don't care," said Mary, turning very red.

"My eye! as if I didn't know you did know and did care."

"Well, give it me," said Mary, impatiently, and anxious in her present mood for her visitor's departure.

Sally relinquished it unwillingly. She had, however, the pleasure of seeing Mary dimple and blush as she read the letter, which seemed to say the writer was not indifferent to her.

"You must tell him I can't come," said Mary, raising her eyes at last. "I have said I won't meet him while father is away, and I won't."

"But Mary, he does so look for you. You'd be quite sorry for him, he's so put out about not seeing you. Besides, you go when your father's at home, without letting on* to him, and what harm would there be in going now?"

"Well, Sally, you know my answer, I won't; and I won't."

"I'll tell him to come and see you himself some evening, instead o' sending me; he'd may be find you not so hard to deal with."

Mary flashed up.

"If he dares to come here while father's away, I'll call the neighbours in to turn him out, so don't be putting him up to that."

"Mercy on us! one would think you were the first girl that ever had a lover; have you never heard what other girls do and think no shame of?"

"Hush, Sally! that's Margaret Jenkins at the door."

And in an instant Margaret was in the room. Mary had begged Job Legh to let her come and sleep with her. In the uncertain fire-light you could not help noticing that she had the groping walk of a blind person.

"Well, I must go, Mary," said Sally. "And that's your last word?"

"Yes, yes; good night." She shut the door gladly on her unwelcome visitor — unwelcome at that time at least.

* "Letting on," informing.

"Oh, Margaret, have ye heard this sad news about George Wilson?"

"Yes, that I have. Poor creatures, they 've been sore tried lately. Not that I think sudden death so bad a thing; it 's easy, and there 's no terrors for him as dies. For them as survives it 's very hard. Poor George! he were such a hearty looking man."

"Margaret," said Mary, who had been closely observing her friend, "thou 'rt very blind to-night, artn't thou? Is it wi' crying? Your eyes are so swollen and red."

"Yes, dear! but not crying for sorrow. Han ye heard where I was last night?"

"No; where?"

"Look here." She held up a bright golden sovereign. Mary opened her large gray eyes with astonishment.

"I 'll tell you all and how about it. You see there 's a gentleman lecturing on music at th' Mechanics, and he wants folks to sing his songs. Well, last night the counter got a sore throat and couldn't make a note. So they sent for me. Jacob Butterworth had said a good word for me, and they asked me would I sing? You may think I was frightened, but I thought now or never, and said I 'd do my best. So I tried o'er the songs wi' th' lecturer, and then th' managers told me I were to make myself decent and be there by seven."

"And what did you put on?" asked Mary. "Oh, why didn't you come in for my pretty pink gingham?"

"I did think on't; but you had na come home then. No! I put on my merino, as was turned last winter, and my white shawl, and did my hair pretty tidy; it did well enough. Well, but as I was saying, I went at seven. I couldn't see to read my music, but I took th' paper in wi' me, to ha' something to do wi' my fingers. Th' folks heads danced, as I stood as right afore 'em all as if I'd been going to play at ball wi' 'em. You may guess I felt squeamish, but mine weren't the first song, and th' music sounded like a friend's voice telling me to take courage. So to make a long story short, when it were all o'er th' lecturer thanked me, and th' managers said as how there never was a new singer so applauded (for they 'd clapped and stamped after I 'd done, till I began to wonder how many pair o' shoes they'd get through a week at that rate, let alone their hands). So I 'm to sing again o' Thursday; and I got a sovereign last night, and am to have half-a-sovereign every night th' lecturer is at th' Mechanics."

"Well, Margaret, I 'm right glad to hear it."

"And I don't think you've heard the best bit yet. Now that a way seemed opened to me, of not being a burden to any one, though it did please God to make me blind, I thought I 'd tell grandfather. I only tell'd him about the singing and the sovereign last night, for I thought I 'd not send him to bed wi' a heavy heart; but this morning I telled him all."

"And how did he take it?"

"He 's not a man of many words; and it took him by surprise like."

"I wonder at that; I 've noticed it in your ways ever since you telled me."

"Ay, that 's it! If I 'd not telled you, and you 'd seen me every day, you'd not ha' noticed the little mite o' difference fra' day to day."

"Well, but what did your grandfather say?"

"Why, Mary," said Margaret, half smiling, "I 'm a bit loth to tell yo, for unless yo knew grandfather's ways like me, yo'd think it strange. He was taken by surprise, and he said: 'Damn yo!' Then he began looking at his book as it were, and were very quiet, while I telled him all about it; how I'd feared, and how downcast I'd been; and how I were now reconciled to it, if it were th' Lord's will; and how I hoped to earn money by singing; and while I were talking, I saw great big tears come dropping on th' book; but in course I never let on that I saw 'em. Dear grandfather! and all day long he 's been quietly moving things out o' my way, as he thought might trip me up, and putting things in my way as he thought I might want; never knowing I saw and felt what he were doing; for, yo see, he thinks I 'm out and out blind, I guess — as I shall be soon."

Margaret sighed in spite of her cheerful and relieved tone.

Though Mary caught the sigh, she felt it was better to let it pass without notice, and began with the tact which true sympathy rarely fails to supply, to ask a variety of questions respecting her friend's musical début, which tended to bring out more distinctly how successful it had been.

"Why, Margaret," at length she exclaimed, "thou 'lt become as famous, may be, as that grand lady fra' London, as we seed one night driving up to th' concert room door in her carriage."

"It looks very like it," said Margaret, with a smile.

"And be sure, Mary, I 'll not forget to give thee a lift now an' then when that comes about. Nay, who knows, if thou 'rt a good girl, but mayhappen I may make thee my lady's maid! Wouldn't that be nice? So I e'en sing to mysel' th' beginning o' one o' my songs,

'An' ye shall walk in silk attire,
An' siller hae to spare.' "

"Nay, don't stop; or else give me something a bit more new, for somehow I never quite liked that part about thinking o' Donald mair."

"Well, though I 'm a bit tir'd, I don't care if I do. Before I come, I were practising well nigh upon two hours this one which I 'm to sing o' Thursday. The lecturer said he were sure it would just suit me, and I should do justice to it; and I should be right sorry to disappoint him, he were so nice and encouraging like to me. Eh! Mary, what a pity there isn't more o' that way, and less scolding and rating i' th' world! It would go a vast deal further. Beside, some o' th' singers said, they were a'most certain that it were a song o' his own, because he were so fidgety and particular about it, and so anxious I should give it th' proper expression. And that makes me care still more. Th' first verse, he said, were to be sung 'tenderly, but joyously!' I 'm afraid I don't quite hit that, but I 'll try.

'What a single word can do!
Thrilling all the heart-strings through,
Calling forth fond memories,
Raining round hope's melodies,
Steeping all in one bright hue —
What a single word can do!'

Now it falls into th' minor key, and must be very sad like. I feel as if I could do that better than t'other.

'What a single word can do!
Making life seem all untrue,
Driving joy and hope away,
Leaving not one cheering ray,
Blighting every flower that grew —
What a single word can do!'"

Margaret certainly made the most of this little song. As a factory worker, listening outside, observed, "She spun it reet* fine!" And if she only sang it at the Mechanics' with half the feeling she put into it that night, the lecturer must have been hard to please, if he did not admit that his expectations were more than fulfilled.

When it was ended, Mary's looks told more than words could have done what she thought of it; and partly to keep in a tear which would fain have rolled out, she brightened into a laugh, and said, "for certain, th' carriage is coming. So let us go and dream on it."

CHAPTER IX.

"A life of self-indulgence is for us,
A life of self-denial is for them;
For us the streets, broad-built and populous,
For them unhealthy corners, garrets dim,
And cellars where the water-rat may swim!
For us green paths refreshed by frequent rain,
For them dark alleys where the dust lies grim!
Not doomed by us to this appointed pain —
God made us rich and poor — of what do these complain?"

MRS. NORTON'S 'CHILD OF THE ISLANDS.'

THE next evening it was a warm, pattering, incessant rain, just the rain to waken up the flowers. But in Man-

* "Reet," right; often used for "very."

chester, where, alas! there are no flowers, the rain had only a disheartening and gloomy effect; the streets were wet and dirty, the drippings from the houses were wet and dirty, and the people were wet and dirty. Indeed, most kept within-doors; and there was an unusual silence of footsteps in the little paved courts.

Mary had to change her clothes after her walk home; and had hardly settled herself before she heard some one fumbling at the door. The noise continued long enough to allow her to get up, and go and open it. There stood — could it be? yes it was, her father!

Drenched and way-worn, there he stood! He came in with no word to Mary in return for her cheery and astonished greeting. He sat down by the fire in his wet things, unheeding. But Mary would not let him so rest. She ran up and brought down his working-day clothes, and went into the pantry to rummage up their little bit of provision while he changed by the fire, talking all the while as gaily as she could, though her father's depression hung like lead on her heart.

For Mary, in her seclusion at Miss Simmonds', — where the chief talk was of fashions, and dress, and parties to be given, for which such and such gowns would be wanted, varied with a slight whispered interlude occasionally about love and lovers, — had not heard the political news of the day: that parliament had refused to listen to the working-men, when they petitioned with all the force of their rough, untutored words to be heard concerning the distress which was riding, like the Conqueror on his Pale Horse, among the people; which was crushing their lives out of them, and stamping woemarks over the land.

When he had eaten and was refreshed, they sat in silence for some time; for Mary wished him to tell her what oppressed him so, yet durst not ask. In this she was wise; for when we are heavy laden in our hearts it falls in better with our humour to reveal our case in our own way, and our own time.

Mary sat on a stool at her father's feet in old childish

guise, and stole her hand into his, while his sadness infected her, and she "caught the trick of grief, and sighed," she knew not why.

"Mary, we mun speak to our God to hear us, for man will not hearken; no, not now, when we weep tears o' blood."

In an instant Mary understood the fact, if not the details, that so weighed down her father's heart. She pressed his hand with silent sympathy. She did not know what to say, and was so afraid of speaking wrongly, that she was silent. But when his attitude had remained unchanged for more than half-an-hour, his eyes gazing vacantly and fixedly at the fire, no sound but now and then a deep drawn sigh to break the weary ticking of the clock, and the drip-drop from the roof without, Mary could bear it no longer. Any thing to rouse her father. Even bad news.

"Father, do you know George Wilson 's dead?" (Her hand was suddenly and almost violently compressed.) "He dropped down dead in Oxford Road yester morning. It 's very sad, isn't it, father?"

Her tears were ready to flow as she looked up in her father's face for sympathy. Still the same fixed look of despair, not varied by grief for the dead.

"Best for him to die," he said, in a low voice.

This was unbearable. Mary got up under pretence of going to tell Margaret that she need not come to sleep with her to-night, but really to ask Job Legh to come and cheer her father.

She stopped outside the door. Margaret was practising her singing, and through the still night air her voice rang out like that of an angel.

"Comfort ye, comfort ye, my people, saith your God."

The old Hebrew prophetic words fell like dew on Mary's heart. She could not interrupt. She stood listening and "comforted," till the little buzz of conversation again began, and then entered and told her errand.

Both grandfather and grand-daughter rose instantly to fulfil her request.

"He 's just tired out, Mary," said old Job. "He 'll be a different man to-morrow."

There is no describing the looks and tones that have power over an aching, heavy laden heart; but in an hour or so John Barton was talking away as freely as ever, though all his talk ran, as was natural, on the disappointment of his fond hope, of the forlorn hope of many.

"Ay, London 's a fine place," said he, "and finer folk live in it than I ever thought on, or ever heerd tell on except in th' story-books. They are having their good things now, that afterwards they may be tormented."

Still at the old parable of Dives and Lazarus! Does it haunt the minds of the rich as it does those of the poor?

"Do tell us all about London, dear father," asked Mary, who was sitting at her old post by her father's knee.

"How can I tell yo a' about it, when I never seed one tenth of it. It 's as big as six Manchesters, they telled me. One-sixth may be made up o' grand palaces, and three-sixths o' middling kind, and th' rest o' holes o' iniquity and filth, such as Manchester knows nought on, I 'm glad to say."

"Well, father, but did you see th' Queen?"

"I believe I didn't, though one day I thought I 'd seen her many a time. You see," said he, turning to Job Legh, "there were a day appointed for us to go to Parliament House. We were most on us biding at a public-house in Holborn, where they did very well for us. Th' morning of taking our petition we 'd such a spread for breakfast as th' Queen hersel might ha' sitten down to. I suppose they thought we wanted putting in heart. There were mutton kidneys, and sausages, and broiled ham, and fried beef and onions; more like a dinner nor a breakfast. Many on our chaps though, I could see, could eat but little. Th' food stuck in their throats when they thought o' them at home, wives and little ones, as had, may be at that very time, nought to eat. Well, after breakfast, we were all set to walk in procession, and a time it took to put us in order, two and two, and the petition, as was yards long, carried by th' foremost pairs. The men looked grave enough, yo may be sure; and such a set of thin, wan, wretched-looking chaps as they were!"

"Yourself is none to boast on."

"Ay, but I were fat and rosy to many a one. Well, we walked on and on through many a street, much the same as Deansgate. We had to walk slowly, slowly, for th' carriages an' cabs as thronged th' streets. I thought by-and-bye we should may be get clear on 'em, but as the streets grew wider they grew worse, and at last we were fairly blocked up at Oxford Street. We getten across at after awhile though, and my eyes! the grand streets we were in then! They 're sadly puzzled how to build houses though in London; there 'd be an opening for a good steady master builder there, as know'd his business. For yo see the houses are many on 'em built without any proper shape for a body to live in; some on 'em they 've after thought would fall down, so they 've stuck great ugly pillars out before 'em. And some on 'em (we thought they must be th' tailor's sign) had getten stone men and women as wanted clothes stuck on 'em. I were like a child, I forgot a' my errant in looking about me. By this it were dinner-time, or better, as we could tell by the sun, right above our heads, and we were dusty and tired, going a step now and a step then. Well, at last we getten into a street grander nor all, leading to th' Queen's palace, and there it were I thought I saw th' Queen. Yo 've seen th' hearses wi' white plumes, Job?"

Job assented.

"Well, them undertaker folk are driving a pretty trade in London. Wellnigh every lady we saw in a carriage had hired one o' them plumes for the day, and had it niddle noddling on her head. It were th' Queen's drawing-room, they said, and th' carriages went bowling along toward her house, some wi' dressed-up gentlemen like circus folk in 'em, and rucks* o' ladies in others. Carriages themselves were great shakes too. Some o' th' gentlemen as couldn't get inside hung on behind, wi' nosegays to smell at, and sticks to keep off folk as might splash their silk stockings. I wondered why they didn't hire

* "Rucks," a great quantity.

a cab rather than hang on like a whip-behind boy; but I suppose they wished to keep wi' their wives, Darby and Joan like. Coachmen were little squat men, wi' wigs like th' oud fashioned parsons. Well, we could na get on for these carriages, though we waited and waited. Th' hosres were too fat to move quick; they never known want o' food, one might tell by their sleek coats; and police pushed us back when we tried to cross. One or two of 'em struck wi' their sticks, and coachmen laughed, and some officers as stood nigh put their spy-glasses in their eye, and left 'em sticking there like mountebanks. One o' th' police struck me. 'Whatten business have you to do that?' said I."

"'You 're frightening them horses,' says he, in his mincing way (for Londoners are mostly all tongue-tied, and can't say their a's and i's properly), 'and it's our business to keep you from molesting the ladies and gentlemen going to her Majesty's drawing-room.'"

"And why are we to be molested," asked I, "going decently about our business, which is life and death to us, and many a little one clemming at home in Lancashire? Which business is of most consequence i' the sight o' God, think yo, our'n or them gran ladies and gentlemen as yo think so much on?

"But I might as well ha' held my peace, for he only laughed."

John ceased. After waiting a little to see if he would go on himself, Job said,

"Well, but that 's not a' your story, man. Tell us what happened when you got to th' Parliament House."

After a little pause, John answered,

"If you please, neighbour, I 'd rather say nought about that. It 's not to be forgotten or forgiven either by me or many another; but I canna tell of our down-casting just as a piece of London news. As long as I live, our rejection of that day will abide in my heart; and as long as I live I shall curse them as so cruelly refused to hear us; but I 'll not speak of it no* more."

* A similar use of a double negative is not unfrequent in Chaucer; as in the "Miller's Tale":

"That of no wife toke he non offering
For curtesie, he sayd, he n'old non."

So, daunted in their inquiries, they sat silent for a few minutes.

Old Job, however, felt that some one must speak, else all the good they had done in dispelling John Barton's gloom was lost. So after a while he thought of a subject, neither sufficiently dissonant from the last to jar on the full heart, nor too much the same to cherish the continuance of the gloomy train of thought.

"Did you ever hear tell," said he to Mary, "that I were in London once?"

"No!" said she, with surprise, and looking at Job with increased respect.

"Ay, but I were though, and Peg there too, though she minds nought about it, poor wench! You must know I had but one child, and she were Margaret's mother. I loved her above a bit, and one day when she came (standing behind me for that I should not see her blushes, and stroking my cheeks in her own coaxing way), and told me she and Frank Jennings (as was a joiner lodging near us) should be so happy if they were married, I could not find it in my heart t' say her nay, though I went sick at the thought of losing her away from my home. However, she was my only child, and I never said nought of what I felt, for fear o' grieving her young heart. But I tried to think o' the time when I 'd been young mysel, and had loved her blessed mother, and how we 'd left father and mother, and gone out into th' world together, and I 'm now right thankful I held my peace, and didna fret her wi' telling her how sore I was at parting wi' her that were the light o' my eyes."

"But," said Mary, "you said the young man were a neighbour."

"Ay, so he were, and his father afore him. But work were rather slack in Manchester, and Frank's uncle sent him word o' London work and London wages, so he were to go there; and it were there Margaret was to follow him. Well, my heart aches yet at thought of those days. She so happy, and he so happy; only the poor father as fretted sadly behind their backs. They were married and stayed some days wi' me afore setting off; and I 've often thought sin' Margaret's heart failed her many a time those few days, and she would fain ha' spoken; but I knew fra' mysel it were better to keep it pent up, and I never let on what I were feeling; I knew what she meant when she came kissing, and holding my hand, and all her old childish ways o' loving me. Well, they went at last. You know them two letters Margaret?"

"Yes, sure," replied his grand-daughter.

"Well, them two were the only letters I ever had fra' her, poor lass. She said in them she were very happy, and I believe she were. And Frank's family heard he were in good work. In one o' her letters, poor thing, she ends wi' saying, 'Farewell, Grandad! wi' a line drawn under grandad, and fra' that an' other hints I knew she were in th' family way; and I said nought, but I screwed up a little money, thinking come Whitsuntide I'd take a holiday and go and see her an' th' little one. But one day towards Whitsuntide, comed Jennings wi' a grave face, and says he, 'I hear our Frank and young Margaret 's both getten the fever.' You might ha' knocked me down wi' a straw, for it seemed as if God told me what th' upshot would be. Old Jennings had gotten a letter you see, fra' the landlady they lodged wi'; a well-penned letter, asking if they 'd no friends to come and nurse them. She 'd caught it first, and Frank, who was as tender o'er her as her own mother could ha' been, had nursed her till he 'd caught it himsel; and she expecting her down-lying* every day. Well, t' make a long story short, old Jennings and I went up by that night's coach. So you see, Mary, that was the way I got to London."

"But how was your daughter when you got there?" asked Mary, anxiously.

"She were at rest, poor wench, and so were Frank. I guessed as much when I see'd th' landlady's face, all swelled wi' crying, when she opened th' door to us. We said, 'Where are they?' and I knew they were dead, fra' her look; but Jennings didn't, as I take it; for when she showed us into a room

* "Down-lying," lying-in.

wi' a white sheet on th' bed, and underneath it, plain to be seen, two still figures, he screeched out as if he 'd been a woman.

"Yet he 'd other children and I 'd none. There lay my darling, my only one. She were dead, and there were no one to love me, no not one. I disremember* rightly what I did; but I know I were very quiet, while my heart were crushed within me.

"Jennings could na' stand being in th' room at all, so the landlady took him down, and I were glad to be alone. It grew dark while I sat there; and at last th' landlady came up again, and said, 'Come, here.' So I got up, and walked into th' light, but I had to hold by th' stair-rails, I were so weak and dizzy. She led me into a room, where Jennings lay on a sofa fast asleep, wi' his pocket handkerchief over his head for a night-cap. She said he'd cried himself fairly off to sleep. There were tea on th' table all ready; for she were a kind-hearted body. But she still said, 'Come here,' and took hold o' my arm. So I went round the table and there were a clothes-basket by th' fire wi' a shawl put o'er it. 'Lift that up,' says she, and I did; and there lay a little wee babby fast asleep. My heart gave a leap, and th' tears comed rushing into my eyes first time that day. 'Is it hers? said I, though I knew it were. 'Yes,' said she. 'She were getting a bit better o' the fever, and th babby were born; aud then the poor young man took worse and died, and she were not many hours behind.'

"Little mite of a thing! and yet it seemed her angel come back to comfort me. I were quite jealous o' Jennings, whenever he went near the babby. I thought it were more my flesh and blood than his 'n, and yet I were afraid he would claim it. However, that were far enough fra' his thoughts; he 'd plenty other childer, and as I found out after all he'd all along been wishing me to take it. Well, we buried Margaret and her husband in a big, crowded, lonely churchyard in London. I were loath to leave them there, as I thought, when they rose again, they 'd feel so strange at first away fra Manchester, and

* "Disremember," forget.

all old friends; but it couldna be helped. Well, God watches o'er their graves there as well as here. That funeral cost a mint o' money, but Jennings and I wished to do th' thing decent. Then we 'd the stout little babby to bring home. We'd not overmuch money left; but it were fine weather, and we thought we 'd take th' coach to Brummagem, and walk on. It were a bright May morning when I last saw London town, looking back from a big hill a mile or two off. And in that big mass o' a place I were leaving my blessed child asleep — in her last sleep. Well, God's will be done! She 's gotten to heaven afore me; but I shall get there at last, please God, though it 's a long while first.

"The babby had been fed afore we set out, and th' coach moving kept it asleep, bless it's little heart. But when th' coach stopped for dinner it were awake, and crying for its pobbies.* So we asked for some bread and milk, and Jennings took it first for to feed it; but it made it 's mouth like a square, and let it run out at each o' th' four corners. 'Shake it, Jennings,' says I; 'that 's the way they make water run through a funnel, when it 's o'er full; and a child's mouth is broad end o' th' funnel, and th' gullet the narrow one.' So he shook it, but it only cried th' more. 'Let me have it,' says I, thinking he were an awkward oud chap. But it were just as bad wi' me. By shaking th' babby we got better nor a gill into its mouth, but more nor that came up again, wetting a' th' nice dry clothes landlady had put on. Well, just as we'd gotten to th' dinner-table, and helped oursels, and eaten two mouthful, came in th' guard, and a fine chap wi' a sample o' calico flourishing in his hand. 'Coach is ready!' says one; 'Half-a-crown your dinner!' says th' other. Well, we thought it a deal for both our dinners, when we'd hardly tasted 'em; but, bless your life, it were half-a-crown a piece, and a shilling for th' bread and milk as were possetted all over babby's clothes. We spoke up again** it; but every body said it were

* "Pobbies," or "pobs," child's porridge.

** "Again," for against. "He that is not with me, he is ageyn me." — *Wickliffe's Version.*

8*

the rule, so what could two poor oud chaps like us do again it? Well, poor babby cried without stopping to take breath, fra' that time till we got to Brummagem for the night. My heart ached for th' little thing. It caught wi' its wee mouth at our coat sleeves and at our mouths, when we tried t' comfort it by talking to it. Poor little wench! It wanted its mammy, as were lying cold in th' grave. 'Well,' says I, 'it 'll be clemmed to death, if it let 's out its supper as it did its dinner. Let 's get some woman to feed it; it comes natural to women to do for babbies. So we asked th' chamber-maid at the inn, and she took quite kindly to it; and we got a good supper, and grew rare and sleepy, what wi' th' warmth, and wi' our long ride i' the open air. Th' chamber-maid said she would like t' have it t' sleep wi' her, only missis would scold so; but it looked so quiet and smiling like, as it lay in her arms, that we thought 't would be no trouble to have it wi' us. I says: 'See, Jennings, how women-folk do quieten babbies; it 's just as I said.' He looked grave; he were always thoughtful-looking, though I never heard him say any thing very deep. At last says he —

"'Young woman! have you gotten a spare night-cap?'

"'Missis always keeps night-caps for gentlemen as does not like to unpack,' says she, rather quick.

"'Ay, but young woman, it 's one of your night-caps I want. Th' babby seems to have taken a mind to yo; and may be in th' dark it might take me for yo if I 'd getten your night-cap on.'

"The chambermaid smirked and went for a cap, but I laughed outright at th' oud bearded chap thinking he 'd make hissel like a woman just by putting on a woman's cap. Howe'er he 'd not be laughed out on 't, so I held th' babby till he were in bed. Such a night as we had on it! Babby began to scream o' th' oud fashion, and we took it in turn and turnabout to sit up and rock it. My heart were very sore for the little one, as it groped about wi' its mouth; but for a' that I could scarce keep fra' smiling at th' thought o' us two oud chaps, th' one wi' a woman's night-cap on, sitting on our hinder ends for half the night, hushabying a babby as wouldn't be hushabied. Toward morning, poor little wench! it fell asleep, fairly tired out wi' crying, but even in its sleep it gave such pitiful sobs, quivering up fra' the very bottom of its little heart, that once or twice I almost wished it lay on its mother's breast, at peace for ever. Jennings fell asleep too; but I began for to reckon up our money. It were little enough we had left, our dinner the day afore had ta'en so much. I didn't know what our reckoning would be for that night lodging, and supper, and breakfast. Doing a sum alway sent me asleep ever sin' I were a lad; so I fell sound, in a short time, and were only wakened by chambermaid tapping at th' door, to say she 'd dress the babby afore her missis were up if we liked. But bless yo', we'd never thought o' undressing it the night afore, and now it were sleeping so sound, and we were so glad o' the peace and quietness, that we thought it were no good to waken it up to screech again.

"Well! (there 's Mary asleep for a good listener!) I suppose you 're getting weary of my tale, so I 'll not be long over ending it. Th' reckoning left us very bare, and we thought we 'd best walk home, for it were only sixty mile, they telled us, and not stop again for nought, save victuals. So we left Brummagem (which is as black a place as Manchester, without looking so like home), and walked a' that day, carrying babby turn and turn about. It were well fed by chambermaid afore we left, and th' day were fine, and folk began to have some knowledge o' th' proper way o' speaking, and we were more cheery at thought o' home (though mine, God knows, were lonesome enough). We stopped none for dinner, but at baggin-time* we getten a good meal at a public-house, an' fed th' babby as well as we could, but that were but poorly. We got a crust too, for it to suck — chambermaid put us up to that. That night, whether we were tired or whatten, I don't know, but it were dree** work, and th' poor little wench had

* "Baggin-time," time of the evening meal.

** "Dree," long and tedious. Anglo-Saxon, "dreogan," to suffer, o endure.

slept out her sleep, and began th' cry as wore my heart out again. Says Jennings, says he,

"'We should na ha' set out so like gentlefolk a top o' the coach yesterday.'

"'Nay, lad! We should ha' had more to walk if we had na ridden, and I 'm sure both you and I 'se* weary o' tramping.'

"So he were quiet a bit. But he were one o' them as were sure to find out somewhat had been done amiss when there were no going back to undo it. So presently he coughs, as if he were going to speak, and I says to mysel, 'At it again, my lad.' Says he,

"'I ax pardon, neighbour, but it strikes me it would ha' been better for my son if he had never begun to keep company wi' your daughter.'

"Well! that put me up, and my heart got very full, and but that I were carrying *her* babby, I think I should ha' struck him. At last I could hold in no longer, and says I,

"'Better say at once it would ha' been better for God never to ha' made th' world, for then we'd never ha' been in it, to have had th' heavy hearts we have now.'

"Well! he said that were rank blasphemy; but I thought his way of casting up again th' events God had pleased to send, were worse blasphemy. Howe'er, I said nought more angry, for th' little babby's sake, as were th' child o' his dead son, as well as o' my dead daughter.

"Th' longest lane will have a turning, and that night came to an end at last; and we were foot-sore and tired enough, and to my mind th' babby were getting weaker and weaker, and it wrung my heart to hear its little wail; I 'd ha' given my right hand for one of yesterday's hearty cries. We were wanting our breakfasts, and so were it too, motherless babby! We could see no public-house, so about six o' clock (only we thought it were later), we stopped at a cottage where a woman were moving about near th' open door. Says I, 'Good wo-

* "I have not been, nor *is*, nor never schal."—*Wickliffe's "Apology*," p. 1.

man, may we rest us a bit?' 'Come in,' says she, wiping a chair, as looked bright enough afore, wi' her apron. It were a cheery, clean room; and we were glad to sit down again, though I thought my legs would never bend at th' knees. In a minute she fell a noticing th' babby, and took it in her arms, and kissed it again and again. 'Missis,' says I, 'we 're not without money, and if yo 'd give us somewhat for breakfast, we'd pay yo honest, and if yo would wash and dress that poor babby, and get some pobbies down its throat, for it 's well-nigh clemmed, I 'd pray for yo' till my dying day.' So she said nought, but gived me th' babby back, and afore yo' could say Jack Robinson, she 'd a pan on th' fire, and bread and cheese on th' table. When she turned round her face looked red, and her lips were thight pressed together. Well! we were right down glad on our breakfast, and God bless and reward that woman for her kindness that day; she fed th' poor babby as gently and softly, and spoke to it as tenderly as its own poor mother could ha' done. It seemed as if that stranger and it had known each other afore, maybe in Heaven, where folk 's spirits come from they say; th' babby looked up so lovingly in her eyes, and made little noises more like a dove than ought else. Then she undressed it (poor darling! it were time), touching it so softly; and washed it from head to foot, and as many on its clothes were dirty; and what bits o' things its mother had gotten ready for it had been sent by th' carrier fra' London, she put 'em aside; and wrapping little naked babby in her apron, she pulled out a key, as were fastened to a black ribbon, and hung down her breast, and unlocked a drawer in th' dresser. I were sorry to be prying, but I could na' help seeing in that drawer some little child's clothes, all strewed wi' lavender, and lying by 'em a little whip an' a broken rattle. I began to have an insight into that woman's heart then. She took out a thing or two, and locked the drawer, and went on dressing babby. Just about then come her husband down, a great big fellow as didn't look half awake, though it were getting late; but he 'd heard all as had been said down-stairs, as were plain to be seen; but he were a gruff chap. We 'd finished our breakfast, and Jennings were looking hard at th' woman as she were getting the babby to sleep wi' a sort of rocking way. At length says he, 'I ha' learnt th' way now; it 's two jiggits and a shake, two jiggits and a shake. I can get that babby asleep now mysel.'

"The man had nodded cross enough to us, and had gone to th' door, and stood there whistling wi' his hands in his breeches-pockets, looking abroad. But at last he turns and says, quite sharp,

"'I say, Missis, I 'm to have no breakfast to-day, I 'spose.'

"So wi' that she kissed th' child, a long, soft kiss; and looking in my face to see if I could take her meaning, gave me th' babby without a word. I were loath to stir, but I saw it were better to go. So giving Jennings a sharp nudge (for he 'd fallen asleep), I says, 'Missis, what 's to pay?' pulling out my money wi' a jingle that she might na guess we were at all bare o' cash. So she looks at her husband, who said ne'er a word, but were listening wi' all his ears nevertheless; and when she saw he would na say, she said, hesitating, as if pulled two ways, by her fear o' him, 'Should you think sixpence over much?' It were so different to public-house reckoning, for we 'd eaten a main deal afore the chap came down. So says I, 'And, Missis, what should we gie you for the babby 's bread and milk?' (I had it once in my mind to say 'and for a' your trouble with it,' but my heart would na let me say it, for I could read in her ways how it had been a work o' love). So says she, quite quick, and stealing a look at her husband's back, as looked all ear, if ever a back did, 'Oh, we could take nought for the little babby's food, if it had eaten twice as much, bless it.' Wi' that he looked at her; such a scowling look! She knew what he meant, and stepped softly across the floor to him, and put her hand on his arm. He seem'd as though he 'd shake it off by a jerk on his elbow, but she said quite low, 'For poor little Johnnie's sake, Richard.' He did not move or speak again, and after looking in his face for a minute, she turned away, swallowing deep in her throat. She kissed th' sleeping babby as she passed, when I paid her. To quieten th' gruff husband, and stop him if he rated her, I could na help slipping another sixpence under th' loaf, and then we set off again. Last look I had o' that woman she were quietly wiping her eyes wi' the corner of her apron, as she went about her husband's breakfast. But I shall know her in heaven."

He stopped to think of that long-ago May morning, when he had carried his grand-daughter under the distant hedgerows and beneath the flowering sycamores.

"There 's nought more to say, wench," said he to Margaret, as she begged him to go on. "That night we reached Manchester, and I 'd found out that Jennings would be glad enough to give up babby to me, so I took her home at once, and a blessing she 's been to me."

They were all silent for a few minutes; each following out the current of their thoughts. Then, almost simultaneously, their attention fell upon Mary. Sitting on her little stool, her head resting on her father's knee, and sleeping as soundly as any infant, her breath (still like an infant's) came and went as softly as a bird steals to her leafy nest. Her half-open mouth was as scarlet as the winter-berries, and contrasted finely with the clear paleness of her complexion, where the eloquent blood flushed carnation at each motion. Her black eye-lashes lay on the delicate cheek, which was still more shaded by the masses of her golden hair, that seemed to form a nest-like pillow for her as she lay. Her father in fond pride straightened one glossy curl, for an instant, as if to display its length and silkiness. The little action awoke her, and, like nine out of ten people in similar circumstances, she exclaimed, opening her eyes to their fullest extent,

"I 'm not asleep. I 've been awake all the time."

Even her father could not keep from smiling, and Job Legh and Margaret laughed outright.

"Come, wench," said Job, "don't look so gloppened* because thou 'st fallen asleep while an oud chap like me was

* "Gloppened," amazed, frightened.

talking on oud times. It were like enough to send thee to sleep. Try if thou canst keep thine eyes open while I read thy father a bit on a poem as is written by a weaver like oursel. A rare chap I 'll be bound is he who could weave verse like this."

So adjusting his spectacles on nose, cocking his chin, crossing his legs, and coughing to clear his voice, he read aloud a little poem of Samuel Bamford's* he had picked up somewhere.

God help the poor, who, on this wintry morn,
  Come forth from alleys dim and courts obscure.
God help yon poor pale girl, who droops forlorn,
  And meekly her affliction doth endure;
God help her, outcast lamb; she trembling stands,
All wan her lips, and frozen red her hands;
Her sunken eyes are modestly down-cast,
Her night-black hair streams on the fitful blast;
Her bosom, passing fair, is half revealed,
And oh! so cold, the snow lies there congealed;
Her feet benumbed, her shoes all rent and worn,
God help thee, outcast lamb, who standst forlorn!
God help the poor!

God help the poor! An infant's feeble wail
  Comes from yon narrow gateway, and behold!
A female crouching there, so deathly pale,
  Huddling her child, to screen it from the cold;
Her vesture scant, her bonnet crushed and torn;
  A thin shawl doth her baby dear enfold:
And so she 'bides the ruthless gale of morn,
  Which almost to her heart hath sent its cold,
And now she, sudden, darts a ravening look,
As one, with new hot bread, goes past the nook;
And, as the tempting load is onward borne,
She weeps. God help thee, helpless one, forlorn!
God help the poor!

God help the poor! Behold yon famished lad,
  No shoes, nor hose, his wounded feet protect;
With limping gait, and looks so dreamy sad,
  He wanders on, stooping to inspect
Each window, stored with articles of food.

* The fine-spirited author of "Passages in the Life of a Radical" — a man who illustrates his order, and shows what nobility may be in a cottage.

He yearns but to enjoy one cheering meal;
Oh! to the hungry palate, viands rude,
Would yield a zest the famished only feel!
He now devours a crust of mouldy bread;
With teeth and hands the precious boon is torn;
Unmindful of the storm that round his head
Impetuous sweeps. God help thee, child forlorn!
God help the poor!

God help the poor! Another have I found —
A bowed and venerable man is he;
Hi· slouched hat with faded crape is bound;
His coat is gray, and threadbare too, I see.
"The rude winds" seem "to mock his hoary hair;"
His shirtless bosom to the blast is bare.
Anon he turns and casts a wistful eye,
And with scant napkin wipes the blinding spray,
And looks around, as if he fain would spy
Friends he had feasted in his better day:
Ah! some are dead; and some have long forbone
To know the poor; and he is left forlorn!
God help the poor!

God help the poor, who in lone valleys dwell,
Or by far hills, where whin and heather grow;
Theirs is a story sad indeed to tell,
Yet little cares the world, and less 't would know
About the toil and want men undergo.
The wearying loom doth call them up at morn,
They work till worn-out nature sinks to sleep,
They taste, but are not fed. The snow drifts deep
Around the fireless cot, and blocks the door;
The night-storm howls a dirge across the moor;
And shall they perish thus — oppressed and lorn?
Shall toil and famine, hopeless, still be borne?
No! God will yet arise and help the poor!

"Amen!" said Barton, solemnly and sorrowfully. "Mary! wench couldst thou copy me them lines, dost think? — that 's to say, if Job there has no objection."

"Not I. More they 're heard and read and the better, say I."

So Mary took the paper. And the next day, on the blank half sheet of a valentine, all bordered with hearts and darts — a valentine she had once suspected to come from Jem Wilson — she copied Bamford's beautiful little poem.

CHAPTER X.

"My heart, once soft as woman's tear, is gnarled
With gloating on the ills I cannot cure." ELLIOTT.

"Then guard and shield her innocence,
Let her not fall like me;
'T were better, oh! a thousand times,
She in her grave should be." 'THE OUTCAST.'

DESPAIR settled down like a heavy cloud; and now and then, through the dead calm of sufferings, came pipings of stormy winds, foretelling the end of these dark prognostics. In times of sorrowful or fierce endurance, we are often soothed by the mere repetition of old proverbs which tell the experience of our forefathers; but now, "it 's a long lane that has no turning," "the weariest day draws to an end," &c., seemed false and vain sayings, so long and so weary was the pressure of the terrible times. Deeper and deeper still sank the poor; it showed how much lingering suffering it takes to kill men, that so few (in comparison) died during those times. But remember! we only miss those who do men's work in their humble sphere; the aged, the feeble, the children, when they die, are hardly noted by the world; and yet to many hearts, their deaths make a blank which long years will never fill up. Remember, too, that though it may take much suffering to kill the able-bodied and effective members of society, it does *not* take much to reduce them to worn, listless, diseased creatures, who thenceforward crawl through life with moody hearts and pain-stricken bodies.

The people had thought the poverty of the preceding years hard to bear, and had found its yoke heavy; but this year added sorely to its weight. Former times had chastised them with whips, but this chastised them with scorpions.

Of course, Barton had his share of mere bodily sufferings. Before he had gone up to London on his vain errand, he had been working short time. But in the hopes of speedy redress by means of the interference of Parliament, he had thrown up his place; and now, when he asked leave to resume his work, he was told they were diminishing their number of hands every week, and he was made aware, by the remarks of fellow workmen, that a Chartist delegate, and a leading member of a Trades' Union, was not likely to be favoured in his search after employment. Still he tried to keep up a brave heart concerning himself. He knew he could bear hunger; for that power of endurance had been called forth when he was a little child, and had seen his mother hide her daily morsel to share it among her children, and when he, being the eldest, had told the noble lie, that "he was not hungry, could not eat a bit more," in order to imitate his mother's bravery, and still the sharp wail of the younger infants. Mary, too, was secure of two meals a day at Miss Simmonds'; though by the way, the dress-maker, too, feeling the effect of bad times, had left off giving tea to her apprentices, setting them the example of long abstinence by putting off her own meal until work was done for the night, however late that might be.

But the rent! It was half-a-crown a week — nearly all Mary's earnings — and much less room might do for them, only two. — (Now came the time to be thankful that the early dead were saved from the evil to come.) — The agricultural labourer generally has strong local attachments; but they are far less common, almost obliterated, among the inhabitants of a town. Still there are exceptions, and Barton formed one. He had removed to his present house just after the last bad times, when little Tom had sickened and died. He had then thought the bustle of a removal would give his poor stunned wife something to do, and he had taken more interest in the details of the proceeding than he otherwise would have done, in the hope of calling her forth to action again. So he seemed to know every brass-headed nail, driven up for her convenience. Only one had been displaced. It was Esther's bonnet nail, which, in his deep revengeful anger against her, after his wife's death, he had torn out of the wall, and cast into the street. It would be hard work to leave the house, which yet seemed hallowed by his wife's presence in the happy days of old. But he was a law unto himself, though sometimes a bad, fierce law; and he resolved to give the rent-collector notice, and look out for a cheaper abode, and tell Mary they must flit. Poor Mary! she loved the house, too. It was wrenching up her natural feelings of home, for it would be long before the fibres of her heart would gather themselves about another place.

This trial was spared. The collector (of himself), on the very Monday when Barton planned to give him notice of his intention to leave, lowered the rent threepence a week, just enough to make Barton compromise and agree to stay on a little longer.

But by degrees the house was stripped of all its little ornaments. Some were broken; and the odd twopences and threepences, wanted to pay for their repairs, were required for the far sterner necessity of food. And by-and-bye Mary began to part with other superfluities at the pawn-shop. The smart tea-tray, and tea-caddy, long and carefully kept, went for bread for her father. He did not ask for it, or complain, but she saw hunger in his shrunk, fierce, animal look. Then the blankets went, for it was summer time, and they could spare them; and their sale made a fund, which Mary fancied would last till better times came. But it was soon all gone; and then she looked around the room to crib it of its few remaining ornaments. To all these proceedings her father said never a word. If he fasted, or feasted (after the sale of some article), on an unusual meal of bread and cheese, he took all with a sullen indifference, which depressed Mary's heart. She often wished he would apply for relief from the Guardians' relieving office; often wondered the Trades' Union did nothing for him. Once when she asked him as he sat, grimed, unshaven, and gaunt, after a day's fasting over the fire, why he did not get relief from the town, he turned round, with grim wrath, and said, "I don't want money, child! D—n their charity and their money! I want work, and it is my right. I want work."

He would bear it all, he said to himself. And he did bear it, but not meekly; that was too much to expect. Real meekness of character is called out by experience of kindness And few had been kind to him. Yet through it all, with stern determination he refused the assistance his Trades' Union would have given him. It had not much to give, but with worldly wisdom, thought it better to propitiate an active, useful member, than to help those who were more unenergetic, though they had large families to provide for. Not so thought John Barton. With him need was right.

"Give it to Tom Darbyshire," he said. "He 's more claim on it than me, for he 's more need of it, with his seven children."

Now Tom Darbyshire was, in his listless, grumbling way, a backbiting enemy of John Barton's. And he knew it; but he was not to be influenced by that in a matter like this.

Mary went early to her work; but her cheery laugh over it was now missed by the other girls. Her mind wandered over the present distress, and then settled, as she stitched, on the visions of the future, where yet her thoughts dwelt more on the circumstances of ease, and the pomps and vanities awaiting her, than on the lover with whom she was to share them. Still she was not insensible to the pride of having attracted one so far above herself in station; not insensible to the secret pleasure of knowing that he, whom so many admired, had often said he would give anything for one of her sweet smiles. Her love for him was a bubble, blown out of vanity; but it looked very real and very bright. Sally Leadbitter, meanwhile, keenly observed the signs of the times; she found out that Mary had begun to affix a stern value to money as the "Purchaser of Life," and many girls had been dazzled and lured by gold, even without the betraying love which she believed to exist in Mary's heart. So she urged young Mr. Carsons, by representations of the want she was sure surrounded Mary, to bring matters more to a point. But he had a kind of instinctive dread of hurting Mary's pride of spirit, and durst not hint his knowledge in any way of the distress that many must be enduring. He felt that for the present he must still be content with stolen meetings and summer evening strolls, and the delight of pouring sweet honeyed words into her ear, while she listened with a blush and a smile that made her look radiant with beauty. No, he would be cautious in order to be certain; for Mary one way, or another, he must make his. He had no doubt of the effect of his own personal charms in the long run; for he knew he was handsome, and believed himself fascinating.

If he had known what Mary's home was, he would not have been so much convinced of his increasing influence over her, by her being more and more ready to linger with him in the sweet summer air. For when she returned for the night her father was often out, and the house wanted the cheerful look it had had in the days when money was never wanted to purchase soap and brushes, black-lead and pipe-clay. It was dingy and comfortless; for, of course, there was not even the dumb familiar home-friend, a fire. And Margaret, too, was now so often from home, singing at some of those grand places. And Alice; oh, Mary wished she had never left her cellar to go and live at Ancoats with her sister-in-law. For in that matter Mary felt very guilty; she had put off and put off going to see the widow after George Wilson's death from dread of meeting Jem, or giving him reason to think she wished to be as intimate with him as formerly; and now she was so much ashamed of her delay that she was likely never to go at all.

If her father was at home it was no better; indeed it was worse. He seldom spoke, less than ever; and often when he did speak they were sharp angry words, such as he had never given her formerly. Her temper was high, too, and her answers not over-mild; and once in his passion he had even beaten her. If Sally Leadbitter or Mr. Carsons had been at hand at that moment, Mary would have been ready to leave home for ever. She sat alone, after her father had flung out of the house, bitterly thinking on the days that were gone; angry with her own hastiness, and believing that her father did not love her; striving to heap up one painful thought on another. Who cared for her? Mr. Carsons might, but in this grief that seemed no comfort. . Mother dead! Father so often angry, so lately cruel (for it was a hard blow, and blistered and reddened Mary's soft white skin with pain): and then her heart turned round, and she remembered with self-reproach how provokingly she had looked and spoken, and how much her father had to bear; and oh, what a kind and loving parent he had been, till these days of trial. The remembrance of one little instance of his fatherly love thronged after another into her mind, and she began to wonder how she could have behaved to him as she had done.

Then he came home; and but for very shame she would have confessed her penitence in words. But she looked sullen, from her effort to keep down emotion; and for some time her father did not know how to begin to speak. At length he gulped down pride, and said:

"Mary, I'm not above saying I'm very sorry I beat thee. Thou wert a bit aggravating, and I'm not the man I was But it were wrong, and I'll try never to lay hands on thee again."

So he held out his arms, and in many tears she told him her repentance for her fault. He never struck her again.

Still, he often was angry. But that was almost better than being silent. Then he sat near the fire-place (from habit), smoking, or chewing opium. Oh, how Mary loathed that smell! And in the dusk, just before it merged into the short summer night, she had learned to look with dread towards the window, which now her father would have kept uncurtained; for there were not seldom seen sights which haunted her in her dreams. Strange faces of pale men, with dark glaring eyes, peered into the inner darkness, and seemed desirous to ascertain if her father was at home. Or, a hand and arm (the body hidden) was put within the door, and beckoned him away. He always went. And once or twice, when Mary was in bed, she heard men's voices below, in earnest, whispered talk.

They were all desperate members of Trades' Unions, ready for any thing; made ready by want.

While all this change for gloom yet struck fresh and heavy on Mary's heart, her father startled her out of a reverie one evening, by asking her when she had been to see Jane Wilson. From his manner of speaking, she was made aware that he had been; but at the time of his visit he had never mentioned any thing about it. Now, however, he gruffly told her to go next day without fail, and added some abuse of her for not having been before. The little outward impulse of her father's speech gave Mary the push, which she, in this instance required; and accordingly, timing her visit so as to avoid Jem's hours at home, she went the following afternoon to Ancoats.

The outside of the well-known house struck her as different; for the door was closed, instead of open, as it once had always stood. The window-plants, George Wilson's pride and especial care, looked withering and drooping. They had been without water for a long time, and now, when the widow had reproached herself severely for neglect, in her ignorant anxiety, she gave them too much. On opening the door, Alice was seen, not stirring about in her habitual way, but knitting by the fire-side. The room felt hot, although the fire burnt gray and dim, under the bright rays of the afternoon sun. Mrs. Wilson was "siding"* the dinner things, and talking all the time, in a kind of whining, shouting voice, which Mary did not at first understand. She understood, at once, however, that her absence had been noted, and talked over; she saw a constrained look on Mrs. Wilson's sorrow-stricken face, which told her a scolding was to come.

"Dear! Mary, is that you?" she began. "Why, who would ha' dreamt of seeing you! We thought you 'd clean forgotten us; and Jem has often wondered if he should know you, if he met you in the street."

Now, poor Jane Wilson had been sorely tried; and at present her trials had had no outward effect, but that of in-

* To "side," to put aside, or in order.

creased acerbity of temper. She wished to show Mary how much she was offended, and meant to strengthen her cause, by putting some of her own sharp speeches into Jem's mouth.

Mary felt guilty, and had no good reason to give as an apology; so for a minute she stood silent, looking very much ashamed, and then turned to speak to aunt Alice, who, in her surprised, hearty greeting to Mary, had dropped her ball of worsted, and was busy trying to set the thread to rights, before the kitten had entangled it past redemption, once round every chair, and twice round the table.

"You mun speak louder than that, if you mean her to hear; she 's become as deaf as a post this last few weeks. I 'd ha' told you, if I 'd remembered how long it were sin' you 'd seen her."

"Yes, my dear, I 'm getting very hard o' hearing of late," said Alice, catching the state of the case, with her quick glancing eyes. "I suppose it 's the beginning of th' end."

"Don't talk o' that way," screamed her sister-in-law. "We 've had enow of ends and deaths without forecasting more." She covered her face with her apron, and sat down to cry.

"He was such a good husband," said she, in a less excited tone, to Mary, as she looked up with tear-streaming eyes from behind her apron. "No one can tell what I 've lost in him, for no one knew his worth like me."

Mary's listening sympathy softened her, and she went on to unburden her heavy laden heart.

"Eh, dear, dear! No one knows what I 've lost. When my poor boys went, I thought the Almighty had crushed me to th' ground, but I never thought o' losing George; I did na think I could ha' borne to ha' lived without him. And yet I 'm here, and he 's" — A fresh burst of crying interrupted her speech.

"Mary," beginning to speak again, — "did you ever hear what a poor creature I were when he married me? And he such a handsome fellow! Jem 's nothing to what his father were at his age."

Yes! Mary had heard, and so she said. But the poor woman's thoughts had gone back to those days, and her little recollections came out, with many interruptions of sighs, and tears, and shakes of the head.

"There were nought about me for him to choose me. I were just well enough afore that accident, but at after I were downright plain. And there was Bessy Witter as would ha' given her eyes for him; she as is Mrs. Carsons now, for she were a handsome lass, although I never could see her beauty then; and Carsons warn't so much above her, as they 're both above us all now."

Mary went very red, and wished she could help doing so, and wished also that Mrs. Wilson would tell her more about the father and mother of her lover; but she durst not ask, and Mrs. Wilson's thoughts soon returned to her husband, and their early married days.

"If you 'll believe me, Mary, there never was such a born goose at house-keeping as I were: and yet he married me! I had been in a factory sin' five years old a'most, and I knew nought about cleaning, or cooking, let alone washing and such-like work. The day after we were married he went to his work at after breakfast, and says he, 'Jenny, we 'll ha' th' cold beef, and potatoes, and that 's a dinner for a prince.' I were anxious to make him comfortable, God knows how anxious. And yet I 'd no notion how to cook a potatoe. I know'd they were boiled, and know'd their skins were taken off, and that were all. So I tidyed my house in a rough kind o' way, then I looked at that very clock up yonder," pointing at one that hung against the wall, "and I seed it were nine o'clock, so, thinks I, th' potatoes shall be well boiled at any rate, and I gets 'em on th' fire in a jiffy (that 's to say, as soon as I could peel 'em, which were a tough job at first), and then I fell to unpacking my boxes! and at twenty minutes past twelve he comes home, and I had the beef ready on th' table, and I went to take the potatoes out o' th' pot; but oh! Mary, th' water had boiled away, and they were all a nasty brown mass, as smelt through all the house. He said nought, and were very gentle; but, oh, Mary, I cried so that afternoon. I shall ne'er forget it; no, never. I made many a blunder at after, but none that fretted me like that."

"Father does not like girls to work in factories," said Mary.

"No, I know he doesn't; and reason good. They oughtn't to go at after they're married, that I'm very clear about. I could reckon up," (counting with her finger) "ay, nine men I know, as has been driven to th' public-house by having wives as worked in factories; good folk, too, as though there was no harm in putting their little ones out at nurse, and letting their house go all dirty, and their fires all out; and that was a place as was tempting for a husband to stay in, was it? He soon finds out gin-shops, where all is clean and bright, and where th' fire blazes cheerily, and gives a man a welcome as it were."

Alice, who was standing near for the convenience of hearing, had caught much of this speech, and it was evident the subject had previously been discussed by the women, for she chimed in.

"I wish our Jem could speak a word to th' Queen about factory work for married women. Eh! but he comes it strong, when once yo get him to speak about it. Wife o' his 'n will never work away fra' home."

"I say it's Prince Albert as ought to be asked how he'd like his missis to be from home when he comes in, tired and worn, and wanting some one to cheer him; and may be, her to come in by-and-bye, just as tired and down in th' mouth; and he'd like for her never to be at home to see to th' cleaning of his house, or to keep a bright fire in his grate. Let alone his meals being all hugger-mugger and comfortless. I'd be bound, prince as he is, if his missis served him so, he'd be off to a gin-palace, or summut o' that kind. So why can't he make a law again poor folks' wives working in factories?"

Mary ventured to say that she thought the Queen and Prince Albert could not make laws, but the answer was,

"Pooh! don't tell me it 's not the Queen as makes laws; and isn't she bound to obey Prince Albert? And if he said they mustn't, why she 'd say they mustn 't, and then all folk would say, oh no, we never shall do any such thing no more."

"Jem 's getten on rarely," said Alice, who had not heard her sister's last bursts of eloquence, and whose thoughts were still running on her nephew, and his various talents. "He 's found out summut about a crank or tank, I forget rightly which it is, but th' master 's made him foreman, and he all the while turning off hands; but he said he could na' part wi' Jem, nohow. He 's good wage now: I tell him he 'll be thinking of marrying soon, and he deserves a right down good wife, that he does."

Mary went very red, and looked annoyed, although there was a secret spring of joy deep down in her heart, at hearing Jem so spoken of. But his mother only saw the annoyed look, and was piqued accordingly. She was not over and above desirous that her son should marry. His presence in the house seemed a relic of happier times, and she had some little jealousy of his future wife, whoever she might be. Still she could not bear any one not to feel gratified and flattered by Jem's preference, and full well she knew how above all others he preferred Mary. Now she had never thought Mary good enough for Jem, and her late neglect in coming to see her, still rankled a little in her breast. So she determined to invent a little, in order to do away with any idea Mary might have that Jem would choose her for "his right down good wife," as aunt Alice called it.

"Ay, he 'll be for taking a wife soon," and then, in a lower voice, as if confidentially, but really to prevent any contradiction or explanation from her simple sister-in-law, she added,

"It 'll not be long afore Molly Gibson (that 's her at th' provision-shop round the corner) will hear a secret as will not displease her I 'm thinking. She 's been casting sheep's eyes at our Jem this many a day, but he thought her father would not give her to a common working man; but now he 's good as her, every bit. I thought once he 'd a fancy for thee, Mary, but I donnot think yo'd ever ha' suited, so it 's best as it is."

By an effort Mary managed to keep down her vexation, and to say, "She hoped he 'd be happy with Molly Gibson. She was very handsome, for certain."

"Ay, and a notable body, too. I 'll just step up-stairs and show you the patchwork quilt she gave me but last Saturday."

Mary was glad she was going out of the room. Her words irritated her; perhaps not the less because she did not fully believe them. Besides, she wanted to speak to Alice, and Mrs. Wilson seemed to think that she, as the widow, ought to absorb all the attention.

"Dear Alice," began Mary, "I 'm so grieved to find you so deaf; it must have come on very rapid."

"Yes, dear, it 's a trial; I 'll not deny it. Pray God give me strength to find out its teaching. I felt it sore one fine day when I thought I 'd go gather some meadow-sweet to make tea for Jane's cough; and the fields seemed so dree and still; and at first I could na' make out what was wanting; and then it struck me it were th' song o' the birds, and that I never should hear their sweet music no more, and I could na' help crying a bit. But I 've much to be thankful for. I think I 'm a comfort to Jane, if I 'm only some one to scold now and then; poor body! It takes off her thoughts from her sore losses when she can scold a bit. If my eyes are left I can do well enough; I can guess at what folk are saying."

The splendid red and yellow patch quilt now made its appearance, and Jane Wilson would not be satisfied unless Mary praised it all over, border, centre, and ground-work, right side and wrong; and Mary did her duty, saying all the more, because she could not work herself up to any very hearty admiration of her rival's present. She made haste, however, with her commendations, in order to avoid encountering Jem. As soon as she was fairly away from the house and street, she slackened her pace, and began to think. Did Jem really care for Molly Gibson? Well, if he did, let him. People seemed all to think he was much too good for her (Mary's own self). Perhaps some one else, far more handsome, and far more grand, would show him one day that she was good enough to be Mrs. Henry Carsons. So temper, or what Mary called "spirit," led her to encourage Mr. Carsons more than ever she had done before.

Some weeks after this there was a meeting of the Trades' Union to which John Barton belonged. The morning of the day on which it was to take place he had lain late in bed, for what was the use of getting up? He had hesitated between the purchase of meal or opium, and had chosen the latter, for its use had become a necessity with him. He wanted it to relieve him from the terrible depression its absence occasioned. A large lump seemed only to bring him into a natural state, or what had been his natural state formerly. Eight o'clock was the hour fixed for the meeting; and at it were read letters, filled with details of woe, from all parts of the country. Fierce, heavy gloom brooded over the assembly; and fiercely and heavily did the men separate, towards eleven o'clock, some irritated by the opposition of others to their desperate plans.

It was not a night to cheer them, as they quitted the glare of the gas-lighted room, and came out into the street. Unceasing, soaking rain was falling; the very lamps seemed obscured by the damp upon the glass, and their light reached but to a little distance from the posts. The streets were cleared of passers-by; not a creature seemed stirring, except here and there a drenched policeman in his oil-skin cape. Barton wished the others good-night, and set off home. He had gone through a street or two, when he heard a step behind him; but he did not care to stop and see who it was. A little further, and the person quickened step, and touched his arm very lightly. He turned, and saw, even by the darkness visible of that badly-lighted street, that the woman who stood by him was of no doubtful profession. It was told by her faded finergy, all unfit to meet the pelting of that pitiless storm; the gauze bonnet, once pink, now dirty white, the muslin gown, all draggled, and soaking wet up to the very knees; the gay-coloured barège shawl, closely wrapped round the form, which yet shivered and shook, as the woman whispered: "I want to speak to you."

He swore an oath, and bade her begone.

"I really do. Don't send me away. I'm so out of breath, I cannot say what I would all at once." She put her hand to her side, and caught her breath with evident pain.

"I tell thee I'm not the man for thee," adding an opprobrious name. "Stay," said he, as a thought suggested by her voice flushed across him. He griped her arm — the arm he had just before shaken off, and dragged her, faintly resisting, to the nearest lamp-post. He pushed the bonnet back, and roughly held the face she would fain have averted, to the light, and in her large, unnaturally bright gray eyes, her lovely mouth, half open, as if imploring the forbearance she could not ask for in words, he saw at once the long-lost Esther; she who had caused his wife's death. Much was like the gay creature of former years; but the glaring paint, the sharp features, the changed expression of the whole! But most of all, he loathed the dress; and yet the poor thing, out of her little choice of attire, had put on the plainest she had, to come on that night's errand.

"So it's thee, is it! It's thee!" exclaimed John, as he ground his teeth, and shook her with passion. "I've looked for thee long at corners o' streets, and such like places. I knew I should find thee at last. Thee 'll may be bethink thee o' some words I spoke, which put thee up at th' time; summut about street-walkers; but oh no! thou art none o' them naughts; no one thinks thou art, who sees thy fine draggle-tailed dress, and thy pretty pink cheeks!" stopping for very want of breath.

"Oh, mercy! John, mercy! listen to me for Mary's sake!"

She meant his daughter, but the name only fell on his ear as belonging to his wife; and it was adding fuel to the fire.

In vain did her face grow deadly pale around the vivid circle of paint, in vain did she gasp for mercy,—he burst forth again.

"And thou names that name to me! and thou thinks the thought of her will bring thee mercy! Dost thou know it was thee who killed her, as sure as ever Cain killed Abel. She'd loved thee as her own, and she trusted thee as her own, and when thou wert gone she never held head up again, but died in less than a three week; and at her judgment day she'll rise, and point to thee as her murderer; or if she don't, I will."

He flung her, trembling, sinking, fainting, from him, and strode away. She fell with a feeble scream against the lamp-post, and lay there in her weakness, unable to rise. A policeman came up in time to see the close of these occurrences, and concluding from Esther's unsteady, reeling fall, that she was tipsy, he took her in her half-unconscious state to the lock-ups for the night. The superintendent of that abode of vice and misery, was roused from his dozing watch through the dark hours, by half-delirious wails and moanings, which he reported as arising from intoxication. If he had listened he would have heard these words, repeated in various forms, but always in the same anxious, muttering way.

"He would not listen to me; what can I do? He would not listen to me, and I wanted to warn him! Oh, what shall I do to save Mary's child! What shall I do? How can I keep her from being such a one as I am; such a wretched, loathsome creature! She was listening just as I listened, and loving just as I loved, and the end will be just like my end. How shall I save her? She won't hearken to warning, or heed it more than I did; and who loves her well enough to watch over her as she should be watched? God keep her from harm! And yet I won't pray for her; sinner that I am! Can my prayers be heard? No! they'll only do harm. How shall I save her? He would not listen to me."

So the night wore away. The next morning she was taken up to the New Bailey. It was a clear case of disorderly vagrancy, and she was committed to prison for a month. How much might happen in that time!

CHAPTER XI.

"Oh Mary, canst thou wreck his peace,
Wha for thy sake wad gladly die?
Or canst thou break that heart of his,
Whase only faut is loving thee?" BURNS.

"I can like of the wealth, I must confess.
Yet more I prize the man though moneyless;
I am not of their humour yet that can
For title or estate affect a man;
Or of myself one body deign to make
With him I loath, for his possessions' sake."
WITHER'S 'FIDELIA.

BARTON returned home after his encounter with Esther, uneasy and dissatisfied. He had said no more than he had been planning to say for years, in case she was ever thrown in his way, in the character in which he felt certain he should meet her. He believed she deserved it all, and yet he now wished he had not said it. Her look, as she asked for mercy haunted him through his broken and disordered sleep; her form, as he last saw her, lying prostrate in helplessness, would not be banished from his dreams. He sat up in bed to try and dispel the vision. Now too late his conscience smote him with harshness. It would have been all very well, he thought, to have said what he did, if he had added some kind words, at last. He wondered if his dead wife was conscious of that night's occurrence; and he hoped not, for with her love for Esther he believed it would embitter Heaven to have seen her so degraded and repulsed. For he now recalled her humility, her tacit acknowledgment of her lost character; and he began to marvel if there was power in the religion he had often heard of, to turn her from her ways. He felt that no earthly power that he knew of could do it, but there glimmered on his darkness, the idea that religion might save her. Still where to find her again? In the wilderness of a large town, where to meet with an individual of so little value or note to any?

And evening after evening he paced those streets in which he had heard those footsteps following him, peering under every fantastic, discreditable bonnet, in the hopes of once more meeting Esther, and addressing her in a far different manner from what he had done before. But he returned, night after night, disappointed in his search, and at last gave it up in despair, and tried to recall his angry feelings towards her, in order to find relief from his present self-reproach.

He often looked at Mary, and wished she were not so like her aunt, for the very bodily likeness seemed to suggest the possibility of a similar likeness in their fate; and then this idea enraged his irritable mind, and he became suspicious and anxious about Mary's conduct. Now hitherto she had been so remarkably free from all control, and almost from all inquiry concerning her actions, that she did not brook this change in her father's behaviour very well. Just when she was yielding more than ever to Mr. Carsons' desire of frequent meetings, it was hard to be so questioned concerning her hours of leaving off work, whether she had come straight home, &c. She could not tell lies; though she could conceal much if she were not questioned. So she took refuge in obstinate silence, alleging as a reason for it her indignation at being so cross-examined. This did not add to the good feeling between father and daughter, and yet they dearly loved each other; and in the minds of each, one principal reason for maintaining such behaviour as displeased the other, was the believing that this conduct would insure that person's happiness.

Her father now began to wish Mary were married. Then this terrible superstitious fear suggested by her likeness to Esther would be done away with. He felt that he could not resume the reins he had once slackened. But with a husband it would be different. If Jem Wilson would but marry her! With his character for steadiness and talent! But he was afraid Mary had slighted him, he came so seldom now to the house. He would ask her.

"Mary, what 's come o'er thee and Jem Wilson? Yo were great friends at one time."

"Oh, folk say he 's going to be married to Molly Gibson,

and of course courting takes up a deal o' time," answered Mary, as indifferently as she could.

"Thou 'st played thy cards badly, then," replied her father, in a surly tone. "At one time he were desperate fond o' thee, or I 'm much mistaken. Much fonder of thee than thou deservedst."

"That 's as people think," said Mary, pertly, for she remembered that the very morning before she had met Mr. Carsons, who had sighed, and swore, and protested all manner of tender vows that she was the loveliest, sweetest, best, &c. And when she had seen him afterwards riding with one of his beautiful sisters, had he not evidently pointed her out as in some way or other an object worthy of attention and interest, and then lingered behind his sister's horse for a moment to kiss his hand repeatedly. So, as for Jem Wilson, she could whistle him down the wind.

But her father was not in the mood to put up with pertness, and he upbraided her with the loss of Jem Wilson till she had to bite her lips till the blood came, in order to keep down the angry words that would rise in her heart. At last her father left the house, and then she might give way to her passionate tears.

It so happened that Jem, after much anxious thought, had determined that day to "put his fortune to the touch, to win or lose it all." He was in a condition to maintain a wife in comfort. It was true his mother and aunt must form part of the household; but such is not an uncommon case among the poor, and if there were the advantages of previous friendship between the parties, it was not, he thought, an obstacle to matrimony. Both mother and aunt he believed would welcome Mary. And oh! what a certainty of happiness the idea of that welcome implied.

He had been absent and abstracted all day long with the thought of the coming event of the evening. He almost smiled at himself for his care in washing and dressing in preparation for his visit to Mary; as if one waistcoat or another could decide his fate in so passionately a momentuous thing.

He believed he only delayed before his little looking-glass for cowardice, for absolute fear of a girl. He would try not to think so much about the affair, and he thought the more.

Poor Jem! it is not an auspicious moment for thee!

"Come in," said Mary, as some one knocked at the door, while she sat sadly at her sewing, trying to earn a few pence by working over hours at some mourning.

Jem entered, looking more awkward and abashed than he had ever done before. Yet here was Mary all alone, just as he had hoped to find her. She did not ask him to take a chair, but after standing a minute or two he sat down near her.

"Is your father at home, Mary?" said he, by way of making an opening, for she seemed determined to keep silence, and went on stitching away.

"No, he 's gone to his Union, I suppose." Another silence. It was no use waiting, thought Jem. The subject would never be led to by any talk he could think of in his anxious fluttered state. He had better begin at once.

"Mary!" said he, and the unusual tone of his voice made her look up for an instant, but in that time she understood from his countenance what was coming, and her heart beat so suddenly and violently she could hardly sit still. Yet one thing she was sure of; nothing he could say should make her have him. She would show them all *who* would be glad to have her. She was not yet calm after her father's irritating speeches. Yet her eyes fell veiled before that passionate look fixed upon her.

"Dear Mary! (for how dear you are, I cannot rightly tell you in words). It 's no new story I 'm going to speak about. You must ha' seen and known it long; for since we were boy and girl, I ha' loved you above father and mother and all; and all I 've thought on by day and dreamt on by night, has been something in which you've had a share. I 'd no way of keeping you for long, and I scorned to try and tie you down; and I lived in terror lest some one else should take you to himself. But now, Mary, I 'm foreman in th' works, and, dear Mary! listen," as she, in her unbearable agitation, stood up and turned away from him. He rose too, and came nearer, trying to take hold of her hand; but this she would not allow. She was bracing herself up to refuse him, for once and for all.

"And now, Mary, I 've a home to offer you, and a heart as true as ever man had to love you and cherish you; we shall never be rich folk, I dare say; but if a loving heart and a strong right arm can shield you from sorrow, or from want, mine shall do it. I cannot speak as I would like; my love won't let itself be put in words. But oh! darling, say you believe me, and that you 'll be mine."

She could not speak at once; her words would not come.

"Mary, they say silence gives consent; is it so?" he whispered.

Now or never the effort must be made.

"No! it does not with me." Her voice was calm, although she trembled from head to foot. "I will always be your friend, Jem, but I can never be your wife."

"Not my wife," said he, mournfully. "Oh, Mary, think awhile! you cannot be my friend if you will not be my wife. At least I can never be content to be only your friend. Do think awhile! If you say No you will make me hopeless, desperate. It 's no love of yesterday. It has made the very groundwork of all that people call good in me. I don't know what I shall be if you won't have me. And Mary! think how glad your father would be! it may sound vain, but he 's told me more than once how much he should like to see us two married!"

Jem intended this for a powerful argument, but in Mary's present mood it told against him more than any thing; for it suggested the false and foolish idea, that her father, in his evident anxiety to promote her marriage with Jem, had been speaking to him on the subject with some degree of solicitation.

"I tell you, Jem, it cannot be. Once for all, I will never marry you."

"And is this the end of all my hopes and fears? the end of my life, I may say, for it is the end of all worth living for!" His agitation rose and carried him into passion. "Mary! you 'll hear, may be, of me as a drunkard, and may be as a thief, and may be as a murderer. Remember! when all are speaking ill of me, you will have no right to blame me, for it 's your cruelty that will have made me what I feel I shall become. You won't even say you 'll try and like me; will you, Mary!" said he, suddenly changing his tone from threatening despair to fond passionate entreaty, as he took her hand and held it forcibly between both of his, while he tried to catch a glimpse of her averted face. She was silent, but it was from deep and violent emotion. He could not bear to wait; he would not hope, to be dashed away again; he rather in his bitterness of heart chose the certainty of despair, and before she could resolve what to answer, he flung away her hand and rushed out of the house.

"Jem! Jem!" cried she, with faint and choking voice. It was too late; he left street after street behind him with his almost winged speed, as he sought the fields, where he might give way unobserved to all the deep despair he felt.

It was scarcely ten minutes since he had entered the house, and found Mary at comparative peace, and now she lay half across the dresser, her head hidden in her hands, and every part of her body shaking with the violence of her sobs. She could not have told at first (if you had asked her, and she could have commanded voice enough to answer) why she was in such agonised grief. It was too sudden for her to analyse, or think upon it. She only felt, that by her own doing her life would be hereafter blank and dreary. By-and-bye her sorrow exhausted her body by its power, and she seemed to have no strength left for crying. She sat down; and now thoughts crowded on her mind. One little hour ago, and all was still unsaid, and she had her fate in her own power. And yet, how long ago had she determined to say pretty much what she did, if the occasion ever offered.

It was as if two people were arguing the matter; that mournful, desponding communion between her former self, and her present self. Herself, a day, an hour ago; and herself now. For we have every one of us felt how a very few minutes of the months and years called life, will sometimes suffice to place all time past and future in an entirely new light; will make us see the vanity or the criminality of the bye-gone, and so change the aspect of the coming time, that we look with loathing on the very thing we have most desired. A few moments may change our character for life, by giving a totally different direction to our aims and energies.

To return to Mary. Her plan had been, as we well know, to marry Mr. Carsons, and the occurrence an hour ago was only a preliminary step. True; but it had unveiled her heart to her; it had convinced her that she loved Jem above all persons or things. But Jem was a poor mechanic, with a mother and aunt to keep; a mother, too, who had shown her pretty clearly that she did not desire her for a daughter-in-law: while Mr. Carsons was rich, and prosperous, and gay, and (she believed) would place her in all circumstances of ease and luxury, where want could never come. What were these hollow vanities to her, now she had discovered the passionate secret of her soul? She felt as if she almost hated Mr. Carsons, who had decoyed her with his baubles. She now saw how vain, how nothing to her, would be all gaieties and pomps, all joys and pleasures, unless she might share them with Jem; yes, with him she had harshly rejected so short a time ago. If he were poor, she loved him all the better. If his mother did think her unworthy of him, what was it but the truth, as she now owned with bitter penitence. She had hitherto been walking in grope-light towards a precipice: but in the clear revelation of that past hour, she saw her danger, and turned away, resolutely, and for ever.

That was some comfort: I mean her clear perception of what she ought not to do; of what no luring temptations should ever again induce her to hearken to. How she could best undo the wrong she had done to Jem and herself by refusing his love, was another anxious question. She wearied herself with proposing plans, and rejecting them.

She was roused to a consciousness of time, by hearing the neighbouring church clock strike twelve. Her father she knew might be expected home any minute, and she was in no mood for a meeting with him. So she hastily gathered up her work, and went to her own little bed-room, leaving him to let himself in.

She put out her candle, that her father might not see its light under the door; and sat down on her bed to think. But again turning things over in her mind again and again, she could only determine at once to put an end to all further communication with Mr. Carsons, in the most decided way she could. Maidenly modesty (and true love is ever modest) seemed to oppose every plan she could think of, for showing Jem how much she repented her decision against him, and how dearly she had now discovered that she loved him. She came to the unusual wisdom of resolving to do nothing, but strive to be patient, and improve circumstances as they might turn up. Surely, if Jem knew of her remaining unmarried, he would try his fortune again. He would never be content with one rejection; she believed she could not in his place. She had been very wrong, but now she would endeavour to do right, and have womanly patience, until he saw her changed and repentant mind in her natural actions. Even if she had to wait for years, it was no more than now it was easy to look forward to, as a penance for her giddy flirting on the one hand, and her cruel mistake concerning her feelings on the other. So anticipating a happy ending to the course of her love, however distant it might be, she fell asleep just as the earliest factory bells were ringing. She had sunk down in her clothes, and her sleep was unrefreshing. She wakened up shivery and chill in body, and sorrow-stricken in mind, though she could not at first rightly tell the cause of her depression.

She recalled the events of the night before, and still resolved to adhere to those determinations she had then formed. But patience seemed a far more difficult virtue this morning.

She hastened down-stairs, and in her earnest sad desire to do right, now took much pains to secure a comfortable though scanty breakfast for her father; and when he dawdled into the room, in an evidently irritable temper, she bore all with the gentleness of penitence, till at last her mild answers turned away wrath.

She loathed the idea of meeting Sally Leadbitter at her daily work; yet it must be done, and she tried to nerve herself for the encounter, and to make it at once understood, that having determined to give up having any thing further to do with Mr. Carsons, she considered the bond of intimacy broken between them.

But Sally was not the person to let these resolutions be carried into effect too easily. She soon became aware of the present state of Mary's feelings, but she thought they merely arose from the changeableness of girlhood, and that the time would come when Mary would thank her for almost forcing her to keep up her meetings and communications with her rich lover.

So, when two days had passed over in rather too marked avoidance of Sally on Mary's part; and when the former was made aware, by Mr. Carsons' complaints that Mary was not keeping her appointments with him, and that unless he detained her by force, he had no chance of obtaining a word as she passed him in the street on her rapid walk home; she resolved to compel Mary to what she called her own good.

She took no notice during the third day of Mary's avoidance as they sat at work; she rather seemed to acquiesce in the coolness of their intercourse. She put away her sewing early, and went home to her mother, who she said, was more ailing than usual. The other girls soon followed her example, and Mary, casting a rapid glance up and down the street, as she stood last on Miss Simmonds' door-step, darted homewards, in hopes of avoiding the person whom she was fast learning to dread. That night she was safe from any encounter on her road, and she arrived at home, which she found as she expected, empty; for she knew it was a club night, which her father would not miss. She sat down to recover breath, and to still her heart, which panted more from nervousness than from over-exertion, although she had walked so quickly. Then she arose, and taking off her bonnet, her eye caught the form of Sally Leadbitter passing the window with a lingering step, and looking into the darkness with all her might as if to ascertain if Mary were returned. In an instant she repassed and knocked at the house-door, but without awaiting an answer, she entered.

"Well, Mary, dear," (knowing well how little "dear" Mary considered her just then); "it 's so difficult to get any comfortable talk at Miss Simmonds', I thought I 'd just step up and see you at home."

"I understood from what you said your mother was ailing, and that you wanted to be with her," replied Mary, in no welcoming tone.

"Ay, but mother 's better now," said the unabashed Sally. "Your father 's out, I suppose?" looking round as well as she could; for Mary made no haste to perform the hospitable offices of striking a match, and lighting a candle.

"Yes, he 's out," said Mary, shortly, and busying herself at last about the candle, without ever asking her visitor to sit down.

"So much the better," answered Sally, "for to tell you the truth, Mary, I 've a friend at th' end of the road, as is anxious to come and see you at home, since you 're grown so particular as not to like to speak to him in the street. He 'll be here directly."

"Oh, Sally, don't let him," said Mary, speaking at last heartily; and running to the door she would have fastened it, but Sally held her hands, laughing meanwhile at her distress.

"Oh, please, Sally," struggling, "dear Sally! don't let him come here, the neighbours will so talk, and father 'll go mad if he hears; he 'll kill me, Sally, he will. Besides, I don't love him — I never did. Oh, let me go," as footsteps approached; and then, as they passed the house, and seemed to give her a respite, she continued, "Do, Sally, dear Sally, go and tell him I don't love him, and that I don't want to have any thing more to do with him. It was very wrong, I dare say, keeping company with him at all, but I 'm very sorry, if I 've led him to think too much of me; and I don't want him to think any more. Will you tell him this, Sally? and I 'll do any thing for you if you will."

"I 'll tell you what I'll do," said Sally, in a more relenting mood, "I'll go back with you to where he 's waiting for us; or rather, I should say, where I told him to wait for a quarter of an hour, till I seed if your father was at home; and if I didn't come back in that time, he said he 'd come here, and break the door open but he 'd see you."

"Oh, let us go, let us go," said Mary, feeling that the interview must be, and had better be anywhere than at home, where her father might return at any minute. She snatched up her bonnet, and was at the end of the court in an instant; but then, not knowing whether to turn to the right or to the left, she was obliged to wait for Sally, who came leisurely up, and put her arm through Mary's with a kind of decided hold, intended to prevent the possibility of her changing her mind, and turning back. But this, under the circumstances, was quite different to Mary's plan. She had wondered more than once if she must not have another interview with Mr. Carsons; and had then determined, while she expressed her resolution that it should be the final one, to tell him how sorry she was if she had thoughtlessly given him false hopes. For be it remembered, she had the innocence, or the ignorance, to believe his intentions honourable; and he, feeling that at any price he must have her, only that he would obtain her as cheaply as he could, had never undeceived her; while Sally Leadbitter laughed in her sleeve at them both, and wondered how it would all end, — whether Mary would gain her point of marriage, with her sly affectation of believing such to be Mr. Carsons' intention in courting her.

Not very far from the end of the street, into which the court where Mary lived opened, they met Mr. Carsons, his hat a good deal slouched over his face as if afraid of being recognised. He turned when he saw them coming, and led the way without uttering a word (although they were close behind) to a street of half-finished houses.

The length of the walk gave Mary time to recoil from the interview which was to follow; but even if her own resolve to go through with it had failed, there was the steady grasp of Sally Leadbitter, which she could not evade, without an absolute struggle.

At last he stopped in the shelter and concealment of a wooden fence, put up to keep the building rubbish from intruding on the foot-pavement. Inside this fence, a minute afterwards, the girls were standing by him; Mary now returning Sally's detaining grasp with interest, for she had determined on the way to make her a witness, willing, or unwilling, to the ensuing conversation. But Sally's curiosity led her to be a very passive prisoner in Mary's hold.

With more freedom than he had ever used before, Mr. Carsons put his arm firmly round Mary's waist, in spite of her indignant resistance.

"Nay, nay! you little witch! Now I have caught you, I shall keep you prisoner. Tell me now what has made you run away from me so fast these few days — tell me, you sweet little coquette!"

Mary ceased struggling, but turned so as to be almost opposite to him, while she spoke out calmly, and boldly.

"Mr. Carsons! I want to speak to you for once and for all. Since I met you last Monday evening, I have made up my mind to have nothing more to do with you. I know I've been wrong in leading you to think I liked you; but I believe I didn't rightly know my own mind; and I humbly beg your pardon, Sir, if I've led you to think too much of me."

For an instant he was surprised; the next, vanity came to his aid, and convinced him that she could only be joking. He, young, agreeable, rich, handsome! No! she was only showing a little womanly fondness for coquetting.

"You 're a darling little rascal to go on in this way! 'Humbly begging my pardon if you 've made me think too much of you.' As if you didn't know I think of you from morning till night. But you want to be told it again and again, do you?"

"No, indeed, Sir, I don't, I would far liefer * that you should say you would never think of me again, than that you should speak of me in this way. For indeed, Sir, I never was more in earnest than I am, when I say to-night is the last night I will ever speak to you."

"Last night, you sweet little equivocator, but not last day. Ha, Mary, I 've caught you, have I?" as she, puzzled by his perseverance in thinking her joking, hesitated in what form she could now put her meaning.

"I mean, Sir," she said, sharply, "that I will never speak to you again, at any time, after to-night."

"And what 's made this change, Mary?" said he, seriously enough now. "Have I done any thing to offend you?" added he, earnestly.

"No, Sir," she answered gently, but yet firmly. "I cannot tell you exactly why I 've changed my mind; but I shall not alter it again; and as I said before, I beg your pardon if I 've done wrong by you. And now, Sir, if you please, good night."

"But I do not please. You shall not go. What have I done, Mary? Tell me. You must not go without telling me how I have vexed you. What would you have me do?"

"Nothing, Sir, but," (in an agitated tone) "oh! let me go! You cannot change my mind; it 's quite made up. Oh, Sir! why do you hold me so tight. If you *will* know why I won't have anything more to do with you, it is that I cannot love you. I have tried, and I really cannot."

* "Liefer," rather.

"Yet had I *levre* unwist for sorrow die."

Chaucer; 'Troilus and Creseide.'

This naive and candid avowal served her but little. He could not understand how it could be true. Some reason lurked behind. He was passionately in love. What should he do to tempt her? A thought struck him.

"Listen! Mary. Nay, I cannot let you go till you have heard me. I do love you dearly; and I won't believe but what you love me a very little, just a very little. Well, if you don't like to own it, never mind! I only want now to tell you how much I love you, by what I am ready to give up for you. You know (or perhaps you are not fully aware) how little my father and mother would like me to marry you. So angry would they be, and so much ridicule should I have to brave, that of course I have never thought of it till now. I thought we could be happy enough without marriage." (Deep sank those words into Mary's heart.) "But now, if you like, I'll get a licence to-morrow morning — nay, to-night, and I'll marry you in defiance of all the world, rather than give you up. In a year or two my father will forgive me, and meanwhile you shall have every luxury money can purchase, and every charm that love can devise to make your life happy. After all, my mother was but a factory girl." (This was said to himself, as if to reconcile himself to this bold step.) "Now, Mary, you see how willing I am to — to sacrifice a good deal for you; I even offer you marriage, to satisfy your little ambitious heart; so, now, won't you say, you can love me a little, little bit?"

He pulled her towards him. To his surprise, she still resisted. Yes! though all she had pictured to herself for so many months in being the wife of Mr. Carsons, was now within her grasp, she resisted. His speech had given her but one feeling, that of exceeding great relief. For she had dreaded, now she knew what true love was, to think of the attachment she might have created; the deep feeling her flirting conduct might have called out. She had loaded herself with reproaches for the misery she might have caused. It was a relief, to gather that the attachment was of that low, despicable kind, which can plan to seduce the object of its affection; that the feeling she had caused was shallow enough, for it only pretended to embrace self, at the expense of the misery, the ruin, of one falsely termed beloved. She need not be penitent to such a plotter! That was the relief.

"I am obliged to you, Sir, for telling me what you have. You may think I am a fool; but I did think you meant to marry me all along; and yet thinking so, I felt I could not love you. Still I felt sorry I had gone so far in keeping company with you. Now, Sir, I tell you, if I had loved you before, I don't think I should have loved you now you have told me you meant to ruin me; for that 's the plain English of not meaning to marry me till just this minute. I said I was sorry, and humbly begged your pardon; that was before I knew what you were. Now I scorn you, Sir, for plotting to ruin a poor girl. Good night."

And with a wrench for which she had reserved all her strength, she flew off like a bolt. They heard her flying footsteps echo down the quiet street. The next sound was Sally's laugh, which grated on Mr. Carsons' ears, and keenly irritated him.

"And what do you find so amusing, Sally?" asked he.

"Oh, Sir, I beg your pardon. I humbly beg your pardon, as Mary says, but I can't help laughing, to think how she 's outwitted us." (She was going to have said, "outwitted you," but changed the pronoun.)

"Why, Sally, had you any idea she was going to fly out in this style?"

"No, I hadn't to be sure. But if you did think of marrying her, why (if I may be so bold as to ask) did you go and tell her you had no thought of doing otherwise by her? That was what put her up at last!"

"Why I had repeatedly before led her to infer that marriage was not my object. I never dreamed she could have been so foolish as to have mistaken me, little provoking romancer though she be! So I naturally wished her to know what a sacrifice of prejudice, of — of myself, in short, I was willing to make for her sake; yet I don't think she was aware of it after all. I believe I might have any lady in Manchester if I liked, and yet I was willing and ready to marry a poor dress-maker. Don't you understand me now? and don't you see what a sacrifice I was making to humour her? and all to no avail."

Sally was silent, so he went on:

"My father would have forgiven any temporary connexion, far sooner than my marrying one so far beneath me in rank."

"I thought you said, Sir, your mother was a factory girl," reminded Sally, rather maliciously.

"Yes, yes! — but then my father was in much such a station; at any rate, there was not the disparity there is between Mary and me."

Another pause.

"Then you mean to give her up, Sir. She made no bones of saying she gave you up."

"No, I do not mean to give her up, whatever you and she may please to think. I am more in love with her than ever; even for this charming capricious ebullition of hers. She'll come round, you may depend upon it. Women always do. They always have second thoughts, and find out that they are best in casting off a lover. Mind I don't say I shall offer her the same terms again."

With a few more words of no importance, the allies parted.

CHAPTER XII.

"I lov'd him not; and yet, now he is gone,
I feel I am alone.
I check'd him while he spoke; yet could he speak,
Alas! I would not check.
For reasons not to love him once I sought,
And wearied all my thought." W. S. LANDOR.

AND now Mary had, as she thought, dismissed both her lovers. But they looked on their dismissals with very different eyes. He who loved her with all his heart and with all his soul, considered his rejection final. He did not comfort himself with the idea, which would have proved so well founded in his case, that women have second thoughts about casting off their lovers. He had too much respect for his own heartiness of love to believe himself unworthy of Mary; that mock humble conceit did not enter his head. He thought he did "not hit Mary's fancy;" and though that may sound a trivial every-day expression, yet the reality of it cut him to the heart. Wild visions of enlistment, of drinking himself into forgetfulness, of becoming desperate in some way or another, entered his mind; but then the thought of his mother stood like an angel with a drawn sword in the way to sin. For, you know, "he was the only son of his mother, and she was a widow;" dependent on him for daily bread. So he could not squander away health and time, which were to him money wherewith to support her failing years. He went to his work, accordingly, to all outward semblance just as usual; but with a heavy, heavy heart within.

Mr. Carsons, as we have seen, persevered in considering Mary's rejection of him as merely a "charming caprice." If she were at work, Sally Leadbitter was sure to slip a passionately loving note into her hand, and then so skilfully move away from her side, that Mary could not all at once return it, without making some sensation among the work-women. She was even forced to take several home with her. But after reading one, she determined on her plan. She made no great resistance to receiving them from Sally, but kept them unopened, and occasionally returned them in a blank half-sheet of paper. But far worse than this, was the being so constantly way-laid as she went home by her persevering lover; who had been so long acquainted with all her habits, that she found it difficult to evade him. Late or early, she was never certain of being free from him. Go this way or that, he might come up some cross street when she had just congratulated herself on evading him for that day. He could not have taken a surer mode of making himself odious to her.

And all this time Jem Wilson never came! Not to see her — that she did not expect — but to see her father; to — she did not know what, but she had hoped he would have come on some excuse, just to see if she hadn't changed her mind. He never came. Then she grew weary and impatient, and her spirits sank. The persecution of the one lover, and the neglect of the other, oppressed her sorely. She could not now sit quietly through the evening at her work; or, if she kept, by a strong effort, from pacing up and down the room, she felt as if she must sing to keep off thought while she sewed. And her songs were the maddest, merriest, she could think of. "Barbara Allen," and such sorrowful ditties, did well enough for happy times; but now she required all the aid that could be derived from external excitement to keep down the impulse of grief.

And her father, too — he was a great anxiety to her, he looked so changed and so ill. Yet he would not acknowledge to any ailment. She knew, that be it as late as it would, she never left off work until (if the poor servants paid her pretty regularly for the odd jobs of mending she did for them) she had earned a few pence, enough for one good meal for her father on the next day. But very frequently, all she could do in the morning, after her late sitting up at night, was to run with the work home, and receive the money from the person for whom it was done. She could not stay often to make purchases of food, but gave up the money at once to her father's eager clutch; sometimes prompted by a savage hunger it is true, but more frequently by a craving for opium.

On the whole he was not so hungry as his daughter. For it was a long fast from the one o'clock dinner-hour at Miss Simmonds' to the close of Mary's vigil, which was often extended to midnight. She was young, and had not yet learned to bear "clemming."

One evening, as she sang a merry song over her work, stopping occasionally to sigh, the blind Margaret came groping in. It had been one of Mary's additional sorrows that her friend had been absent from home, accompanying the lecturer on music in his round among the manufacturing towns of Yorkshire and Lancashire. Her grandfather, too, had seen this a good time for going his expeditions in search of specimens; so that the house had been shut up for several weeks.

"Oh! Margaret, Margaret! how glad I am to see you. Take care. There, now you 're all right, that 's father's chair. Sit down." — She kissed her over and over again.

"It seems like the beginning o' brighter times, to see you again, Margaret. Bless you! And how well you look!"

"Doctors always send ailing folk for change of air: and you know I 've had plenty o' that same lately."

"You 've been quite a traveller for sure! Tell us all about it, do, Margaret. Where have you been to, first place?"

"Eh, lass, that would take a long time to tell. Half o'er the world I sometimes think. Bolton, and Bury, and Owdham, and Halifax, and — but Mary, guess who I saw there? May be you know though, so it 's not fair guessing."

"No, I donnot. Tell me, Margaret, for I cannot abide waiting, and guessing."

"Well, one night as I were going fra' my lodgings wi' the help on a lad as belonged to th' landlady, to find the room where I were to sing, I heard a cough before me, walking along. Think's I, that 's Jem Wilson's cough, or I 'm much mistaken. Next time came a sneeze and cough, and then I were certain. First I hesitated whether I should speak, thinking if it were a stranger he 'd may be think me forrard.* But I knew blind folks must not be nesh about using their tongues, so says I, 'Jem Wilson, is that you?' And sure enough it was and nobody else. Did you know he were in Halifax, Mary?"

"No;" she answered, faintly and sadly; for Halifax was all the same to her heart as the Antipodes; equally inaccessible by humble penitent looks and maidenly tokens of love.

"Well, he 's there, however; he 's putting up an engine for some folks there, for his master. He 's doing well, for he 's getten four or five men under him; we 'd two or three

* "Forrard," forward.

meetings, and he telled me all about his invention for doing away wi' the crank, or somewhat. His master bought it from him, and ta 'en out a patent, and Jem 's a gentleman for life wi' the money his master gied him. But you 'll ha' heard all this, Mary."

No! she had not.

"Well, I thought it all happened afore he left Manchester, and then in course you 'd ha' known. But may be it were all settled after he got to Halifax; however, he 's gotten two or three hunder pounds for his invention. But what 's up with you Mary? you 're sadly out o' sorts You 've never been quarrelling wi' Jem, surely."

Now Mary cried outright; she was weak in body, and unhappy in mind, and the time was come when she might have the relief of telling her grief. She could not bring herself to confess how much of her sorrow was caused by her having been vain and foolish; she hoped that need never be known, and she could not bear to think of it.

"Oh, Margaret; do you know Jem came here one night when I were put out, and cross. Oh, dear! dear! I could bite my tongue out when I think on it. And he told me how he loved me, and I thought I did not love him, and I told him I didn't; and, Margaret, — he believed me, and went away so sad, and so angry; and now I 'd do any thing, — I would indeed," her sobs choked the end of her sentence. Margaret looked at her with sorrow, but with hope; for she had no doubt in her own mind, that it was only a temporary estrangement.

"Tell me, Margaret," said Mary, taking her apron down from her eyes, and looking at Margaret with eager anxiety, "What can I do to bring him back to me? Should I write to him?"

"No," replied her friend, "that would not do. Men are so queer, they like to have a' the courting to themselves."

"But I did not mean to write him a courting letter," said Mary, somewhat indignantly.

"If you wrote at all, it would be to give him a hint you 'd taken the rue, and would be very glad to have him now. I believe now he 'd rather find that out himself."

"But he won't try," said Mary, sighing. "How can he find it out when he 's at Halifax?"

"If he 's a will he 's a way, depend upon it. And you would not have him if he 's not a will to you, Mary! No, dear!" changing her tone from the somewhat hard way in which sensible people too often speak, to the soft accents of tenderness which come with such peculiar grace from them; "you must just wait and be patient. You may depend upon it, all will end well, and better than if you meddled in it now."

"But it 's so hard to be patient," pleaded Mary.

"Ay, dear; being patient is the hardest work we, any on us, have to do through life, I take it. Waiting is far more difficult than doing. I 've known that about my sight, and many a one has known it in watching the sick; but it 's one of God's lessons we all must learn, one way or another." After a pause. "Have ye been to see his mother of late?"

"No; not for some weeks. When last I went she was so frabbit* with me, that I really thought she wish'd I'd keep away."

"Well! if I were you I 'd go. Jem will hear on 't, and it will do you far more good in his mind than writing a letter, which, after all, you would find a tough piece of work when you came to settle to it. 'T would be hard to say neither too much nor too little. But I must be going, grandfather is at home, and it 's our first night together, and he must not be sitting wanting me any longer."

She rose up from her seat, but still delayed going.

"Mary! I 've somewhat else I want to say to you, and I don't rightly know how to begin. You see, grandfather and I know what bad times is, and we know your father is out o'work, and I 'm getting more money than I can well manage; and dear, would you just take this bit o' gold, and pay me

* "Frabbit," ill-tempered.

back in good times." The tears stood in Margaret's eyes as she spoke.

"Dear Margaret, we're not so bad pressed as that." (The thought of her father, and his ill looks, and his one meal a day, rushed upon Mary.) "And yet, dear, if it would not put you out o' your way, — I would work hard to make it up to you; — but would not your grandfather be vexed?"

"Not he, wench! It were more his thought than mine, and we have gotten ever so many more at home, so don't hurry yourself about paying. It 's hard to be blind, to be sure, else money comes in so easily now to what it used to do; and it 's downright pleasure to earn it, for I do so like singing."

"I wish I could sing," said Mary, looking at the sovereign.

"Some has one kind of gifts, and some another. Many 's the time when I could see, that I longed for your beauty, Mary! We 're like childer, ever wanting what we han not got. But now I must say just one more word. Remember, if you 're sore pressed for money, we shall take it very unkind if you donnot let us know. Good bye to ye."

In spite of her blindness she hurried away, anxious to rejoin her grandfather, and desirous also to escape from Mary's expressions of gratitude.

Her visit had done Mary good in many ways. It had strengthened her patience and her hope. It had given her confidence in Margaret's sympathy; and last, and really least in comforting power (of so little value are silver and gold in comparison to love, that gift in every one's power to bestow), came the consciousness of the money-value of the sovereign she held in her hand. The many things it might purchase! First of all came the thought of a comfortable supper for her father that very night; and acting instantly upon the idea, she set off in hopes that all the provision-shops might not yet be closed, although it was so late.

That night the cottage shone with unusual light, and fire-gleam; and the father and daughter sat down to a meal they thought almost extravagant. It was so long since they had had enough to eat.

"Food gives heart," say the Lancashire people; and the next day Mary made time to go and call on Mrs. Wilson, according to Margaret's advice. She found her quite alone, and more gracious than she had been the last time Mary had visited her. Alice was gone out, she said.

"She would just step up to the post-office, all for no earthly use. For it were to ask if they hadn't a letter lying there for her from her foster-son Will Wilson, the sailor-lad."

"What made her think there were a letter?" asked Mary.

"Why yo see, a neighbour as has been in Liverpool, telled us Will's ship were come in. Now he said last time he were in Liverpool, he 'd ha' come to ha' seen Alice, but his ship had but a week holiday, and hard work for the men in that time, too. So Alice makes sure he 'll come this, and has had her hand behind her ear at every noise in th' street, thinking it were him. And to-day she were neither to have nor to hold, but off she would go to th' post, and see if he had na sent her a line to th' old house near yo. I tried to get her to give up going, for let alone her deafness she 's getten so dark, she cannot see five yards afore her; but no, she would go, poor old body."

"I did not know her sight failed her; she used to have good eyes enough when she lived near us."

"Ay, but it 's gone lately a good deal. But you never ask after Jem" — anxious to get in a word on the subject nearest her heart.

"No," replied Mary, blushing scarlet. "How is he?"

"I cannot justly say how he is, seeing he 's at Halifax; but he were very well when he wrote last Tuesday. Han ye heard o' his good luck?"

Rather to her disappointment, Mary owned she had heard of the sum his master had paid him for his invention.

"Well! and did not Margaret tell you what he 'd done wi' it? It 's just like him though, ne'er to say a word about it. Why, when he were paid what does he do, but get his master to help him to buy an income for me and Alice. He had her name put down for her life; but, poor thing, she 'll not be long to the fore, I 'm thinking. She 's sadly failed of late. And so, Mary, yo see, we 're two ladies o' property. It 's a matter o' twenty pound a year, they tell me. I wish the twins had lived, bless 'em," said she, dropping a few tears. "They should ha' had the best o' schooling, and their belly-fulls o' food. I suppose they 're better off in heaven, only I should so like to see 'em."

Mary's heart filled with love at this new proof of Jem's goodness; but she could not talk about it. She took Jane Wilson's hand and pressed it with affection; and then turned the subject to Will, her sailor nephew. Jane was a little bit sorry, but her prosperity had made her gentler, and she did not resent what she felt as Mary's indifference to Jem, and his merits.

"He 's been in Africa, and that neighbourhood, I believe. He 's a fine chap, but he 's not gotten Jem's hair. His has too much o' the red in it. He sent Alice (but, maybe, she telled you) a matter o' five pound when he were over before; but that were nought to an income, yo know."

"It 's not every one that can get a hundred or two at a time," said Mary.

"No! no! that 's true enough. There 's not many a one like Jem. That 's Alice's step," said she, hastening to open the door to her sister-in-law. Alice looked weary, and sad, and dusty. The weariness and the dust would not have been noticed either by her, or the others, if it had not been for the sadness.

"No letters?" said Mrs. Wilson.

"No, none! I must just wait another day to hear fra' my lad. It 's very dree work, waiting," said Alice.

Margaret's words came into Mary's mind. Every one has their time and kind of waiting.

"If I but knew he were safe, and not drowned!" spoke Alice. "If I but knew he *were* drowned, I would ask grace to say, Thy will be done. It 's the waiting."

"It 's hard work to be patient to all of us," said Mary; "I know I find it so, but I did not know one so good as you did, Alice; I shall not think so badly of myself for being a bit impatient, now I 've heard you say you find it difficult."

The idea of reproach to Alice was the last in Mary's mind; and Alice knew it was. Nevertheless, she said,

"Then, my dear, I beg your pardon, and God's pardon, too, if I 've weakened your faith, by showing you how feeble mine was. Half our life 's spent in waiting, and it ill becomes one like me, wi' so many mercies, to grumble. I'll try and put a bridle o'er my tongue, and my thoughts too." She spoke in a humble and gentle voice, like one asking forgiveness.

"Come, Alice," interposed Mrs. Wilson, "don't fret yoursel for e'er a trifle wrong said here or there. See! I 've put th' kettle on, and you and Mary shall ha' a dish o' tea in no time."

So she bustled about, and brought out a comfortable-looking substantial loaf, and set Mary to cut bread and butter, while she rattled out the tea-cups — always a cheerful sound.

Just as they were sitting down, there was a knock heard at the door, and without waiting for it to be opened from the inside, some one lifted the latch, and in a man's voice asked, if one George Wilson lived there?

Mrs. Wilson was entering on a long and sorrowful explanation of his having once lived there, but of his having dropped down dead; when Alice, with the instinct of love (for in all usual and common instances sight and hearing failed to convey impressions to her until long after other people had received them), arose, and tottered to the door.

"My bairn! — my own dear bairn!" she exclaimed, falling on Will Wilson's neck.

You may fancy the hospitable, and welcoming commotion that issued; how Mrs. Wilson laughed, and talked, and cried, altogether, if such a thing can be done; and how Mary gazed with wondering pleasure at her old playmate; now, a dashing, bronzed-looking, ringletted sailor, frank, and hearty, and affectionate.

But it was something different from common to see Alice's joy at once more having her foster-child with her. She did not speak, for she really could not; but the tears came coursing down her old withered cheeks, and dimmed the horn spectacles she had put on, in order to pry lovingly into his face. So what with her failing sight, and her tear-blinded eyes, she gave up the attempt of learning his face by heart through the medium of that sense, and tried another. She passed her sodden, shrivelled hands, all trembling with eagerness, over his manly face, bent meekly down in order that she might more easily make her strange inspection. At last, her soul was satisfied.

After tea, Mary, feeling sure there was much to be said on both sides, at which it would be better none should be present, not even an intimate friend like herself, got up to go away. This seemed to arouse Alice from her dreamy consciousness of exceeding happiness, and she hastily followed Mary to the door. There, standing outside, with the latch in her hand, she took hold of Mary's arm, and spoke nearly the first words she had uttered since her nephew's return.

"My dear! I shall never forgive mysel, if my wicked words to-night are any stumbling-block in your path. See how the Lord has put coals of fire on my head! Oh! Mary, don't let my being an unbelieving Thomas weaken your faith. Wait patiently on the Lord, whatever your trouble may be."

CHAPTER XIII.

"The mermaid sat upon the rocks
All day long,
Admiring her beauty and combing her locks
And singing a mermaid song.

And hear the mermaid's song you may,
As sure as sure can be,
If you will but follow the sun all day,
And souse with him into the sea."

W. S. Landor.

It was perhaps four or five days after the events mentioned in the last chapter, that one evening, as Mary stood lost in reverie at the window, she saw Will Wilson enter the court, and come quickly up to her door. She was glad to see him, for he had always been a friend of hers, perhaps too much like her in character ever to become any thing nearer or dearer. She opened the door in readiness to receive his frank greeting, which she as frankly returned.

"Come Mary! on with bonnet and shawl, or whatever rigging you women require before leaving the house. I'm sent to fetch you, and I can't lose time when I'm under orders."

"Where am I to go to?" asked Mary, as her heart leaped up at the thought of who might be waiting for her.

"Not very far," replied he. "Only to old Job Legh's round the corner there. Aunt would have me come and see these new friends of hers, and then we meant to ha' come on here to see you and your father, but the old gentleman seems inclined to make a night of it, and have you al there. Where is your father? I want to see him. He must come too."

"He 's out, but I 'll leave word next door for him to follow me; that 's to say, if he comes home afore long." She added, hesitatingly, "Is any one else at Job's?

"No! My aunt Jane would not come for some maggot or other; and as for Jem! I don't know what you 've all been doing to him, but he 's as down-hearted a chap as I 'd wish to see. He 's had his sorrows sure enough, poor lad! But it 's time for him to be shaking off his dull looks, and not go moping like a girl."

"Then he 's come fra' Halifax, is he?" asked Mary.

"Yes! his body 's come, but I think he 's left his heart behind him. His tongue I'm sure he has, as we used to say to childer, when they would not speak. I try to rouse him up a bit, and I think he likes having me with him, but still he 's as gloomy and as dull as can be. 'T was only yesterday he took me to the works, and you 'd ha' thought us two Quakers as the spirit hadn't moved, all the way down we were so mum. It 's a place to craze a man certainly; such a noisy black hole!

There were one or two things worth looking at, the bellows for instance, or the gale they called a bellows. I could ha' stood near it a whole day; and if I 'd a berth in that place, I should like to be bellows-man, if there is such a one. But Jem weren't diverted even with that; he stood as grave as a judge while it blew my hat out o' my hand. He 's lost all relish for his food, too, which frets my aunt sadly. Come! Mary, ar'n't you ready?"

She had not been able to gather if she were to see Jem at Job Legh's; but when the door was opened, she at once saw and felt he was not there. The evining then would be a blank; at least so she thought for the first five minutes; but she soon forgot ber disappointment in the cheerful meeting of old friends, all, except herself, with some cause for rejoicing at that very time. Margaret, who could not be idle, was knitting away, with her face looking full into the room, away from her work. Alice sat meek and patient with her dimmed eyes and gentle look, trying to see and to hear, but never complaining; indeed, in her inner self she was blessing God for her happiness; for the joy of having her nephew, her child, near her, was far more present to her mind, than her deprivations of sight and hearing.

Job was in the full glory of host and hostess too, for by a tacit agreement he had roused himself from his habitual abstraction, and had assumed many of Margaret's little household duties. While he moved about he was deep in conversation with the young sailor, trying to extract from him any circumstances connected with the natural history of the different countries he had visited.

"Oh! if you are fond of grubs, and flies, and beetles, there 's no place for 'em like Sierra Leone. I wish you 'd had some of ours; we had rather too much of a good thing; we drank them with our drink, and could scarcely keep from eating them with our food. I never thought any folk could care for such fat green beasts as those, or I would ha' brought you them by the thousand. A plate full o' peas soup would ha' been full enough for you, I dare say; it were often too full for us."

"I would ha' given a good deal for some on 'em," said Job.

"Well, I knew folk at home liked some o' the queer things one meets with abroad; but I never thought they 'd care for them nasty slimy things. I were always on the look out for a mermaid, for that, I knew, were a curiosity."

"You might ha' looked long enough," said Job, in an under-tone of contempt, which, however, the quick ears of the sailor caught.

"Not so long, master, in some latitudes, as you think. It stands to reason th' sea hereabouts is too cold for mermaids; for women here don't go half-naked on account o' climate. But I 've been in lands where muslin were too hot to wear on land, and where the sea were more than milk-warm; and though I'd never the good luck to see a mermaid in that latitude, I know them that has."

"Do tell us about it," cried Mary.

"Pooh, pooh!" said Job, the naturalist.

Both speeches determined Will to go on with his story. What could a fellow who had never been many miles from home know about the wonders of the deep, that he should put him down in that way?

"Well, it were Jack Harris, our third mate, last voyage, has many and many a time telled us all about it. You see he were becalmed of Chatham Island (that 's in the Great Pacific, and a warm enough latitude for mermaids, and sharks, and such like perils). So some of the men took the long boat, and pulled for the island to see what it were like; and when they got near, they heard a puffing, like a creature come up to take breath; you 've never heard a diver? No! Well! you 've heard folks in th' asthma, and it were for all the world like that. So they looked around, and what should they see but a mermaid, sitting on a rock, and sunning herself. The water is always warmer when it 's rough, you know, so I suppose in the calm she felt it rather chilly, and had come up to warm herself."

"What was she like? asked Mary, breathlessly.

Job took his pipe off the chimney-piece and began to smoke with very audible puffs, as if the story were not worth listening to.

"Oh! Jack used to say she was for all the world as beautiful as any of the wax ladies in the barbers' shops; only, Mary, there were one little difference: her hair was bright grass green."

"I should not think that was pretty," said Mary, hesitatingly; as if not liking to doubt the perfection of any thing belonging to such an acknowledged beauty.

"Oh! but it is when you 're used to it. I always think when first we get sight of land, there 's no colour so lovely as grass green. However, she had green hair sure enough; and were proud enough of it, too; for she were combing it out full-length when first they saw her. They all thought she were a fair prize, and may be as good as a whale in ready money (they were whale-fishers you know). For some folk think a deal of mermaids, whatever other folk do." This was a hit at Job, who retaliated in a series of sonorous spittings and puffs.

"So, as I were saying, they pulled towards her, thinking to catch her. She were all the while combing her beautiful hair, and beckoning to them, while with the other hand she held a looking-glass."

"How many hands had she?" asked Job.

"Two, to be sure, just like any other woman," answered Will, indignantly.

"Oh! I thought you said she beckoned with one hand, and combed her hair with another, and held a looking-glass with a third," said Job, with provoking quietness.

"No! I didn't! at least if I did, I meant she did one thing after another, as any one but" (here he mumbled a word or two) "could understand. Well, Mary," turning very decidedly towards her; "when she saw them coming near, whether it were she grew frightened at their fowling-pieces, as they had on board for a bit o' shooting on the island, or whether it were she were just a fickle jade as did not rightly know her own mind (which seeing one half of her was woman, I think myself was most probable), but when they were only about two oars' length from the rock where she sat, down she plopped into the water, leaving nothing but her hinder end of a fish-tail sticking up for a minute, and then that disappeared too.

"And did they never see her again?" asked Mary.

"Never so plain; the man who had the second watch one night declared he saw her swimming round the ship, and holding up her glass for him to look in; and then he saw the little cottage near Aber in Wales (where his wife lived) as plain as ever he saw it in life, and his wife standing outside, shading her eyes as if she were looking for him. But Jack Harris gave him no credit, for he said he were always a bit of romancer and beside that, were a home-sick, down-hearted chap."

"I wish they had caught her," said Mary, musing.

"They got one thing as belonged to her," replied Will, "and that I 've often seen with my own eyes, and I reckon it 's a sure proof of the truth of their story; for them that wants proof."

"What was it?" asked Margaret, almost anxious her grandfather should be convinced.

"Why, in her hurry she left her comb on the rock, and one o' the men spied it; so they thought that were better than nothing, and they rowed there and took it, and Jack Harris had it on board the *John Cropper*, and I saw him comb his hair with it every Sunday morning."

"What was it like?" asked Mary, eagerly; her imagination running on coral combs, studded with pearls.

"Why, if it had not had such a strange yarn, belonging to it, you 'd never ha' noticed it from any other small-tooth comb."

"I should rather think not," sneered Job Legh.

The sailor bit his lips to keep down his anger against an old man. Margaret felt very uneasy, knowing her grandfather so well, and not daring to guess what caustic remark might come next to irritate the young sailor guest.

"Mary, however, was too much interested by the wonders of the deep to perceive the incredulity with which Job Legh received Wilson's account of the mermaid, and when he left off, half offended, and very much inclined not to open his lips again through the evening, she eagerly said,

"Oh, do tell us something more of what you hear and see on board ship. Do, Will!"

"What 's the use, Mary, if folk won't believe one. There are things I saw with my own eyes, that some people would pish and pshaw at, as if I were a baby to be put down by cross noises. But I 'll tell you, Mary," with an emphasis on *you*, "some more of the wonders of the sea, sin' you 're not too wise to believe me. I have seen a fish fly."

This did stagger Mary. She had heard of mermaids as signs of inns and as sea-wonders, but never of flying fish. Not so Job. He put down his pipe, and nodding his head as a token of approbation, he said,

"Ay, ay! young man. Now you 're speaking truth."

"Well now! you 'll swallow that, old gentleman. You 'll credit me when I say I 've seen a critter half fish, half bird, and you won't credit me when I say there be such beasts as mermaids, half fish, half woman. To me, one 's just as strange as t'other."

"You never saw the mermaid yoursel," interposed Margaret, gently. But "love me, love my dog," was Will Wilson's motto, only his version was "believe me, believe Jack Harris;" and the remark was not so soothing to him, as it was intended to have been.

"It 's the Exocetus; one of the Malacopterygii Abdominales," said Job, much interested.

"Ay, there you go! You're one o' them folks as never knews beasts unless they 're called out o' their names. Put 'em in Sunday clothes and you know 'em, but in their work-a-day English you never know nought about 'em. I 've met wi' many o' your kidney; and if I 'd ha known it, I 'd ha christened poor Jack's mermaid wi' some grand gibberish of a name. Mermaidicus Jack Harrisensis; that 's just like their new-fangled words. D'ye believe there 's such a thing as the Mermaidicus, master?" asked Will, enjoying his own joke uncommonly, as most people do.

"Not I! tell me about the —"

"Well!" said Will, pleased at having excited the old gentleman's faith and credit at last. "It were on this last voyage, about a day's sail from Madeira, that one of our men —"

"Not Jack Harris, I hope," murmured Job.

"Called me," continued Will, not noticing the interruption, "to see the what d'ye call it — flying fish I say it is. It were twenty feet out o' water, and it flew near on to a hundred yards. But I say, old gentleman, I ha' gotten one dried, and if you 'll take it, why I 'll give it you; only," he added, in a lower tone, "I 'd wish you'd just gie me credit for the Mermaidicus."

I really believe if the assuming faith in the story of the mermaid had been made the condition of receiving the flying fish, Job Legh, sincere man as he was, would have pretended belief; he was so much delighted at the idea of possessing this specimen. He won the sailor's heart by getting up to shake both his hands in his vehement gratitude, puzzling poor old Alice, who yet smiled through her wonder; for she understood the action to indicate some kindly feeling towards her nephew.

Job wanted to prove his gratitude, and was puzzled how to do it. He feared the young man would not appreciate any of his duplicate Araneides; not even the great American Mygale, one of his most precious treasures; or else he would gladly have bestowed any duplicate on the donor of a real dried Exocetus. What could he do for him? He could ask Margaret to sing. Other folks beside her old doating grandfather thought a deal of her songs. So Margaret began some of her noble old-fashioned songs. She knew no modern music (for which her auditors might have been thankful), but she poured her rich voice out in some of the old canzonets she had lately learnt while accompanying the musical lecturer on his tour.

Mary was amused to see how the young sailor sat entranced; mouth, eyes, all open, in order to catch every breath of sound. His very lids refused to wink, as if afraid in that brief proverbial interval to lose a particle of the rich music that floated through the room. For the first time the idea crossed Mary's mind that it was possible the plain little sensible Margaret, so prim and demure, might have power over the heart of the handsome, dashing, spirited Will Wilson.

Job, too, was rapidly changing his opinion of his new guest. The flying fish went a great way, and his undisguised admiration for Margaret's singing carried him still further.

It was amusing enough to see these two, within the hour so barely civil to each other, endeavouring now to be ultra-agreeable. Will, as soon as he had taken breath (a long, deep gasp of admiration) after Margaret's song, sidled up to Job, and asked him in a sort of doubting tone,

"You wouldn't like a live Manx cat, would ye, master?"

"A what?" exclaimed Job.

"I don't know its best name," said Will, humbly. "But we call 'em just Manx cats. They 're cats without tails."

Now Job, in all his natural history, had never heard of such animals; so Will continued,

"Because I 'm going afore joining my ship, to see mother's friends in the island, and would gladly bring you one, if so be you 'd like to have it. They look as queer, and out o' nature as flying fish, or" — he gulped the words down that should have followed. "Especially when you see 'em walking a roof-top, right again the sky, when a cat, as is a proper cat, is sure to stick her tail stiff out behind, like a slack rope dancer a-balancing; but these cats having no tail, cannot stick it out, which captivates some people uncommonly. If yo 'll allow me, I 'll bring one for Miss there," jerking his head at Margaret. Job assented with grateful curiosity, wishing much to see the tail-less phenomenon.

"When are you going to sail?" asked Mary.

"I cannot justly say; our ship 's bound for America next voyage, they tell me. A mess-mate will let me know when her sailing-day is fixed; but I 've got to go to th' Isle o' Man first. I promised uncle last time I were in England to go this next time. I may have to hoist the blue Peter any day; so, make much of me while you have me, Mary."

Job asked him if he had been in America.

"Haven't I? North and South both! This time we 're bound to North. Yankee-Land, as we call it, where Uncle Sam lives."

"Uncle who?" said Mary.

"Oh, it 's a way sailors have of speaking. I only mean I 'm going to Boston, U. S., that 's Uncle Sam."

Mary did not understand, so she left him, and went to sit by Alice, who could not hear conversation unless expressly addressed to her. She had sat patiently silent the greater part of the night, and now greeted Mary with a quiet smile.

"Where 's yo'r father?" asked she.

"I guess he 's at his Union; he 's there most evenings."

Alice shook her head; but whether it were that she did not hear, or that she did not quite approve of what she heard, Mary could not make out. She sat silently watching Alice, and regretting over her dimmed and veiled eyes, formerly so bright and speaking. As if Alice understood by some other sense what was passing in Marry's mind, she turned suddenly round, and answered Mary's thought.

"Yo 're mourning for me, my dear; and there 's no need, Mary. I 'm as happy as a child. I sometimes think I am a child, whom the Lord is hushabying to my long sleep. For when I were a nurse-girl, my missis alway telled me to speak very soft and low, and to darken the room that her little one might go to sleep; and now all noises are hushed and still to me, and the bonny earth seems dim and dark, and I know it 's my Father lulling me away to my long sleep. I 'm very well content, and yo mustn't fret for me. I 've had well nigh every blessing in life I could desire."

Mary thought of Alice's long-cherished, fond wish to revisit the home of her childhood, so often and often deferred, and now probably never to take place. Or if it did, how changed from the fond anticipation of what it was to have been! It would be a mockery to the blind and deaf Alice.

The evening came quickly to an end. There was the humble cheerful meal, and then the bustling merry farewell, and Mary was once more in the quietness and solitude of her own dingy, dreary-looking home; her father still out, the fire extinguished, and her evening's task of work lying all undone upon the dresser. But it had been a pleasant little interlude to think upon. It had distracted her attention for a few hours from the pressure of many uneasy thoughts, of the dark, heavy, oppressive times, when sorrow and want seemed to surround her on every side; of her father, his changed and altered looks, telling so plainly of broken health, and an embittered heart; of the morrow, and the morrow beyond that, to be spent in that close monotonous work-room, with Sally Leadbitter's odious whispers hissing in her ear; and of the hunted look, so full of dread, from Miss Simmonds' door-step up and down the street, lest her persecuting lover should be near: for he lay in wait for her with wonderful perseverance, and of late had made himself almost hateful, by the unmanly force which he had used to detain her to listen to him, and the indifference with which he exposed her to the remarks of the passers-by, any one of whom might circulate reports which it would be terrible for her father to hear — and worse than death should they reach Jem Wilson. And all this she had drawn upon herself by her giddy flirting. Oh! how she loathed the recollection of the hot summer evening, when, worn out by stitching, and sewing, she had loitered homewards with weary languor, and first listened to the voice of the tempter.

And Jem Wilson! Oh, Jem, Jem, why did you not come to receive some of the modest looks and words of love which Mary longed to give you, to try and make up for the hasty rejection which you as hastily took to be final, though both mourned over it with many tears. But day after day passed away, and patience seemed of no avail; and Mary's cry was ever the old moan of the Moated Grange.

> "Why comes he not," she said,
> "I am aweary, aweary.
> I would that I were dead."

CHAPTER XIV.

"Know the temptation ere you judge the crime!
Look on this tree — 't was green, and fair and graceful;
Yet now, save these few shoots, how dry and rotten!
Thou canst not tell the cause. Not long ago,
A neighbour oak, with which its roots were twined,
In falling wrenched them with such cruel force,
That though we covered them again with care,
Its beauty withered, and it pined away.
So, could we look into the human breast,
How oft the fatal blight that meets our view,
Should we trace down to the torn, bleeding fibres
Of a too trusting heart — where it were shame,
For pitying tears, to give contempt or blame."

'Street Walks.'

The month was over; — the honeymoon to the newly-married; the exquisite convalescence to the "living mother of a living child;" the "first dark days of nothingness" to the widow and the child-bereaved; the term of penance, of hard labour, and solitary confinement, to the shrinking, shivering, hopeless prisoner.

"Sick, and in prison, and ye visited me." Shall you, or I, receive such blessing? I know one who will. An overseer of a foundry, an aged man, with hoary hair, has spent his Sabbaths, for many years, in visiting the prisoners and the afflicted, in Manchester New Bailey; not merely advising, and comforting, but putting means into their power of regaining the virtue and the peace they had lost; becoming himself their guarantee in obtaining employment, and never deserting those who have once asked help from him.*

Esther's term of imprisonment was ended. She received a good character in the governor's books; she had picked her daily quantity of oakum, had never deserved the extra punishment of the tread-mill, and had been civil and decorous in her language. And once more she was out of prison. The door closed behind her with a ponderous clang, and in her desolation she felt as if shut out of home — from the only

* Vide *Manchester Guardian*, of Wednesday, March 18, 1846; and also the Reports of Captain Williams, prison inspector.

shelter she could meet with, houseless and pennyless as she was, on that dreary day.

But it was but for an instant that she stood there doubting. One thought had haunted her both by night and by day, with monomaniacal incessancy; and that thought was how to save Mary (her dead sister's only child, her own little pet in the days of her innocence) from following in the same downward path to vice. To whom could she speak and ask for aid? She shrank from the idea of addressing John Barton again; her heart sank within her, at the remembrance of his fierce repulsing action, and far fiercer words. It seemed worse than death to reveal her condition to Mary, else she sometimes thought that this course would be the most terrible, the most efficient warning. She must speak; to that she was soul-compelled; but to whom? She dreaded addressing any of her former female acquaintance, even supposing they had sense, or spirit, or interest enough to undertake her mission.

To whom shall the outcast prostitute tell her tale! Who will give her help in the day of need? Here is the leper-sin, and all stand aloof dreading to be counted unclean.

In her wild night wanderings, she had noted the haunts and habits of many a one who little thought of a watcher in the poor forsaken woman. You may easily imagine that a double interest was attached by her, to the ways and companionships of those with whom she had been acquainted in the days which, when present, she had considered hardly-worked and monotonous, but which now in retrospection seemed so happy and unclouded. Accordingly, she had, as we have seen, known where to meet with John Barton on that unfortunate night, which had only produced irritation in him, and a month's imprisonment to her. She had also observed that he was still intimate with the Wilsons. She had seen him walking and talking with both father and son; her old friends too; and she had shed unregarded, unvalued tears, when some one had casually told her of George Wilson's sudden death. It now flashed across her mind that to the son, to Mary's playfellow, her elder brother in the days of childhood, her tale might be told, and listened to with interest, and some mode of action suggested by him by which Mary might be guarded and saved.

All these thoughts had passed through her mind while yet she was in prison; so when she was turned out, her purpose was clear, and she did not feel her desolation of freedom as she would otherwise have done.

That night she stationed herself early near the foundry where she knew Jem worked; he stayed later than usual, being detained by some arrangements for the morrow. She grew tired and impatient; many workmen had come out of the door in the long, dead, brick wall, and eagerly had she peered into their faces, deaf to all insult or curse. He must have gone home early; one more turn in street, and she would go.

During that turn he came out, and in the quiet of that street of workshops and warehouses, she directly heard his steps. How her heart failed her for an instant; but still she was not daunted from her purpose, painful as its fulfilment was sure to be. She laid her hand on his arm. As she expected, after a momentary glance at the person who thus endeavoured to detain him, he made an effort to shake it off, and pass on. But trembling as she was, she had provided against this by a firm and unusual grasp.

"You must listen to me, Jem Wilson," she said, with almost an accent of command.

"Go away, missis; I 've nought to do with you, either in hearkening or talking."

He made another struggle.

"You must listen," she said again, authoritatively, "for Mary Barton's sake."

The spell of her name was as potent as that of the mariner's glittering eye. "He listened like a three-year child."

"I know you care enough for her to wish to save her from harm."

He interrupted his earnest gaze into her face, with the exclamation —

"And who can yo be to know Mary Barton, or to know that she 's ought to me?"

There was a strife in Esther's mind for an instant, between the shame of acknowledging herself, and the additional weight to her revelation which such acknowledgment would give. Then she spoke.

"Do you remember Esther, the sister of John Barton's wife? the aunt to Mary? And the Valentine I sent you last February ten years?"

"Yes, I mind her well! But yo are not Esther, are you?" He looked again into her face, and seeing that indeed it was his boyhood's friend, he took her hand, and shook it with a cordiality that forgot the present in the past.

"Why, Esther! Where han ye been this many a year? Where han ye been wandering that we none of us could find you out?"

The question was asked thoughtlessly, but answered with fierce earnestness.

"Where have I been? What have I been doing? Why do you torment me with questions like these? Can you not guess? But the story of my life is wanted to give force to my speech, afterwards I will tell it you. Nay! don't change your fickle mind now, and say you don't want to hear it. You must hear it, and I must tell it; and then see after Mary, and take care she does not become like me. As she is loving now, so did I love once; one above me far." She remarked not, in her own absorption, the change in Jem's breathing, the sudden clutch at the wall which told the fearfully vivid interest he took in what she said. "He was so handsome, so kind! Well, the regiment was ordered to Chester (did I tell you he was an officer?), and he could not bear to part from me, nor I from him, so he took me with him. I never thought poor Mary would have taken it so to heart! I always meant to send for her to pay me a visit when I was married; for, mark you! he promised me marriage. They all do. Then came three years of happiness. I suppose I ought not to have been happy, but I was. I had a little girl, too. Oh! the sweetest darling that ever was seen! But I must not think of her," putting her hand wildly up to her forehead, "or I shall go mad; I shall."

"Don't tell me any more about yoursel," said Jem, soothingly.

"What! you 're tired already, are you? but I will tell you; as you 've asked for it, you shall hear it. I won't recall the agony of the past for nothing. I will have the relief of telling it. Oh, how happy I was!"—sinking her voice into a plaintive child-like manner. "It went like a shot through me when one day he came to me and told me he was ordered to Ireland, and must leave me behind; at Bristol we then were."

Jem muttered some words; she caught their meaning, and in a pleading voice continued,

"Oh, don't abuse him; don't speak a word against him! You don't know how I love him yet; yet, when I am sunk so low. You don't guess how kind he was. He gave me fifty pounds before we parted, and I knew he could ill spare it. Don't Jem, please," as his muttered indignation rose again. For her sake he ceased. "I might have done better with the money; I see now. But I did not know the value of it then. Formerly I had earned it easily enough at the factory, and as I had no more sensible wants, I spent it on dress and on eating. While I lived with him, I had it for asking; and fifty pounds would, I thought go a long way. So I went back to Chester, where I 'd been so happy, and set up a small-ware shop, and hired a room near. We should have done well, but alas! alas! my little girl fell ill, and I could not mind my shop and her too; and things grew worse and worse. I sold my goods any how to get money to buy her food and medicine; I wrote over and over again to her father for help, but he must have changed his quarters, for I never got an answer. The landlord seized the few bobbins and tapes I had left, for shop-rent; and the person to whom the mean little room, to which we had been forced to remove, belonged, threatened to turn us out unless his rent was paid; it had run

12*

on many weeks, and it was winter, cold bleak winter; and my child was so ill, so ill, and I was starving. And I could not bear to see her suffer, and forgot how much better it would be for us to die together; — oh her moans, her moans, which money could give the means of relieving! So I went out into the street one January night — Do you think God wlll punish me for that?" she asked with wild vehemence, almost amounting to insanity, and shaking Jem's arm in order to force an answer from him.

But before he could shape his heart's sympathy into words, her voice had lost its wildness, and she spoke with the quiet of despair.

"But it's no matter! I've done that since, which separates us as far asunder as heaven and hell can be." Her voice rose again to the sharp pitch of agony. "My darling! my darling! even after death I may not see thee, my own sweet one! she was so good — like a little angel. What is that text, I don't remember, — the text mother used to teach me when I sat on her knee long ago; it begins 'Blessed are the pure'" —

"Blessed are the pure in heart, for they shall see God."

"Ay, that's it! It would break mother's heart if she knew what I am now — it did break Mary's heart, you see. And now I recollect it was about her child I wanted to see you, Jem. You know Mary Barton, don't you?" said she, trying to collect her thoughts.

Yes, Jem knew her. How well, his beating heart could testify!

"Well, there's something to do for her; I forget what; wait a minute! She is so like my little girl;" said she, raising her eyes, glistening with unshed tears, in search of the sympathy of Jem's countenance.

He deeply pitied her; but oh! how he longed to recall her mind to the subject of Mary, and the lover above her in rank, and the service to be done for her sake. But he controlled himself to silence. After awhile, she spoke again, and in a calmer voice.

"When I came to Manchester (for I could not stay in Chester after her death), I found you all out very soon. And yet I never thought my poor sister was dead. I suppose I would not think so. I used to watch about the court where John lived, for many and many a night, and gather all I could about them from the neighbours' talk; for I never asked a question, I put this and that together, and followed one, and listened to another; many 's the time I 've watched the policeman off his beat, and peeped through the chink of the window-shutter to see the old room, and sometimes Mary or her father sitting up late for some reason or another. I found out Mary went to learn dress-making, and I began to be frightened for her; for it 's a bad life for a girl to be out late at night in the streets, and after many an hour of weary work, they 're ready to follow after any novelty that makes a little change. But I made up my mind, that bad as I was, I could watch over Mary, and perhaps keep her from harm. So I used to wait for her at nights, and follow her home, often when she little knew any one was near her. There was one of her companions I never could abide, and I'm sure that girl is at the bottom of some mischief. By-and-bye, Mary's walks homewards were not alone. She was joined soon after she came out, by a man; a gentleman. I began to fear for her, for I saw she was light-hearted, and pleased with his attentions; and I thought worse of him for having such long talks with that bold girl I told you of. But I was laid up for a long time with spitting of blood; and could do nothing. I 'm sure it made me worse, thinking about what might be happening to Mary. And when I came out, all was going on as before, only she seemed fonder of him than ever; and oh Jem! her father won't listen to me, and it 's you must save Mary! You 're like a brother to her, and maybe could give her advice and watch over her, and at any rate John will hearken to you; only he 's so stern and so cruel." She began to cry a little at the remembrance of his harsh words; but Jem cut her short by his hoarse, stern inquiry,

"Who is this spark that Mary loves? Tell me his name!"

"It 's young Carsons, old Carsons' son, that your father worked for."

There was a pause. She broke the silence.

"Oh! Jem, I charge you with the care of her! I suppose it would be murder to kill her, but it would be better for her to die than to live to lead such a life as I do. Do you hear me, Jem?"

"Yes! I hear you. It would be better. Better we were all dead." This was said as if thinking aloud; but he immediately changed his tone, and continued,

"Esther, you may trust to my doing all I can for Mary. That I have determined on. And now listen to me! you loathe the life you lead, else you would not speak of it as you do. Come home with me. Come to my mother. She and my aunt Alice live together. I will see that they give you a welcome. And to-morrow I will see if some honest way of living cannot be found for you. Come home with me."

She was silent for a minute, and he hoped he had gained his point. Then she said,

"God bless you, Jem, for the words you have just spoken. Some years ago you might have saved me, as I hope and trust you will yet save Mary. But it is too late now; — too late," she added, with accents of deep despair.

Still he did not relax his hold. "Come home," he said.

"I tell you, I cannot. I could not lead a virtuous life if I would. I should only disgrace you. If you will know all," said she, as he still seemed inclined to urge her, "I must have drink. Such as live like me could not bear life if they did not drink. It 's the only thing to keep us from suicide. If we did not drink, we could not stand the memory of what we have been, and the thought of what we are for a day. If I go without food, and without shelter, I must have my dram. Oh! you don't know the awful nights I have had in prison for want of it;" said she, shuddering, and glaring round with terrified eyes, as if dreading to see some spiritual creature, with dim form, near her.

"It is so frightful to see them," whispering in tones of

wildness, although so low spoken. "There they go round and round my bed the whole night through. My mother, carrying little Annie (I wonder how they got together) and Mary — and all looking at me with their sad, stony eyes; oh Jem! it is so terrible! They don't turn back either, but pass behind the head of the bed, and I feel their eyes on me everywhere. If I creep under the clothes I still see them; and what is worse," hissing out her words with fright, "they see me. Don't speak to me of leading a better life — I must have drink. I cannot pass to-night without a dram; I dare not."

Jem was silent from deep sympathy. O! could he, then, do nothing for her! She spoke again, but in a less excited tone, although it was thrillingly earnest.

"You are grieved for me! I know it better than if you told me in words. But you can do nothing for me. I am past hope. You can yet save Mary. You must. She is innocent, except for the great error of loving one above her in station. Jem! you *will* save her?"

With heart and soul, though in few words, Jem promised that if aught earthly could keep her from falling, he would do it. Then she blessed him, and bade him good-night.

"Stay a minute," said he, as she was on the point of departure. "I may want to speak to you again. I mun know where to find you — where do you live?"

She laughed strangely. "And do you think one sunk so low as I am has a home? Decent, good people have homes. We have none. No, if you want me, come at night, and look at the corners of the streets about here. The colder, the bleaker, the more stormy the night, the more certain you will be to find me. For then," she added, with a plaintive fall in her voice, "it is so cold sleeping in entries, and on door-steps, and I want a dram more than ever."

Again she rapidly turned off, and Jem also went on his way. But before he reached the end of the street, even in the midst of the jealous anguish that filled his heart, his conscience smote him. He had not done enough to save her. One more effort, and she might have come. Nay, twenty efforts would have been well rewarded by her yielding. He turned back, but she was gone. In the tumult of his other feelings, his self-reproach was deadened for the time. But many and many a day afterwards he bitterly regretted his omission of duty; his weariness of well-doing.

Now, the great thing was to reach home, and solitude. Mary loved another! Oh! how should he bear it? He had thought her rejection of him a hard trial, but that was nothing now. He only remembered it, to be thankful that he had not yielded to the temptation of trying his fate again, not in actual words, but in a meeting, where her manner should tell far more than words, that her sweeter smiles, her dainty movements, her pretty household ways, were all to be reserved to gladden another's eyes and heart. And he must live on; that seemed the strangest. That a long life (and he knew men did live long, even with deep, biting sorrow corroding at their hearts) must be spent without Mary; nay, with the consciousness she was another's! That hell of thought he would reserve for the quiet of his own room, the dead stillness of night. He was on the threshold of home now.

He entered. There were the usual faces, the usual sights. He loathed them, and then he cursed himself because he loathed them. His mother's love had taken a cross turn, because he had kept the tempting supper she had prepared for him waiting until it was nearly spoilt. Alice, her dulled senses deadening day by day, sat mutely near the fire; her happiness bounded by the consciousness of the presence of her foster child, knowing that his voice repeated what was passing to her deafened ear, that his arm removed each little obstacle to her tottering steps. And Will, out of the very kindness of his heart, talked more and more merrily than ever. He saw Jem was downcast, and fancied his rattling might cheer him; at any rate, it drowned his aunt's muttered grumblings, and in some measure concealed the blank of the evening. At last, bed-time came; and Will withdrew to his neighbouring lodging; and Jane and Alice Wilson had raked the fire, and fastened doors and shutters, and pattered up stairs, with their tottering foot-steps and shrill voices. Jem, too, went to the closet termed his bed-room. There was no bolt to the door; but by one strong effort of his right arm, a heavy chest was moved against it, and he could sit down on the side of his bed, and think.

Mary loved another! That idea would rise uppermost in his mind, and had to be combated in all its forms of pain. It was, perhaps, no great wonder that she should prefer one, so much above Jem in the external things of life. But the gentleman; why did he, with his range of choice, among the ladies of the land, why did he stoop down to carry off the poor man's darling? With all the glories of the garden at his hand, why did he prefer to cull the wild-rose,—Jem's own fragrant wild-rose?

His *own!* Oh! never now his own! — Gone for evermore!

Then uprose the guilty longing for blood! — The frenzy of jealousy!—Some one should die. He would rather Mary were dead, cold in her grave, than that she were another's. A vision of her pale, sweet face, with her bright hair, all bedabbled with gore, seemed to float constantly before his aching eyes. But hers were ever open, and contained, in their soft, deathly look, such mute reproach! What had she done to deserve such cruel treatment from him? She had been wooed by one, whom Jem knew to be handsome, gay, and bright, and she had given him her love. That was all! It was the wooer who should die. Yes, die, knowing the cause of his death. Jem pictured him (and gloated on the picture), lying smitten, yet conscious; and listening to the upbraiding accusation of his murderer. How he had left his own rank, and dared to love a maiden of low degree; and—oh! stinging agony of all— how she, in return, had loved him! Then the other nature spoke up, and bade him remember the anguish he should so prepare for Mary! At first he refused to listen to that better voice; or listened only to pervert. He would glory in her wailing grief! he would take pleasure in her desolation of heart!

No! he could not, said the still small voice. It would be worse, far worse to have caused such woe, than it was now to bear his present heavy burden.

But it was too heavy, too grievous to be borne, and live.

He would slay himself and the lovers should love on, and the sun shine bright, and he with his burning, woeful heart would be at rest. "Rest that is reserved for the people of God."

Had he not promised with such earnest purpose of soul, as makes words more solemn than oaths, to save Mary from becoming such as Esther? Should he shrink from the duties of life, into the cowardliness of death? Who would then guard Mary, with her love, and her innocence? Would it not be a goodly thing to serve her, although she loved him not; to be her preserving angel, through the perils of life; and she, unconscious all the while?

He braced up his soul, and said to himself, that with God's help he would be that earthly keeper.

And now the mists and the storms seemed clearing away from his path, though it still was full of stinging thorns. Having done the duty nearest to him (of reducing the tumult of his own heart to something like order), the second became more plain before him.

Poor Esther's experience had led her, perhaps, too hastily to the conclusion, that Mr. Carsons' intentions were evil towards Mary; at least she had given no just ground for the fears she entertained that such was the case. It was possible, nay, to Jem's heart, very probable, that he might only be too happy to marry her. She was a lady by right of nature, Jem thought; in movement, grace, and spirit; what was birth to a Manchester manufacturer, many of whom glory, and justly too, in being the architects of their own fortunes? And, as far as wealth was concerned, judging another by himself, Jem could only imagine it a great privilege to lay it at the feet of the loved one. Harry Carsons' mother had been a factory girl; so, after all, what was the great reason for doubting his intentions towards Mary?

There might probably be some little awkwardness about the affair at first: Mary's father having such strong prejudices on the one hand; and something of the same kind being likely to exist on the part of Mr. Carsons' family. But Jem knew he had power over John Barton's mind; and it would be something to exert that power in promoting Mary's happiness, and to relinquish all thought of self in so doing.

Oh! why had Esther chosen him for this office? It was beyond his strength to act rightly! Why had she singled him out?

The answer came when he was calm enough to listen for it. Because Mary had no other friend capable of the duty required of him; the duty of a brother, as Esther imagined him to be in feeling, from his long friendship. He would be unto her as a brother.

As such, he ought to ascertain Harry Carsons' intentions towards her in winning her affections. He would ask him, straightforwardly, as became man speaking to man, not concealing, if need were, the interest he felt in Mary.

Then, with the resolve to do his duty to the best of his power, peace came into his soul; he had left the windy storm and tempest behind.

Two hours before day-dawn he fell asleep.

CHAPTER XV.

"What thoughtful heart can look into this gulf
That darkly yawns 'twixt rich and poor,
And not find food for saddest meditation!
Can see without a pang of keenest grief,
Them fiercely battling (like some natural foes)
Whom God had made, with help and sympathy,
To stand as brothers, side by side, united!
Where is the wisdom that shall bridge this gulf,
And bind them once again in trust and love?"

'LOVE-TRUTHS.'

WE must return to John Barton. Poor John! He never got over his disappointing journey to London. The deep mortification he then experienced (with, perhaps, as little selfishness for its cause as mortification ever had), was of no temporary nature; indeed few of his feelings were.

Then came a long period of bodily privation; of daily hunger after food; and though he tried to persuade himself he could bear want himself with stoical indifference, and did care about it as little as most men, yet the body took its revenge for its uneasy feelings. The mind became soured and morose, and lost much of its equipoise. It was no longer elastic, as in the days of youth, or in times of comparative happiness; it ceased to hope. And it is hard to live on when one can no longer hope.

The same state of feeling which John Barton entertained, if belonging to one who had had leisure to think of such things, and physicians to give names to them, would have been called monomania; so haunting, so incessant, were the thoughts that pressed upon him. I have somewhere read a forcibly described punishment among the Italians, worthy of a Borgia. The supposed or real criminal was shut up in a room, supplied with every convenience and luxury; and at first mourned little over his imprisonment. But day by day he became aware that the space between the walls of his apartment was narrowing, and then he understood the end. Those painted walls would come into hideous nearness, and at last crush the life out of him.

And so day by day, nearer and nearer, came the diseased thoughts of John Barton. They excluded the light of heaven, the cheering sounds of earth. They were preparing his death.

It is true, much of their morbid power might be ascribed to the use of opium. But before you blame too harshly this use, or rather abuse, try a hopeless life, with daily cravings of the body for food. Try, not alone being without hope yourself, but seeing all around you reduced to the same despair, arising from the same circumstances; all around you telling (though they use no words or language), by their looks and feeble actions, that they are suffering and sinking under the pressure of want. Would you not be glad to forget life, and its burdens? And opium gives forgetfulness for a time.

It is true they who thus purchase it pay dearly for their oblivion; but can you expect the uneducated to count the cost of their whistle? Poor wretches! They pay a heavy price. Days of oppressive weariness and languor, whose realities have the feeble sickliness of dreams; nights, whose dreams are fierce realities of agony; sinking health, tottering frames, incipient madness, and worse, the *consciousness* of incipient madness; this is the price of their whistle. But have you taught them the science of consequences?

John Barton's overpowering thought, which was to work out his fate on earth, was rich and poor; why are they so separate, so distinct, when God has made them all? It is not His will, that their interests are so far apart. Whose doing is it?

And so on into the problems and mysteries of life, until, bewildered and lost, unhappy and suffering, the only feeling that remained clear and undisturbed in the tumult of his heart, was hatred to the one class, and keen sympathy with the other.

But what availed his sympathy? No education had given him wisdom; and without wisdom, even love, with all its effects, too often works but harm. He acted to the best of his judgment, but it was a widely-erring judgment.

The actions of the uneducated seem to me typified in those of Frankenstein, that monster of many human qualities, ungifted with a soul, a knowledge of the difference between good and evil.

The people rise up to life; they irritate us, they terrify us, and we become their enemies. Then, in the sorrowful moment of our triumphant power, their eyes gaze on us with a mute reproach. Why have we made them what they are; a powerful monster, yet without the inner means for peace and happiness?

John Barton became a Chartist, a Communist, all that is commonly called wild and visionary. Ay! but being visionary is something. It shows a soul, a being not altogether sensual; a creature who looks forward for others, if not for himself.

And with all his weakness he had a sort of practical power, which made him useful to the bodies of men to whom he belonged. He had a ready kind of rough Lancashire eloquence, arising out of the fulness of his heart, which was very stirring to men similarly circumstanced, who liked to hear their feelings put into words. He had a pretty clear head at times, for method and arrangement; a necessary talent to large combinations of men. And what perhaps more than all made him relied upon and valued, was the consciousness which every one who came in contact with him felt, that he was actuated by no selfish motives; that his class, his order, was what he stood by, not the rights of his own paltry self. For even in great and noble men, as soon as self comes into prominent existence, it becomes a mean and paltry thing.

A little time before this, there had come one of those occasions for deliberation among the employed, which deeply interested John Barton, and the discussions concerning which had caused his frequent absence from home of late.

I am not sure if I can express myself in the technical terms of either masters or workmen, but I will try simply to state the case on which the latter deliberated.

An order for coarse goods came in from a new foreign market. It was a large order, giving employment to all the mills engaged in that species of manufacture: but it was necessary to execute it speedily, and at as low prices as possible, as the masters had reason to believe that a duplicate order had been sent to one of the continental manufacturing towns, where there were no restrictions on food, no taxes on building or machinery, and where consequently they dreaded that the goods could be made at a much lower price than they could afford them for; and that, by so acting and charging, the rival manufactures would obtain undivided possession of the market. It was clearly their interest to buy cotton as cheaply, and to beat down wages as low as possible. And in the long run the interests of the workmen would have been thereby benefited. Distrust each other as they may, the employers and the employed must rise or fall together. There may be some difference as to chronology, none as to fact.

But the masters did not choose to make all these circumstances known. They stood upon being the masters, and that they had a right to order work at their own prices, and they believed that in the present depression of trade, and unemployment of hands, there would be no great difficulty in getting it done.

Now let us turn to the workmen's view of the question. The masters (of the tottering foundation of whose prosperity they were ignorant) seemed doing well, and like gentlemen, "lived at home in ease," while they were starving, gasping on from day to day; and there was a foreign order to be executed, the extent of which, large as it was, was greatly exaggerated; and it was to be done speedily. Why were the masters offering such low wages under these circumstances? Shame upon them! It was taking advantage of their work-people being almost starved; but they would starve entirely rather than come into such terms. It was bad enough to be poor, while by the labour of their thin hands, the sweat of their brows, the masters were made rich; but they would not be utterly ground down to dust. No! they would fold their hands and sit idle, and smile at the masters, whom even in death they could baffle. With Spartan endurance they determined to let the employers know their power, by refusing to work.

So class distrusted class, and their want of mutual confidence wrought sorrow to both. The masters would not be bullied, and compelled to reveal why they felt it wisest and best to offer only such low wages; they would not be made to tell that they were even sacrificing capital to obtain a decisive victory over the continental manufacturers. And the workmen sat silent and stern with folded hands refusing to work for such pay. There was a strike in Manchester.

Of course it was succeeded by the usual consequences. Many other Trades' Unions, connected with different branches of business, supported with money, countenance, and encouragement of every kind, the stand which the Manchester power-loom weavers were making against their masters. Delegates from Glasgow, from Nottingham, and other towns, were sent to Manchester, to keep up the spirit of resistance; a committee was formed, and all the requisite officers elected; chairman, treasurer, honorary secretary: — among them was John Barton.

The masters, meanwhile, took their measures. They placarded the walls with advertisements for power-loom weavers. The workmen replied by a placard in still larger letters, stating their grievances. The masters met daily in town, to mourn over the time (so fast slipping away) for the fulfilment of the foreign orders; and to strengthen each other in their resolution not to yield. If they gave up now, they might give up always. It would never do. And amongst the most energetic of the masters, the Carsons, father and son, took their places. It is well known, that there is no religionist so zealous as a convert; no masters so stern, and regardless of the interests of their work people, as those who have risen from such a station themselves. This would account for the elder Mr. Carsons' determination not to be bullied into yielding; not even to be bullied into giving reasons for acting as the masters did. It was the employers will, and that should be enough for the employed. Harry Carsons did not trouble himself much about the grounds for his conduct. He liked the excitement of the affair. He liked the attitude of resistance. He was brave, and he liked the idea of personal danger, with which some of the more cautious tried to intimidate the violent among the masters.

Meanwhile, the power-loom weavers living in the more remote parts of Lancashire, and the neighbouring counties heard of the masters' advertisement for workmen; and in their solitary dwellings grew weary of starvation, and resolved to come to Manchester. Foot-sore, way-worn, half-starved looking men they were, as they tried to steal into town in the early dawn, before people were astir, or in the dusk of the evening. And now began the real wrong-doing of the Trades' Unions. As to their decision to work, or not, at such a particular rate of wages, that was either wise or unwise; all error of judgment at the worst. But they had no right to tyrannise over others, and tie them down to their own procrustean bed. Abhorring what they considered oppression in the masters, why did they oppress others? Because, when men get excited, they know not what they do. Judge, then, with something of the mercy of the Holy One, whom we all love.

In spite of policemen, set to watch over the safety of the poor country weavers — in spite of magistrates, and prisons, and severe punishments, — the poor depressed men tramping in from Burnley, Padiham, and other places, to work at the condemned "Starvation Prices," were waylaid, and beaten, and left by the roadside almost for dead. The police broke up every lounging knot of men: — they separated quietly, to reunite half-a-mile out of town.

Of course the feeling between the masters and workmen did not improve under these circumstances.

Combination is an awful power. It is like the equally mighty agency of steam; capable of almost unlimited good or evil. But to obtain a blessing on its labours, it must work under the direction of a high and intelligent will; incapable of being misled by passion, or excitement. The will of the operatives had not been guided to the calmness of wisdom.

So much for generalities. Let us now return to individuals.

A note, respectfully worded, although its tone of determination was strong, had been sent by the power-loom weavers, requesting that a "deputation" of them might have a meeting with the masters, to state the conditions they must have fulfilled before they would end the turn-out. They thought they had attained a sufficiently commanding position to dictate. John Barton was appointed one of the deputation.

The masters agreed to this meeting, being anxious to end the strife, although undetermined among themselves how far they should yield, or whether they should yield at all. Some of the old, whose experience had taught them sympathy, were for concession. Others, white headed men too, had only learnt hardness and obstinacy from the days of the years of their lives, and sneered at the more gentle and yielding. The younger men were one and all for an unflinching resistance to claims urged with so much violence. Of this party Harry Carsons was the leader.

But like all energetic people, the more he had to do the more time he seemed to find. With all his letter-writing, his calling, his being present at the New Bailey, when investigations of any case of violence against knob-sticks * was going on, he beset Mary more than ever. She was weary of her life for him. From blandishments he had even gone to threats—threats that whether she would or not she should be his; he showed an indifference that was almost insulting to every thing which might attract attention and injure her character.

And still she never saw Jem. She knew he had returned home. She heard of him occasionally through his cousin, who roved gaily from house to house, finding and making friends everywhere. But she never saw him. What was she to think? Had he given her up? Were a few hasty words, spoken in a moment of irritation, to stamp her lot through life? At times she thought that she could bear this meekly, happy in her own constant power of loving. For of change or of forgetfulness she did not dream. Then at other times her state of impatience was such, that it required all her self-restraint to prevent her from going and seeking him out, and (as man would do to man, or woman to woman) begging him to forgive her hasty words, and allow her to retract them, and bidding him accept of the love that was filling her whole heart. She wished Margaret had

* "Knob-sticks," those who consent to work at lower wages.

not advised her against such a manner of proceeding; she believed it was her friend's words that seemed to make such a simple action impossible, in spite of all the internal urgings. But a friend's advice is only thus powerful, when it puts into language the secret oracle of our souls. It was the whisperings of her womanly nature that caused her to shrink from any unmaidenly action, not Margaret's counsel.

All this time, this ten days or so, of Will's visit to Manchester, there was something going on which interested Mary even now, and which, in former times, would have exceedingly amused and excited her. She saw as clearly as if told in words, that the merry, random, boisterous sailor had fallen deeply in love with the quiet, prim, somewhat plain Margaret: she doubted if Margaret was aware of it, and yet, as she watched more closely, she began to think some instinct made the blind girl feel whose eyes were so often fixed upon her pale face; that some inner feeling made the delicate and becoming rose-flush steal over her countenance. She did not speak so decidedly as before; there was a hesitation in her manner that seemed to make her very attractive; as if something softer, more loveable than excellent sense, were coming in as a motive for speech; her eyes had always been soft, and were in no ways disfigured by her blindness, and now seemed to have a new charm, as they quivered under their white downcast lids. She must be conscious, thought Mary, — heart answering to heart.

Will's love had no blushings, no downcast eyes, no weighing of words; it was as open and undisguised as his nature; yet he seemed afraid of the answer its acknowledgment might meet with. It was Margaret's angelic voice that had entranced him, and which made him think of her as a being of some other sphere, that he feared to woo. So he tried to propitiate Job in all manner of ways. He went over to Liverpool to rummage in his great sea-chest for the flying-fish (no very odorous present by the way). He hesitated over a child's caul for some time, which was, in his eyes, a far greater treasure than any Exocetus. What use could it be of to a landsman? Then Margaret's voice rang in his ears; and he determined to sacrifice it, his most precious possession, to one whom she loved, as she did her grandfather.

It was rather a relief to him, when, having put it and the flying-fish together in a brown paper parcel, and sat upon them for security all the way in the rail-road, he found that Job was so indifferent to the precious caul, that he might easily claim it again. He hung about Margaret, till he had received many warnings and reproaches from his conscience in behalf of his dear aunt Alice's claims upon his time. He went away, and then he bethought him of some other little word with Job. And he turned back, and stood talking once more in Margaret's presence, door in hand, only waiting for some little speech of encouragement to come in and sit down again. But as the invitation was not given, he was forced to leave at last, and go and do his duty.

Four days had Jem Wilson watched for Mr. Harry Carsons without success; his hours of going and returning to his home were so irregular, owing to the meetings and consultations among the masters, which were rendered necessary by the turn-out. On the fifth, without any purpose on Jem's part, they met.

It was the workman's dinner hour, the interval between twelve and one; when the streets of Manchester are comparatively quiet, for a few shopping ladies, and lounging gentlemen, count for nothing in that busy, bustling, living place. Jem had been on an errand for his master, instead of returning to his dinner; and in passing along a lane, a road (called in compliment to the intentions of some future builder, a street), he encountered Harry Carsons, the only person, as far as he saw, beside himself, treading the unfrequented path. Along one side ran a high broad fence, blackened over by coal-tar, and spiked and stuck with pointed nails at the top, to prevent any one from climbing over into the garden beyond. By this fence was the foot-path. The carriage road was such as no carriage, no, not even a cart, could possibly have passed along, without Hercules to assist in lifting it out of the deep clay ruts. On the other side of the way was a dead brick wall; and a field after that, where there was a sawpit, and joiner's shed.

Jem's heart beat violently, when he saw the gay, handsome young man approaching, with a light, buoyant step. This then, was he whom Mary loved. It was, perhaps, no wonder; for he

13*

seemed to the poor smith, so elegant, so well-appointed, that he felt the superiority in externals, strangely and painfully, for an instant. Then something uprose within him, and told him, that "a man 's a man for a' that, for a' that, and twice as much as a' that." And he no longer felt troubled by the outward appearance of his rival.

Harry Carsons came on, lightly bounding over the dirty places with almost a lad's buoyancy. To his surprise the dark, sturdy-looking artisan stopped him, by saying respectfully,

"May I speak a word wi' you, Sir?"

"Certainly, my good man," looking his astonishment; then finding that the promised speech did not come very quickly, he added, "But make haste for I 'm in a hurry."

Jem had cast about for some less abrupt way of broaching the subject uppermost in his mind than he now found himself obliged to use. With a husky voice that trembled as he spoke, he said,

"I think, Sir, yo 're keeping company wi' a young woman called Mary Barton?"

A light broke in upon Henry Carsons' mind, and he paused before he gave the answer for which the other waited.

Could this man be a lover of Mary's? And (strange stinging thought) could he be beloved by her, and so have caused her obstinate rejection of himself? He looked at Jem from head to foot, a black, grimy mechanic, in dirty fustian clothes, strongly built, and awkward (according to the dancing-master); then he glanced at himself, and recalled the reflection he had so lately quitted in his bed-room. It was impossible. No woman with eyes could choose the one when the other wooed. It was Hyperion to a Satyr. That quotation came aptly; he forgot "That a man's a man for a' that." And yet here was a clue, which he had often wanted, to her changed conduct towards him. If she loved this man. If — he hated the fellow, and longed to strike him. He would know all.

"Mary Barton! let me see. Ay, that is the name of the girl. An arrant flirt the little hussy is; but very pretty. Ay, Mary Barton is her name."

Jem bit his lips. Was it then so; that Mary was a flirt; the giddy creature of whom he spoke? He would not believe it, and yet how he wished the suggestive words unspoken. That thought must keep now, though. Even if she were, the more reason for there being some one to protect her; poor faulty darling.

"She 's a good girl, Sir, though may be a bit set up with her beauty; but she 's her father's only child, Sir, and —" he stopped; he did not like to express suspicion, and yet he was determined he would be certain there was ground for none. What should he say?

"Well, my fine fellow, and what have I to do with that! It 's but loss of my time, and yours, too, if you've only stopped me to tell me Mary Barton is very pretty; I know that well enough."

He seemed as though he would have gone on, but Jem put his black, working, right hand upon his arm to detain him. The haughty young man shook it off, and with his glove pretended to brush away the sooty contamination that might be left upon his light greatcoat sleeve. The little action aroused Jem.

"I will tell you, in plain words what I have got to say to you, young man. It 's been telled me by one as knows, and has seen, that you walk with this same Mary Barton, and are known to be courting her; and her as spoke to me about it, thinks as how Mary loves you. That may be, or may not. But I 'm an old friend of hers, and her father's; and I just wished to know if you mean to marry the girl. Spite of what you said of her lightness, I ha' known her long enough to be sure she 'll make a noble wife for any one, let him be what he may; and I mean to stand by her like a brother; and if you mean rightly, you 'll not think the worse on me for what I 've now said; and if — but no, I 'll not say what I 'll do to the man who wrongs a hair of her head. He shall rue it to the longest day he lives, that 's all. Now, Sir, what I ask of you is this. If you mean fair and honourable by her, well and good; but if not, for your own sake as well as hers, leave her alone, and never speak to her more." Jem's voice quivered with the earnestness with which he spoke, and he eagerly waited for some answer.

Harry Carsons, meanwhile, instead of attending very particularly to the purpose the man had in addressing him, was trying to gather from his speech what was the real state of the case. He succeeded so far as to comprehend that Jem inclined to believe that Mary loved his rival; and consequently, that if the speaker were attached to her himself, he was not a favoured admirer. The idea came into Mr. Carsons' mind, that perhaps after all, Mary loved him in spite of her frequent and obstinate rejections; and that she had employed this person (whoever he was) to bully him into marrying her. He resolved to try and ascertain more correctly the man's relation to her. Either he was a lover, and if so, not a favoured one (in which case Mr. Carsons could not at all understand the man's motives for interesting himself in securing her marriage); or he was a friend, an accomplice, whom she had employed to bully him. So little faith in goodness have the mean and selfish!

"Before I make you into my confidant, my good man," said Mr. Carsons, in a contemptuous tone, "I think it might be as well to inquire your right to meddle with our affairs. Neither Mary nor I, as I conceive, called you in as a mediator." He paused: he wanted a distinct answer to this last supposition. None came; so he began to imagine he was to be threatened into some engagement, and his angry spirit rose.

"And so, my fine fellow, you will have the kindness to leave us to ourselves, and not meddle with what does not concern you. If you were a brother, or father of hers, the case might have been different. As it is, I can only consider you an impertinent meddler."

Again he would have passed on, but Jem stood in a determined way before him, saying,

"You say if I had been her brother, or her father, you 'd have answered me what I ask. Now, neither father nor brother could love her as I have loved her, ay, and as I love her still; if love gives a right to satisfaction, it 's next to impossible any one breathing can come up to my right. Now, Sir, tell me! do you mean fair by Mary or not? I 've proved my claim to know, and, by G —, I will know."

"Come, come, no impudence," replied Mr. Carsons, who having discovered what he wanted to know (namely, that Jem was a lover of Mary's, and that she was not encouraging his suit), wished to pass on.

"Father, brother, or rejected lover" (with an emphasis on the word rejected), "no one has a right to interfere between my little girl and me. No one shall. Confound you, man! get out of my way, or I'll make you," as Jem still obstructed his path with dogged determination.

"I won't, then, till you've given me your word about Mary," replied the mechanic, grinding his words out between his teeth, and the livid paleness of the anger he could no longer keep down covering his face till he looked ghastly.

"Won't you?" (with a taunting laugh), "then I'll make you." The young man raised his slight cane, and smote the artisan across the face with a stinging stroke. An instant afterwards he lay stretched in the muddy road, Jem standing over him, panting with rage. What he would have done next in his moment of ungovernable passion, no one knows; but a policeman from the main street, into which this road led, had been sauntering about for some time, unobserved by either of the parties, and expecting some kind of conclusion like the present to the violent discussion going on between the two young men. In a minute he had pinioned Jem, who sullenly yielded to the surprise.

Mr. Carsons was on his feet directly, his face glowing with rage or shame.

"Shall I take him to the lock-ups for assault, Sir?" said the policeman.

"No, no," exclaimed Mr. Carsons; "I struck him first. It was no assault on his side: though," he continued, hissing out his words to Jem, who even hated freedom procured for him, however justly, at the intervention of his rival, "I will never forgive or forget your insult. Trust me," he gasped the words in excess of passion, "Mary shall fare no better for your insolent interference." He laughed, as if with the consciousness of power.

Jem replied with equal excitement —

"And if you dare to injure her in the least, I will await you where no policeman can step in between. And God shall judge between us two."

The policeman now interfered with persuasions and warnings. He locked his arm in Jem's to lead him away in an opposite direction to that in which he saw Mr. Carsons was going. Jem submitted, gloomily, for a few steps, then wrenched himself free. The policeman shouted after him.

"Take care, my man! there 's no girl on earth worth what you 'll be bringing on yourself, if you don't mind."

But Jem was out of hearing.

CHAPTER XVI.

"Not for a moment take the scorner's chair;
While seated there, thou know'st not how a word,
A tone, a look, may gall thy brother's heart,
And make him turn in bitterness against thee."

'Love Truths.'

The day arrived on which the masters were to have an interview with a deputation of the work-people. The meeting was to take place in a public room, at an hotel; and there, about eleven o'clock, the mill-owners, who had received the foreign orders, began to collect.

Of course, the first subject, however full their minds might be of another, was the weather. Having done their duty by all the showers and sunshine which had occurred during the past week, they fell to talking about the business which brought them together. There might be about twenty gentlemen in the room, including some by courtesy, who were not immediately concerned in the settlement of the present question; but who, nevertheless, were sufficiently interested to attend. These were divided into little groups, who did not seem by any means unanimous. Some were for a slight concession, just a sugar plum to quieten the naughty child, a sacrifice to peace and quietness. Some were steadily and vehemently opposed to the dangerous precedent of yielding one jot or one tittle to the outward force of a turn-out. It was teaching the work-people how to become masters, said they. Did they want the wildest thing hereafter, they would know that the way to obtain their wishes would be to strike work. Besides, one or two of those present had only just returned from the New Baily, where one of the turn-outs had been tried for a cruel assault on a poor north-country weaver, who had attempted to work at the low price. They were indignant, and justly so, at the merciless manner in which the poor fellow had been treated; and their indignation at wrong, took (as it often does) the extreme form of revenge. They felt as if, rather than yield to the body of men who were resorting to such cruel measures towards their fellow-workmen, they, the masters, would sooner relinquish all the benefits to be derived from the fulfilment of the commission, in order that the workmen might suffer keenly. They forgot that the strike was in this instance the consequence of want and need, suffered unjustly, as the endurers believed; for, however insane, and without ground of reason, such was their belief, and such was the cause of their violence. It is a great truth that you cannot extinguish violence by violence. You may put it down for a time; but while you are crowing over your imaginary success, see if it does not return with seven devils worse than its former self!

No one thought of treating the workmen as brethren and friends, and openly, clearly, as appealing to reasonable men, stating exactly and fully the circumstances which led the masters to think it was the wise policy of the time to make sacrifices themselves, and to hope for them from the operatives.

In going from group to group in the room, you caught such a medley of sentences as the following:

"Poor devils! they 're near enough to starving, I 'm afraid. Mrs. Aldred makes two cows' heads into soup every week, and people come many miles to fetch it; and if these times last we must try and do more. But we must not be bullied into any thing!"

"A rise of a shilling or so won't make much difference, and they will go away thinking they 've gained their point."

"That 's the very thing I object to. They 'll think so, and whenever they 've a point to gain, no matter how unreasonable, they 'll strike work."

"It really injures them more than us."

"I don't see how our interests can be separated."

"The d — d brute had thrown vitriol on the poor fellow's ancles, and you know what a bad part that is to heal. He had to stand still with the pain, and that left him at the mercy of the cruel wretch who beat him about the head till you 'd hardly have known he was a man. They doubt if he 'll live."

"If it were only for that, I 'll stand out against them, even if it were the cause of my ruin."

"Aye, I for one, won't yield one farthing to the cruel brutes; they 're more like wild beasts than human beings."

(Well! who might have made them different?)

"I say, Carsons, just go and tell Duncombe of this fresh instance of their abominable conduct. He 's wavering, but I think this will decide him."

The door was now opened, and the waiter announced that the men were below, and asked if it were the pleasure of the gentlemen that they should be shown up.

They assented, and rapidly took their places round the official table; looking, as like as they could, to the Roman senators who awaited the irruption of Brennus and his Gauls.

Tramp, tramp, came the heavy clogged feet up the stairs; and in a minute five wild, earnest-looking men, stood in the room. John Barton, from some mistake as to time, was not among them. Had they been larger boned men, you would have called them gaunt; as it was, they were little of stature, and their fustian clothes hung loosely upon their shrunk limbs. In choosing their delegates, too, the operatives had had more regard to their brains, and power of speech, than to their wardrobes; they might have read the opinions of that worthy Professor Teufelsdreck, in Sartor Resartus, to judge from the dilapidated coats and trousers, which yet clothed men of parts and of power. It was long since many of them had known the luxury of a new article of dress; and air-gaps were to be seen in their garments. Some of the masters were rather affronted at such a ragged detachment coming between the wind and their nobility; but what cared they?

At the request of a gentleman hastily chosen to officiate as chairman, the leader of the delegates read, in a high-pitched, psalm-singing voice, a paper, containing the operatives' statement of the case at issue, their complaints, and their demands, which last were not remarkable for moderation.

He was then desired to withdraw for a few minutes, with his

fellow-delegates to another room, while the masters considered what should be their definitive answer.

When the men had left the room, a whispered earnest consultation took place, every one re-urging his former arguments. The conceders carried the day; but only by a majority of one. The minority haughtily and audibly expressed their dissent from the measures to be adopted, even after the delegates re-entered the room; their words and looks did not pass unheeded by the quick-eyed operatives; their names were registered in bitter hearts.

The masters could not consent to the advance demanded by the workmen. They would agree to give one shilling per week more than they had previously offered. Were the delegates empowered to accept such offer?

They were empowered to accept or decline any offer made that day by the masters.

Then it might be as well for them to consult among themselves as to what should be their decision. They again withdrew.

It was not for long. They came back, and positively declined any compromise of their demands.

Then up sprang Mr. Henry Carsons, the head and voice of the violent party among the masters, and addressing the chairman, even before the scowling operatives, he proposed some resolutions, which he, and those who agreed with him, had been concocting during this last absence of the deputation.

They were, firstly, withdrawing the proposal just made, and declaring all communication between the masters and that particular Trades' Union at an end; secondly, declaring that no master would employ any workman in future, unless he signed a declaration that he did not belong to any Trades' Union, and pledged himself not to assist or subscribe to any society, having for its object interference with the masters' powers; and, thirdly, that the masters should pledge themselves to protect and encourage all workmen willing to accept employment on those conditions, and at the rate of wages first offered. Considering that the men who now stood listening with lowering brows of defiance were all of them leading members of the Union, such resolutions were in themselves sufficiently provocative of animosity: but not content with simply stating them, Harry Carsons went on to characterise the conduct of the workmen in no measured terms; every word he spoke rendering their looks more livid, their glaring eyes more fierce. One among them would have spoken, but checked himself in obedience to the stern glance and pressure on his arm, received from the leader. Mr. Carsons sat down, and a friend instantly got up to second the motion. It was carried, but far from unanimously. The chairman announced it to the delegates (who had been once more turned out of the room for a division). They received it with deep brooding silence, but spake never a word, and left the room without even a bow.

Now there had been some by-play at this meeting, not recorded in the Manchester newspapers, which gave an account of the more regular part of the transaction.

While the men had stood grouped near the door, on their first entrance, Mr. Harry Carsons had taken out his silver pencil, and had drawn an admirable caricature of them — lank, ragged, dispirited, and famine-stricken. Underneath he wrote a hasty quotation from the fat knight's well-known speech in Henry IV. He passed it to one of his neighbours, who acknowledged the likeness instantly, and by him it was sent round to others, who all smiled and nodded their heads. When it came back to its owner he tore the book of the letter on which it was drawn, in two; twisted them up, and flung them into the fire-place; but, careless whether they reached their aim or not, he did not look to see that they fell just short of any consuming cinders.

This proceeding was closely observed by one of the men.

He watched the masters as they left the hotel (laughing, some of them were, at passing jokes), and when all had gone, he re-entered. He went to the waiter, who recognised him.

"There 's a bit on a picture up yonder, as one o' the gentlemen threw away; I 've a little lad at home as dearly loves a picture; by your leave I 'll go up for it."

The waiter, good-natured and sympathetic, accompanied him up-stairs; saw the paper picked up, and untwisted, and then being convinced, by a hasty glance at its contents, that it was only what the man had called it, "a bit of a picture," he allowed him to bear away his prize.

Towards seven o'clock that evening many operatives began to assemble in a room in the Weavers' Arms public-house, a room appropriated for festive "occasions," as the landlord, in his circular, on opening the premises, had described it. But, alas! it was on no festive occasion that they met there on this night. Starved, irritated, despairing men, they were assembling to hear the answer that morning given by the masters to their delegates; after which, as was stated in the notice, a gentleman from London would have the honour of addressing the meeting on the present state of affairs between the employers and the employed, or (as he chose to term them) the idle and the industrious classes. The room was not large, but its bareness of furniture made it appear so. Unshaded gas flared down upon the lean and unwashed artisans as they entered, their eyes blinking at the excess of light.

They took their seats on benches, and awaited the deputation. The latter, gloomily and ferociously, delivered the masters' ultimatum, adding thereunto not one word of their own; and it sank all the deeper into the sore hearts of the listeners for their forbearance.

Then the "gentleman from London," (who had been previously informed of the masters' decision) entered. You would have been puzzled to define his exact position, or what was the state of his mind as regarded education. He looked so self-conscious, so far from earnest, among the group of eager, fierce, absorbed men, among whom he now stood. He might have been a disgraced medical student of the Bob Sawyer class, or an unsuccessful actor, or a flashy shopman. The impression he would have given you would have been unfavourable, and yet there was much about him that could only be characterised as doubtful.

He smirked in acknowledgment of their uncouth greetings, and sat down; then glancing round, he inquired whether it would not be agreeable to the gentlemen present to have pipes and liquor handed round; adding, that he would stand treat.

As the man who has had his taste educated to love reading,

falls devouringly upon books after a long abstinence, so these poor fellows, whose tastes had been left to educate themselves into a liking for tobacco, beer, and similar gratifications, gleamed up at the proposal of the London delegate. Tobacco and drink deaden the pangs of hunger, and make one forget the miserable home, the desolate future.

They were now ready to listen to him with approbation. He felt it; and rising like a great orator, with his right arm outstretched, his left in the breast of his waitscoat, he began to declaim, with a forced theatrical voice.

After a burst of eloquence, in which he blended the deeds of the elder and the younger Brutus, and magnified the resistless might of the "millions of Manchester," the Londoner descended to matter-of-fact business, and in his capacity this way he did not belie the good judgment of those who had sent him as delegate. Masses of people when left to their own free choice, seem to have discretion in distinguishing men of natural talent; it is a pity they so little regard temper and principles. He rapidly dictated resolutions, and suggested measures. He wrote out a stirring placard for the walls. He proposed sending delegates to entreat the assistance of other Trades' Unions in other towns. He headed the list of subscribing Unions, by a liberal donation from that with which he was especially connected in London; and what was more, and more uncommon, he paid down the money in real, clinking, blinking, golden sovereigns! The money, alas, was cravingly required; but before alleviating any private necessities on the morrow, small sums were handed to each of the delegates, who were in a day or two to set out on their expeditions to Glasgow, Newcastle, Nottingham, &c. These men were most of them members of the deputation, who had that morning waited upon the masters. After he had drawn up some letters, and spoken a few more stirring words, the gentleman from London withdrew, previously shaking hands all round; and many speedily followed him out of the room, and out of the house.

The newly-appointed delegates, and one or two others, remained behind to talk over their respective missions, and to give and exchange opinions in more homely and natural language than they dared to use before the London orator.

"He 's a rare chap, yon," began one, indicating the departed delegate by a jerk of his thumb towards the door. "He 's getten the gift of the gab, anyhow!"

"Ay! ay! he knows what he 's about. See! how he poured it into us about that there Brutus. He were pretty hard, too, to kill his own son!"

"I could kill mine if he took part with the masters; to be sure, he 's but a step-son, but that makes no odds," said another.

But how tongues were hushed, and all eyes were directed towards the member of the deputation who had that morning returned to the hotel, to obtain possession of Harry Carsons' clever caricature of the operatives.

The heads clustered together, to gaze at, and detect the likenesses.

"That 's John Slater! I 'd ha' known him anywhere, by his big nose. Lord! how like; that 's me, by G—d, it 's the very way I 'm obligated to pin my waistcoat up, to hide that I 've getten no shirt. That *is* a shame, and I 'll not stand it."

"Well!" said John Slater, after having acknowledged his nose and his likeness; "I could laugh at a jest as well as e'er the best on 'em, though it did tell agin mysel, if I were not clemming" (his eyes filled with tears; he was a poor, pinched, sharp-featured man, with a gentle and melancholy expression of countenance,) "and if I could keep from thinking of them at home, as is clemming; but with their cries for food ringing in my ears, and making me afeard of going home, and wonder if I should hear 'em wailing out, if I lay cold and drowned at th' bottom o' th' canal, there, — why, man, I cannot laugh at ought. It seems to make me sad that there is any as can make game on what they've never knowed; as can make such laughable pictures on men, whose very hearts within 'em are so raw and sore as ours were and are, God help us."

John Barton began to speak; they turned to him with great attention. "It makes me more than sad, it makes my heart burn within me, to see that folk can make a jest of earnest men;

for chaps, who comed to ask for a bit o' fire for th' old granny, as shivers i' th' cold; for a bit o' bedding, and some warm clothing to the poor wife who lies in labour on th' damp flags; and for victuals for the childer, whose little voices are getting too faint and weak to cry aloud wi' hunger. For, brothers, is not them the things we ask for when we ask for more wage? We donnot want dainties, we want bellyfuls; we donnot want gimcrack coats and waistcoats, we want warm clothes, and so that we get 'em we 'd not quarrel wi' what they 're made on. We donnot want their grand houses, we want a roof to cover us from the rain, and the snow, and the storm; ay, and not alone to cover us, but the helpless ones that cling to us in the keen wind, and ask us with their eyes why we brought 'em into th' world to suffer?" He lowered his deep voice almost to a whisper.

"I 've seen a father who had killed his child rather than let it clem before his eyes; and he were a tender-hearted man."

He began again in his usual tone. "We come to th' masters wi' full hearts, to ask for them things I named afore. We know that they 've getten money, as we 've earned for 'em; we know trade is mending, and they 've large orders, for which they 'll be well paid; we ask for our share o' th' payment; for, say we, if th' masters get our share of payment it will only go to keep servants and horses, to more dress and pomp. Well and good, if yo choose to be fools we 'll not hinder you, so long as you 're just; but our share we must and will have; we 'll not be cheated. *We* want it for daily bread, for life itself; and not for our own lives neither (for there 's many a one here, I know by mysel, as would be glad and thankful to lie down and die out o' this weary world), but for the lives of them little ones, who don't yet know what life is, and are afeard of death. Well, we come before th' masters to state what we want, and what we must have, afore we 'll set shoulder to their work; and they say, 'No.' One would think that would be enough of hard-heartedness, but it isn't. They go and make jesting pictures on us! I could laugh at mysel, as well as poor John Slater there; but then I must be easy in my mind to laugh. Now I only know that I would give the last drop of my blood to avenge us on yon chap, who had so little feeling in him as to make game on earnest, suffering men!"

A low angry murmur was heard among the men, but it did not yet take form or words. John continued —

"You'll wonder, chaps, how I came to miss the time this morning; I'll just tell you what I was a-doing. Th' chaplain at the New Bailey sent and gived me an order to see Jonas Higginbotham; he as was taken up last week for throwing vitriol in a knob-stick's face. Well, I couldn't help but go; and I din't reckon it would ha' kept me so late. Jonas were like one crazy when I got to him; he said he could na' get rest night or day for th' face of the poor fellow he had damaged; then he thought on his weak, clemmed look, as he tramped, foot-sore, into town; and Jonas thought, may be, he had left them at home as would look for news, and hope and get none, but, haply, tidings of his death. Well, Jonas had thought on these things till he could not rest, but walked up and down continually like a wild beast in his cage. At last he bethought him on a way to help a bit, and he got th' chaplain to send for me; and he telled me this; and that th' man were lying in th' Infirmary, and he bade me go (to-day's the day as folk may be admitted into th' Infirmary) and get his silver watch, as was his mother's, and sell it as well as I could, and take the money, and bid the poor knob-stick send it to his friends beyond Burnley, and I were to take him Jonas's kind regards, and he humbly axed him to forgive him. So I did what Jonas wished. But bless your life, none on us would ever throw vitriol again (at least at a knob-stick) if they could see the sight I saw to-day. The man lay, his face all wrapped in cloths, so I didn't see *that;* but not a limb, nor a bit of a limb, could keep from quivering with pain. He would ha' bitten his hand to keep down his moans, but couldn't, his face hurt him so if he moved it e'er so little. He could scarce mind me when I telled him about Jonas; he did squeeze my hand when I jingled the money, but when I axed his wife's name he shrieked out, 'Mary, Mary, shall I never see you again. Mary, my darling, they've made me blind because I wanted to work for you and our own baby; oh, Mary, Mary!' Then the nurse came, and said he were raving, and that I had made him worse. And I 'm afeard it was true; yet I were loth to go without knowing where to send the money . . . . So that kept me beyond my time, chaps."

"Did you hear where the wife lived at last?" asked many anxious voices.

"No! he went on talking to her, till his words cut my heart like a knife. I axed th' nurse to find out who she was, and where she lived. But what I 'm more especial naming it now for is this, — for one thing I wanted you all to know why I weren't at my post this morning; for another, I wish to say, that I, for one, ha' seen enough of what comes of attacking knob-sticks, and I 'll ha' nought to do with it no more."

There were some expressions of disapprobation, but John did not mind them.

"Nay! I 'm no coward," he replied, "and I 'm true to th' backbone. What I would like, and what I would do, would be to fight the masters. There 's one among yo called me a coward. Well! every man has a right to his opinion; but since I 've thought on th' matter to-day, I 've thought we han all on us been more like cowards in attacking the poor like ourselves; them as has none to help, but mun choose between vitriol and starvation. I say we 're more cowardly in doing that than in leaving them alone. No! what I would do is this. Have at the masters!" Again he shouted, "Have at the masters!" He spoke lower; all listened with hushed breath.

"It 's the masters as has wrought this woe; it 's the masters as should pay for it. Him as called me coward just now, may try if I am one or not. Set me to serve out the masters, and see if there 's ought I 'll stick at."

"It would give the masters a bit on a fright if one on them were beaten within an inch of his life," said one.

"Ay! or beaten till no life were left in him," growled another.

And so with words, or looks that told more than words, they built up a deadly plan. Deeper and darker grew the import of their speeches, as they stood hoarsely muttering their meaning out, and glaring, with eyes that told the terror their own thoughts were to them, upon their neighbours. Their clenched fists, their set teeth, their livid looks, all told the suffering which their minds were voluntarily undergoing in the contemplation of crime, and in familiarising themselves with its details.

Then came one of those fierce terrible oaths which bind members of Trades' Unions to any given purpose. Then, under the flaring gaslight, they met together to consult further. With the distrust of guilt, each was suspicious of his neighbour; each dreaded the treachery of another. A number of pieces of paper (the identical letter on which the caricature had been drawn that very morning) were torn up, and *one was marked.* Then all were folded up again, looking exactly alike. They were shuffled together in a hat. The gas was extinguished; each drew out a paper. The gas was relighted. Then each went as far as he could from his fellows, and examined the paper he had drawn without saying a word, and with a countenance as stony and immoveable as he could make it.

Then, still rigidly silent, they each took up their hats and went every one his own way.

He who had drawn the marked paper had drawn the lot of the assassin! and he had sworn to act according to his drawing! But no one save God and his own conscience knew who was the appointed murderer!

CHAPTER XVII.

"Mournful is 't to say Farewell,
Though for few brief hours we part;
In that absence, who can tell
What may come to wring the heart!" ANONYMOUS.

THE events recorded in the last chapter took place on a Tuesday. On Thursday afternoon Mary was surprised, in the midst of some little bustle in which she was engaged, by the entrance of Will Wilson. He looked strange, at least it was strange to see any different expression on his face to his usual joyous beaming appearance. He had a paper parcel in his hand. He came in, and sat down, more quietly than usual.

"Why, Will! what 's the matter with you? You seem quite cut up about something!"

"And I am, Mary! I'm come to say good-bye; and few folk like to say good-bye to them they love."

"Good-bye! Bless me, Will! that 's sudden, isn't it?"

Mary left off ironing, and came and stood near the fire-place. She had always liked Will; but now it seemed as if a sudden spring of sisterly love had gushed up in her heart, so sorry did she feel to hear of his approaching departure.

"It 's very sudden, isn't it?" said she, repeating the question.

"Yes, it 's very sudden," said he, dreamily. "No, it isn't;" rousing himself, to think of what he was saying. "The captain told me in a fortnight he would be ready to sail again; but it comes very sudden on me, I had got so fond of you all."

Mary understood the particular fondness that was thus generalised. She spoke again.

"But it 's not a fortnight since you came. Not a fortnight since you knocked at Jane Wilson's door, and I was there, you remember. Nothing like a fortnight!"

"No; I know it 's not. But, you see, I got a letter this afternoon from Jack Harris, to tell me our ship sails on Tuesday next; and it 's long since I promised my uncle (my mother's brother, him that lives at Kirk-Christ, beyond Ramsay, in the Isle of Man) that I 'd go and see him and his, this time of coming ashore. I must go. I'm sorry enough; but I mustn't slight poor mother's friends. I must go. Don't try to keep me," said he, evidently fearing the strength of his own resolution, if hard pressed by entreaty.

"I 'm not a-going, Will. I dare say you 're right; only I can't help feeling sorry you 're going away. It seems so flat to be left behind. When do you go?"

"To-night. I shan't see you again."

"To-night! and you go to Liverpool! May be you and father will go together. He 's going to Glasgow, by way of Liverpool."

"No! I'm walking; and I don't think your father will be up to walking."

"Well! and why on earth are you walking? You can get by railway for three-and-sixpence."

"Ay, but Mary! (thou mustn't tell what I 'm going to tell thee) I haven't got three shillings, no, nor even a sixpence left, at least not here; before I came I gave my landlady enough to carry me to the island and back, and may be a trifle for presents, and I brought the rest here; and it 's all gone but this," jingling a few coppers in his hand.

"Nay, never fret over my walking a matter of thirty mile," added he, as he saw she looked grave and sorry. "It 's a fine clear night, and I shall set off betimes, and get in afore the Manx packet sails. Where 's your father going? To Glasgow, did you say? Perhaps he and I may have a bit of a trip together then, for, if the Manx boat has sailed when I get into Liverpool, I shall go by a Scotch packet. What 's he going to do in Glasgow? — Seek for work? Trade is as bad there as here folk say."

"No; he knows that," answered Mary sadly. "I sometimes think he 'll never get work again, and that trade will never mend. It 's very hard to keep up one's heart. I wish I were a boy, I 'd go to sea with you. It would be getting away from bad news at any rate; and now, there 's hardly a creature that crosses the door-step, but has something sad and unhappy to tell one. Father is going as a delegate from his Union, to ask help from the Glasgow folk. He 's starting this evening."

Mary sighed, for the feeling again came over her that it was very flat to be left alone.

"You say no one crosses the threshold but has something sad to say; you don't mean that Margaret Jennings has any trouble?" asked the young sailor, anxiously.

"No!" replied Mary, smiling a little, she 's the only one I know, I believe, who seems free from care. Her blindness almost appears a blessing sometimes; she was so downhearted when she dreaded it, and now she seems so calm and happy when it 's downright come. No! Margaret 's happy, I do think."

"I could almost wish it had been otherwise," said Will, thoughtfully. "I could have been so glad to comfort her, and cherish her, if she had been in trouble."

"And why can't you cherish her, even though she is happy?" asked Mary.

"Oh! I don't know. She seems so much better than I am!

And her voice! When I hear it, and think of the wishes that are in my heart, it seems as much out of place to ask her to be my wife, as it would be to ask an angel from heaven."

Mary could not help laughing outright, in spite of her depression, at the idea of Margaret as an angel; it was so difficult (even to her dress-making imagination), to fancy where, and how, the wings would be fastened to the brown stuff gown, or the blue and yellow print.

Will laughed, too, a little, out of sympathy with Mary's pretty merry laugh. Then he said —

"Ay, you may laugh, Mary; it only shows you 've never been in love."

In an instant Mary was carnation colour, and the tears sprang to her soft gray eyes. She that was suffering so much from the doubts arising from love! It was unkind of him. He did not notice her change of look and of complexion. He only noticed that she was silent, so he continued:

"I thought — I think, that when I come back from this voyage, I will speak. It 's my fourth voyage in the same ship and with the same captain, and he 's promised he 'll make me a second mate after this trip, then I shall have something to offer Margaret; and her father, and aunt Alice, shall live with her, and keep her from being lonesome while I 'm at sea. I 'm speaking as if she cared for me, and would marry me; d'ye think she does care at all for me, Mary?" asked he, anxiously.

Mary had a very decided opinion of her own on the subject, but she did not feel as if she had any right to give it. So she said —

"You must ask Margaret, not me, Will; she 's never named your name to me." His countenance fell. "But I should say that was a good sign from a girl like her; I 've no right to say what I think; but, if I was you, I would not leave her now without speaking."

"No! I cannot speak! I have tried. I 've been in to wish them good-bye, and my voice stuck in my throat. I could say nought of what I 'd planned to say; and I never thought of being so bold as to offer her marriage till I 'd been my next trip, and been made mate. I could not even offer her this box," said he, undoing his paper parcel and displaying a gaudily ornamented accordion; "I longed to buy her something, and I thought, if it were something in the music line, she would may be fancy it more. So, will you give it to her, Mary, when I 'm gone? and, if you can slip in something tender, — something, you know, of what I feel, — may be she would listen to you, Mary."

Mary promised that she would do all that he asked.

"I shall be thinking on her many and many a night, when I 'm keeping my watch in mid-sea; I wonder if she will ever think on me, when the wind is whistling, and the gale rising. You 'll often speak of me to her, Mary? And if I should meet with any mischance, tell her how dear, how very dear, she was to me, and bid her, for the sake of one who loved her well, try and comfort my poor aunt Alice. Dear old aunt! you and Margaret will often go and see her, won't you. She 's sadly failed since I was last ashore. And so good as she has been! When I lived with her, a little wee chap, I used to be awakened by the neighbours knocking her up; this one was ill, and that body's child was restless; and, for as tired as ever she might be, she would be up and dressed in a twinkling, never thinking of the hard day's wash afore her next morning. Them were happy times! How pleased I used to be when she would take me into the fields with her to gather herbs! I 've tasted tea in China since then, but it wasn't half so good as the herb tea she used to make for me o' Sunday nights. And she knew such a deal about plants and birds, and their ways! She used to tell me long stories about her childhood, and we used to plan how we would go sometime, please God (that was always her word), and live near her old home beyond Lancaster; in the very cottage where she was born if we could get it. Dear! and how different it is! Here is she still in a back street o' Manchester, never likely to see her own home again; and I, a sailor, off for America next week. I wish she had been able to go to Burton once afore she died."

"She would maybe have found all sadly changed," said Mary, though her heart echoed Will's feeling.

"Ay! ay! I dare say it 's best. One thing I do wish though, and I have often wished it when out alone on the deep sea, when even the most thoughtless can't choose but think on th' past and th' future; and that is, that I 'd never grieved her. Oh Mary! many a hasty word comes sorely back on the heart, when one thinks one shall never see the person whom one has grieved again!"

They both stood thinking. Suddenly Mary started.

"That 's father's step. And his shirt 's not ready!"

She hurried to her irons, and tried to make up for lost time.

John Barton came in. Such a haggard and wildly anxious looking man, Will thought he had never seen. He looked at Will, but spoke no word of greeting or welcome.

"I 'm come to bid you good-bye," said the sailor, and would in his sociable friendly humour have gone on speaking. But John answered abruptly,

"Good-bye to ye, then."

There was that in his manner which left no doubt of his desire to get rid of the visitor, and Will accordingly shook hands with Mary, and looked at John, as if doubting how far to offer to shake hands with him. But he met with no answering glance or gesture, so he went his way, stopping for an instant at the door to say,

"You 'll think on me on Tuesday, Mary. That 's the day we shall hoist our blue Peter, Jack Harris says."

Mary was heartily sorry when the door closed; it seemed like shutting out a friendly sunbeam. And her father! what could be the matter with him? He was so restless; not speaking (she wished he would), but starting up and then sitting down, and meddling with her irons; he seemed so fierce, too, to judge from his face. She wondered if he disliked Will being there; or if he were vexed to find that she had not got further on with her work. At last she could bear his nervous way no longer, it made her equally nervous and fidgety. She would speak.

"When are you going, father? I don't know the time o' the trains."

"And why shouldst thou know?" replied he, gruffly. "Meddle with thy ironing, but donnot be asking questions about what doesn't concern thee."

"I wanted to get you something to eat first," answered she, gently.

"Thou dost not know that I'm larning to do without food," said he.

Mary looked at him to see if he spoke jestingly. No! he looked savagely grave.

She finished her bit of ironing, and began preparing the food she was sure her father needed; for by this time her experience in the degrees of hunger had taught her that his present irritability was increased, if not caused, by want of food.

He had had a sovereign given him to pay his expenses as delegate to Glasgow, and out of this he had given Mary a few shillings in the morning; so she had been able to buy a sufficient meal, and now her care was to cook it so as to tempt him.

"If thou 'rt doing that for me, Mary, thou may'st spare thy labour. I telled thee I were not for eating."

"Just a little bit, father, before starting," coaxed Mary, perseveringly.

At that instant who should come in but Job Legh. It was not often he came, but when he did pay visits, Mary knew from past experience they were any thing but short. Her father's countenance fell back into the deep gloom from which it was but just emerging at the sound of Mary's sweet voice, and pretty pleading. He became again restless and fidgety, scarcely giving Job Legh the greeting necessary for a host in his own house. Job, however, did not stand upon ceremony. He had come to pay a visit, and was not to be daunted from his purpose. He was interested in John Barton's mission to Glasgow, and wanted to hear all about it; so he sat down, and made himself comfortable, in a manner that Mary saw was meant to be stationary.

"So thou 'rt off to Glasgow, art thou?" he began his catechism.

"Ay."

"When art starting?"

"To-night."

"That I knowed. But by what train?"

That was just what Mary wanted to know; but what apparently her father was in no mood to tell. He got up without speaking, and went up-stairs. Mary knew from his step, and his way, how much he was put out, and feared Job would see it too. But no! Job seemed imperturbable. So much the better, and perhaps she could cover her father's rudeness by her own civility to so kind a friend.

So half listening to her father's movements up-stairs (passionate, violent, restless motions they were), and half attending to Job Legh, she tried to pay him all due regard.

"When does your father start, Mary?"

That plaguing question again.

"Oh! very soon. I'm just getting him a bit of supper. Is Margaret very well?"

"Yes, she's well enough. She's meaning to go and keep Alice Wilson company for an hour or so this evening; as soon as she thinks her nephew will have started for Liverpool; for she fancies the old woman will feel a bit lonesome. Th' Union is paying for your father, I suppose?"

"Yes, they've giv'n him a sovereign. You're one of th' Union, Job?"

"Ay! I'm one, sure enough; but I'm but a sleeping partner in the concern. I were obliged to become a member for peace, else I don't go along with 'em. Yo see they think themselves wise, and me silly, for differing with them! well! there's no harm in that. But then they won't let me be silly in peace and quietness, but will force me to be as wise as they are; now that's not British liberty, I say. I'm forced to be wise according to their notions, else they parsecute me, and sarve me out."

What could her father be doing up-stairs? Tramping and banging about. Why did he not come down? Or why did not Job go? The supper would be spoilt.

But Job had no notion of going.

"You see my folly is this, Mary. I would take what I could get; I think half a loaf is better than no bread. I would work for low wages rather than sit idle and starve. But, comes the Trades' Union, and says, 'Well, if you take the half-loaf, we'll worry you out of your life. Will you be clemmed, or will you be worried?' Now clemming is a quiet death, and worrying isn't, so I choose clemming, and come into th' Union. But I wish they'd leave me free, if I am a fool."

Creak, creak, went the stairs. Her father was coming down at last.

Yes, he came down, but more doggedly fierce than before, and made up for his journey, too; with his little bundle on his arm. He went up to Job, and, more civilly than Mary expected, wished him good-bye. He then turned to her, and in a short cold manner, bade her farewell.

"Oh! father, don't go yet. Your supper is all ready. Stay one moment!"

But he pushed her away, and was gone. She followed him to the door, her eyes blinded by sudden tears; she stood there looking after him. He was so strange, so cold, so hard. Suddenly, at the end of the court, he turned, and saw her standing there; he came back quickly, and took her in his arms.

"God bless thee, Mary! — God in heaven bless thee, poor child!" She threw her arms round his neck.

"Don't go yet, father; I can't bear you to go yet. Come in, and eat some supper; you look so ghastly; dear father, do!"

"No," he said, faintly and mournfully. "It 's best as it is. I couldn't eat, and it 's best to be off. I cannot be still at home. I must be moving."

So saying, he unlaced her soft twining arms, and kissing her once more, set off on his fierce errand.

And he was out of sight! She did not know why, but she had never before felt so depressed, so desolate. She turned in to Job, who sat there still. Her father, as soon as he was out of sight, slackened his pace, and fell into that heavy listless step, which told as well as words could do, of hopelessness and weakness. It was getting dark, but he loitered on, returning no greeting to any one.

A child's cry caught his ear. His thoughts were running on little Tom; on the dead and buried child of happier years. He followed the sound of wail, that might have been *his*, and found a poor little mortal, who had lost his way, and whose grief had choked up his thoughts to the single want, "Mammy, mammy.' With tender address, John Barton soothed the little laddie, and with beautiful patience he gathered fragments of meaning from the half-spoken words which came mingled with sobs from the terrified little heart. So, aided by inquiries here and there from a passer-by, he led and carried the little fellow home, where his mother had been too busy to miss him, but now received him with thankfulness, and with an eloquent Irish blessing. When John heard the words of blessing, he shook his head mournfully, and turned away to retrace his steps.

Let us leave him.

Mary took her sewing after he had gone, and sat on, and sat on, trying to listen to Job, who was more inclined to talk than usual. She had conquered her feeling of impatience towards him so far as to be able to offer him her father's rejected supper; and she even tried to eat herself. But her heart failed her. A leaden weight seemed to hang over her; a sort of presentiment of evil, or perhaps only an excess of low-spirited feeling in consequence of the two departures which had taken place that afternoon.

She wondered how long Job Legh would sit. She did not like putting down her work, and crying before him, and yet she had never in her life longed so much to be alone in order to indulge a good hearty burst of tears.

"Well, Mary," she suddenly caught him saying, "I thought you'd be a bit lonely to-night; and as Margaret were going to cheer th' old woman, I said I 'd go and keep th' young un' company; and a very pleasant, chatty evening we 've had; very. Only I wonder as Margaret is not come back."

"But perhaps she is," suggested Mary.

"No, no, I took care o' that. Look ye here!" and he pulled out the great house-key. "She 'll have to stand waiting i' th' street, and that I 'm sure she wouldn't do, when she knew where to find me."

"Will she come back by hersel?" asked Mary.

"Ay. At first I were afraid o' trusting her, and I used to follow her a bit behind; never letting on, of course. But bless you! she goes along as steadily as can be; rather slow to be sure, and her head a bit on one side as if she were listening. And it 's real beautiful to see her cross the road. She 'll wait above a bit to hear that all is still; not that she 's so dark as not to see a coach or a cart like a big black thing, but she can't rightly judge how far off it is by sight, so she listens. Hark! that 's her!"

Yes; in she came with her usually calm face, all tear-stained and sorrow-marked.

"What 's the matter, my wench?" said Job, hastily.

"Oh; grandfather! Alice Wilson 's so bad!" She could say no more, for her breathless agitation. The afternoon, and the parting with Will, had weakened her nerves for any after-shock.

"What is it? Do tell us, Margaret?" said Mary, placing her in a chair, and loosening her bonnet-strings.

"I think it 's a stroke o' the palsy. Any rate she has lost the use of one side."

"Was it afore Will had set off?" asked Mary.

"No; he were gone before I got there," said Margaret; "and she were much about as well as she has been for many a day. She spoke a bit, but not much; but that were only natural, for Mrs. Wilson likes to have the talk to hersel, you know. She got up to go across the room, and then I heard a drag wi' her leg, and presently a fall, and Mrs. Wilson came running, and set up such a cry! I stopped wi' Alice, while she fetched a doctor; but she could not speak, to answer me, though she tried, I think."

"Where was Jem? Why didn't he go for the doctor?"

"He were out when I got there, and he never came home while I stopped."

"Thou 'st never left Mrs. Wilson alone wi' poor Alice?" asked Job, hastily.

"No, no," said Margaret. "But, oh! grandfather, it 's now I feel how hard it is to have lost my sight. I should have so loved to nurse her; and I did try, until I found I did more harm than good. Oh! grandfather; if I could but see!"

She sobbed a little; and they let her give that ease to her heart. Then she went on —

"No! I went round by Mrs. Davenport's, and she were hard at work; but, the minute I told my errand, she were ready and willing to go to Jane Wilson, and stop up all night with Alice."

"And what does the doctor say?" asked Mary.

"O! much what all doctors say: he puts a fence on this side, and a fence on that, for fear he should be caught tripping in his judgment. One moment he does not think there 's much hope — but while there is life there is hope; th' next he says he should think she might recover partial, but her age is again her. He 's ordered her leeches to her head."

Margaret having told her tale, leant back with weariness, both of body and mind. Mary hastened to make her a cup of tea; while Job, lately so talkative, sat quiet and mournfully silent.

"I 'll go first thing to-morrow morning, and learn how she is; and I 'll bring word back before I go to work," said Mary.

"It 's a bad job Will 's gone," said Job.

"Jane does not think she knows any one," replied Margaret. "It 's perhaps as well he shouldn't see her now, for they say her face is sadly drawn. He 'll remember her with her own face better, if he does not see her again."

With a few more sorrowful remarks they separated for the night, and Mary was left alone in her house, to meditate on the heavy day that had passed over her head. Every thing seemed going wrong. Will gone; her father gone — and so strangely too! And to a place so mysteriously distant as Glasgow seemed to be to her! She had felt his presence as a protection against Harry Carsons and his threats; and now she dreaded lest he should learn she was alone. Her heart began to despair, too, about Jem. She feared he had ceased to love her; and she — she only loved him more and more for his seeming neglect. And, as if all this aggregate of sorrowful thoughts was not enough, here was this new woe, of poor Alice's paralytic stroke.

CHAPTER XVIII.

"But in his pulse there was no throb,
Nor on his lips one dying sob;
Sigh, nor word, nor struggling breath
Heralded his way to death." SIEGE OF CORINTH.

"My brain runs this way and that way; 't will not fix
On aught but vengeance." DUKE OF GUISE.

I MUST now go back to an hour or two before Mary and her friends parted for the night. It might be about eight o'clock that evening, and the three Miss Carsons were sitting in their father's drawing-room. He was asleep in the dining-room, in his own comfortable chair. Mrs. Carsons was (as was usual with her, when no particular excitement was going on), very poorly, and sitting up-stairs in her dressing-room, indulging in the luxury of a headache. She was not well, certainly. "Wind in the head," the servants called it. But it was but the natural consequence of the state of mental and bodily idleness in which she was placed. Without education enough to value the resources of wealth and leisure, she was so circumstanced as to command both. It would have done her more good than all the æther and sal-volatile she was daily in the habit of swallowing, if she might have taken the work of one of her own housemaids for a week; made beds, rubbed tables, shaken carpets, and gone out into the fresh morning air, without all the paraphernalia of shawl, cloak, boa, fur boots, bonnet, and veil, in which she was equipped before setting out for an "airing," in the closely shut-up carriage.

So the three girls were by themselves in the comfortable, elegant, well-lighted, drawing-room; and, like many similarly-situated young ladies, they did not exactly know what to do to while away the time until the tea-hour. The elder two had been at a dancing-party the night before, and were listless and sleepy in consequence. One tried to read "Emerson's Essays," and fell asleep in the attempt; the other was turning over a parcel of new songs, in order to select what she liked. Amy, the youngest, was copying some manuscript music. The air was heavy with the fragrance of strongly-scented flowers, which sent out their night odours from an adjoining conservatory.

The clock on the chimney-piece chimed eight. Sophy, (the sleeping sister) started up at the sound.

"What o'clock is that?" she asked.

"Eight," said Amy.

"Oh, dear! how tired I am! Is Harry come in? Tea will rouse one up a little. Are you not worn out, Helen?"

"Yes; I am tired enough. One is good for nothing the day after a dance. Yet I don't feel weary at the time; I suppose it is the lateness of the hours."

"And yet, how could it be managed otherwise? So many don't dine till five or six, that one cannot begin before eight or nine; and then it takes a long time to get into the spirit of the evening. It is always more pleasant after supper than before."

"Well, I 'm too tired to-night to reform the world in the matter of dances or balls. What are you copying, Amy?"

"Only that little Spanish air you sing — 'Quien quiera.'"

"What are you copying it for?" asked Helen.

"Harry asked me to do it for him, this morning at breakfast-time, — for Miss Richardson, he said."

"For Jane Richardson!" said Sophy, as if a new idea were receiving strength in her mind.

"Do you think Harry means any thing by his attention to her?" asked Helen.

"Nay, I do not know any thing more than you do; I can only observe and conjecture. What do you think, Helen?"

"Harry always likes to be of consequence to the belle of the room. If one girl is more admired than another, he likes to flutter about her, and seem to be on intimate terms with her. This is his way, and I have not noticed any thing beyond that in his manner to Jane Richardson."

"But I don't think she knows it 's only his way. Just watch her the next time we meet her when Harry is there, and see how she crimsons, and looks another way when she feels he is coming up to her. I think he sees it, too, and I think he is pleased with it."

"I dare say Harry would like well enough to turn the head of such a lovely girl as Jane Richardson. But I 'm not convinced that he is in love, whatever she may be."

"Well, then!" said Sophy, indignantly, "though it is our own brother, I do think he is behaving very wrongly. The more I think of it the more sure I am that she thinks he means something, and that he intends her to think so. And then, when he leaves off paying her attention —"

"Which will be as soon as a prettier girl makes her appearance," interrupted Helen.

"As soon as he leaves off paying her attention," resumed Sophy, "she will have many and many a heart-ache, and then she will harden herself into being a flirt, a feminine flirt, as he is masculine flirt. Poor girl!"

"I don't like to hear you speak so of Harry," said Amy, looking up at Sophy.

"And I don't like to have to speak so, Amy, for I love him dearly. He is a good, kind brother, but I do think him vain, and I think he hardly knows the misery, the crime to which indulged vanity may lead him."

Helen yawned.

"Oh! do you think we may ring for tea? Sleeping after dinner makes me so feverish."

"Yes, surely. Why should not we?" said the more energetic Sophy, pulling the bell with some determination.

"Tea, directly, Parker," said she, authoritatively, as the man entered the room.

She was too little in the habit of reading expressions on the faces of others to notice Parker's countenance.

Yet it was striking. It was blanched to a dead whiteness; the lips compressed as if to keep within some tale of horror; the eyes distended and unnatural. It was a terror stricken face.

The girls began to put away their music and books, in preparation for tea. The door slowly opened again, and this time it was the nurse who entered. I call her nurse, for such had been her office in by-gone days, though now she held rather an anomalous situation in the family. Seamstress, attendant on the young ladies, keeper of the stores; only "Nurse" was still her name. She had lived longer with them than any other servant, and to her their manner was far less haughty than to the other domestics. She occasionally came into the drawing-room to look for things belonging to their father or mother, so it did not excite any surprise when she advanced into the room. They went on arranging their various articles of employment.

She wanted them to look up. She wanted them to read something in her face — her face so full of woe, of horror. But they went on without taking any notice. She coughed; not a natural cough; but one of those coughs which ask so plainly for remark.

"Dear nurse, what is the matter?" asked Amy. "Are not you well?"

"Is mamma ill?" asked Sophy, quickly.

"Speak, speak, nurse!" said they all, as they saw her efforts to articulate, choked by the convulsive rising in her throat. They clustered round her with eager faces, catching a glimpse of some terrible truth to be revealed.

"My dear young ladies! my dear girls," she gasped out at length, and then she burst into tears.

"Oh! do tell us what it is, nurse," said one. "Any thing is better than this. Speak!"

"My children! I don't know how to break it to you. My dears, poor Mr. Harry is brought home —"

"Brought home — *brought* home — how?" Instinctively they sank their voices to a whisper; but a fearful whisper it was. In the same low tone, as if afraid lest the walls, the furniture, the inanimate things which told of preparation for life and comfort, should hear, she answered,

"Dead!"

Amy clutched her nurse's arm, and fixed her eyes on her as if to know if such a tale could be true; and when she read its confirmation in those sad, mournful, unflinching eyes, she sank, without word or sound, down in a faint upon the floor. One sister sat down on an ottoman, and covered her face, to try and realise it. That was Sophy. Helen threw herself on the sofa, and burying her head in the pillows, tried to stifle the screams and moans which shook her frame.

The nurse stood silent. She had not told *all*.

"Tell me," said Sophy, looking up, and speaking in a hoarse voice, which told of the inward pain, "tell me, nurse! Is he *dead*, did you say? Have you sent for a doctor? Oh! send for one, send for one," continued she, her voice rising to shrillness, and starting to her feet. Helen lifted herself up, and looked, with breathless waiting, towards nurse.

"My dears, he is dead! But I have sent for a doctor. I have done all I could."

"When did he — when did they bring him home?" asked Sophy.

"Perhaps ten minutes ago. Before you rang for Parker."

"How did he die? Where did they find him? He looked so well. He always seemed so strong. Oh! are you sure he is dead?"

She went towards the door. Nurse laid her hand on her arm

"Miss Sophy, I have not told you all. Can you bear to hear it? Remember, master is in the next room, and he knows nothing yet. Come you must help me to tell him. Now, be quiet, dear! It was no common death he died!" She looked in her face as if trying to convey her meaning by her eyes.

Sophy's lips moved, but nurse could hear no sound.

"He has been shot as he was coming home along Turner Street, to-night."

Sophy went on with the motion of her lips, twitching them almost convulsively.

"My dear, you must rouse yourself, and remember your father and mother have yet to be told. Speak! Miss Sophy."

But she could not; her whole face worked involuntarily. The nurse left the room, and almost immediately brought back some sal-volatile and water. Sophy drank it eagerly, and gave one or two deep gasps. Then she spoke in a calm, unnatural voice.

"What do you want me to do, nurse? Go to Helen, and poor Amy. See, they want help."

"Poor creatures! we must let them alone for a bit. You must go to master; that's what I want you to do, Miss Sophy. You must break it to him, poor old gentleman. Come, he's asleep in the dining-room, and the men are waiting to speak to him."

Sophy went mechanically to the dining-room door.

"Oh! I cannot go in. I cannot tell him. What must I say?"

"I'll come with you, Miss Sophy. Break it to him by degrees."

"I can't nurse. My head throbs so, I shall be sure to say the wrong thing."

However, she opened the door. There sat her father, the shaded light of the candle-lamp falling upon, and softening his marked features, while his snowy hair contrasted well with the deep crimson morocco of the chair. The newspaper he had been reading had dropped on the crapet by his side. He breathed regularly and deeply.

At that instant the words of Mrs. Hemans' song came full in Sophy's mind: —

"Ye know not what ye do,
That call the slumberer back
From the realms unseen by you,
To life's dim weary track."

But this life 's track would be to the bereaved father something more than dim and weary, hereafter.

"Papa," said she, softly. He did not stir.

"Papa!" she exclaimed, somewhat louder.

He started up, half awake.

"Tea is ready, is it?" and he yawned.

"No! papa, but something very dreadful — very sad, has happened!"

He was gaping so loud that he did not catch the words she uttered, and did not see the expression of her face.

"Master Henry has not come back," said nurse. Her voice heard inunusual speech to him, arrested his attention, and rubbing his eyes, he looked at the servant.

"Harry! oh no! he had to attend a meeting of the masters about these cursed turn-outs. I don't expect him yet. What are you looking at me so strangely for, Sophy?"

"Oh, papa, Harry is come back," said she, bursting into tears.

"What do you mean?" said he, startled into an impatient consciousness that something was wrong. "One of you says he is not come home, and the other says he is. Now that 's nonsense! Tell me at once what 's the matter. Did he go on horseback to town! Is he thrown? Speak, child, can't you?"

"No! he 's not been thrown, papa," said Sophy, sadly.

"But he 's badly hurt," put in the nurse, desirous to be drawing his anxiety to a point.

"Hurt? Where? How? Have you sent for a doctor?" said he, hastily rising, as if to leave the room.

"Yes, papa, we've sent for a doctor — but I 'm afraid — I believe it 's of no use."

He looked at her for a moment, and in her face he read the truth. His son, his only son was dead.

He sank back in his chair, and hid his face in his hands, and bowed his head upon the table. The strong mahogany dining-table, shook and rattled under his agony.

Sophy went and put her arms round his bowed neck.

"Go! you are not Harry," said he; but the action roused him.

"Where is he? where is the — " said he, with his strong face set into the lines of anguish, by two minutes of such intense woe.

"In the servants' hall," said nurse. "Two policemen and another man brought him home. They would be glad to speak to you when you are able, Sir."

"I am now able," replied he. At first when he stood up he tottered. But steadying himself, he walked, as firmly as a soldier on drill, to the door. Then he turned back and poured out a glass of wine from the decanter which yet remained on the table. His eye caught the wine-glass which Harry had used but two or three hours before. He sighed a long quivering sigh. And then mastering himself again, he left the room.

"You had better go back to your sisters, Miss Sophy," said nurse.

Miss Carsons went. She could not face death yet.

The nurse followed Mr. Carsons to the servants' hall. There on their dinner-table lay the poor dead body. The men who had brought it were sitting near the fire, while several of the servants stood round the table, gazing at the remains.

The remains!

One or two were crying; one or two were whispering; awed into a strange stillness of voice and action by the presence of the dead. When Mr. Carsons came in they all drew back and looked at him with the reverence due to sorrow.

He went forward and gazed long and fondly on the calm, dead face; then he bent down and kissed the lips yet crimson with life. The policeman had advanced, and stood ready to be questioned. But at first the old man's mind could only take in the idea of death; slowly, slowly came the conception of violence, of murder. "How did he die?" he groaned forth.

The policemen looked at each other. Then one began, and stated that having heard the report of a gun in Turner Street, he had turned down that way (a lonely unfrequented way Mr. Carsons knew, but a short cut to his garden door, of which Harry had a key); that as he (the policeman) came nearer he had heard footsteps as of a man running away; but the evening was so dark (the moon not having yet risen) that he could see no one twenty yards off. That he had even been startled when close to the body, by seeing it lying across the path at his feet. That he had sprung his rattle; and when another policeman came up, by the light of the lantern they had discovered who it was that had been killed. That they believed him to be dead when they first took him up, as he had never moved, spoken, or breathed. That intelligence of the murder had been sent to the superintendent who would probably soon be here. That two or three policemen were still about the place where the murder was committed, seeking out for some trace of the murderer. Having said this, they stopped speaking.

Mr. Carsons had listened attentively, never taking his eyes off the dead body. When they had ended he said,

"Where was he shot?"

They lifted up some of the thick chesnut curls and showed a blue spot (you could hardly call it a hole, the flesh had closed so much over it) in the left temple. A deadly aim! And yet it was so dark a night!

"He must have been close upon him," said one policeman.

"And have had him between him and the sky," added the other.

There was a little commotion at the door of the room, and there stood poor Mrs. Carsons, the mother.

She had heard unusual noises in the house, and had sent down her maid (much more a companion to her than her highly educated daughters) to discover what was going on. But the maid either forgot, or dreaded, to return; and with nervous impatience Mrs. Carsons came down herself, and had traced the hum and buzz of voices to the servants' hall.

Mr. Carsons turned round. But he could not leave the dead for any one living.

"Take her away, nurse. It is no sight for her. Tell Miss Sophy to go to her mother." His eyes were again fixed on the dead face of his son.

Presently Mrs. Carsons' hysterical cries were heard all over the house. Her husband shuddered at the outward expression of the agony which was rending his heart.

Then the police superintendent came, and after him the

doctor. The latter went through all the forms of ascertaining death, without uttering a word, and when at the conclusion of the operation of opening a vein, from which no blood flowed, he shook his head, all present understood the confirmation of their previous belief. The superintendent asked to speak to Mr. Carsons in private.

"It was just what I was going to request of you," answered he, so he led the way into the dining-room, with the wine-glass still on the table.

The door was carefully shut, and both sat down, each apparently waiting for the other to begin.

At last Mr. Carsons spoke.

"You probably have heard that I am a rich man."

The superintendent bowed in assent.

"Well, Sir, half — nay, if necessary, the whole of my fortune I will give to have the murderer brought to the gallows."

"Every exertion, you may be sure, Sir, shall be used on our part; but probably offering a handsome reward might accelerate the discovery of the murderer. But what I wanted particularly to tell you, Sir, is that one of my men has already got some clue, and that another (who accompanied me here) has within this quarter of an hour found a gun in the field which the murderer crossed, and which he probably threw away when pursued, as encumbering his flight. I have not the smallest doubt of discovering the murderer."

"What do you call a handsome reward?" said Mr. Carsons

"Well, Sir, three, or five hundred pounds is a munificent reward: more than will probably be required as a temptation to any accomplice."

"Make it a thousand," said Mr. Carsons, decisively. "It 's the doing of those damned turn-outs."

"I imagine not," said the superintendent. "Some days ago the man I was naming to you before, repeated to the inspector when he came on his beat, that he had to separate your son from a young man, who by his dress he believed to be employed in a foundry; that the man had thrown Mr. Carsons down, and seemed inclined to proceed to more violence, when the policeman came up and interfered. Indeed, my man wished to give him in charge for an assault, but Mr. Carsons would not allow that to be done."

"Just like him! — noble fellow!" murmured the father.

"But after your son had left, the man made use of some pretty strong threats. And it 's rather a curious coincidence that this scuffle took place in the very same spot where the murder was committed; in Turner Street."

There was some one knocking at the door of the room. It was Sophy, who beckoned her father out, and then asked him, in an awe-struck whisper, to come up-stairs and speak to her mother.

"She will not leave Harry, and talks so strangely. Indeed — indeed — papa, I think she has lost her senses."

And the poor girl sobbed bitterly.

"Where is she?" asked Mr. Carsons.

"In his room."

They went up-stairs rapidly, and silently. It was a large comfortable bedroom; too large to be well lighted by the flaring, flickering kitchen-candle which had been hastily snatched up, and now stood on the dressing-table.

On the bed, surrounded by its heavy, pall-like green curtains, lay the dead son. They had carried him up, and laid him down, as tenderly as though they feared to waken him; and, indeed, it looked more like sleep than death, so very calm and full of repose was the face. You saw, too, the chiselled beauty of the features much more perfectly than when the brilliant colouring of life had distracted your attention. There was a peace about him, which told that death had come too instantaneously to give any previous pain.

In a chair, at the head of the bed, sat the mother, — smiling. She held one of the hands (rapidly stiffening, even in her warm grasp), and gently stroked the back of it, with the endearing caress she had used to all her children when young.

"I am glad you are come," said she, looking up at her husband, and still smiling. "Harry is so full of fun, he always has something new to amuse us with; and now he pretends he is asleep, and that we can't waken him. Look! he is smiling now, he hears I have found him out. Look!"

And, in truth, the lips, in the rest of death, did look as though they wore a smile, and the waving light of the unsnuffed candle almost made them seem to move.

"Look, Amy," said she to her youngest child, who knelt at her feet, trying to soothe her, by kissing her garments.

"Oh, he was always a rogue! You remember, don't you, love? how full of play he was as a baby; hiding his face under my arm, when you wanted to play with him. Always a rogue, Harry!"

"We must get her away, Sir," said nurse; "you know there is much to be done, before —"

"I understand, nurse," said the father, hastily interrupting her in dread of the distinct words which would tell of the changes of mortality.

"Come love," said he to his wife. "I want you to come with me. I want to speak to you down stairs."

"I 'm coming," said she, rising; "perhaps, after all, nurse, he 's really tired, and would be glad to sleep. Don't let him get cold, though, — he feels rather chilly," continued she, after she had bent down, and kissed the pale lips.

Her husband put his arm round her waist, and they left the room. Then the three sisters burst into unrestrained wailings. They were startled into the reality of life and death. And yet in the midst of shricks and moans, of shivering and chattering of teeth, Sophy's eye caught the calm beauty of the dead; so calm amidst such violence, and she hushed her emotion.

"Come," said she to her sisters, "nurse wants us to go; and besides, we ought to be with mamma. Papa told the man he was talking to, when I went for him, to wait, and she must not be left."

Meanwhile, the superintendent had taken a candle, and was examinings the engravings that hnng round the dining-room. It was so common to him to be acquainted with crime, that he was far from feeling all his interest absorbed in the present case of violence, although he could not help having much anxiety to detect the murderer. He was busy looking at the only oil-painting in the room (a youth of eighteen or so, in a fancy dress), and conjecturing its identity with the young man so mysteriously dead; when the door opened, and Mr. Carsons returned. Stern as he had looked before leaving the room, he looked far sterner now. His face was hardened into deep-purposed wrath.

"I beg your pardon, Sir, for leaving you." The superintendent bowed. They sat down, and spoke long together. One by one the policemen were called in, and questioned.

All through the night there was bustle and commotion in the house. Nobody thought of going to bed. It seemed strange to Sophy to hear nurse summoned from her mother's side to supper, in the middle of the night, and still stranger that she could go. The necessity of eating and drinking seemed out of place in the house of death.

When night was passing into morning, the dining-room door opened, and two persons' steps were heard along the hall. The superintendent was leaving at last. Mr. Carsons stood on the front door-step, feeling the refreshment of the cooler morning air, and seeing the starlight fade away into dawn.

"You will not forget," said he. "I trust to you." The policeman bowed.

"Spare no money. The only purpose for which I now value wealth is to have the murderer arrested, and brought to justice. My hope in life now is to see him sentenced to death. Offer any rewards. Name a thousand pounds in the placards. Come to me at any hour, night or day, if that be required. All I ask of you, is, to get the murderer hanged. Next week, if possible — to-day is Friday. Surely with the clues you already possess, you can muster up evidence sufficient to have him tried next week."

"He may easily request an adjournment of his trial, on the ground of the shortness of the notice," said the superintendent.

"Oppose it, if possible. I will see that the first lawyers are employed. I shall know no rest while he lives."

"Every thing shall be done, Sir."

"You will arrange with the coroner. Ten o'clock, if convenient."

The superintendent took leave.

Mr. Carsons stood on the step, dreading to shut out the light and air, and return into the haunted, gloomy house.

"My son! my son!" he said, at last. "But you shall be avenged, my poor murdered boy."

Ay! to aveege his wrongs the murderer had singled out his victim, and with one fell action had taken away the life that God had given. To avenge his child's death, the old man lived on; with the single purpose in his heart of vengeance on the murderer. True, his vengeance was sanctioned by law, but was it the less revenge?

Are ye worshippers of Christ? or of Alecto?

Oh! Orestes, you would have made a very tolerable Christian of the nineteenth century!

CHAPTER XIX.

"Deeds to be hid which were not hid,
Which, all confused, I could not know,
Whether I suffered or I did,
For all seemed guilt, remorse, or woe." COLERIDGE.

I LEFT Mary, on that same Thursday night which left its burden of woe at Mr. Carsons' threshold, haunted with depressing thoughts. All through the night she tossed restlessly about; trying to get quit of the ideas that harrassed her, and longing for the light when she could rise, and find some employment. But just as dawn began to appear, she became more quiet, and fell into a sound heavy sleep, which lasted till she was sure it was late in the morning by the full light that shone in.

She dressed hastily, and heard the neighbouring church clock strike eight. It was far too late to do as she had planned (after inquiring how Alice was, to return and tell Margaret), and she accordingly went in to inform the latter of her change of purpose, and the cause of it; but on entering the house she found Job sitting alone, looking sad enough. She told him what she came for.

"Margaret, wench! why she 's been gone to Wilson's these two hours. Ay! sure, you did say last night you would go; but she could na rest in her bed, so was off betimes this morning."

Mary could do nothing but feel guilty of her long morning nap, and hasten to follow Margaret's steps; for late as it was, she felt she could not settle well to her work, unless she learnt how kind good Alice Wilson was going on.

So, eating her crust-of-bread breakfast, she passed rapidly along the streets. She remembered afterwards the little groups of people she had seen, eagerly hearing, and imparting news; but at the time her only care was to hasten on her way, in dread of a reprimand from Miss Simmonds.

She went into the house at Jane Wilson's, her heart at the instant giving a strange knock, and sending the rosy flush into her face, at the thought that Jem might possibly be inside the door. But I do assure you, she had not thought of it before. Impatient and loving as she was, her solicitude about Alice on that hurried morning had not been mingled with any thought of him.

Her heart need not have leaped, her colour need not have rushed so painfully to her cheeks, for he was not there. There was the round table, with a cup and saucer, which had evidently been used, and there was Jane Wilson sitting on the other side, crying quietly, while she ate her breakfast with a sort of unconscious appetite. And there was Mrs. Davenport washing away at a night-cap or so, which, by their simple, old-world make, Mary knew at a glance were Alice's. But nothing — no one else.

Alice was much the same, or rather better of the two, they told her; at any rate she could speak, though it was sad rambling talk. Would Mary like to see her?

Of course she would. Many are interested by seeing their friends under the new aspect of illness: and among the poor there is no wholesome fear of injury or excitement to restrain this wish.

So Mary went up-stairs, accompanied by Mrs. Davenport, wringing the suds off her hands, and speaking in a loud whisper far more audible than her usual voice.

"I mun be hastening home, but I'll come again to-night, time enough to iron her cap; 't would be a sin and a shame if we let her go dirty now she 's ill, when she 's been so rare and clean all her life-long. But she 's sadly forsaken, poor thing! She 'll not know you, Mary, she knows none of us."

The room up-stairs held two beds, one superior in the grandeur of four posts and checked curtains to the other, which had been occupied by the twins in their brief life-time. The smaller had been Alice's bed since she had lived there; but with the natural reverence to one "stricken of God and afflicted," she had been installed, since her paralytic stroke the evening before, in the larger and grander bed; while Jane Wilson had taken her short broken rest on the little pallet.

Margaret came forwards to meet her friend, whom she half expected, and whose step she knew. Mrs. Davenport returned to her washing.

The two girls did not speak, the presence of Alice awed them into silence. There she lay with the rosy colour, absent from her face since the days of childhood, flushed once more into it by her sickness nigh unto death. She lay on the affected side, and with her other arm she was constantly sawing the air, not exactly in a restless manner, but in a monotonous, incessant way, very trying to a watcher. She was talking away, too, almost as constantly, in a low, indistinct tone. But her face, her profiled countenance, looked calm and smiling, even interested by the ideas that were passing through her clouded mind.

"Listen!" said Margaret, as she storped her head down to catch the muttered words more distinctly.

"What will mother say? The bees are turning homeward for th' last time, and we've a terrible long bit to go yet. See! here's a linnet's nest in this gorse bush. Th' hen bird is on it. Look at her bright eyes, she won't stir. Ay! we mun hurry home. Won't mother be pleased with the bonny lot of heather we've got. Make haste, Sally, may be we shall have cockles for supper. I saw th' cockle-man's donkey turn up our way fra' Arnside."

Margaret touched Mary's hand, and the pressure in return told her that they understood each other; that they knew how in this illness to the old, world-weary woman, God had sent her a veiled blessing: she was once more in the scenes of her childhood, unchanged and bright as in those long departed days; once more with the sister of her youth, the playmate of fifty years ago, who had for nearly as many years slept in a grassy grave in the little church-yard beyond Burton.

Alice's face changed; she looked sorrowful, almost penitent.

"Oh, Sally! I wish we'd told her. She thinks we were in church all morning, and we've gone on deceiving her. If we'd told her at first how it was — how sweet th' hawthorn smelt through the open church-door, and how we were on th' last bench in the aisle, and how it were the first butterfly we'd seen this spring, and how it flew into th' very church itself; oh! mother is so gentle, I wish we'd told her. I 'll go to her next time she comes in sight, and say, 'Mother, we were naughty last sabbath.'"

She stopped, and a few tears came stealing down the old withered cheek, at the thought of the temptation and deceit of her childhood. Surely, many sins could not have darkened that innocent child-like spirit since. Mary found a red-spotted pocket-handkerchief, and put it into the hand, which sought about for something to wipe away the trickling tears. She took it, with a gentle murmur.

"Thank you, mother."

Mary pulled Margaret away from the bed.

"Don't you think she 's happy, Margaret?"

"Ay! that I do, bless her. She feels no pain, and knows nought of her present state. Oh! that I could see, Mary! I try and be patient with her afore me, but I 'd give aught I have to see her, and see what she wants. I am so useless! I mean to stay here as long as Jane Wilson is alone; and I would fain be here all to-night, but—"

"I 'll come," said Mary, decidedly.

"Mrs. Davenport said she 'd come again, but she 's hard-worked all day—"

"I 'll come," repeated Mary.

"Do!" said Margaret, "and I 'll be here till you come. May be, Jem and you could take th' night between you, and Jane Wilson might get a bit of sound sleep in his bed; for she were up and down the better part of last night, and just when she were in a sound sleep this morning, between two and three, Jem came home, and th' sound o' his voice roused her in a minute."

"Where had he been till that time o' night?" asked Mary.

"Nay! it were none of my business; and, indeed, I never saw him till he came in here to see Alice. He were in again this morning, and seemed sadly downcast. But you 'll, may be, manage to comfort him to-night, Mary," said Margaret, smiling, while a ray of hope glimmered in Mary's heart, and she almost felt glad, for an instant, of the occasion which would at last bring them together. Oh! happy night! when would it come? Many hours had yet to pass.

Then she saw Alice, and repented, with a bitter self-reproach. But she could not help having gladness in the depths of her heart, blame herself as she would. So she tried not to think, as she hurried along to Miss Simmonds', with a dancing step of lightness.

She was late — that she knew she should be. Miss Simmonds was vexed and cross. That also she had anticipated, and had intended to smooth her raven down by extraordinary diligence and attention. But there was something about the girls she did not understand — had not anticipated. They stopped talking when she came in; or rather, I should say, stopped listening, for Sally Leadbitter was the talker to whom they were hearkening with deepest attention. At first they eyed Mary, as if she had acquired some new interest to them, since the day before. Then they began to whisper; and, absorbed as Mary had been in her own thoughts, she could not help becoming aware that it was of her they spoke.

At last Sally Leadbitter asked Mary if she had heard the news?

"No! What news?" answered she.

The girls looked at each other with gloomy mystery. Sally went on.

"Have you not heard that young Mr. Carsons was murdered last night?"

Mary's lips could not utter a negative, but no one who looked at her pale and terror-stricken face could have doubted that she had not heard before of the fearful occurrence.

Oh, it is terrible, that sudden information, that one you have known has met with a bloody death! You seem to shrink from the world where such deeds can be committed, and to grow sick with the idea of the violent and wicked men of earth. Much as Mary had learned to dread him lately, now he was dead (and dead in such a manner), her feeling was that of oppressive sorrow for him.

The room went round and round, and she felt as though she should faint; but Miss Simmonds came in, bringing a waft of fresher air as she opened the door, to refresh the body, and the certainty of a scolding for inattention to brace the sinking mind. She, too, was full of the morning's news.

"Have you heard any more of this horrid affair, Miss Barton?" asked she, as she settled to her work.

Mary tried to speak; at first she could not, and when she succeeded in uttering a sentence, it seemed as though it were not her own voice that spoke.

"No, Ma'am, I never heard of it till this minute."

"Dear! that 's strange, for every one is up about it. I hope the murderer will be found out, that I do. Such a handsome young man to be killed as he was. I hope the wretch that did it may be hanged as high as Haman."

One of the girls reminded them that the assizes came on next week.

"Ay," replied Miss Simmonds, "and the milk-man told me they will catch the wretch, and have him tried and hung in less than a week. Serve him right, whoever he is. Such a handsome young man as he was."

Then each began to communicate to Miss Simmonds the various reports they had heard.

Suddenly she burst out—

"Miss Barton! as I live, dropping tears on that new silk gown of Mrs. Hawkes'! Don't you know they will stain, and make it shabby for ever? Crying like a baby, because a handsome young man meets with an untimely end. For shame of yourself. Miss. Mind your character and your work if you please. Or, if you must cry" (seeing her scolding rather increased the flow of Mary's tears, than otherwise), "take this print to cry over. That won't be marked like this beautiful silk," rubbing it, as if she loved it, with a clean pocket-handkerchief, in order to soften the edges of the hard round drops.

Mary took the print, and naturally enough, having had leave given her to cry over it, rather checked the inclination to weep.

Everybody was full of the one subject. The girl sent out to match silk, came back with the account gathered at the shop, of the coroner's inquest then sitting; the ladies, who called to speak about gowns first began about the murder, and mingled details of that, with directions for their dresses. Mary felt as though the haunting horror were a nightmare, a fearful dream, from which awakening would relieve her. The picture of the murdered body, far more ghastly than the reality, seemed to swim in the air before her eyes. Sally Leadbitter looked and spoke of her, almost accusingly, and made no secret now of Mary's conduct, more blameable to her fellow workwomen for its latter changeableness, than for its former giddy flirting.

"Poor young gentleman," said one, as Sally recounted Mary's last interview with Mr. Carsons.

"What a shame!" exclaimed another, looking indignantly at Mary.

"That 's what I call regular jilting," said a third, "And he lying cold and bloody in his coffin now!"

Mary was more thankful than she could express, when Miss Simmonds returned, to put a stop to Sally's communications, and to check the remarks of the girls.

She longed for the peace of Alice's sick room. No more thinking with infinite delight of her anticipated meeting with Jem, she felt too much shocked for that now; but longing for peace and kindness, for the images of rest and beauty, and sinless times long ago, which the poor old woman's rambling presented, she wished to be as near death as Alice; and to have struggled through this world, whose sufferings she had early learnt, and whose crimes now seemed pressing close upon her. Old texts from the Bible that her mother used to read (or rather spell out) aloud in the days of childhood, came up to her memory. "Where the wicked cease from troubling, and the weary are at rest." "The tears shall be wiped away from all eyes," &c. And it was to that world Alice was hastening! Oh! that she were Alice.

I must return to the Wilsons' house, which was far from being the abode of peace that Mary was picturing it to herself. You remember the reward Mr. Carsons offered for the apprehension of the murderer of his son? It was in itself a temptation, and to aid its efficacy came the natural sympathy for the aged parents mourning for their child, for the young man cut off in the flower of his days; and besides this, there is always a pleasure in unravelling a mystery, in catching at the gossamer clue which will guide to certainty. This feeling, I am sure, gives much impetus to the police. Their senses are ever and always on the qui-vive, and they enjoy the collecting and collating evidence, and the life of adventure they experience; a continual unwinding of Jack Sheppard romances always interesting to the vulgar and uneducated mind, to which the outward signs and tokens of crime are ever exciting.

There was no lack of clue or evidence at the coroner's inquest that morning. The shot, the finding of the body, the subsequent discovery of the gun, were rapidly deposed to; and then the policeman who had interrupted the quarrel between Jem Wilson and the murdered young man was brought forward, and gave his evidence, clear, simple, and straightforward. The coroner had no hesitation, the jury had none, but the verdict was cautiously worded. "Wilful murder against some person unknown."

This very cautiousness, when he deemed the thing so sure as to require no caution, irritated Mr. Carsons. It did not soothe him that the superintendent called the verdict a mere form,—exhibited a warrant empowering him to seize the body of Jem Wilson committed on suspicion, — declared his intention of employing a well-known officer in the Detective Service to ascertain the ownership of the gun, and collect other evidence especially as regarded the young woman, about whom the policeman deposed that the quarrel had taken place; Mr. Carsons was still excited and irritable; restless in body and mind. He made every preparation for the accusation of Jem the following morning before the magistrates: he engaged attorneys skilled in criminal practice to watch the case and prepare briefs; he wrote to celebrated barristers coming the Northern circuit, to bespeak their services. A speedy conviction, a speedy execution, seemed to be the only things that would satisfy his craving thirst for blood. He would have fain been policeman, magistrate, accusing speaker, all; but most of all, the judge, rising with full sentence of death on his lips.

That afternoon, as Jane Wilson had begun to feel the effect of a night's disturbed rest, evinced in frequent droppings off to sleep while she sat by her sister-in-law's bed-side, lulled by the incessant crooning of the invalid's feeble voice, she was startled by a man speaking in the house-place below, who, wearied o knocking at the door, without obtaining any answer, had entered and was calling lustily for

"Missis! Missis!"

When Mrs. Wilson caught a glimpse of the intruder through thè stair-rails, she at once saw he was a stranger, a working-man, it might be a fellow-labourer with her son, for his dress was grimy enough for the supposition. He held a gun in his hand.

"May I make bold to ask if this gun belongs to your son?"

She first looked at the man, and then, weary and half asleep, not seeing any reason for refusing to answer the inquiry, she moved forward to examine it, talking while she looked for certain old-fashioned ornaments on the stock. "It looks like his; ay, it is his, sure enough. I could speak to it anywhere by these marks. You see it were his grandfather's as were gamekeeper to some one up in th' north; and they don't make guns so smart now-a-days. But, how comed you by it? He sets great store on it. Is he bound for th' shooting gallery? He is not, for sure, now his aunt is so ill, and me left all alone;" and the immediate cause for her anxiety being thus recalled to her mind, she entered on a long story of Alice's illness, interspersed with recollections of her husband's and her children's deaths.

The disguised policeman listened for a minute or two, to glean any further information he could; and then, saying he was in a hurry, he turned to go away. She followed him to the door, still telling him her troubles, and was never struck, until it was too late to ask the reason, with the unaccountableness o his conduct, in carrying the gun away with him. Then, as she heavily climbed the stairs, she put away the wonder and the thought about his conduct, by determining to believe he was some workman with whom her son had made some arrangement about shooting at the gallery; or mending the old weapon; or something or other. She had enough to fret her, without moidering herself about old guns. Jem had given it to him to bring to her; so it was safe enough; or, if it was not, why she should be glad never to set eyes on it again, for she could not abide fire-arms, they were so apt to shoot people.

So, comforting herself for the want of thought in not making further inquiry, she fell off into another doze, feverish, dream-haunted, and unrefreshing.

Meanwhile, the policeman walked off with his prize, with an odd mixture of feelings; a little contempt, a little disappointment, and a good deal of pity. The contempt and the disappointment were caused by the widow's easy admission of the gun being her son's property, and her manner of identifying it by the ornaments. He liked an attempt to baffle him; he was accustomed to it, it gave some exercise to his wits and his shrewdness. There would be no fun in fox-hunting, if Reynard yielded himself up without any effort to escape. Then, again, his mother's milk was yet in him, policeman, officer of the Detective Service though he was; and he felt sorry for the old woman, whose "softness" had given such material assistance in identifying her son as the murderer. However, he conveyed the gun, and the intelligence he had gained, to the superintendent; and the result was, that, in a short time afterwards, three policemen went to the works at which Jem was foreman, and announced their errand to the astonished overseer, who directed them to the part of the foundry where Jem was then superintending a casting.

Dark, black were the walls, the ground, the faces around them, as they crossed the yard. But, in the furnace-house a deep and lurid red glared over all; the furnace roared with mighty flame. The men, like demons, in their fire-and-soot colouring, stood swart around, awaiting the moment when the tons of solid iron should have melted down into fiery liquid, fit to be poured, with still, heavy sound, into the delicate moulding of fine black sand, prepared to receive it. The heat was intense, and the red glare grew every instant more fierce; the policemen stood awed with the novel sight. Then, black figures, holding strange-shaped bucket shovels, came athwart the deep-red furnace light, and clear and brilliant flowed forth the iron into the appropriate mould. The buzz of voices rose again; there was time to speak, and gasp, and wipe the brows; and then, one by one, the men dispersed to some other branch of their employment.

No. B. 72, pointed out Jem as the man he had seen engaged

in a scuffle with Mr. Carsons, and then the other two stepped forward and arrested him, stating of what he was accused, and the grounds of the accusation. He offered no resistance, though he seemed surprised; but calling a fellow-workman to him, he briefly requested him to tell his mother he had got into trouble, and could not return home at present. He did not wish her to hear more at first.

So Mrs. Wilson's sleep was next interrupted in almost an exactly similar way to the last, like a recurring nightmare.

"Missis! Missis!" some one called out from below.

Again it was a workman, but this time a blacker-looking one than before.

"What don ye want?" said she, peevishly.

"Only, nothing but—" stammered the man, a kind-hearted matter-of-fact person, with no invention, but a great deal of sympathy.

"Well! speak out, can't ye, and ha' done with it?"

"Jem's in trouble," said he, repeating Jem's very words, as he could think of no others.

"Trouble?" said the mother, in a high-pitched voice of distress. "Trouble! God help me, trouble will never end, I think. What d'ye mean by trouble? Speak out man, can't ye? Is he ill? My boy! tell me, is he ill?" in a hurried voice of terror.

"Na, na, that 's not it. He 's well enough. All he bade me say was, 'tell mother I 'm in trouble, and can't come home to-night.'"

"Not come home to-night! And what am I to do with Alice? I can't go on, wearing my life out wi' watching. He might come and help me."

"I tell you he can't," said the man.

"Can't; and he is well, you say. Stuff! It 's just that he 's getten like other young men, and wants to go a larking. But I 'll give it him when he comes back."

The man turned to go; he durst not trust himself to speak in Jem's justification. But she would not let him off.

She stood between him and the door, as she said,

"Yo shall not go, till yo 've told me what he 's after. I can see plain enough you know, and I'll know too, before I've done."

"You 'll know soon enough, Missis!"

"I 'll know now, I tell ye. What 's up that he can't come home and help me nurse? Me, as never got a wink o'sleep last night wi' watching."

"Well, if you will have it out," said the poor badgered man, "the police have got hold on him."

"On my Jem!" said the enraged mother. "You 're a downright liar, and that 's what you are. My Jem, as never did harm to any one in his life. You 're a liar, that 's what you are."

"He 's done harm enough now," said the man, angry in his turn, "for there 's good evidence he murdered young Carsons, as was shot last night."

She staggered forward to strike the man for telling the terrible truth; but the weakness of old age, of motherly agony, overcame her, and she sank down on a chair, and covered her face. He could not leave her.

When next she spoke, it was in an imploring, feeble, childlike voice.

"Oh, Master, say you 're only joking. I ax your pardon if I have vexed ye, but please say you 're only joking. You don't know what Jem is to me."

She looked humbly, anxiously up at him.

"I wish I were only joking, Missis, but it 's true as I say. They 've taken him up on charge of murder. It were his gun as were found near th' place; and one o' the police heard him quarrelling with Mr. Carsons a few days back, about a girl."

"About a girl!" broke in the mother, once more indignant, though too feeble to show it as before. "My Jem was as steady as —" she hesitated for a comparison wherewith to finish, and then repeated, "as steady as Lucifer, and he were an angel, you know. My Jem was not one to quarrel about a girl."

"Ay, but it was that though. They 'd got her name quite pat. The man had heard all they said. Mary Barton was her name, whoever she may be."

"Mary Barton! the dirty hussey! to bring my Jem into trouble of this kind. I 'll give it her well when I see her: that I will. Oh! my poor Jem!" rocking herself to and fro. "And what about the gun? What did ye say about that?"

"His gun were found on th' spot where the murder were done."

"That 's a lie for one, then. A man has got the gun now, safe and sound; I saw it not an hour ago."

The man shook his head.

"Yes, he has indeed. A friend o' Jem's, as he'd lent it to."

"Did you know the chap?" asked the man, who was really anxious for Jem's exculpation, and caught a gleam of hope from her last speech.

"No! I can't say as I did. But he were put on as a workman."

"It 's may be only one of them policemen, disguised."

"Nay; they 'd never go for to do that, and trick me into telling on my own son. It would be like seething a kid in its mother's milk; and that th' Bible forbids."

"I don't know," replied the man.

Soon afterwards he went away, feeling unable to comfort, yet distressed at the sight of sorrow; she would fain have detained him, but go he would. And she was alone.

She never for an instant believed Jem guilty; she would have doubted if the sun were fire, first: but sorrow, desolation, and at times, anger, took possession of her mind. She told the unconscious Alice, hoping to rouse her to sympathy; and then was disappointed, because, still smiling and calm, she murmured of her mother, and the happy days of infancy.

CHAPTER XX.

"I saw where stark and cold he lay,
Beneath the gallows-tree,
And every one did point and say,
''T was there he died for thee!'
*   *   *   *
"Oh! weeping heart! Oh! bleeding heart!
What boots thy pity now?
Bid from his eyes that shade depart,
That death-damp from his brow!"

'The Birtle Tragedy.'

So there was no more peace in the house of sickness except to Alice, the dying Alice.

But Mary knew nothing of the afternoon's occurrences; and gladly did she breathe in the fresh air, as she left Miss Simmonds' house, to hasten to the Wilsons'. The very change from the in-door to the out-door atmosphere, seemed to alter the current of her thoughts. She thought less of the dreadful subject which had so haunted her all day; she cared less for the upbraiding speeches of her fellow-workwomen; the old association of comfort and sympathy received from Alice gave her the idea that, even now, her bodily presence would soothe and compose those who were in trouble, changed, unconscious, and absent though her spirit might be.

Then, again, she reproached herself a little for the feeling of pleasure she experienced, in thinking that he whom she dreaded could never more beset her path; in the security with which she could pass each street corner — each shop, where he used to lie in ambush. Oh! beating heart! was there no other little thought of joy lurking within, to gladden the very air without? Was she not going to meet, to see, to hear Jem; and could they fail at last to understand each other's loving hearts!

She softly lifted the latch, with the privilege of friendship. *He* was not there, but his mother was standing by the fire, stirring some little mess or other. Never mind! he would come soon: and with an unmixed desire to do her graceful duty to all belonging to him, she stepped lightly forwards, unheard by the old lady, who was partly occupied by the simmering, bubbling sound of her bit of cookery; but more with her own sad thoughts, and wailing, half-uttered murmurings.

Mary took off bonnet and shawl with speed, and advancing, made Mrs. Wilson conscious of her presence, by saying,

"Let me do that for you. I 'm sure you mun be tired."

Mrs. Wilson slowly turned round, and her eyes gleamed like those of a pent-up wild beast, as she recognised her visitor.

"And is it thee that dares set foot in this house, after what has come to pass? Is it not enough to have robbed me of my boy with thy arts and thy profligacy, but thou must come here to crow over me — me — his mother? Dost thou know where he is, thou bad hussey, with thy great blue eyes and yellow hair, to lead men on to ruin? Out upon thee with thy angel's face, thou whited sepulchre. Dost thou know where Jem is, all through thee?"

"No!" quivered out poor Mary, scarcely conscious that she

spoke, so daunted, so terrified was she by the indignant mother's greeting.

"He 's lying in th' New Bailey," slowly and distinctly spoke the mother, watching the effect of her words, as if believing in their infinite power to pain, "There he lies, waiting to take his trial for murdering young Mr. Carsons."

There was no answer; but such a blanched face, such wild, distended eyes, such trembling limbs, instinctively seeking support!

"Did you know Mr. Carsons as now lies dead?" continued the merciless woman. "Folk say you did, and knew him but too well. And that for the sake of such as you, my precious child shot yon chap. But he did not. I know he did not. They may hang him, but his mother will speak to his innocence with her last dying breath."

She stopped more from exhaustion than want of words. Mary spoke, but in so changed and choked a voice that the old woman almost started. It seemed as if some third person must be in the room, the voice was so hoarse and strange.

"Please, say it again. I don't quite understand you. What has Jem done? Please to tell me."

"I never said he had done it. I said, and I 'll swear that he never did do it. I don't care who heard 'em quarrel, or if it is his gun as were found near the body. It 's not my own Jem as would go for to kill any man, choose how a girl had jilted him. My own good Jem, as was a blessing sent upon the house where he was born." Tears came into the mother's burning eyes as her heart recurred to the days when she had rocked the cradle of her "first-born;" and then, rapidly passing over events, till the full consciousness of his present situation came upon her, and perhaps annoyed at having shown any softness of character in the presence of the Dalilah who had lured him to his danger, she spoke again, and in a sharp tone.

"I told him, and told him to leave off thinking on thee; but he wouldn't be led by me. Thee! wench! thou wert not good enough to wipe the dust off his feet. A vile, flirting quean as thou art. It 's well thy mother does not know (poor body) what a good-for-nothing thou art."

"Mother! oh mother!" said Mary, as if appealing to the merciful dead. "But I was not good enough for him! I know I was not," added she, in a voice of touching humility.

For through her heart went tolling the ominous, prophetic words he had used when he had last spoken to her.

"Mary! you 'll may be hear of me as a drunkard and may be as a thief, and may be as a murderer. Remember! when all are speaking ill of me, yo will have no right to blame me, for it 's your cruelty that will have made me what I feel I shall become."

And she did not blame him, though she doubted not his guilt; she felt how madly she might act if once jealous of him, and how much cause had she not given him for jealousy, miserable guilty wretch that she was! Speak on, desolate mother. Abuse her as you will. Her broken spirit feels to have merited all.

But her last humble, self-abased words had touched Mrs. Wilson's heart, sore as it was; and she looked at the snow-pale girl with those piteous eyes, so hopeless of comfort, and she relented in spite of herself.

"Thou seest what comes of light conduct, Mary! It 's thy doing that suspicion has lighted on him, who is as innocent as the babe unborn. Thou 'lt have much to answer for if he 's hung. Thou 'lt have my death too at thy door!"

Harsh as these words seem, she spoke them in a milder tone of voice than she had yet used. But the idea of Jem on the gallows, Jem dead, took possession of Mary, and she covered her eyes with her wan hands, as if indeed to shut out the fearful sight.

She murmured some words, which though spoken low, as if choked up from the depths of agony, Jane Wilson caught. "My heart is breaking," said she feebly. "My heart is breaking."

"Nonsense!" said Mrs. Wilson. "Don't talk in that silly way. My heart has a better right to break than yours, and yet I hold up you see. But, oh dear! oh dear!" with a sudden revulsion of feeling, as the reality of the danger in which her son was placed, pressed upon her. "What am I saying? How could I hold up if thou wert gone, Jem? Though I 'm as sure as I stand here of thy innocence, if they hang thee, my lad, I will lie down and die!"

She wept aloud with bitter consciousness of the fearful chance awaiting her child. She cried more passionately still.

Mary roused herself up.

"Oh, let me stay with you, at any rate, till we know the end. Dearest Mrs. Wilson, mayn't I stay?"

The more obstinately and upbraidingly Mrs. Wilson refused, the more Mary pleaded, with ever the same soft, entreating cry, "Let me stay with you." Her stunned soul seemed to bound its wishes, for the hour at least, to remaining with one who loved and sorrowed for the same human being that she did.

But no. Mrs. Wilson was inflexible.

"I 've may be been a bit hard on you, Mary, I 'll own that. But I cannot abide you yet with me. I cannot but remember it 's your giddiness as has wrought this woe. I 'll stay with Alice, and perhaps Mrs. Davenport may come help a bit. I cannot put up with you about me. Good-night. To-morrow I may look on you different, may be. Good night."

And Mary turned out of the house, which had been *his* home, where *he* was loved, and mourned for, into the busy, desolate, crowded street, where they were crying half-penny broadsides, giving an account of the bloody murder, the coroner's inquest, and a raw-head-and-bloody-bones picture of the suspected murderer, James Wilson.

But Mary heard not, she heeded not. She staggered on like one in a dream. With hung head and tottering steps, she instinctively chose the shortest cut to that home which was to her, in her present state of mind, only the hiding place of four walls, where she might vent her agony, unseen and unnoticed by the keen, unkind world without, but where no welcome, no love, no sympathising tears awaited her.

As she neared that home, within two minutes' walk of it, her impetuous course was arrested by a light touch on her arm, and turning hastily, she saw a little Italian boy, with his humble show-box, — a white mouse, or some such thing. The setting sun cast its red glow on his face, otherwise the olive complexion would have been very pale; and the glittering tear-drops hung on the long curled eye-lashes. With his soft voice, and pleading looks, he uttered, in his pretty broken English, the word

"Hungry! so hungry."

'And, as if to aid by gesture the effect of the solitary word, he pointed to his mouth, with its white quivering lips.

Mary answered him impatiently,

"Oh, lad, hunger is nothing — nothing!"

And she rapidly passed on. But her heart upbraided her the next minute with her unrelenting speech, and she hastily entered her door and seized the scanty remnant of food which the cupboard contained, and she retraced her steps to the place where the little hopeless stranger had sunk down by his mute companion in loneliness and starvation, and was raining down tears as he spoke in some foreign tongue, with low cries for the far distant "Mamma mia!"

With the elasticity of heart belonging to childhood he sprang up as he saw the food the girl brought; she whose face, lovely in its woe, had tempted him first to address her; and, with the graceful courtesy of his country, he looked up and smiled while he kissed her hand, and then poured forth his thanks, and shared her bounty with his little pet companion. She stood an instant, diverted from the thought of her own grief by the sight of his infantine gladness; and then bending down and kissing his smooth forehead, she left him, and sought to be alone with her agony once more.

She re-entered the house, locked the door, and tore off her bonnet, as if greedy of every moment which took her from the full indulgence of painful, despairing thought.

Then she threw herself on the ground, yes, on the hard flags she threw her soft limbs down; and the comb fell out of her hair, and those bright tresses swept the dusty floor, while she pillowed and hid her face on her arms, and burst forth into hard, suffocating sobs.

Oh, earth! thou didst seem but a dreary dwelling-place for thy poor child that night. None to comfort, none to pity! And self-reproach gnawing at her heart.

Oh, why did she ever listen to the tempter? Why did she ever give ear to her own suggestions, and cravings after wealth and grandeur? Why had she thought it a fine thing to have a rich lover?

She — she had deserved it all; but he was the victim, — he the beloved. She could not conjecture, she could not even pause to think who had revealed, or how he had discovered her acquaintance with Harry Carsons. It was but too clear, some way or another, he had learnt all; and what would he think of her? No hope of his love, — oh, that she would give up, and be content; it was his life, his precious life, that was threatened? Then she tried to recall the particulars, which, when Mrs. Wilson had given them, had fallen but upon a deafened ear, — something about a gun, a quarrel, which she could not remember clearly. Oh, how terrible to think of his crime, his blood-guiltiness; he who had hitherto been so good, so noble, and now an assassin! And then she shrank from him in thought; and then, with bitter remorse, clung more closely to his image with passionate self-upbraiding. Was it not she who had led him to the pit into which he had fallen? Was she to blame him? She to judge him? Who could tell how maddened he might have been by jealousy; how one moment's uncontrollable passion might have led him to become a murderer! And she had blamed him in her heart after his last deprecating, imploring, prophetic speech!

Then she burst out crying afresh; and when weary of crying, fell to thinking again. The gallows! The gallows! Black it stood against the burning light which dazzled her shut eyes, press on them as she would. Oh! she was going mad; and for awhile she lay outwardly still, but with the pulses careering through her head with wild vehemence.

And then came a strange forgetfulness of the present, in thought of the long-past times; — of those days when she hid her face on her mother's pitying, loving bosom, and heard tender words of comfort, be her grief or her error what it might; — of those days when she had felt as if her mother's love was too mighty not to last for ever; — of those days when hunger had been to her (as to the little stranger she had that evening relieved) something to be thought about, and mourned over; — when Jem and she had played together; he, with the condescension of an older child, and she, with unconscious earnestness, believing that he was as much gratified with important trifles as she was; — when her father was a cheery-hearted man, rich in the love of his wife, and the companionship of his friend; — when (for it still worked round to that), when mother was alive, and *he* was not a murderer.

And then Heaven blessed her unaware, and she sank from remembering, to wandering, unconnected thought, and thence to sleep. Yes! it was sleep, though in that strange posture, on that hard cold bed; and she dreamt of the happy times of long ago, and her mother came to her, and kissed her as she lay, and once more the dead were alive again in that happy world of dreams. All was restored to the gladness of childhood, even to the little kitten which had been her playmate and bosom friend then, and which had been long forgotten in her waking hours. All the loved ones were there!

She suddenly wakened! Clear and wide awake! Some noise had startled her from sleep. She sat up, and put her hair (still wet with tears) back from her flushed cheeks, and listened. At first she could only hear her beating heart. All was still without, for it was after midnight, such hours of agony had passed away; but the moon shone clearly in at the unshuttered window, making the room almost as light as day, in its cold ghastly radiance. There was a low knock at the door! A strange feeling crept over Mary's heart, as if something spiritual were near; as if the dead so lately present in her dreams, were yet gliding and hovering round her, with their dim, dread forms. And yet, why dread? Had they not loved her? — and who loved her now? Was she not lonely enough to welcome the spirits of the dead, who had loved her while here? If her mother had conscious being, her love for her child endured. So she quietened her fears, and listened — listened still.

"Mary! Mary! open the door!" as a little movement on her part seemed to tell the being outside of her wakeful, watchful state. They were the accents of her mother's voice; the very south-country pronunciation, that Mary so well remembered; and which she had sometimes tried to imitate when alone, with the fond mimicry of affection.

So, without fear, without hesitation, she rose and unbarred the door. There, against the moonlight, stood a form, so closely resembling her dead mother, that Mary never doubted the identity, but exclaiming (as if she were a terrified child, secure of safety when near the protecting care of its parent) —

"Oh! mother! mother! You are come at last?" she threw herself, or rather fell, into the trembling arms, of her long-lost, unrecognised Aunt Esther.

CHAPTER XXI.

"My rest is gone,
 My heart is sore,
Peace find I never,
 And never more."

MARGARET'S SONG IN 'FAUST.'

I MUST go back a little to explain the motives which caused Esther to seek an interview with her niece.

The murder had been committed early on Thursday night, and between then and the dawn of the following day, there was ample time for the news to spread far and wide among all those whose duty, or whose want, or whose errors, caused them to be abroad in the streets of Manchester.

Among those who listened to the tale of violence was Esther.

A craving desire to know more took possession of her mind. Far away as she was from Turner Street, she immediately set off to the scene of the murder, which was faintly lighted by the gray dawn as she reached the spot. It was so quiet and still that she could hardly believe it to be the place. The only vestige of any scuffle or violence was a trail on the dust, as if somebody had been lying there, and then been raised by extraneous force. The little birds were beginning to hop and twitter in the leafless hedge, making the only sound that was near and distinct. She crossed into the field where she guessed the murderer to have stood; it was easy of access, for the worn, stunted hawthorn-hedge had many gaps in it. The night-smell of bruised grass came up from under her feet, as she went towards the saw-pit and carpenter's shed, which, as I have said before, were in a corner of the field near the road, and where one of her informants had told her it was supposed by the police that the murderer had lurked while waiting for his victim. There was no sign, however, that any one had been about the place. If the grass had been bruised or bent where he had trod, it had had enough of the elasticity of life to raise itself under the dewy influences of night. She hushed her breath in involuntary awe, but nothing else told of the violent deed by which a fellow-creature had passed away. She stood still for a minute, imagining to herself the position of the parties, guided by the only circumstance which afforded any evidence, the trailing mark on the dust in the road.

Suddenly (it was before the sun had risen above the horizon) she became aware of something white in the hedge. All other colours wore the same murky hue, though the forms of objects were perfectly distinct. What was it? It could not be a flower; — that, the time of year made clear. A frozen lump of snow, lingering late in one of the gnarled tufts of the hedge? She stepped forwards to examine. It proved to be a little piece of stiff writing-paper compressed into a round shape. She understood it instantly; it was the paper that had served as wadding for the murderer's gun. Then she had been standing just where the murderer must have been but a few hours before; probably (as the rumour had spread through the town, reaching her ears) one of the poor maddened turn-outs, who hung about everywhere, with black, fierce looks, as if contemplating some deed of violence. Her sympathy was all with them, for she had known what they suffered; and besides this there was her own individual dislike of Mr. Carsons, and dread of him for Mary's sake. Yet, poor Mary! Death was a terrible, though sure, remedy for the evil Esther had dreaded for her; and how would she stand the shock, loving as her aunt believed her to do? Poor Mary! who would comfort her? Esther's thoughts began to picture her sorrow, her despair, when the news of her lover's death should reach her; and she longed to tell her there might have been a keener grief yet had he lived.

Bright, beautiful came the slanting rays of the morning sun. It was time for such as she to hide themselves, with the other obscene things of night, from the glorious light of day, which was only for the happy. So she turned her steps towards town, still holding the paper. But in getting over the hedge it encumbered her to hold it in her clasped hand, and she threw it down. She passed on a few steps, her thoughts still of Mary, till the idea crossed her mind, could it (blank as it appeared to be) give any clue to the murderer? As I said before, her sympathies were all on that side, so she turned back and picked it up; and then feeling as if in some measure an accessory, she hid it unexamined in her hand, and hastily passed out of the street at the opposite end to that by which she had entered it.

And what do you think she felt, when, having walked some distance from the spot, she dared to open the crushed paper, and saw written on it Mary Barton's name, and not only that, but the street in which she lived! True, a letter or two was torn off, but, nevertheless, there was the name clear to be recognised. And oh! what terrible thought flashed into her mind; or was it only fancy? But it looked very like the writing which she had once known well — the writing of Jem Wilson, who, when she lived at her brother-in-law's, and he was a near neighbour, had often been employed by her to write her letters to people, to whom she was ashamed of sending her own misspelt scrawl. She remembered the wonderful flourishes she had so much admired in those days, while she sat by dictating, and Jem, in all the pride of newly-acquired penmanship, used to dazzle her eyes by extraordinary graces and twirls.

If it were his!

Oh! perhaps it was merely that her head was running so on Mary, that she was associating every trifle with her. As if only one person wrote in that flourishing, meandering style!

It was enough to fill her mind to think from what she might have saved Mary by securing the paper. She would look at it just once more, and see if some very dense and stupid policeman could have mistaken the name, or if Mary would certainly have been dragged into notice in the affair.

No! no one could have mistaken the "ry Barton," and it *was* Jem's handwriting!

Oh! if it was so, she understood it all, and she had been the cause! With her violent and unregulated nature, rendered morbid by the course of life she led, and her consciousness of her degradation, she cursed herself for the interference which she believed had led to this; for the information and the warning she had given to Jem, which had roused him to this murderous action. How could she, the abandoned and polluted outcast, ever have dared to hope for a blessing, even on her efforts to do good? The black curse of Heaven rested on all her doings, were they for good or for evil.

Poor, diseased mind! and there were none to minister to thee!

So she wandered about, too restless to take her usual heavy morning's sleep; up and down the streets, greedily listening to every word of the passers by, and loitering near each group of talkers, anxious to scrape together every morsel of information, or conjecture, or suspicion, though without possessing any definite purpose in all this. And ever and always she clenched the scrap of paper which might betray so much, until her nails had deeply indented the palm of her hand; so fearful was she in her nervous dread, lest unawares she should let it drop.

Towards the middle of the day she could no longer evade the body's craving want of rest and refreshment; but the rest was taken in a spirit vault, and the refreshment was a glass of gin.

Then she started up from the stupor she had taken for repose; and suddenly driven before the gusty impulses of her mind, she pushed her way to the place where at that very time the police were bringing the information they had gathered with regard to the all-engrossing murder. She listened with painful acuteness of comprehension to dropped words and unconnected sentences, the meaning of which became clearer, and yet more clear to her. Jem was suspected. Jem was ascertained to be the murderer.

She saw him (although he, absorbed in deep sad thought, saw her not), she saw him brought hand-cuffed, and guarded out of the coach. She saw him enter the station, — she gasped for breath till he came out, still hand-cuffed, and still guarded, to be conveyed to the New Bailey.

He was the only one who had spoken to her with hope that she might win her way back to virtue. His words had lingered in her heart with a sort of call to Heaven, like distant Sabbath bells, although in her despair she had turned away from his voice. He was the only one who had spoken to her kindly. The murder, shocking though it was, was an absent, abstract thing, on which her thoughts could not, and would not dwell: all that was present in her mind was Jem's danger, and his kindness.

Then Mary came to remembrance. Esther wondered till she was sick of wondering, in what way she was taking the affair. In some manner it would be a terrible blow for the poor, motherless girl; with her dreadful father, too, who was to Esther a sort of accusing angel.

She set off towards the court where Mary lived, to pick up what she could there of information. But she was ashamed to enter in where once she had been innocent, and hung about the neighbouring streets, not daring to question, so she learnt but little; nothing in fact but the knowledge of John Barton's absence from home.

She went up a dark entry to rest her weary limbs on a doorstep and think. Her elbows on her knees, her face hidden in her hands, she tried to gather together and arrange her thoughts. But still every now and then she opened her hand to see if the paper were yet there.

She got up at last. She had formed a plan, and had a course of action to look forward to that would satisfy one craving desire at least. The time was long gone by when there was much wisdom or consistency in her projects.

It was getting late, and that was so much the better. She went to a pawn-shop, and took off her finery in a back room. She was known by the people and had a character for honesty, so she had no very great difficulty in inducing them to let her have a suit of outer clothes, befitting the wife of a working-man, a black silk bonnet, a printed gown, a plaid shawl, dirty and rather worn to be sure, but which had a sort of sanctity to the eyes of the street-walker, as being the appropriate garb of that happy class to which she could never, never more belong.

She looked at herself in the little glass which hung against the wall, and sadly shaking her head, thought how easy were the duties of that Eden of innocence from which she was shut out; how she would work, and toil, and starve, and die, if necessary, for a husband, a home, — for children, — but that thought she could not bear; a little form rose up, stern in its innocence, from the witches' cauldron of her imagination, and she rushed into action again.

You know now how she came to stand by the threshold of Mary's door, waiting, trembling, until the latch was lifted, and her niece, with words that spoke of such desolation among the living, fell into her arms.

She had felt as if some holy spell would prevent her (even as the unholy Lady Geraldine was prevented, in the abode of Christabel) from crossing the threshold of that home of her early innocence; and she had meant to wait for an invitation. But Mary's helpless action did away with all reluctant feeling, and she bore or dragged her to her seat, and looked on her bewildered eyes, as, puzzled with the likeness, which was not identity, she gazed on her aunt's features.

In pursuance of her plan, Esther meant to assume the manners and character, as she had done the dress, of a mechanic's wife; but then, to account for her long absence, and her long silence towards all that ought to have been dear to her, it was necessary that she should put on an indifference far distant from her heart, which was loving and yearning, in spite of all its faults. And, perhaps, she overacted her part, for certainly Mary felt a kind of repugnance to the changed and altered aunt, who so suddenly re-appeared on the scene; and it would have cut Esther to the very core, could she have known how her little darling of former days was feeling towards her.

"You don't remember me I see, Mary!" she began. "It's a long while since I left you all, to be sure, and I, many a time, thought of coming to see you, and — and your father. But I live so far off, and am always so busy, I cannot do just what I wish. You recollect aunt Esther, don't you, Mary?"

"Are you aunt Hetty?" asked Mary, faintly, still looking at the face which was so different from the old recollections of her aunt's fresh dazzling beauty.

"Yes! I am aunt Hetty. Oh! it's so long since I heard that name," sighing forth the thoughts it suggested; then recovering herself, and striving after the hard character she wished to assume, she continued: "and to-day I heard a friend of yours, and of mine too, long ago, was in trouble, and I guessed you would be in sorrow, so I thought I would just step this far and see you."

Mary's tears flowed afresh, but she had no desire to open her heart to her strangely-found aunt, who had, by her own confession, kept aloof from and neglected them for so many years. Yet she tried to feel grateful for kindness (however late) from any one, and wished to be civil. Moreover, she had a strong disinclination to speak on the terrible subject, uppermost in her mind. So, after a pause, she said,

"Thank you. I dare say you mean very kind. Have you had a long walk? I 'm so sorry," said she, rising with a sudden thought, which was as suddenly checked by recollection, "but I 've nothing to eat in the house, and I 'm sure you must be hungry, after your walk."

For Mary concluded that certainly her aunt's residence must be far away on the other side of the town, out of sight or hearing. But after all, she did not think much about her; her heart was so aching-full of other things, that all besides seemed like a dream. She received feelings and impressions from her conversation with her aunt, but did not, could not put them together, or think, or argue about them.

And Esther! How scanty had been her food for days and weeks, her thinly-covered bones and pale lips might tell, but her words should never reveal! So, with a little unreal laugh, she replied,

"Oh! Mary, my dear! don't talk about eating. We 've the best of every thing, and plenty of it, for my husband is in good work. I 'd such a supper before I came out. I couldn't touch a morsel if you had it."

Her words shot a strange pang through Mary's heart. She had always remembered her aunt's loving and unselfish disposition; how was it changed, if, living in plenty, she had never thought it worth while to ask after relations who were all but starving! She shut up her heart instinctively against her aunt.

And all the time poor Esther was swallowing her sobs, and over-acting her part, and controlling herself more than she had done for many a long day, in order that her niece might not be shocked and revolted, by the knowledge of what her aunt had become: — a prostitute; an outcast.

She had longed to open her wretched, wretched heart, so hopeless, so abandoned by all living things, to one who had loved her once; and yet she refrained, from dread of the averted eye, the altered voice, the internal loathing, which she feared such disclosure might create. She would go straight to the subject of the day. She could not tarry long, for she felt unable to support the character she had assumed for any length of time.

They sat by the little round table, facing each other. The candle was placed right between them, and Esther moved it in order to have a clearer view of Mary's face, so that she might read her emotions, and ascertain her interests. Then she began:

"It 's a bad business, I 'm afraid, this of Mr. Carsons' murder."

Mary winced a little.

"I hear Jem Wilson is taken up for it."

Mary covered her eyes with her hands, as if to shade them from the light, and Esther herself, less accustomed to self-command, was getting too much agitated for calm observation of another.

"I was taking a walk near Turner Street, and I went to see the spot," continued Esther, "and, as luck would have it, I spied this bit of paper in the hedge," producing the precious piece still folded in her hand. "It has been used as wadding for the gun, I reckon; indeed, that 's clear enough, from the shape it 's crammed into. I was sorry for the murderer, whoever he might be (I didn't then know of Jem's being suspected), and I thought I would never leave a thing about, as might help, if ever so little, to convict him; the police are so 'cute about straws. So I carried it a little way, and then I opened it, and saw your name, Mary."

Mary took her hands away from her eyes, and looked with surprise at her aunt's face, as she uttered these words. She *was* kind after all, for was she not saving her from being summoned, and from being questioned, and examined; a thing to be dreaded above all others: as she felt sure that her unwilling answers, frame them how she might, would add to the suspicions against Jem; her aunt was indeed kind, to think of what would spare her this.

Esther went on, without noticing Mary's look. The very action of speaking was so painful to her, and so much interrupted by the hard, raking little cough, which had been her constant annoyance for months, that she was too much engrossed by the physical difficulty of utterance, to be a very close observer.

"There could be no mistake if they had found it. Look at your name, together with the very name of this court! And in Jem's handwriting too, or I'm much mistaken. Look Mary!"

And now she did watch her.

Mary took the paper and flattened it; then suddenly stood stiff up, with irrepressible movement, as if petrified by some horror abruptly disclosed; her face, strung and rigid; her lips compressed tight, to keep down some rising exclamation. She dropped on her seat, as suddenly as if the braced muscles had in an instant given way. But she spoke no word.

"It is his hand-writing — isn't it?" asked Esther, though Mary's manner was almost confirmation enough.

"You will not tell. You never will tell," demanded Mary, in a tone so sternly earnest, as almost to be threatening.

"Nay, Mary," said Esther, rather reproachfully, "I am not so bad as that. Oh! Mary, you cannot think I would do that, whatever I may be."

The tears sprang to her eyes, at the idea that she was suspected of being one who would help to inform against an old friend.

Mary caught her sad and upbraiding look.

"No! I know you would not tell, aunt. I don't know what I say, I am so shocked. But say you will not tell. Do."

"No, indeed I willn't tell, come what may."

Mary sat still looking at the writing, and turning the paper round with careful examination, trying to hope, but her very fears belying her hopes.

"I thought you cared for the young man that 's murdered," observed Esther, half-aloud; but feeling that she could not mistake this strange interest in the suspected murderer, implied by Mary's eagerness to screen him from anything which might strengthen suspicion against him. She had come, desirous to know the extent of Mary's grief for Mr. Carsons, and glad of the excuse afforded her by the important scrap of paper. Her remark about its being Jem's hand-writing, she had, with this view of ascertaining Mary's state of feeling, felt to be most imprudent the instant after she had uttered it; but Mary's anxiety that she should not tell, was too great, and too decided, to leave a doubt as to her interest for Jem. She grew more and more bewildered, and her dizzy head refused to reason. Mary never spoke. She held the bit of paper firmly, determined to retain possession of it, come what might; and anxious, and impatient, for her aunt to go. As she sat, her face bore a likeness to Esther's dead child.

"You are so like my little girl, Mary!" said Esther, weary of the one subject on which she could get no satisfaction, and recurring, with full heart, to the thought of the dead.

Mary looked up. Her aunt had children, then. That was all the idea she received. No faint imagination of the love and the woe of that poor creature crossed her mind, or she would have taken her, all guilty and erring, to her bosom, and tried to bind up the broken heart. No! it was not to be. Her aunt had children, then; and she was on the point of putting some question about them, but before it could be spoken another thought turned it aside, and she went back to her task of unravelling the mystery of the paper, and the hand-writing. Oh! how she wished her aunt would go.

As if, according to the believers in mesmerism, the intenseness of her wish gave her power over another, although the wish was unexpressed, Esther felt herself unwelcome, and that her absence was desired.

She felt this some time before she could summon up resolution to go. She was so much disappointed in this longed-for, dreaded interview with Mary; she had wished to impose upon her with her tale of married respectability, and yet she had yearned and craved for sympathy in her real lot. And she had imposed upon her well. She should perhaps be glad of it afterwards; but her desolation of hope seemed for the time redoubled. And she must leave the old dwelling-place, whose very walls, and flags, dingy and sordid as they were, had a charm for her. Must leave the abode of poverty, for the more terrible abodes of vice. She must — she would go.

"Well, good-night, Mary. That bit of paper is safe enough with you, I see. But you made me promise I would not tell about it, and you must promise me to destroy it before you sleep."

"I promise," said Mary, hoarsely, but firmly. "Then you are going?"

"Yes. Not if you wish me to stay. Not if I could be of any comfort to you, Mary;" catching at some glimmering hope.

"Oh, no," said Mary, anxious to be alone. "Your husband will be wondering where you are. Some day you must tell me all about yourself. I forget what your name is?"

"Fergusson," said Esther, sadly.

"Mrs. Fergusson," repeated Mary, half unconsciously. "And where did you say you lived?"

"I never did say," muttered Esther; then aloud, "In Angel's Meadow, 145, Nicholas Street."

"145, Nicholas Street, Angel Meadow. I shall remember."

As Esther drew her shawl around her, and prepared to depart, a thought crossed Mary's mind that she had been cold and hard in her manner towards one, who had certainly meant to act kindly in bringing her the paper (that dread, terrible piece of paper), and thus saving her from — she could not rightly think how much, or how little she was spared. So, desirous of making up for her previous indifferent manner, she advanced to kiss her aunt before her departure.

But, to her surprise, her aunt pushed her off with a frantic kind of gesture, and saying the words,

"Not me. You must never kiss me. You!"

She rushed into the outer darkness of the street; and there wept long and bitterly.

CHAPTER XXII.

"There was a listening fear in her regard,
As if calamity had but begun;
As if the vanward clouds of evil days
Had spent their malice, and the sullen rear
Was, with its stored thunder, labouring up."

KEATS' 'HYPERION.'

No sooner was Mary alone than she fastened the door, and put the shutters up against the window, which had all this time remained shaded only by the curtains hastily drawn together on Esther's entrance, and the lighting of the candle.

She did all this with the same compressed lips, and the same stony look that her face had assumed on the first examination of the paper. Then she sat down for an instant to think; and rising directly, went, with a step rendered firm by inward resolution of purpose, up the stairs; — passed her own door, two steps, into her father's room. What did she want there?

I must tell you; I must put into words the dreadful secret which she believed that bit of paper had revealed to her.

Her father was the murderer!

That corner of stiff, shining, thick writing-paper, she recognised as a part of the sheet on which she had copied Samuel Bamford's beautiful lines so many months ago — copied (as you perhaps remember) on the blank part of a valentine sent to her by Jem Wilson, in those days when she did not treasure and hoard up every thing he had touched, as she would do now.

That copy had been given to her father for whom it was made, and she had occasionally seen him reading it over, not a fortnight ago she was sure. But she resolved to ascertain if the other part still remained in his possession. He might, it was just possible he *might*, have given it away to some friend; and if so, that person was the guilty one, for she could swear to the paper anywhere.

First of all she pulled out every article from the little old chest of drawers. Amongst them were some things which had belonged to her mother, but she had no time now to examine and try and remember them. All the reverence she could pay them was to carry them and lay them on the bed carefully, while the other things were tossed impatiently out upon the floor.

The copy of Bamford's lines was not there. Oh! perhaps he might have given it away; but then must it not have been to Jem? It was his gun.

And she set to with redoubled vigour to examine the deal-box which served as chair, and which had once contained her father's Sunday clothes, in the days when he could afford to have Sunday clothes.

He had redeemed his better coat from the pawn-shop before

he left, that she had noticed. Here was his old one. What rustled under her hand in the pocket?

The paper! "Oh! Father!"

Yes, it fitted; jagged end to jagged end, letter to letter; and even the part which Esther had considered blank had its tallying mark with the larger piece, its tails of *ys* and *gs*. And then, as if that were not damning evidence enough, she felt again, and found some little bullets or shot (I don't know which you would call them) in that same pocket, along with a small paper parcel of gunpowder. As she was going to replace the jacket, having abstracted the paper, and bullets, &c., she saw a woollen gun-case, made of that sort of striped horse-cloth you must have seen a thousand times appropriated to such a purpose. The sight of it made her examine still further, but there was nothing else that could afford any evidence, so she locked the box, and sat down on the floor to contemplate the articles; now with a sickening despair, now with a kind of wondering curiosity, how her father had managed to evade observation. After all it was easy enough. He had evidently got possession of some gun (was it really Jem's? was he an accomplice? No! she did not believe it; he never, never would deliberately plan a murder with another, however he might be wrought up to it by passionate feeling at the time. Least of all would he accuse her to her father, without previously warning her; it wss out of his nature).

Then having obtained possession of the gun, her father had loaded it at home, and might have carried it away with him some time, when the neighbours were not noticing, and she was out, or asleep; and then he might have hidden it somewhere to be in readiness when he should want it. She was sure he had no such thing with him when he went away the last time

She felt it was of no use to conjecture his motives. His actions had become so wild and irregular of late, that she could not reason upon them. Besides, was it not enough to know that he was guilty of this terrible offence? Her love for her father seemed to return with painful force, mixed up as it was with horror at his crime. That dear father who was once so kind, so warm-hearted, so ready to help either man or beast in distress, to murder! But in the desert of misery with which these thoughts surrounded her, the arid depths of whose gloom she dared not venture to contemplate, a little spring of comfort was gushing up at her feet, unnoticed at first, but soon to give her strength and hope.

And *that* was the necessity for exertion on her part which this discovery enforced.

Oh! I do not think that the necessity for exertion, for some kind of action (bodily or mentally) in time of distress, is a most infinite blessing, although the first efforts at such seasons are painful. Something to be done implies that there is yet hope of some good thing to be accomplished, or some additional evil that may be avoided; and by degrees the hope absorbs much of the sorrow.

It is the woes that cannot in any earthly way be escaped that admit least earthly comforting. Of all trite, worn-out, hollow mockeries of comfort that were ever uttered by people who will not take the trouble of sympathising with others, the one I dislike the most is the exhortation not to grieve over an event, "for it cannot be helped." Do you think if I could help it, I would sit still with folded hands, content to mourn? Do you not believe that as long as hope remained I would be up and doing? I mourn because what has occurred cannot be helped. The reason you give me for not grieving, is the very and sole reason of my grief. Giver me nobler and higher reasons for enduring meekly what my Father sees fit to send, and I will try earnestly and faithfully to be patient; but mock me not, or any other mourner, with the speech, "Do not grieve, for it cannot be helped. It is past remedy."

But some remedy to Mary's sorrow came with thinking. If her father was guilty, Jem was innocent. If innocent, there was a possibility of saving him. He must be saved. And she must do it; for, was not she the sole depository of the terrible secret? Her father was not suspected; and never should be, if by any foresight or any exertions of her own she could prevent it.

She did not yet know how Jem was to be saved, while her father was also to be considered innocent. It would require much thought, and much prudence. But with the call upon her exertions, and her various qualities of judgment and discretion, came the answering consciousness of innate power to meet the emergency. Every step now, nay, the employment of every minute, was of consequence; for you must remember she had learnt at Miss Simmonds' the probability that the murderer would be brought to trial the next week. And you must remember. too, that never was so young a girl so friendless, or so penniless, as Mary was at this time. But the lion accompanied Una through the wilderness and the danger; and so will a high, resolved purpose of right doing ever guard and accompany the helpless.

It struck two; deep, mirk, night.

It was of no use bewildering herself with plans this weary, endless night. Nothing could be done before morning: and, at first in her impatience, she began to long for day; but then she felt in how unfit a state her body was for any plan of exertion, and she resolutely made up her mind to husband her physical strength.

First of all she must burn the tell-tale paper. The powder, bullets, and gun-case, she tied into a bundle, and hid in the sacking of the bed for the present, although there was no likelihood of their affording evidence against any one. Then she carried the paper down-stairs, and burnt it on the hearth, powdering the very ashes with her fingers, and dispering the fragments of fluttering black films among the cinders of the grate. Then she breathed again.

Her head ached with dizzying violence; she must get quit of the pain or it would incapacitate her for thinking and planning. She looked for food, but there was nothing but a little raw oatmeal in the house: still, although it almost choked her, she ate some of this, knowing from experience, how often headaches were caused by long fasting. Then she sought for some water to bathe her throbbing temples, and quench her feverish thirst. There was none in the house, so she took the jug and went out to the pump at the other end of the court, whose echoes resounded her light footsteps in the quiet stillness of the night. The hard, square outlines of the houses cut sharply against the cold bright sky, from which myriads of stars were shining down in eternal repose. There was little sympathy in the outward scene, with the internal trouble. All was so still, so motionless, so hard! Very different to this lovely night in the country in which I am now writing, where the distant horizon is soft and undulating in the moonlight, and the nearer trees sway gently to and fro in the night-wind with something of almost human motion; and the rustling air makes music among their branches, as if speaking soothingly to the weary ones, who lie awake in heaviness of heart. The sights and sounds of such a night lull pain and grief to rest.

But Mary re-entered her home after she had filled her pitcher, with a still stronger sense of anxiety, and a still clearer conviction of how much rested upon her unassisted and friendless self, alone with her terrible knowledge, in the hard, cold, populous world.

She bathed her forehead, and quenched her thirst, and then, with wise deliberation of purpose, went up-stairs, and undressed herself, as if for a long night's slumber, although so few hours intervened before day-dawn. She believed she never could sleep, but she lay down, and shut her eyes; and before many minutes she was in as deep and sound a slumber as if there was no sin or sorrow in the world.

She woke up, as it was natural, much refreshed in body; but with a consciousness of some great impending calamity. She sat up in bed to recollect, and when she did remember, she sank down again with all the helplessness of despair. But it was only the weakness of an instant; for were not the very minutes precious, for deliberation if not for action?

Before she had finished the necessary morning business of dressing, and setting her house in some kind of order, she had disentangled her ravelled ideas, and arranged some kind of a plan for action. If Jem was innocent (and now, of his guilt, even his slightest participation in, or knowledge of the murder, she acquitted him with all her heart and soul), he must have been somewhere else when the crime was committed; probably with some others, who might bear witness to the fact, if she only knew where to find them. Every thing rested on her. She had heard of an alibi, and believed it might mean the deliverance she wished to accomplish; but she was not quite sure, and determined to apply to Job, as one of the few among her acquaintance gifted with the knowledge of hard words, for to her, all terms of law, or natural history, were alike many-syllabled mysteries.

No time was to be lost. She went straight to Job Legh's house, and found the old man and his granddaughter sitting at breakfast; as she opened the door she heard their voices speaking in a grave, hushed, subdued tone, as if something grieved their hearts. They stopped talking on her entrance, and then she knew they had been conversing about the murder; about Jem's probable guilt; and (it flashed upon her for the first time) on the new light they would have obtained regarding herself: for until now they had never heard of her giddy flirting with Mr. Carsons; not in all her confidential talk with Margaret had she ever spoken of him. And now, Margaret would hear her conduct talked of by all, as that of a bold, bad girl; and even if she did not believe every thing that was said, she could hardly help feeling wounded, and disappointed in Mary.

So it was in a timid voice that Mary wished her usual good-morrow, and her heart sank within her a little, when Job, with a form of civility, bade her welcome in that dwelling, where, until now, she had been too well assured to reqnire to be asked to sit down.

She took a chair. Margaret continued silent.

"I 'm come to speack to you about this — about Jem Wilson."

"It 's a bad business, I 'm afeared," replied Job, sadly.

"Ay, it 's bad enough anyhow. But Jem 's innocent. Indeed he is; I 'm as sure as sure can be."

"How can you know, wench? Facts bear strong again him, poor fellow, though he 'd a deal to put him up, and aggravate him, they say. Ay, poor lad, he 's done for himself, I'm afeared."

"Job!" said Mary, rising from her chair in her eagerness, "you must not say he did it. He didn't; I 'm sure and certain he didn't. Oh! why do you shake your head? Who is to believe me, — who is to think him innocent, if you, who know'd him so well, stick to it he 's guilty?"

"I 'm loth enough to do it, lass," replied Job; "but I think he 's been ill-used, and — jilted (that 's plain truth, Mary, hard as it may seem), and his blood has been up — many a man has done the like afore, from like causes."

"Oh, God! Then you won't help me, Job, to prove him innocent? Oh! Job, Job; believe me, Jem never did harm to no one."

"Not afore; — and mind, wench! I don't over-blame him for this." Job relapsed into silence.

Mary thought a moment.

"Well, Job, you 'll not refuse me this, I know. I won't mind what you think, if you 'll help me as if he was innocent. Now suppose I know — I knew he was innocent, — it 's only supposing, Job, — what must I do to prove it? Tell me, Job! Isn't it called an *alibi*, the getting folk to swear to where he really was at the time?"

"Best way, if you know 'd him innocent, would be to find out the real murderer. Some one did it, that 's clear enough. If it wasn't Jem, who was it?"

"How can I tell?" answered Mary, in agony of terror, lest Job's question was prompted by any suspicion of the truth.

But he was far enough from any such thought. Indeed, he had no doubt in his own mind that Jem had, in some passionate moment, urged on by slighted love and jealousy, been the murderer. And he was strongly inclined to believe, that Mary was aware of this, only that, too late repentant of her light conduct which had led to such fatal consequences, she was now most anxious to save her old playfellow, her early friend, from the doom awaiting the shedder of blood.

"If Jem 's not done it, I don't see as any on us can tell who did it. We might find out something if we 'd time; but they say he 's to be tried on Tuesday. It 's no use hiding it, Mary; things looks strong against him."

"I know they do! I know they do! But, oh! Job! isn't an *alibi* a proving where he really was at th' time of the murder; and how must I set about an *alibi?*"

"An *alibi* is that, sure enough." He thought a little. "You mun ask his mother his doings, and his whereabouts that night; the knowledge of that will guide you a bit."

For he was anxious that on another should fall the task of enlightening Mary on the hopelessness of the case, and he felt that her own sense would be more convinced by inquiry and examination than any mere assertion of his.

Margaret had sat silent and grave all this time. To tell the truth, she was surprised and disappointed by the disclosure of Mary's conduct, with regard to Mr. Henry Carsons. Gentle, reserved, and prudent herself, never exposed to the trial of being admired for her personal appearance, and unsusceptible enough to be in doubt even yet, whether the fluttering, tender, infinitely-joyous feeling, she was for the first time experiencing, at sight, or sound, or thought of Will Wilson, was love or not, — Margaret had no sympathy with the temptations to which loveliness, vanity, ambition, or the desire of being admired, exposes so many; no sympathy with flirting girls, in short. Then, she had no idea of the strength of the conflict betwеen will and principle in some who were differently constituted from herself. With her, to be convinced that an action was wrong, was tantamount to a determination not to do so again; and she had little or no difficulty in carrying out her determination. So she could not understand how it was that Mary had acted wrongly, and had felt too much ashamed, in spite of internal sophistry, to speak of her actions. Margaret considered herself deceived; felt aggrieved; and, at the time of which I am now telling you, was strongly inclined to give Mary up altogether, as a girl devoid of the modest proprieties of her sex, and capable of gross duplicity, in speaking of one lover as she had done of Jem, while she was encouraging another in attentions, at best of a very doubtful character.

But now Margaret was drawn into the conversation. Suddenly it flashed across Mary's mind, that the night of the murder was the very night, or rather the same early morning, that Margaret had been with Alice. She turned sharp round, with —

"Oh! Margaret, you can tell me; you were there when he came back that night; were you not? No! you were not; but you were there not many hours after. Did not you hear where he'd been? He was away the night before, too, when Alice was first taken; when you were there for your tea. Oh! where was he, Margaret?"

"I don't know," she answered. "Stay! I do remember something about his keeping Will company, in his walk to Liverpool. I can't justly say what it was, so much happened that night."

"I 'll go to his mother's," said Mary, resolutely.

They neither of them spoke, either to advise or dissuade. Mary felt she had no sympathy from them, and braced up her soul to act without such loving aid of friendship. She knew that their advice would be willingly given at her demand, and that was all she really required for Jem's sake. Still her courage failed a little as she walked to Jane Wilson's, alone in the world with her secret.

Jane Wilson's eyes were swelled with crying; and it was sad to see the ravages which intense anxiety and sorrow had made on her appearance in four-and-twenty hours. All night long she and Mrs. Davenport had crooned over their sorrows, always recurring, like the burden of an old song, to the dreadest sorrow of all, which was now impending over Mrs. Wilson. She had grown — I hardly know what word to use — but, something like proud of her martyrdom; she had grown to hug her grief; to feel an excitement in her agony of anxiety about her boy.

"So, Mary, you 're here! Oh! Mary, lass! He 's to be tried on Tuesday."

She fell to sobbing, in the convulsive breath-catching manner which tells so of much previous weeping.

"Oh! Mrs. Wilson, don't take on so! We 'll get him off, you 'll see. Don't fret; they can't prove him guilty!"

"But I tell thee they will," interrupted Mrs. Wilson, half-irritated at the light way, as she considered it, in which Mary spoke; and a little displeased that another could hope when she had almost brought herself to find pleasure in despair.

"It may suit thee well," continued she, "to make light o' the misery thou hast caused; but I shall lay his death at thy door, as long as I live, and die I know he will; and all for what he never did — no, he never did; my own blessed boy!"

She was too weak to be angry long; her wrath sank away to feeble sobbing and worn-out moans.

Mary was most anxious to soothe her from any violence of either grief or anger; she did so want her to be clear in her recollection; and, besides, her tenderness was great towards Jem's mother. So she spoke in a low gentle tone the loving entences, which sound so broken and powerless in repetition and which yet have so much power, when accompanied with caressing looks and actions, fresh from the heart; and the old woman insensibly gave herself up to the influence of those sweet, loving blue eyes, those tears of sympathy, those words of love and hope, and was lulled into a less morbid state of mind.

"And now, dear Mrs. Wilson, can you remember where he said he was going on Thursday night? He was out when Alice was taken ill; and he did not come home till early in the morning, or, to speak true, in the night: did he?"

"Ay! he went out near upon five; he went out with Will; he said he were going to set* him a part of the way, for Will were hot upon walking to Liverpool, and wouldn't hearken to Jem's offer of lending him five shillings for his fare. So the two lads set off together. I mind it all now; but, thou seest, Alice's illness, and this business of poor Jem's, drove it out of my head; they went off together, to walk to Liverpool; that 's to say, Jem were to go a part o' th' way. But, who knows" (falling back into the old desponding tone) "if he really went? He might be led off on the road. Oh! Mary, wench! they 'll hang him for what he 's never done."

"No, they won't — they shan't! I see my way a-bit now. We mun get Will to help; there 'll be time. He can swear that Jem were with him. Where is Jem?"

"Folk said he were taken to Kirkdale, i' th' prison van, this morning; without my seeing him, poor chap! Oh! wench! but they 've hurried on the business at a cruel rate."

"Ay! they 've not let grass grow under their feet, in hunting out the man that did it," said Mary, sorrowfully and bitterly. "But keep up your heart. They got on the wrong scent when they took to suspecting Jem. Don't be afeared. You 'll see it will end right for Jem."

"I should mind it less if I could do aught," said Jane Wilson; "but I 'm such a poor weak old body, and my head 's so gone, and I 'm so daz 'd like, what with Alice and all, that I think and think, and can do nought to help my child. I might ha' gone and seen him last night, they tell me now, and then I missed it. Oh! Mary, I missed it; and I may never see the lad again."

* "To set," to accompany.

She looked so piteously in Mary's face with her miserable eyes, that Mary felt her heart giving way, and, dreading the weakness of her powers, which the burst of crying she longed for would occasion, hastily changed the subject to Alice; and Jane, in her heart, feeling that there was no sorrow like a mother's sorrow, replied,

"She keeps on much the same, thank you. She 's happy, for she knows nothing of what 's going on; but th' doctor says she grows weaker and weaker. Thou 'lt may be like to see her?"

Mary went up-stairs: partly because it is the etiquette in humble life, to offer to friends a last opportunity of seeing the dying or the dead, while the same etiquette forbids a refusal of the invitation; and partly because she longed to breathe, for an instant, the atmosphere of holy calm, which seemed ever to surround the pious good old woman. Alice lay, as before, without pain, or at least any outward expression of it; but totally unconscious of all present circumstances, and absorbed in recollections of the days of her girlhood, which were vivid enough to take the place of reality to her. Still she talked of green fields, and still she spoke to the long-dead mother and sister, low-lying in their graves this many a year, as if they were with her and about her, in the pleasant places where her youth had passed.

But the voice was fainter, the motions were more languid; she was evidently passing away; but *how* happily!

Mary stood for a time in silence, watching and listening. Then she bent down and reverently kissed Alice's cheek; and drawing Jane Wilson away from the bed, as if the spirit of her who lay there were yet cognizant of present realities, she whispered a few words of hope to the poor mother, and kissing her over and over again in a warm, loving manner, she bade her good-bye, went a few steps, and then once more came back to bid her keep up her heart.

And when she had fairly left the house, Jane Wilson felt as if a sun-beam had ceased shining into the room.

Yet oh! how sorely Mary's heart ached; for more and more the fell certainty came on her that her father was the murderer! She struggled hard not to dwell on this conviction; to think alone on the means of proving Jem's innocence; that was her first duty, and that should be done.

CHAPTER XXIII.

"And must it then depend on this poor eye
And this unsteady hand, whether the bark,
That bears my all of treasured hope and love,
Shall find a passage through these frowning rocks
To some fair port where peace and safety smile,—
Or whether it shall blindly dash against them,
And miserably sink? Heaven be my help;
And clear my eye, and nerve my trembling hand!"
'The Constant Woman.'

Her heart beating, her head full of ideas, which required time and solitude to be reduced into order, Mary hurried home. She was like one who finds a jewel of which he cannot all at once ascertain the value, but who hides his treasure until some quiet hour when he may ponder over the capabilities its possession unfolds. She was like one who discovers the silken clue which guides to some bower of bliss, and secure of the power within his grasp, has to wait for a time before he may tread the labyrinth.

But no jewel, no bower of bliss was ever so precious to miser or lover as was the belief which now pervaded Mary's mind, that Jem's innocence might be proved, without involving any suspicion of that other—that dear one—so dear, although so criminal—on whose part in this cruel business she dared not dwell even in thought. For if she did, there arose the awful question,—if all went against Jem the innocent, if judge and jury gave the verdict forth which had the looming gallows in the rear, what ought she to do, possessed of her terrible knowledge? Surely not to inculpate her father—and yet—and yet—she almost prayed for the blessed unconsciousness of death or madness, rather than that awful question should have to be answered by her.

But now a way seemed opening, opening yet more clear. She was thankful she had thought of the *alibi*, and yet more thankful to have so easily obtained the clue to Jem's whereabouts that miserable night. The bright light that her new hope threw over all, seemed also to make her thankful for the early time appointed for the trial. It would be easy to catch Will Wilson on his return from the Isle of Man, which he had planned should be on the Monday; and on the Tuesday all would be made clear — all that she dared to wish to be made clear.

She had still to collect her thoughts and freshen her memory enough to arrange how to meet with Will — for to the chances of a letter she would not trust; to find out his lodgings when in Liverpool; to try and remember the name of the ship in which he was to sail: and the more she considered these points, the more difficulty she found there would be in ascertaining these minor but important facts. For you are aware that Alice, whose memory was clear and strong on all points in which her heart was interested, was lying in a manner senseless: that Jane Wilson was (to use her own word, so expressive to a Lancashire ear) "dazed,"* that is to say, bewildered, lost in the confusion of terrifying and distressing thoughts; incapable of concentrating her mind; and at the best of times Will's proceedings were a matter of little importance to her (or so she pretended), she was so jealous of aught which distracted attention from her pearl of price, her only son Jem. So Mary felt hopeless of obtaining any intelligence of the sailor's arrangements from her.

Then, should she apply to Jem himself! No! she knew him too well. She felt how thoroughly he must ere now have had it in his power to exculpate himself at another's expense. And his tacit refusal so to do had assured her of what she had never doubted, that the murderer was safe from any impeachment of his. But then neither would he consent, she feared, to any steps which might tend to proving himself innocent. At any rate, she could not consult him. He was removed to Kirkdale, and time pressed. Already it was Saturday at noon. And even if she could have gone to him, I believe she would not. She longed to do all herself, to be his liberator, his deliverer; to win him life, though she might never regain his lost love by her own exertions. And oh! how could she see him to discuss a subject in which both knew who was the blood-stained man; and yet whose name might not be breathed by either, so dearly with all his faults, his sins, was he loved by both.

* "They make him so amazed,
And his eyes so dazed." — *Skelton.*

All at once, when she had ceased to try and remember, the name of Will's ship flashed across her mind. The *John Cropper*. He had named it, she had been sure, all along. He had named it in his conversation with her that last, that fatal Thursday evening. She repeated it over and over again, through a nervous dread of again forgetting it. The *John Cropper*.

And then, as if she were rousing herself out of some strange stupor, she bethought her of Margaret. Who so likely as Margaret to treasure every little particular respecting Will, now Alice was dead to all the stirring purposes of life?

She had gone thus far in her process of thought, when a neighbour stepped in; she with whom they had usually deposited the house-key, when both Mary and her father were absent from home, and who consequently took upon herself to answer all inquiries, and receive all messages which any friends might make, or leave, on finding the house shut up.

"Here 's somewhat for you, Mary! A policeman left it."

A bit of parchment.

Many people have a dread of those mysterious pieces of parchment. I am one. Mary was another. Her heart misgave her as she took it, and looked at the unusual appearance of the writing, which, though legible enough, conveyed no idea to her, or rather her mind shut itself up against receiving any idea, which after all was rather a proof she had some suspicion of the meaning that awaited her.

"What is it?" asked she, in a voice from which all the pith and marrow seemed extracted.

"Nay! how should I know? Policeman said he 'd call again towards evening, and see if you 'd gotten it. He were loth to leave it, though I telled him who I was, and all about my keeping th' key, and taking messages."

"What is it about?" asked Mary again, in the same hoarse, feeble voice, and turning it over in her fingers, as if she dreaded to inform herself of its meaning.

"Well! yo can read word of writing and I cannot, so it 's queer I should have to tell you. But my master says it 's a summons for yo to bear witness again Jem Wilson, at th' trial at Liverpool Assize."

"God pity me!", said Mary, faintly, as white as a sheet.

"Nay, wench, never take on so. What yo can say will go little way either to help or hinder, for folk say he's certain to be hung; and sure enough it was t' other one as was your sweetheart."

Mary was beyond any pang this speech would have given at another time. Her thoughts were all busy picturing to herself the terrible occasion of their next meeting — not as lovers meet should they meet!

"Well!" said the neighbour, seeing no use in remaining with one who noticed her words or her presence so little; "thou 'lt tell policeman thou 'st getten his precious bit of paper. He seemed to think I should be for keeping it mysel; he 's th' first as has ever misdoubted me about giving messages, or notes. Good day."

She left the house, but Mary did not know it. She sat still with the parchment in her hand.

All at once she started up. She would take it to Job Legh, and ask him to tell her the true meaning, for it could not be *that*.

So she went, and choked out her words of inquiry.

"It 's a sub-pœna," he replied, turning the parchment over with the air of a connoisseur; for Job loved hard words, and lawyer-like forms, and even esteemed himself slightly qualified for a lawyer, from the smattering of knowledge he had picked up from an odd volume of Blackstone that he had once purchased at a book-stall.

"A sub-pœna — what is that?" gasped Mary, still in suspense.

Job was struck with her voice, her changed, miserable voice, and peered at her countenance from over his spectacles.

"A sub-pœna is neither more nor less than this, my dear. It 's a summonsing you to attend, and answer such questions as may be asked of you regarding the trial of James Wilson, for the murder of Henry Carsons; that 's the long and short of it, only more elegantly put, for the benefit of them who knows how to value the gift of language. I 've been at witness before-time myself; there 's nothing much to be afeared on; if they are impudent, why, just you be impudent, and give 'em tit for tat."

"Nothing much to be afeared on!" echoed Mary, but in such a different tone.

"Ay, poor wench, I see how it is. It 'll go hard with thee a bit, I dare say; but keep up thy heart. Yo cannot have much to tell 'em, that can go either one way or th' other. Nay! may be thou may do him a bit o' good, for when they set eyes on thee, they 'll see fast enough how he came to be so led away by jealousy; for thou'rt a pretty creature, Mary, and one look at thy face will let 'em into th' secret of a young man's madness, and make 'em more ready to pass it over."

"Oh! Job, and won't you ever believe me when I tell you he 's innocent? Indeed, and indeed I can prove it; he was with Will all that night; he was, indeed, Job!"

"My wench! whose word hast thou for that?" said Job, pityingly.

"Why! his mother told me, and I 'll get Will to bear witness to it. But, oh! Job" (bursting into tears), "it is hard if you won't believe me. How shall I clear him to strangers, when those who know him, and ought to love him, are so set against his being innocent?"

"God knows, I 'm not against his being innocent," said Job, solemnly. "I 'd give half my remaining days on earth,— I'd give them all, Mary (and but for the love I bear to my poor blind girl, they 'd be no great gift), if I could save him. You 've thought me hard, Mary, but I 'm not hard at bottom, and I 'll help you if I can; that I will, right or wrong," he added; but in a low voice, and coughed the uncertain words away the moment afterwards.

"Oh, Job! if you will help me," exclaimed Mary, brightening up (though it was but a wintry gleam after all), "tell me what to say, when they question me; I shall be so gloppened,* I sha'n't know what to answer."

"Thou canst do nought better than tell the truth. Truth 's best at all times, they say; and for sure it is when folk have to do with lawyers; for they 're 'cute and cunning enough to get it out sooner or later, and it makes folk look like Tom Noddies, when truth follows falsehood, against their will."

"But I don't know the truth; I mean — I can't say rightly what I mean; but I 'm sure, if I were pent up, and stared at by hundreds of folk, and asked ever so simple a question, I should

* "Gloppened," terrified.

be for answering it wrong; if they asked me if I had seen you on a Saturday, or a Tuesday, or any day, I should have clean forgotten all about it, and say the very thing I should not."

"Well, well, don't go for to get such notions into your head; they 're what they call 'narvous,' and talking on 'em does no good. Here 's Margaret! bless the wench! Look, Mary, how well she guides hersel."

Job fell to watching his grand-daughter, as with balancing, measured steps, timed almost as if to music, she made her way across the street.

Mary shrank as if from a cold blast — shrank from Margaret! The blind girl, with her reserve, her silence, seemed to be a severe judge; she, listening, would be such a check to the trusting earnestness of confidence, which was beginning to unlock the sympathy of Job. Mary knew herself to blame; felt her errors in every fibre of her heart; but yet she would rather have had them spoken about, even in terms of severest censure, than have been treated in the icy manner in which Margaret had received her that morning.

"Here 's Mary," said Job, almost as if he wished to propitiate his grand-daughter, "come to take a bit of dinner with us, for I 'll warrant she 's never thought of cooking any for herself to-day; and she looks as wan and pale as a ghost."

It was calling out the feeling of hospitality, so strong and warm in most of those who have little to offer, but whose heart goes eagerly and kindly with that little. Margaret came towards Mary with a welcoming gesture, and a kinder manner by far than she had used in the morning.

"Nay, Mary, thou know'st thou 'st getten nought at home," urged Job.

And Mary, faint and weary, and with a heart too aching-full of other matters to be pertinacious in this, withdrew her refusal.

They ate their dinner quietly; for to all it was an effort to speak, and after one or two attempts they had subsided into silence.

When the meal was ended Job began again on the subject they all had at heart.

"Yon poor lad at Kirkdale will want a lawyer to see they don't put on him, but do him justice. Hast thought of that?"

Mary had not, and felt sure his mother had not.

Margaret confirmed this last supposition.

"I 've but just been there, and poor Jane is like one dateless; so many griefs come on her at once. One time she seems to make sure he 'll be hung; and if I took her in that way, she flew out (poor body!) and said, that in spite of what folks said, there were them as could, and would prove him guiltless. So I never knew where to have her. The only thing she was constant in, was declaring him innocent."

"Mother-like!" said Job.

"She meant Will, when she spoke of them that could prove him innocent. He was with Will on Thursday night; walking a part of the way with him to Liverpool; now the thing is to lay hold on Will, and get him to prove this." So spoke Mary, calm, from the earnestness of her purpose.

"Don't build too much on it, my dear," said Job.

"I do build on it," replied Mary, "because I know it 's the truth, and I mean to try and prove it, come what may. Nothing you can say will daunt me, Job, so don't you go and try. You may help, but you cannot hinder me doing what I'm resolved on."

They respected her firmness of determination, and Job almost gave into her belief, when he saw how steadfastly she was acting upon it. Oh! surest way of conversion to our faith, whatever it may be, — regarding either small things, or great, — when it is beheld as the actuating principle, from which we never swerve! When it is seen that, instead of over-much profession, it is worked into the life, and moves every action!

Mary gained courage as she instinctively felt she had made way with one at least of her companions.

"Now I 'm clear about this much," she continued, "he was with Will when the — shot was fired (she could not bring herself to say, when the murder was committed, when she remembered *who* it was that, she had every reason to believe, was the taker-away of life). Will can prove this, I must find Will. He wasn't to sail till Tuesday. There 's time enough. He was to come back from his uncle's, in the Isle of Man, on Monday. I must meet him in Liverpool, on that day, and tell him what has happened, and how poor Jem is in trouble, and that he must prove an *alibi*, come Tuesday. All this I can and will do, though perhaps I don't clearly know how, just at present. But surely God will help me. When I know I'm doing right, I will have no fear, but put my trust in Him; for I 'm acting for the innocent and good, and not for my own self, who have done so wrong. I have no fear when I think of Jem, who is so good."

She stopped, oppressed with the fulness of her heart. Margaret began to love her again; to see in her the same, sweet, faulty, impulsive, loveable creature she had known in the former Mary Barton, but with more of dignity, self-reliance, and purpose.

Mary spoke again.

"Now I know the name of Will's vessel — the *John Cropper;* and I know that she is bound to America. That is something to know. But I forget, if I ever heard, where he lodges in Liverpool. He spoke of his landlady, as a good, trustworthy woman; but if he named her name, it has slipped my memory. Can you help me Margaret?"

She appealed to her friend calmly and openly, as if perfectly aware of, and recognising the unspoken tie which bound her and Will together; she asked her in the same manner in which she would have asked a wife where her husband dwelt. And Margaret replied in the like calm tone, two spots of crimson on her cheeks alone bearing witness to any internal agitation.

"He lodges at a Mrs. Jones's, Milk-House Yard, out of Nicholas Street. He has lodged there ever since he began to go to sea; she is a very decent kind of woman, I believe."

"Well, Mary! I 'll give you my prayers," said Job. "It 's not often I pray regular, though I often speak a word to God, when I 'm either very happy, or very sorry; I 've catched myself thanking him at odd hours when I 've found a rare insect, or had a fine day for an out; but I cannot help it, no more than I can talking to a friend. But this time I 'll pray regular for Jem, and for you. And so will Margaret, I 'll be bound. Still wench! what think yo of a lawyer? I know one, Mr. Cheshire, who 's rather given to th' insect line — and a good kind o'chap. He and

I have swopped specimens many's the time, when either of us had a duplicate. He 'll do me a kind turn, I 'm sure. I 'll just take my hat, and pay him a visit."

No sooner said, than done.

Margaret and Mary were left alone. And this seemed to bring back the feeling of awkwardness, not to say estrangement.

But Mary, excited to an unusual pitch of courage, was the first to break silence.

"Oh, Margaret!" said she, "I see — I feel how wrong you think I have acted; you cannot think me worse than I think myself, now my eyes are opened." Here her sobs came choking up her voice.

"Nay," Margaret began, "I have no right to —"

"Yes, Margaret you have a right to judge; you cannot help it; only in your judgment remember mercy, as the Bible says. You, who have been always good, cannot tell how easy it is at first to go a little wrong, and then how hard it is to go back. Oh! I little thought when I was first pleased with Mr. Carsons' speeches, how it would all end; perhaps in the death of him I love better than life."

She burst into a passion of tears. The feelings pent up through the day would have vent. But checking herself with a strong effort, and looking up at Margaret as piteously as if those calm, stony eyes could see her imploring face, she added,

"I must not cry; I must not give way; there will be time enough for that, hereafter, if — I only wanted you to speak kindly to me, Margaret, for I am very, very wretched; more wretched than any one can ever know; more wretched, I sometimes fancy, than I have deserved, — but that 's wrong, isn't it, Margaret? Oh! I have done wrong, and I am punished; you cannot tell how much."

Who could resist her voice, her tones of misery, of humility? Who would refuse the kindness for which she begged so penitently? Not Margaret. The old friendly manner came back. With it, may be, more of tenderness.

"Oh! Margaret, do you think he can be saved, do you think they can find him guilty, if Will comes forward as a witness? Won't that be a good *alibi?*"

Margaret did not answer for a moment.

"Oh, speak! Margaret, said Mary," with anxious impatience.

"I know nought about law, or *alibis*," replied Margaret, meekly; but, Mary, as grandfather says, aren't you building too much on what Jane Wilson has told you about his going with Will? Poor soul, she 's gone dateless, I think, with care, and watching, and overmuch trouble; and who can wonder? Or Jem may have told her he was going, by way of a blind."

"You don't know Jem," said Mary, starting from her seat in a hurried manner, "or you would not say so."

"I hope I may be wrong; but think, Mary, how much there is against him. The shot was fired with his gun; he it was as threatened Mr. Carsons not many days before; he was absent from home at that very time, as we know, and, as I 'm much afeard, some one will be called on to prove; and there 's no one else to share suspicion with him."

Mary heaved a deep sigh.

"But, Margaret, he did not do it," Mary again asserted.

Margaret looked unconvinced.

"I can do no good, I see, by saying so, for none on you believe me, and I won't say so again till I can prove it. Monday morning I 'll go to Liverpool. I shall be at hand for the trial. Oh dear! dear! And I will find Will; and then, Margaret, I think you 'll be sorry for being so stubborn about Jem."

"Don't fly off, dear Mary, I 'd give a deal to be wrong. And now I 'm going to be plain spoken. You 'll want money. Them lawyers is no better than a spunge for sucking up money; let alone your hunting out Will, and your keep in Liverpool, and what not. You must take some of the mint I 've got laid by in the old tea-pot. You have no right to refuse, for I offer it to Jem, not to you; it 's for his purposes you 're to use it."

"I know — I see. Thank you Margaret; you 're a kind one, at any rate. I take it for Jem; and I 'll do my very best with it for him. Not all, though; don't think I 'll take all. They 'll pay me for my keep. I 'll take this," accepting a sovereign from the hoard which Margaret produced out of its accustomed place in the cupboard. "Your grandfather will pay the lawyer, I 'll have nought to do with him," shuddering as she remembered Job's words, about lawyer's skill in always discovering the truth, sooner or later; and knowing what was the secret she had to hide.

"Bless you! don't make such ado about it," said Margaret, cutting short Mary's thanks. "I sometimes think there 's two sides to the commandment; and that we may say, 'Let others do unto you, as you would do unto them,' for pride often prevents our giving others a great deal of pleasure, in not letting them be kind, when their hearts are longing to help; and when we ourselves should wish to do just the same, if we were in their place. Oh! how often I 've been hurt, by being coldly told by persons not to trouble myself about their care, or sorrow, when I saw them in great grief, and wanted to be of comfort. Our Lord Jesus was not above letting folk minister to Him, for he knew how happy it makes one to do ought for another. It 's the happiest work on earth."

Mary had been too much engrossed by watching what was passing in the street to attend very closely to that which Margaret was saying. From her seat she could see out of the window pretty plainly, and she caught sight of a gentleman walking alongside of Job, evidently in earnest conversation with him, and looking keen and penetrating enough to be a lawyer. Job was laying down something to be attended to she could see, by his up-lifted fore-finger, and his whole gesture; then he pointed and nodded across the street to his own house, as if inducing his companion to come in. Mary dreaded lest he should; and she be subjected to a closer cross-examination than she had hitherto undergone, as to why she was so certain that Jem was innocent. She feared he was coming; he stepped a little towards the spot. No! it was only to make way for a child, tottering along, whom Mary had overlooked. Now Job took him by the button, so earnestly familiar had he grown. The gentleman looked "fidging fain" to be gone, but submitted in a manner that made Mary like him in spite of his profession. Then came a volley of last words, answered by briefest nods, and monosyllables; and then the stranger went off with redoubled quickness of pace, and Job crossed the street with a little satisfied air of importance on his kindly face.

"Well! Mary," said he, on entering, "I 've seen the lawyer, not Mr. Cheshire though; trials for murder, it seems, are not his line o' business. But he gived me a note to another 'torney; a fine fellow enough, only too much of a talker; I could hardly get a word in, he cut me so short. However, I 've just been going over the principal points again to him; may be you saw us? I wanted him just come over and speak to you himsel, Mary, but he was pressed for time; and he said your evidence would not be much either here or there. He 's going to the 'sizes first train on Monday morning, and will see Jem, and hear the ins and outs from him, and he 's gived me his address, Mary, and you and Will are to call on him (Will 'special) on Monday, at two o'clock. Thou 'rt taking it in, Mary; thou'rt to call on him in Liverpool at two, Monday afternoon?"

Job had reason to doubt if she fully understood him; for all this minuteness of detail, these satisfactory arrangements, as he considered them, only seemed to bring the circumstances in which she was placed more vividly home to Mary. They convinced her that it was real, and not all a dream, as she had sunk into fancying it for a few minutes, while sitting in the old accustomed place, her body enjoying the rest, and her frame sustained by food, and listening to Margaret's calm voice. The gentleman she had just beheld would see and question Jem in a few hours, and what would be the result?

Monday: that was the day after to-morrow, and on Tuesday, life and death would be tremendous realities to her lover; or else death would be an awful certainty to her father.

No wonder Job went over his main points again: —

"Monday; at two o'clock mind; and here 's his card. 'Mr. Bridgenorth, 41, Renshaw Street, Liverpool.' He 'll be lodging there."

Job ceased talking, and the silence roused Mary up do thank him.

"You 're very kind, Job; very. You and Margaret won't desert me, come what will."

"Pooh! pooh! wench; don't lose heart, just as I 'm beginning to get it. He seems to think a deal on Will's evidence. You 're sure, girls, you 're under no mistake about Will?"

"I'm sure," said Mary, "he went straight from here, purposing to go to see his uncle at the Isle of Man, and be back Sunday night, ready for the sailing on Tuesday."

"So am I," said Margaret. "And the ship's name was the *John Cropper*, and he lodged where I told Mary before. Have you got it down, Mary?" Mary wrote it on the back of Mr. Bridgenorth's card.

"He was not over willing to go," said she, as she wrote, "for he knew little about his uncle, and said he didn't care if he never know'd more. But he said kinsfolk was kinsfolk, and promises was promises, so he'd go for a day or so, and then it would be over."

Margaret had to go and practise some singing in town; so, though loth to depart and be alone, Mary bade her friends good-bye.

CHAPTER XXIV.

"O sad and solemn is the trembling watch
Of those who sit and count the heavy hours,
Beside the fevered sleep of one they love!
O awful is it in the hushed mid night,
While gazing on the pallid, moveless form,
To start and ask, 'Is it now sleep — or death?'"

ANONYMOUS.

MARY could not be patient in her loneliness; so much painful thought weighed on her mind; the very house was haunted with memories, and foreshadowings.

Having performed all duties to Jem, as far as her weak powers, yet loving heart could act; and a black veil being drawn over her father's past, present, and future life, beyond which she could not penetrate to judge of any filial service she ought to render; her mind unconsciously sought after some course of action in which she might engage. Any thing, any thing, rather than leisure for reflection.

And then came up the old feeling which first bound Ruth to Naomi; the love they both held towards one object; and Mary felt that her cares would be most lightened by being of use, or of comfort to his mother. So she once more locked up the house, and set off towards Ancoats; rushing along with down-cast head, for fear lest any one should recognise her and arrest her progress.

Jane Wilson sat quietly in her chair as Mary entered; so quietly, as to strike one by the contrast it presented to her usual bustling, and nervous manner.

She looked very pale and wan; but the quietness was the thing that struck Mary most. She did not rise as Mary came in, but sat still and said something in so gentle, so feeble a voice, that Mary did not catch it.

Mrs. Davenport, who was there, plucked Mary by the gown, and whispered,

"Never heed her; she 's worn out, and best let alone. I 'll tell you all about it, up-stairs."

But Mary, touched by the anxious look with which Mrs. Wilson gazed at her, as if waiting the answer to some question, went forward to listen to the speech she was again repeating.

"What is this? will you tell me?"

Then Mary looked, and saw another ominous slip of parchment in the mother's hand, which she was rolling up and down in a tremulous manner between her fingers.

Mary's heart sickened within her; and she could not speak.

"What is it?" she repeated. "Will you tell me?" She still looked at Mary, with the same child-like gaze of wonder and patient entreaty.

What could she answer?

"I telled ye not to heed her," said Mrs. Davenport, a little angrily. "She knows well enough what it is, — too well, belike. I was not in when they sarved it; but Mrs. Heming (her as lives next door) was, and she spelled out the meaning, and made it all clear to Mrs. Wilson. It 's a summons to be a witness on Jem's trial — Mrs. Heming thinks to swear to the gun; for yo see, there 's nobbut* her as can testify to its being his, and she let on so easily to the policeman that it was his, that there 's no getting off her word now. Poor body; she takes it very hard, I dare say!"

Mrs. Wilson had waited patiently while this whispered speech was being uttered, imagining, perhaps, that it would end in some explanation addressed to her. But when both were silent, though

* "Nobbut," none-but. "No man sigh evere Goe *no but* the oon bigetun sone." — *Wiclif's Version.*

their eyes, without speech or language, told their heart's pity, she spoke again in the same unaltered gentle voice (so different from the irritable impatience she had been ever apt to show to every one except her husband — he who had wedded her, broken-down and injured) in a voice so different, I say, from the old, hasty manner, she spoke now the same anxious words.

"What is this? Will you tell me?"

"Yo'd better give it me at once, Mrs. Wilson, and let me put it out of your sight. Speak to her, Mary, wench, and ask for a sight on it; I 've tried and better-tried to get it from her, and she takes no heed of words, and I 'm loth to pull it by force out of her hands."

Mary drew the little "cricket" * out from under the dresser, and sat down at Mrs. Wilson's knee, and, coaxing one of her tremulous ever moving hands into hers, began to rub it soothingly; there was a little resistance — a very little, but that was all; and presently, in the nervous movement of the imprisoned hand, the parchment fell to the ground.

Mary calmly and openly picked it up, without any attempt at concealment, and quietly placing it in sight of the anxious eyes that followed it with a kind of spell-bound dread, went on with her soothing caresses.

"She has had no sleep for many nights," said the girl to Mrs. Davenport, "and all this woe and sorrow,—it 's no wonder."

"No, indeed!" Mrs. Davenport answered.

"We must get her fairly to bed; we must get her undressed, and all; and trust to God in His mercy, to send her to sleep, or else, —"

For, you see, they spoke before her as if she were not there; her heart was so far away.

Accordingly they almost lifted her from the chair, in which she sat motionless, and taking her up as gently as a mother carries her sleeping baby, they undressed her poor, worn form, and laid her in the little bed up-stairs. They had once thought of placing her in Jem's bed, to be out of sight or sound of any disturbance of Alice's, but then again they remembered the shock she might receive in awakening in so unusual a place, and

* "Cricket," a stool.

also that Mary, who intended to keep vigil that night in the house of mourning, would find it difficult to divide her attention in the possible cases that might ensue.

So they laid her, as I said before, on that little pallet-bed; and, as they were slowly withdrawing from the bed-side, hoping and praying that she might sleep, and forget for a time her heavy burden, she looked wistfully after Mary, and whispered,

"You haven't told me what it is. What is it?"

And gazing in her face for the expected answer, her eye-lids slowly closed, and she fell into a deep, heavy sleep, almost as profound a rest as death.

Mrs. Davenport went her way, and Mary was alone, — for I cannot call those who sleep allies, against the agony of thought which solitude sometimes brings up.

She dreaded the night before her. Alice might die; the doctor had that day declared her case hopeless, and not far from death; and at times the terror, so natural to the young, not of death, but of the remains of the dead, came over Mary; and she bent and listened anxiously for the long-drawn, pausing breath of the sleeping Alice.

Or Mrs. Wilson might awake in a state which Mary dreaded to anticipate, and anticipated while she dreaded; — in a state of complete delirium. Already her senses had been severely stunned by the full explanation of what was required of her, — of what she had to prove against her son, her Jem, her only child, — which Mary could not doubt the officious Mrs. Heming had given; and what if in dreams (that land into which no sympathy nor love can penetrate with another, either to share its bliss or its agony, — that land whose scenes are unspeakable terrors, are hidden mysteries, are priceless treasures to one alone, — that land where alone I may see, while yet I tarry here, the sweet looks of my dead child), — what if, in the horrors of her dreams, her brain should go still more astray, and she should waken crazy with her visions, and the terrible reality that begot them?

How much worse is anticipation sometimes than reality! How Mary dreaded that night, and how calmly it passed by! Even more so than if Mary had not had such claims upon her care!

Anxiety about them deadened her own peculiar anxieties.

She thought of the sleepers whom she was watching, till overpowered herself by the want of rest, she fell off into short slumbers in which the night wore imperceptibly away. To be sure Alice spoke, and sang during her waking moments, like the child she deemed herself; but so happily with the dearly-loved ones around her, with the scent of the heather, and the song of the wild bird hovering about her in imagination — with old scraps of ballads, or old snatches of primitive versions of the Psalms (such as are sung in country churches half draperied over with ivy, and where the running brook, or the murmuring wind among the trees makes fit accompaniment to the chorus of human voices uttering praise and thanksgiving to their God) — that the speech and the song gave comfort and good cheer to the listener's heart, and the gray dawn began to dim the light of the rush-candle, before Mary thought it possible that day was already trembling in the horizon.

Then she got up from the chair where she had been dozing, and went, half-asleep, to the window to assure herself that morning was at hand. The streets were unusually quiet with a Sabbath stillness. No factory bells that morning; no early workmen going to their labours; no slip-shod girls cleaning the windows of the little shops which broke the monotony of the street; instead, you might see here and there some operative sallying forth for a breath of country air, or some father leading out his wee toddling bairns for the unwonted pleasure of a walk with "Daddy," in the clear frosty morning. Men with more leisure on week days would perhaps have walked quicker than they did through the fresh sharp air of this Sunday morning; but to them there was a pleasure, an absolute refreshment in the dawdling gait they, one and all of them had.

To be sure, there were one or two passengers on that morning whose objects were less innocent and less praiseworthy than those of the people I have already mentioned, and whose animal state of mind and body clashed jarringly on the peacefulness of the day, but upon them I will not dwell; as you and I, and almost every one, I think, may send up our individual cry of self-reproach that we have not done all that we could for the stray and wandering ones of our brethren.

When Mary turned from the window, she went to the bed of each sleeper, to look and listen. Alice looked perfectly quiet and happy in her slumber, and her face seemed to have become much more youthful during the painless approach to death.

Mrs. Wilson's countenance was stamped with the anxiety of the last few days, although she, too, appeared sleeping soundly; but as Mary gazed on her, trying to trace a likeness to her son in her face, she awoke and looked up into Mary's eyes, while the expression of consciousness came back into her own.

Both were silent for a minute or two. Mary's eyes had fallen beneath that penetrating gaze, in which the agony of memory seemed every minute to find fuller vent.

"Is it a dream?" the mother asked at last in a low voice.

"No!" replied Mary, in the same tone.

Mrs. Wilson hid her face in the pillow.

She was fully conscious of every thing this morning; it was evident that the stunning effect of the subpœna, which had affected her so much last night in her weak, worn-out state, had passed away. Mary offered no opposition when she indicated by languid gesture and action that she wished to rise. A sleepless bed is a haunted place.

When she was dressed with Mary's aid, she stood by Alice for a minute or two looking at the slumberer.

"How happy she is!" said she, quietly and sadly.

All the time that Mary was getting breakfast ready, and performing every other little domestic office she could think of, to add to the comfort of Jem's mother, Mrs. Wilson sat still in the arm-chair, watching her silently. Her old irritation of temper and manner seemed to have suddenly disappeared, or perhaps she was too depressed in body and mind to show it.

Mary told her all that had been done with regard to Mr. Bridgenorth; all her own plans for seeking out Will; all her hopes; and concealed as well as she could all the doubts and fears that would rise unbidden. To this Mrs. Wilson listened without much remark, but with deep interest and perfect comprehension. When Mary ceased she sighed and said, "Oh wench! I am his mother, and yet I do so little, I can do so little! That 's what frets me! I seem like a child as sees its mammy ill, and moans and cries its little heart out, yet does nought to help. I think my sense has left me all at once, and I can't even find strength to cry like the little child."

Hereupon she broke into a feeble wail of self-reproach, that her outward show of misery was not greater; as if any cries, or tears, or loud-spoken words could have told of such pangs at the heart as that look, and that thin, piping, altered voice!

But think of Mary and what she was enduring! Picture to yourself (for I cannot tell you) the armies of thoughts that met and clashed in her brain; and then imagine the effort it cost her to be calm, and quiet, and even in a faint way, cheerful and smiling at times.

After a while she began to stir about in her own mind for some means of sparing the poor mother the trial of appearing as a witness in the matter of the gun. She had made no allusion to her summons this morning, and Mary almost thought she must have forgotten it; and surely some means might be found to prevent that additional sorrow. She must see Job about it; nay, if necessary, she must see Mr. Bridgenorth, with all his truth-compelling powers; for, indeed, she had so struggled and triumphed (though a sadly-bleeding victor at heart) over herself these two last days, had so concealed agony, and hidden her inward woe and bewilderment, that she began to take confidence, and to have faith in her own powers of meeting any one with a passably fair show, whatever might be rending her life beneath the cloak of her deception.

Accordingly, as soon as Mrs. Davenport came in after morning church, to ask after the two lone women, and she had heard the report Mary had to give (so much better as regarded Mrs. Wilson than what they had feared the night before it would have been) — as soon as this kind-hearted, grateful woman came in, Mary, telling her her purpose, went off to fetch the doctor who attended Alice.

He was shaking himself after his morning's round, and happy in the anticipation of his Sunday's dinner; but he was a good-tempered man, who found it difficult to keep down his jovial easiness even by the bed of sickness or death. He had mischosen his profession; for it was his delight to see every one around him in full enjoyment of life.

However, he subdued his face to the proper expression of sympathy, befitting a doctor listening to a patient, or a patient's friend (and Mary's sad, pale, anxious face, might be taken for either the one, or the other).

"Well, my girl! and what brings you here?" said he, as he entered his surgery. "Not on your own account, I hope."

"I wanted you to come and see Alice Wilson, — and then I thought you would may be take a look at Mrs. Wilson."

He bustled on his hat and coat, and followed Mary, instantly.

After shaking his head over Alice (as if it was a mournful thing for one so pure and good, so true, although so humble a Christian, to be nearing her desired heaven), and muttering the accustomed words intended to destroy hope, and prepare anticipation, he went in compliance with Mary's look to ask the usual questions of Mrs. Wilson, who sat passively in her arm-chair. She answered his questions, and submitted to his examination.

"How do you think her?" asked Mary, eagerly.

"Why — a," began he, perceiving that he was desired to take one side in his answer, and unable to find out whether his listener was anxious for a favourable verdict or otherwise; but thinking it most probable that she would desire the former, he continued,

"She is weak, certainly; the natural result of such a shock as the arrest of her son would be, — for I understand this James Wilson, who murdered Mr. Carsons, was her son. Sad thing to have such a reprobate in the family."

"You say '*who murdered,*' Sir!" said Mary, indignantly. "He is only taken up on suspicion, and many have no doubt of his innocence — those who know him, Sir."

"Ah, well, well! doctors have seldom time to read newspapers, and I dare say I 'm not very correct in my story. I dare say he 's innocent; I 'm sure I had no right to say otherwise, — only words slip out. — No! indeed, young woman, I see no cause for apprehension about this poor creature in the next room; — weak — certainly; but a day or two's good nursing will set her up, and I 'm sure you 're a good nurse, my dear, from your pretty kind-hearted face, — I'll send a couple of pills and a draught, but don't alarm yourself, — there's no occasion, I assure you."

"But you don't think her fit to go to Liverpool?" asked Mary, still in the anxious tone of one who wishes earnestly for some particular decision.

"To Liverpool — yes," replied he. "A short journey like that couldn't fatigue, and might distract her thoughts. Let her go by all means, — it would be the very thing for her."

"Oh, Sir!" burst out Mary, almost sobbing; "I did so hope you would say she was too ill to go."

"Whew—" said he, with a prolonged whistle, trying to understand the case, but, being, as he said, no reader of newspapers, utterly unaware of the peculiar reasons there might be for so apparently unfeeling a wish, — "Why did you not tell me so sooner? It might certainly do her harm in her weak state! there is always some risk attending journeys — draughts, and what not. To her, they might prove very injurious, — very. I disapprove of journeys, or excitement, in all cases where the patient is in the low, fluttered state in which Mrs. Wilson is. If you take *my* advice, you will certainly put a stop to all thoughts of going to Liverpool." He really had completely changed his opinion, though quite unconsciously; so desirous was he to comply with the wishes of others.

"Oh, Sir, thank you! And will you give me a certificate of her being unable to go, if the lawyer says we must have one? The lawyer, you know," continued she, seeing him look puzzled, "who is to defend Jem, — it was as a witness against him — "

"My dear girl?" said he, almost angrily, "why did you not state the case fully at first? one minute would have done it, — and my dinner waiting all this time. To be sure she can't go, — it would be madness to think of it; if her evidence could have done good, it would have been a different thing. Come to me for the certificate any time; that is to say, if the lawyer advises you. I second the lawyer; take counsel with both the learned professions — ha, ha, ha, — "

And laughing at his own joke, he departed, leaving Mary, accusing herself of stupidity in having imagined that every one was as well acquainted with the facts concerning the trial as she was herself; for indeed she had never doubted that the doctor would have been aware of the purpose of poor Mrs. Wilson's journey to Liverpool.

Presently she went to Job (the ever ready Mrs. Davenport keeping watch over the two old women), and told him her fears, her plans, and her proceedings.

To her surprise he shook his head, doubtfully.

"It may have an awkard look, if we keep her back. Lawyers is up to tricks."

"But it is no trick," said Mary. "She is so poorly, she was last night so, at least; and to-day she 's so faded and weak."

"Poor soul! I dare say. I only mean for Jem's sake; and so much is known, it won't do now to hang back. But I'll ask Mr. Bridgenorth. I 'll e'en take your doctor's advice. Yo tarry at home, and I 'll come to yo in an hour's time. Go thy ways, wench."

CHAPTER XXV.

"Something there was, what, none presumed to say,
Clouds lightly passing on a smiling day, —
Whispers and hints which went from ear to ear,
And mixed reports no judge on earth could clear." CRABBE.

"Curious conjectures he may always make,
And either side of dubious questions take." IB.

MARY went home. Oh! how her head did ache, and how dizzy her brain was growing! But there would be time enough she felt for giving way, hereafter.

So she sat quiet and still by an effort; sitting near the window, and looking out of it, but seeing nothing, when all at once she caught sight of something which roused her up, and made her draw back.

But it was too late. She had been seen.

Sally Leadbitter flaunted into the little dingy room, making it gaudy with the Sunday excess of colouring in her dress.

She was really curious to see Mary; her connexion with a murderer seemed to have made her into a sort of *lusus naturæ*, and was almost, by some, expected to have made a change in her personal appearance, so earnestly did they stare at her. But Mary had been too much absorbed the last day or two to notice this.

Now Sally had a grand view, and looked her over and over (a very different thing from looking her through and through), and almost learnt her off by heart: — "her every-day gown (Hoyle's print you know, that lilac thing with the high body) she was so fond of; a little black silk handkerchief just knotted round her neck, like a boy; her hair all taken back from her face, as if she wanted to keep her head cool — she would always keep that hair of hers so long; and her hands twitching continually about. —"

Such particulars would make Sally into a Gazette Extraordinary the next morning at the work-room, and were worth coming for, even if little else could be extracted from Mary.

"Why, Mary!" she began. "Where have you hidden yourself? You never showed your face all yesterday at Miss Simmonds'. You don't fancy we think any the worse of you for what 's come and gone. Some on us, indeed, were a bit sorry for the poor young man, as lies stiff and cold for your sake, Mary; but we shall ne'er cast it up against you. Miss Simmonds, too, will be mighty put out if you don't come, for there 's a deal of mourning, agait."

"I can't," Mary said, in a low voice. "I don't mean ever to come again."

"Why, Mary!" said Sally, in unfeigned surprise. "To be sure you 'll have to be in Liverpool, Tuesday, and may be Wednesday; but after that you 'll surely come, and tell us all about it. Miss Simmonds knows you 'll have to be off those two days. But between you and me, she 's a bit of a gossip, and will like hearing all how and about the trial, well enough to let you off very easy for your being absent a day or two. Besides, Betsy Morgan was saying yesterday, she shouldn't wonder but you'd prove quite an attraction to customers. Many a one would come and have their gowns made by Miss Simmonds just to catch a glimpse at you, at after the trial 's over. Really, Mary, you 'll turn out quite a heroine."

The little fingers twitched worse than ever; the large soft eyes looked up pleadingly into Sally's face; but she went on in the same strain, not from any unkind or cruel feeling towards Mary, but solely because she was incapable of comprehending her suffering.

She had been shocked, of course, at Mr. Carsons' death, though at the same time the excitement was rather pleasant than otherwise; and dearly now would she have enjoyed the conspicuous notice which Mary was sure to receive.

"How shall you like being cross-examined, Mary?"

"Not at all," answered Mary, when she found she must answer.

"La! what impudent fellows those lawyers are! And their clerks, too, not a bit better. I shouldn't wonder" (in a comforting tone, and really believing she was giving comfort) "if you picked up a new sweetheart in Liverpool. What gown are you going in, Mary?"

"Oh, I don't know and don't care," exclaimed Mary, sick and weary of her visitor.

"Well, then! take my advice, and go in that blue merino. It 's old to be sure, and a bit worn at elbows, but folk won't notice that, and th' colour suits you. Now mind, Mary. And I 'll lend you my black watered scarf," added she, really good-naturedly, according to her sense of things, and withal, a little bit pleased at the idea of her pet article of dress figuring away on the person of a witness at a trial for murder.

"I 'll bring it to-morrow before you start."

"No, don't!" said Mary; "thank you, but I don't want it."

"Why, what can you wear? I know all your clothes as well as I do my own, and what is there you can wear? Not your old plaid shawl, I do hope? You would not fancy this I have on, more nor the scarf, would you?" said she, brightening up at the thought, and willing to lend it, or any thing else.

"Oh, Sally! don't go on talking a-that-ns; how can I think on dress at such a time? When it 's a matter of life and death to Jem?"

"Bless the girl! It 's Jem, is it? Well, now I thought there was some sweetheart in the back ground, when you flew off so with Mr. Carsons. Then what in the name of goodness made him shoot Mr. Harry? After you had given up going with him, I mean? Was he afraid you 'd be on again?"

"How dare you say he shot Mr. Harry?" asked Mary, firing up from the state of languid indifference into which she had sunk while Sally had been settling about her dress. "But it 's no matter what you think, as did not know him. What grieves me is, that people should go on thinking him guilty as did know him," she said, sinking back into her former depressed tone and manner.

"And don't you think he did it?" asked Sally."

Mary paused; she was going on too fast with one so curious and so unscrupulous. Besides she remembered how even she herself had, at first, believed him guilty; and she felt it was not for her to cast stones at those who, on similar evidence, inclined to the same belief. None had given him much benefit of a doubt. None had faith in his innocence. None but his mother; and there the heart loved more than the head reasoned, and her yearning affection had never for an instant entertained the idea that her Jem was a murderer. But Mary disliked the whole conversation; the subject, the manner in which it was treated, were all painful, and she had a repugnance to the person with whom she spoke.

She was thankful, therefore, when Job Legh's voice was heard at the door, as he stood with the latch in his hand, talking to a neighbour, and when Sally jumped up in vexation and said, "There 's that old fogey coming in here as I 'm alive! Did your father set him to look after you while he was away? or what brings the old chap here? However, I 'm off; I never could abide either him or his prim grand-daughter. Good-bye, Mary.'

So far in a whisper, then louder.

"If you think better of my offer about the scarf, Mary, just step in to-morrow before nine, and you're quite welcome to it."

She and Job passed each other at the door, with mutual looks of dislike, which neither took any pains to conceal.

"Yon's a bold, bad girl," said Job to Mary.

"She 's very good-natured," replied Mary, too honourable to abuse a visitor who had only that instant crossed her threshold, and gladly dwelling on the good quality most apparent in Sally's character.

"Ay, ay! good-natured, generous, jolly, full of fun; there are a number of other names for the good qualities the devil leaves his childer, as baits to catch gudgeons with. D'ye think folk could be led astray by one who was every way bad? How-e'er, that 's not what I came to talk about. I 've seen Mr. Bridge-north, and he is in a manner of the same mind as we; he thinks it would have an awkward look, and might tell against the poor lad on his trial; still if she 's ill she' s ill, and it can't be helped."

"I don't know if she 's so bad as all that," said Mary, who began to dread her part in doing any thing which might tell against her poor lover.

"Will you come and see her Job? the doctor seemed to say as I liked, not as he thought."

"That's because he had no great thought on the subject, either one way or t' other," replied Job, whose contempt for medical men pretty nearly equalled his respect for lawyers. "But I'll go and welcome. I han not seen th' ould ladies since their sorrows and it 's but manners to go and ax after them. Come along."

The room at Mrs. Wilson's had that still, changeless look you must have often observed in the house of sickness or mourning No particular employment going on; people watching and waiting rather than acting, unless in the more sudden and violent attacks; what little movement is going on, so noiseless and hushed; the furniture all arranged and stationary, with a view to the comfort of the afflicted; the window-blinds drawn down, to keep out the disturbing variety of a sun-beam; the same saddened serious look on the faces of the in-dwellers: you fall back into the same train of thought with all these associations, and forget the street, the outer world in the contemplation of the one stationary, absorbing interest within.

Mrs. Wilson sat quietly in her chair, with just the same look Mary had left on her face; Mrs. Davenport went about with creaking shoes which made all the more noise from her careful and lengthened tread, annoying the ears of those who were well, in this instance, far more than the dull senses of the sick and the sorrowful. Alice's voice still was going on cheerfully in the upper room with incessant talking and little laughs to herself, or perhaps in sympathy with her unseen companions; "unseen," I say, in preference to "fancied," for who knows whether God does not permit the forms of those who were dearest when living, to hover round the bed of the dying?

Job spoke, and Mrs. Wilson answered.

So quietly that it was unnatural under the circumstances. It made a deeper impression on the old man than any token of mere bodily illness could have done. If she had raved in delirium, or moaned in fever, he could have spoken after his wont, and given his opinion, his advice and his consolation; now he was awed into silence.

At length he pulled Mary aside into a corner of the house-place where Mrs. Wilson was sitting, and began to talk to her.

"Yo 're right, Mary! She 's no ways fit to go to Liverpool, poor soul. Now I 've seen her I only wonder the doctor could ha' been unsettled in his mind at th' first. Choose how it goes wi' poor Jem, she cannot go. One way or another it will soon be over, the best to leave her in the state she is till then."

"I was sure you would think so," said Mary.

But they were reckoning without their host. They esteemed her senses gone, while in fact, they were only inert, and could not convey impressions rapidly to the over-burdened, troubled brain. They had not noticed that her eyes had followed them (mechanically it seemed at first) as they had moved away to the corner of the room; that her face hitherto so changeless, had begun to work with one or two of the old symptoms of impatience.

But when they were silent she stood up, and startled them almost as if a dead person had spoken, by saying clearly and decidedly — "I go to Liverpool. I hear you and your plans; and I tell you I shall go to Liverpool. If my words are to kill my son, they have already gone forth out of my mouth, and nought can bring them back. But I will have faith. Alice (up above) has often telled me I wanted faith, and now I will have it. They cannot — they will not kill my child, my only child. I will not be afeared. Yet oh! I am so sick with terror. But if he is to die, think ye not that I will see him again; ay! see him at his trial. When all are hating him, he shall have his poor mother near him, to give him all the comfort, eyes, and looks, and tears, and a heart that is dead to all but him, can give; his poor old mother, who knows how free he is from sin — in the sight of man at least. They 'll let me go to him, maybe, the very minute it 's over; and

I know many Scripture texts (though you would not think it), that may keep up his heart. I missed seeing him ere he went to yon prison, but nought shall keep me away again one minute when I can see his face; for maybe the minutes are numbered, and the count but small. I know I can be a comfort to him, poor lad. You would not think it now, but he'd always speak as kind and soft to me as if he were courting me, like. He loved me above a bit; and I am to leave him now to dree all the cruel slander they 'll put upon him? I can pray for him at each hard word they say against him, if I can do nought else; and he 'll know what his mother is doing for him, poor lad, by the look on my face."

Still they made some look, or gesture of opposition to her wishes. She turned sharp round on Mary, the old object of her pettish attacks, and said,

"Now wench! once for all, I tell you this. *He* could never guide me; and he 'd sense enough not to try. What he could na do, don't you try. I shall go to Liverpool to-morrow, and find my lad, and stay with him through thick and thin; and if he dies, why, perhaps, God of His mercy, will take me too. The grave is a sure cure for an aching heart!"

She sank back in her chair, quite exhausted by the sudden effort she had made; but if they even offered to speak, she cut them short (whatever the subject might be), with the repetition of the same words, "I shall go to Liverpool."

No more could be said, the doctor's opinion had been so undecided; Mr. Bridgenorth had given his legal voice in favour of her going, and Mary was obliged to relinquish the idea of persuading her to remain at home, if indeed under all the circumstances it could be thought desirable.

"Best way will be," said Job, "for me to hunt out Will, early to-morrow morning, and yo, Mary, come at after with Jane Wilson. I know a decent woman where yo two can have a bed, and where we may meet together when I 've found Will, afore going to Mr. Bridgenorth's at two o'clock; for, I can tell him, I 'll not trust none of his clerks for hunting up Will, if Jem's life 's to depend on it."

Now Mary disliked this plan inexpressibly; her dislike was partly grounded on reason, and partly on feeling. She could not bear the idea of deputing to any one the active measures necessary to be taken in order to save Jem. She felt as if they were her duty, her right. She durst not trust to any one the completion of her plan: they might not have energy, or perseverance, or desperation enough to follow out the slightest chance; and her love would endow her with all these qualities, independently of the terrible alternative which awaited her in case all failed and Jem was condemned. No one could have her motives; and consequently no one could have her sharpened brain, her despairing determination. Beside (only that was purely selfish), she could not endure the suspense of remaining quiet, and only knowing the result when all was accomplished.

So with vehemence and impatience she rebutted every reason Job adduced for his plan; and, of course, thus opposed, by what appeared to him wilfulness, he became more resolute, and angry words were exchanged, and a feeling of estrangement rose up between them for a time, as they walked homewards.

But then came in Margaret with her gentleness, like an angel of peace, so calm and reasonable, that both felt ashamed of their irritation, and tacitly left the decision to her (only, by the way, I think Mary could never have submitted if it had gone against her, penitent and tearful as was her manner now to Job, the good old man who was helping her to work for Jem, although they differed as to the manner).

"Mary had better go," said Margaret to her grandfather, in a low tone, "I know what she 's feeling, and it will be a comfort to her soon, may be, to think she did all she could herself. She would perhaps fancy it might have been different; do, grandfather, let her."

Margaret had still, you see, little or no belief in Jem's innocence; and besides she thought if Mary saw Will, and heard herself from him that Jem had not been with him that Thursday night, it would in a measure break the force of the blow which was impending.

"Let me lock up house, grandfather, for a couple of days, and go and stay with Alice. It 's but little one like me can do, I know" (she added softly); "but, by the blessing o' God, I 'll do it and welcome; and here comes one kindly use o' money, I can hire them as will do for her what I cannot. Mrs. Davenport is a willing body, and one who knows sorrow and sickness, and I can pay her for her time, and keep her there pretty near altogether. So let that be settled. And you take Mrs. Wilson, dear grandad, and let Mary go find Will, and you can all meet together at after, and I 'm sure I wish you luck."

Job consented with only a few dissenting grunts; but on the whole, with a very good grace for an old man who had been so positive only a few minutes bofore.

Mary was thankful for Margaret's interference. She did not speak, but threw her arms round Margaret's neck, and put up her rosy-red mouth to be kissed, and even Job was attracted by the pretty, child-like gesture; and when she drew near him, afterwards, like a little creature sidling up to some person whom it feels to have offended, he bent down and blessed her, as if she had been a child of his own.

To Mary the old man's blessing came like words of power.

CHAPTER XXVI.

"Like a bark upon the sea,
   Life is floating over death;
Above, below, encircling thee',
   Danger lurks in every breath.

Parted art thou from the grave
   Only by a plank most frail;
Tossed upon the restless wave,
   Sport of every fickle gale.

Let the skies be e'er so clear,
   And so calm and still the sea,
Shipwreck yet has he to fear
   Who life's voyager will be."

RÜCKERT.

THE early trains for Liverpool, on Monday morning, were crowded by attorneys, attorneys' clerks, plaintiffs, defendants, and witnesses, all going to the Assizes. They were a motley assembly, each with some cause for anxiety stirring at his heart; though, after all, that is saying little or nothing, for we are all of us in the same predicament through life; each with a fear and a hope from childhood to death. Among the passengers there was Mary Barton,dressed in the blue gown and obnoxious plaid shawl.

Common as railroads are now in all places as a means of transit, and especially in Manchester, Mary had never been on one before; and she felt bewildered by the hurry, the noise of people and bells, and horns; the whiz and the scream of the arriving trains.

The very journey itself seemed to her a matter of wonder. She had a back seat, and looked towards the factory-chimneys, and the cloud of smoke which hovers over Manchester, with a feeling akin to the "Heimweh." She was losing sight of the familiar objects of her childhood for the first time; and unpleasant as those objects are to most, she yearned after them with some of the same sentiment which gives pathos to the thoughts of the emigrant.

The cloud-shadows which give beauty to Chat-Moss, the picturesque old houses of Newton, what were they to Mary, whose heart was full of many things. Yet she seemed to look at them earnestly as they glided past; but she neither saw nor heard.

She neither saw nor heard till some well-known names fell upon her ear.

Two lawyers' clerks were discussing the cases to come on that Assizes; of course, "the murder case," as it had come to be termed, held a conspicuous place in their conversation.

They had no doubt of the result.

"Juries are always very unwilling to convict on circumstantial evidence, it is true," said one, "but here there can hardly be any doubt."

"If it had not been so clear a case," replied the other, "I should have said they were injudicious in hurrying on the trial so much. Still, more evidence might have been collected."

"They tell me," said the first speaker, "the people in Gardener's office I mean, that it was really feared the old gentleman would have gone out of his mind, if the trial had been delayed. He was with Mr. Gardener as many as seven times on Saturday, and called him up at night to suggest that some letter should be written, or something done to secure the verdict."

"Poor old man," answered his companion, "who can wonder? — an only son, — such a death, — the disagreeable circumstances attending it; I had not time to read the *Guardian* on Saturday, but I understand it was some dispute about a factory girl?"

"Yes, some such person. Of course she 'll be examined, and Williams will do it in style. I shall slip out from our court to hear him if I can hit the nick of time."

"And if you can get a place you mean, for depend upon it the court will be crowded."

"Ay, ay, the ladies (sweet souls) will come in shoals to hear a trial for murder, and see the murderer, and watch the judge put on his black cap."

"And then go home, and groan over the Spanish ladies who take delight in bull-fights — 'such unfememinine creatures!'"

Then they went on to other subjects.

It was but another drop to Mary's cup; but she was nearly in that state which Crabbe describes,

> "For when so full the cup of sorrows flows
> Add but a drop, it instantly o'erflows."

And now they were in the tunnel! — and now they were in Liverpool; and she must rouse herself from the torpor of mind and body, which was creeping over her; the result of much anxiety and fatigue, and several sleepless nights.

She asked a policeman the way to Milk House Yard, and following his directions with the *savoir faire* of a town-bred girl, she reached a little court leading out of a busy, thronged street, not far from the Docks.

When she entered the quiet little yard she stopped to regain her breath, and to gather strength, for her limbs trembled, and her heart beat violently.

All the unfavourable contingencies she had, until now, forbidden herself to dwell upon, came forward to her mind — the possibility, the bare possibility, of Jem being an accomplice in the murder — the still greater possibility that he had not fulfilled his intention of going part of the way with Will, but had been led off by some little accidental occurrence from his original intention; and that he had spent the evening with those, whom it was now too late to bring forward as witnesses.

But sooner or later she must know the truth; so taking courage she knocked at the door of a house.

"Is this Mrs. Jones's?" she inquired.

"Next door but one," was the curt answer.

And even this extra minute was a reprieve.

Mrs. Jones was busy washing, and would have spoken angrily to the person who knocked so gently at the door, if anger had been in her nature; but she was a soft, helpless kind of woman, and only sighed over the many interruptions she had had to her business that unlucky Monday morning.

But the feeling which would have been anger in a more impatient temper, took the form of prejudice against the disturber, whoever he or she might be.

Mary's fluttered and excited appearance strengthened this prejudice in Mrs. Jones's mind, as she stood, stripping the soap-suds off her arms, while she eyed her visitor, and waited to be told what her business was.

But no words would come. Mary's voice seemed choked up in her throat.

"Pray what do you want young woman?" coldly asked Mrs. Jones at last.

"I want — Oh! is Will Wilson here?"

"No, he is not," replied Mrs. Jones, inclining to shut the door in her face.

"Is he not come back from the Isle of Man?" asked Mary, sickening.

"He never went; he stayed in Manchester too long; as perhaps you know, already."

And again the door seemed closing.

But Mary bent forwards with suppliant action (as some young tree bends, when blown by the rough, autumnal wind), and gasped out,

"Tell me — tell me — where is he?"

Mrs. Jones suspected some love affair, and, perhaps, one of not the most creditable kind; but the distress of the pale young creature before her was so obvious, and so pitiable, that were she ever so sinful, Mrs. Jones could no longer uphold her short, reserved manner.

"He 's gone this very morning, my poor girl. Step in, and I 'll tell you about it."

"Gone!" cried Mary. "How gone? I must see him, — it 's

a matter of life and death: he can save the innocent from being hanged, — he cannot be gone, — how gone?"

"Sailed, my dear! sailed in the *John Cropper* this very blessed morning."

"Sailed!"

CHAPTER XXVII.

"Yon is your quay!
Hark to the clamour in that miry road,
Bounded and narrowed by yon vessel's load;
The lumbering wealth she empties round the place,
Package and parcel, hogshead, chest, and case:
While the loud seaman and the angry hind,
Mingling in business, bellow to the wind."
CRABBE.

MARY staggered into the house. Mrs. Jones placed her tenderly in a chair, and there stood bewildered by her side.

"Oh, father! father!" muttered she, "what have you done? — What must I do? must the innocent die? — or he — whom I fear — I fear — oh! what am I saying?" said she, looking round affrighted, and seemingly reassured by Mrs. Jones's countenance, "I am so helpless, so weak, — but a poor girl after all. How can I tell what is right? Father! you have always been so kind to me, — and you to be — never mind — never mind, all will come right in the grave."

"Save us, and bless us!" exclaimed Mrs. Jones, "if I don't think she 's gone out of her wits!"

"No, I 'm not!" said Mary, catching at the words, and with a strong effort controlling the mind she felt to be wandering, while the red blood flushed to scarlet the heretofore white cheek, 'I 'm not out of my senses; there is so much to be done — so much — and no one but me to do it, you know, — though I can't rightly tell what it is," looking up with bewilderment into Mrs. Jones's face. "I must not go mad whatever comes — at least not yet. No!" (bracing herself up), "something may yet be done, and I must do it. Sailed! did you say? The *John Cropper?* Sailed?"

"Ay! she went out of dock last night, to be ready for the morning's tide."

"I thought she was not to sail till to-morrow," murmured Mary.

"So did Will; (he 's lodged here long, so we all call him 'Will,')" replied Mrs. Jones. "The mate had told him so, I believe, and he never knew different till he got to Liverpool on Friday morning; but as soon as he heard, he gave up going to the Isle o' Man, and just ran over to Rhyl with the mate, one John Harris, as has friends a bit beyond Abergele; you may have heard him speak on him, for they are great chums, though I 've my own opinion of Harris.

"And he 's sailed," repeated Mary, trying by repetition to realise the fact to herself.

"Ay, he went on board last night to be ready for the morning's tide, as I said afore, and my boy went to see the ship go down the river, and came back all agog with the sight. Here, Charley, Charley." She called out loudly for her son: but Charley was one of those boys who are never "far to seek," as the Lancashire people say, when anything is going on; a mysterious conversation, an unusual event, a fire, or a riot, any thing, in short; such boys are the little omnipresent people of this world.

Charley had, in fact, been spectator and auditor all this time; though for a little while he had been engaged in 'dollying' and a few other mischievous feats in the washing line, which had prevented his attention from being fully given to his mother's conversation with the strange girl who had entered.

"Oh, Charley! there you are! Did you not see the *John Cropper* sail down the river this morning? Tell the young woman about it, for I think she hardly credits me."

"I saw her tugged down the river by a steam-boat, which comes to same thing," replied he.

"Oh! if I had but come last night!" moaned Mary. "But I never thought of it. I never thought but what he knew right when he said he would be back from the Isle of Man on Monday morning, and not afore — and now some one must die for my negligence!"

"Die!" exclaimed the lad. "How?"

"Oh! Will would have proved an *alibi*, — but he 's gone, — and what am I to do?"

"Don't give it up yet," cried the energetic boy, interested

at once in the case; "let 's have a try for him. We are but where we were if we fail."

Mary roused herself. The sympathetic "we" gave her heart and hope. "But what can be done? You say he 's sailed; what can be done?" But she spoke louder, and in a more life-like tone.

"No! I did not say he 'd sailed; mother said that, and women know nought about such matters. You see," (proud of his office of instructor, and insensibly influenced, as all about her were, by Mary's sweet, earnest, lovely countenance) "there 's sand-banks at the mouth of the river, and ships can't get over them but at high-water; especially ships of heavy burden, like the *John Cropper*. Now, she was tugged down the river at low water, or pretty near, and will have to lie some time before the water will be high enough to float her over the banks. So hold up your head, — you 've a chance yet, though may be but a poor one."

"But what must I do?" asked Mary, to whom all this explanation had been a vague mystery.

"Do!" said the boy, impatiently, "why, have not I told you? Only women (begging your pardon) are so stupid at understanding about any thing relating to the sea; — you must get a boat, and make all haste, and sail after him, — after the *John Cropper*. You may overtake her, or you may not. It 's just a chance; but she 's heavy laden, and that 's in your favour. She 'll draw many feet of water."

Mary had humbly and eagerly (oh, how eagerly!) listened to this young Sir Oracle's speech; but try as she would, she could only understand that she must make haste, and sail — somewhere —

"I beg your pardon," (and her little acknowledgment of inferiority in this speech pleased the lad, and made him her still more zealous friend.) "I beg your pardon," said she, "but I don't know where to get a boat. Are there boat-stands?"

The lad laughed outright.

"You 're not long in Liverpool, I guess. Boat-stands! No; go down to the pier, — any pier will do, and hire a boat, — you 'll be at no loss when once you are there. Only make haste."

"Oh, you need not tell me that, if I but knew how," said Mary, trembling with eagerness. "But you say right, — I never was here before, and I don't know my way to the place you speak on; only tell me, and I 'll not lose a minute."

"Mother!" said the wilful lad, "I 'm going to show her the way to the pier; I 'll be back in an hour, — or so, —" he added, in a lower tone.

And before the gentle Mrs. Jones could collect her scattered wits sufficiently to understand half of the hastily formed plan, her son was scudding down the street, closely followed by Mary's half-running steps.

Presently he slackened his pace sufficiently to enable him to enter into conversation with Mary, for once escaped from the reach of his mother's recalling voice, he thought he might venture to indulge his curiosity.

"Ahem! — What 's your name? It 's so awkward to be calling you young woman."

"My name is Mary, — Mary Barton," answered she, anxious to propitiate one who seemed so willing to exert himself in her behalf, or else she grudged every word which caused the slightest relaxation in her speed, although her chest seemed tightened, and her head throbbing, from the rate at which they were walking.

"And you want Will Wilson to prove an *alibi* — is that it?"

"Yes — oh, yes — can we not cross now?"

"No, wait a minute; it 's the teagle hoisting above your head I 'm afraid of; — and who is it that 's to be tried?"

"Jem; oh, lad! can't we get past?"

They rushed under the great bales quivering in the air above their heads, and pressed onwards for a few minutes, till Master Charley again saw fit to walk a little slower, and ask a few more questions.

"Mary, is Jem your brother, or your sweetheart, that you 're so set upon saving him?"

"No — no," replied she, but with something of hesitation, that made the shrewd boy yet more anxious to clear up the mystery.

"Perhaps he 's your cousin then? Many a girl has a cousin who has not a sweetheart."

"No, he 's neither kith nor kin to me. What 's the matter? What are you stopping for?" said she, with nervous terror, as Charley turned back a few steps, and peered up a side street.

"Oh, nothing to flurry you so, Mary. I heard you say to mother you had never been in Liverpool before, and if you 'll only look up this street you may see the back windows of our Exchange. Such a building as yon is! with 'natomy hiding under a blanket, and Lord Admiral Nelson, and a few more people in the middle of the court! No! come here," as Mary, in her eagerness, was looking at any window that caught her eye first, to satisfy the boy. "Here then, now you can see it. You can say now, you 've seen Liverpool Exchange."

"Yes, to be sure — it 's a beautiful window, I 'm sure. But are we near the boats? I 'll stop as I come back, you know; only I think we 'd better get on now."

"Oh! if the wind 's in your favour you 'll be down the river in no time, and catch Will, I 'll be bound; and if it 's not, why, you know, the minute it took you to look at the Exchange will be neither here nor there."

Another rush onwards, till one of the long crossings near the docks caused a stoppage, and gave Mary time for breathing, and Charley leisure to ask another question.

"You 've never said where you come from?"

"Manchester," replied she.

"Eh, then! you 've a power of things to see. Liverpool beats Manchester hollow, they say. A nasty, smoky hole, bean't it? Are you bound to live there?"

"Oh, yes! it 's my home."

"Well, I don't think I could abide a home in the middle of smoke. Look there! now you see the river! That 's something now you 'd give a deal for in Manchester. Look!"

And Mary did look, and saw down an opening made in the forest of masts belonging to the vessels in dock, the glorious river, along which white-sailed ships were gliding with the ensigns of all nations not "braving the battle," but telling of the distant lands, spicy or frozen, that sent to that mighty mart for their comforts or their luxuries; she saw small boats passing to and fro on that glittering highway, but she also saw such puffs and clouds of smoke from the countless steamers, that she wondered at Charley's intolerance of the smoke of Manchester. Across the swing-bridge, along the pier, — and they stood breathless by a magnificent dock, where hundreds of ships lay motionless during the process of loading and unloading. The cries of the sailors, the variety of languages used by the passers-by, and the entire novelty of the sight compared with any thing which Mary had ever seen, made her feel most helpless and forlorn; and she clung to her young guide as to one who alone by his superior knowledge could interpret between her and the new race of men by whom she was surrounded, — for a new race sailors might reasonably be considered, to a girl who had hitherto seen none but inland dwellers, and those for the greater part factory people.

In that new world of sight and sound, she still bore one prevailing thought, and though her eye glanced over the ships and the wide-spreading river, her mind was full of the thought of reaching Will.

"Why are we here?" asked she, of Charley. "There are no little boats about, and I thought I was to go in a little boat; those ships are never meant for short distances, are they?"

"To be sure not," replied he, rather contemptuously. "But the *John Cropper* lay in this dock, and I know many of the sailors, and if I could see one I knew, I 'd ask him to run up the mast, and see if he could catch a sight of her in the offing. If she 's weighed her anchor no use for your going, you know."

Mary assented quietly to this speech, as if she were as careless as Charley seemed now to be about her overtaking Will; but in truth her heart was sinking within her, and she no longer felt the energy which had hitherto upheld her. Her bodily strength was giving way, and she stood cold and shivering, although the noon-day sun beat down with considerable power on the shadeless spot where she was standing.

"Here 's Tom Bourne!" said Charley; and altering his manner from the patronising key in which he had spoken to Mary, he addressed a weather-beaten old sailor who came rolling along the pathway where they stood, his hands in his pockets, and his quid in his mouth, with very much the air of one who had nothing to do but look about him, and spit right and left; addressing this old tar, Charley made known to him his wish in slang, which to Mary was almost inaudible, and quite unintelligible, and which I am too much of a land-lubber to repeat correctly.

Mary watched looks and actions with a renovated keenness of perception.

She saw the old man listen attentively to Charley; she saw him eye her over from head to foot, and wind up his inspection with a little nod of approbation (for her very shabbiness and poverty of dress were creditable signs to the experienced old sailor), and then she watched him leisurely swing himself on to a ship in the basin, and borrowing a glass run up the mast with the speed of a monkey.

"He 'll fall!" said she, in affright, clutching at Charley's arm, and judging the sailor, from his storm-marked face and unsteady walk on land, to be much older than he really was.

"Not he!" said Charley. "He 's at the mast-head, now. See! he 's looking through his glass, and using his arms as steady as if he were on dry land. Why I 've been up the mast, many and many a time; only don't tell mother. She thinks I'm to be a shoemaker, but I've made up my mind to be a sailor; only there's no good arguing with a woman. You'll not tell her, Mary?"

"Oh, see!" exclaimed she (his secret was very safe with her, for, in fact, she had not heard it), "See! he 's coming down; he 's down. Speak to him, Charley."

But unable to wait another instant she called out herself,

"Can you see the *John Cropper?* Is she there yet?"

"Ay, ay," he answered, and coming quickly up to them, he hurried them away to seek for a boat, saying the bar was already covered, and in an hour the ship would hoist her sails, and be off. "You 've the wind right against you, and must use oars. No time to lose."

They ran to some steps leading down to the water. They beckoned to some watermen, who, suspecting the real state of the case, appeared in no hurry for a fare, but leisurely brought their boat alongside the stairs, as if it were a matter of indifference to them whether they were engaged or not, while they conversed together in few words, and in an under-tone, respecting the charge they should make.

"Oh, pray make haste," called Mary. "I want you to take me to the *John Cropper*. Where is she, Charley? Tell them — I don't rightly know the words, — only make haste!"

"In the offing she is, sure enough, Miss," answered one of the men, shoving Charley on one side, regarding him as too young to be a principal in the bargain.

"I don't think we can go, Dick," said he, with a wink to his companion, "there 's the gentleman over at New Brighton as wants us."

"But mayhap, the young woman will pay us handsome for giving her a last look at her sweetheart," interposed the other.

"Oh, how much do you want? Only make haste — I 've enough to pay you, but every moment is precious," said Mary.

"Ay, that it is. Less than an hour won't take us to the mouth of the river, and she 'll be off by two o'clock!"

"Poor Mary's ideas of "plenty of money," however, were different to those entertained by the boatmen. Only fourteen or fifteen shillings remained out of the sovereign Margaret had lent her, and the boatman imagining "plenty," to mean no less than several pounds, insisted upon receiving a sovereign (an exorbitant fare by-the-bye, although reduced from their first demand of thirty shillings).

While Charley, with a boy's impatience of delay, and disregard to money, kept urging,

"Give it 'em, Mary; they 'll none of them take you for less. It 's your only chance. There 's St. Nicholas ringing one!

"I 've only got fourteen and ninepence," cried she, in despair, after counting over her money; but I 'll give you my shawl, and you can sell it for four or five shillings, — oh! won't that much do?" asked she, in such a tone of voice, that they must indeed have had hard hearts who could refuse such agonised entreaty.

They took her on board.

And in less than five minutes she was rocking and tossing in a boat for the first time in her life, alone with two rough hard-looking men.

CHAPTER XXVIII.

"A wet sheet and a flowing sea,
A wind that follows fast
And fills the white and rustling sail,
And bends the gallant mast!
And bends the gallant mast, my boys,
While, like the eagle free,
Away the good ship flies, and leaves
Old England on the lee." ALLAN CUNNINGHAM.

MARY had not understood that Charley was not coming with her. In fact, she had not thought about it, till she perceived his absence, as they pushed off from the landing-place, and remembered that she had never thanked him for all his kind interest in her behalf, and now his absence made her feel most lonely — even his, the little mushroom friend of an hour's growth.

The boat threaded her way through the maze of larger vessels which surrounded the shore, bumping against one, kept off by the oars from going right against another, overshadowed by a third, until at length they were fairly out on the broad river, away from either shore; the sights, and sounds of land being lost in the distance.

And then came a sort of pause.

Both wind and tide were against the two men, and labour as they would they made but little way. Once Mary in her impatience had risen up to obtain a better view of the progress they had made, but the men had roughly told her to sit down immediately, and she had dropped on her seat like a chidden child, although the impatience was still at her heart.

But now she grew sure they were turning off from the straight course which they had hitherto kept on the Cheshire side of the river, whither they had gone to avoid the force of the current, and after a short time she could not help naming her conviction, as a kind of nightmare dread and belief came over her, that every thing animate and inanimate was in league against her one sole aim and object of overtaking Will.

They answered gruffly. They saw a boatman whom they knew, and were desirous of obtaining his services as steersman, so that both might row with greater effect. They knew what they were about. So she sat silent with clenched hands while the parley went on, the èxplanation was given, the favour asked and granted. But she was sickening all the time with nervous fear.

They had been rowing a long, long time — half a day it seemed, at least — yet Liverpool appeared still close at hand, and Mary began almost to wonder that the men were not as much disheartened as she was, when the wind which had been hitherto against them, dropped, and thin clouds began to gather over the sky, shutting out the sun, and casting a chilly gloom over every thing.

There was not a breath of air, and yet it was colder than when the soft violence of the westerley wind had been felt.

The men renewed their efforts. The boat gave a bound forwards at every pull of the oars. The water was glassy and motionless, reflecting tint by tint of the Indian ink sky above. Mary shivered, and her heart sank within her. Still now they evidently were making progress. Then the steersman pointed to a rippling line in the river only a little way off, and the men disturbed Mary, who was watching the ships that lay in what appeared to her the open sea, to get at their sails.

She gave a little start, and rose. Her patience, her grief, and perhaps her silence, had begun to win upon the men.

"Yon second to the norrard is the *John Cropper*. Wind 's right now, and sails will soon carry us along-side of her."

He had forgotten (or perhaps he did not like to remind Mary), that the same wind which now bore their little craft along with easy, rapid motion, would also be favourable to the *John Cropper*.

But as they looked with straining eyes, as if to measure the decreasing distance that separated them from her, they saw her sails unfurled and flap in the breeze, till catching the right point, they bellied forth into white roundness, and the ship began to plunge and heave, as if she were a living creature, impatient to be off.

"They 're heaving anchor!" said one of the boatmen to the other, as the faint musical cry of the sailors came floating over the waters that still separated them.

Full of the spirit of the chase, though as yet ignorant of Mary's motives, the men sprung to hoist another sail. It was fully as much as the boat could bear, in the keen, gusty east wind which was now blowing, and she bent and laboured, and ploughed, and creaked upbraidingly as if tasked beyond her strength; but she sped along with a gallant swiftness.

They drew nearer, and they heard the distant "ahoy" more clearly. It ceased. The anchor was up, and the ship was away.

Mary stood up, steadying herself by the mast, and stretched out her arms, imploring the flying vessel to stay its course, by that mute action, while the tears streamed down her cheeks. The men caught up their oars, and hoisted them in the air, and shouted to arrest attention.

They were seen by the men aboard the larger craft; but they were too busy with all the confusion prevalent in an outward-bound vessel to pay much attention. There were coils of ropes and seamen's chests to be stumbled over at every turn; there were animals, not properly secured, roaming bewildered about the deck, adding their pitiful lowings and bleatings to the aggregate of noises. There were carcases not cut up, looking like corpses of sheep and pigs rather than like mutton and pork; there were sailors running here and there and everywhere, having had no time to fall into method, and with their minds divided between thoughts of the land and the people they had left, and the present duties on board ship; while the captain strove hard to procure some kind of order by hasty commands given in a loud, impatient voice, to right and left, starboard, and larboard, cabin and steerage.

As he paced the deck with a chafed step, vexed at one or two little mistakes on the part of the mate, and suffering himself from the pain of separation from wife and children, but showing his suffering only by his outward irritation, he heard a hail from the shabby little river boat that was striving to overtake his winged ship. For the men fearing that, as the ship was now fairly over the bar, they should only increase the distance between them, and being now within shouting range, had asked of Mary her more particular desire.

Her throat was dry, all musical sound had gone out of her voice; but in a loud harsh whisper she told the men her errand of life and death, and they hailed the ship.

"We 're come for one William Wilson who is wanted to prove an *alibi* in Liverpool Assize Courts to-morrow. James Wilson is to be tried for a murder done on Thursday night when he was with William Wilson. Any thing more missus?" asked the boatman of Mary, in a lower voice, and taking his hands down from his mouth.

"Say I 'm Mary Barton. Oh, the ship is going on! Oh, for the love of Heaven, ask them to stop."

The boatman was angry at the little regard paid to his summons, and called out again; repeating the message with the name of the young woman who sent it, and interlarding it with sailor's oaths.

The ship flew along — away, — the boat struggled after.

They could see the captain take his speaking-trumpet. And oh! and alas! they heard his words.

He swore a dreadful oath; he called Mary a disgraceful name; and he said he would not stop his ship for any one, nor could he part with a single hand, whoever swung for it.

The words came in unpitying clearness with their trumpet-sound. Mary sat down looking like one who prays in the death agony. For her eyes were turned up to that Heaven, where mercy dwelleth, while her blue lips quivered, though no sound came. Then she bowed her head and hid it in her hands.

"Hark! yon sailor hails us."

She looked up. And her heart stopped its beating to listen.

William Wilson stood as near the stern of the vessel as he could get; and unable to obtain the trumpet from the angry captain, made a tube of his own hands.

"So help me God, Mary Barton, I 'll come back in the pilot boat, time enough to save the life of the innocent."

"What does he say?" asked Mary, wildly, as the voice died away in the increasing distance, while the boatmen cheered, in their kindled sympathy with their passenger.

"What does he say?" repeated she. "Tell me. I could not hear."

She had heard with her ears, but her brain refused to recognise the sense.

They repeated his speech, all three speaking at once, with many comments; while Mary looked at them and then at the vessel far away.

"I don't rightly know about it," said she, sorrowfully. "What is the pilot-boat?"

They told her, and she gathered the meaning out of the sailors' slang which enveloped it. There was a hope still, although so slight and faint.

"How far does the pilot go with the ship?"

To different distances they said. Some pilots would go as far as Holyhead for the chance of the homeward-bound vessels; others only took the ships over the Banks. Some captains were more cautious than others, and the pilots had different ways. The wind was against the homeward-bound vessels, so perhaps the pilot aboard the *John Cropper* would not care to go far out.

"How soon would he come back?"

There were three boatmen, and three opinions, varying from twelve hours to two days. Nay, the man who gave his vote for the longest time, on having his judgment disputed, grew stubborn, and doubled the time, and thought it might be the end of the week before the pilot-boat came home.

They began disputing, and urging reasons; and Mary tried to understand them; but independently of their nautical language, a veil seemed drawn over her mind, and she had no clear perception of any thing that passed. Her very words seemed not her own, and beyond her power of control, for she found herself speaking quite differently to what she meant.

One by one her hopes had fallen away, and left her desolate; and though a chance yet remained, she could no longer hope. She felt certain it, too, would fade and vanish. She sank into a kind of stupor. All outward objects harmonised with her despair, — the gloomy leaden sky, — the deep, dark waters below, of a still heavier shade of colour, — the cold, flat, yellow shore in the distance, which no ray lightened up, — the nipping cutting wind.

She shivered with her depression of mind and body.

The sails were taken down, of course, on the return to Liverpool, and the progress they made, rowing, and tacking was very slow. The men talked together, disputing about the pilots at first, and then about matters of local importance, in which Mary would have taken no interest at any time, and she gradually became drowsy; irrepressibly so, indeed, for in spite of her jerking efforts to keep awake she sank away to the bottom of the boat, and there lay couched on a rough heap of sails, ropes, and tackle of various kinds.

The measured beat of the waters against the sides of the boat, and the musical boom of the more distant waves, were more lulling than silence, and she slept sound.

Once she opened her eyes heavily, and dimly saw the old gray, rough boatman (who had stood out the most obstinately for the full fare) covering her with his thick pea jacket. He had taken it off on purpose, and was doing it tenderly in his way, but before she could rouse herself up to thank him she had dropped off to sleep again.

At last, in the dusk of evening, they arrived at the landing-place from which they had started some hours before. The men spoke to Mary, but though she mechanically replied, she did not stir; so, at length, they were obliged to shake her. She stood up, shivering and puzzled as to her whereabouts.

"Now tell me where you are bound to, missus," said the gray old man, "and maybe I can put you in the way."

She slowly comprehended what he said, and went through the process of recollection; but very dimly, and with much labour. She put her hand into her pocket and pulled out her purse, and shook its contents into the man's hand; and then began meekly to unpin her shawl, although they had turned away without asking for it.

"No, no!" said the older man, who lingered on the step before springing into the boat, and to whom she mutely offered the shawl.

"Keep it! we donnot want it. It were only for to try you, — some folks say they 've no more blunt, when all the while they 've getten a mint.

"Thank you," said she, in a dull, low tone.

"Where are you bound to? I axed that question afore," said the gruff old fellow.

"I don't know. I'm a stranger," replied she, quietly, with a strange absence of anxiety under the circumstances.

"But you mun find out, then," said he, sharply, "pier-head's no place for a young woman to be standing on, gape-saying."

"I've a card somewhere as will tell me," she answered, and the man partly relieved, jumped into the boat, which was now pushing off to make way for the arrivals from some steamer.

Mary felt in her pocket for the card, on which was written the name of the street where she was to have met Mr. Bridgenorth at two o'clock; where Job and Mrs. Wilson were to have been, and where she was to have learnt from the former the particulars of some respectable lodging. It was not to be found.

She tried to brighten her perceptions, and felt again, and took out the little articles her pocket contained, her empty purse, her pocket-handkerchief, and such little things, but it was not there.

In fact she had dropped it when, so eager to embark, she had pulled out her purse to reckon up her money.

She did not know this, of course. She only knew it was gone.

It added but little to the despair that was creeping over her. But she tried a little more to help herself, though every minute her mind became more cloudy. She strove to remember where Will had lodged, but she could not; name, street, every thing had passed away, and it did not signify; better she were lost than found.

She sat down quietly on the top step of the landing, and gazed down into the dark, dank water below. Once or twice a spectral thought loomed among the shadows of her brain; a wonder whether beneath that cold dismal surface there would not be rest from the troubles of earth. But she could not hold an idea before her for two consecutive moments; and she forgot what she thought about before she could act upon it.

So she continued sitting motionless, without looking up, or regarding in any way the insults to which she was subjected.

Through the darkening light the old boatman had watched her: interested in her in spite of himself, and his scoldings of himself.

When the landing-place was once more comparatively clear, he made his way towards it, across boats, and along planks, swearing at himself while he did so for an old fool.

He shook Mary's shoulder violently.

"D— you, I ask you again where you 're bound to? Don't sit there, stupid. Where are you going to?"

"I don't know," sighed Mary.

"Come, come; avast with that story. You said a bit ago you 'd a card, which was to tell you where to go."

"I had, but I 've lost it. Never mind."

She looked again down upon the black mirror below.

He stood by her, striving to put down his better self; but he could not. He shook her again. She looked up, as if she had forgotten him.

"What do you want?" asked she wearily.

"Come with me and be d—d to you!" replied he, clutching her arm to pull her up.

She arose and followed him, with the unquestioning docility of a little child.

CHAPTER XXIX.

"There are who, living by the legal pen,
Are held in honour — honourable men." CRABBE.

AT five minutes before two, Job Legh stood upon the door-step of the house where Mr. Bridgenorth lodged at Assize time. He had left Mrs. Wilson at the dwelling of a friend of his, who had offered him a room for the old woman and Mary: a room which had frequently been his, on his occasional visits to Liverpool, but which he was thankful now to have obtained for them, as his own sleeping-place was a matter of indifference to him, and the town appeared crowded and disorderly, on the eve of the Assizes.

He was shown in to Mr. Bridgenorth, who was writing. Mary and Will Wilson had not yet arrived, being, as you know, far away on the broad sea; but of this Job of course knew nothing and he did not as yet feel much anxiety about their non-appearance; he was more curious to know the result of Mr. Bridgenorth's interview that morning with Jem.

"Why, yes," said Mr. Bridgenorth, putting down his pen, "I have seen him, but to little purpose, I 'm afraid. He 's very impracticable — very. I told him, of course, that he must be perfectly open with me, or else I could not be prepared for the weak points. I named your name with the view of unlocking his confidence, but — "

"What did he say?" asked Job, breathlessly.

"Why, very little. He barely answered me. Indeed, he refused to answer some questions — positively refused. I don't know what I can do for him."

"Then you think him guilty, Sir," said Job, despondingly.

"No, I don't," replied Mr. Bridgenorth, quickly and decisively, "Much less than I did before I saw him. The impression (mind, 't is only impression; I rely upon your caution, not to take it for fact) — the impression," with an emphasis on the word, "he gave me is, that he knows something about the affair, but what, he will not say; and so, the chances are, if he persists in his obstinacy, he'll be hung. That 's all."

He began to write again, for he had no time to lose.

"But he must not be hung," said Job, with vehemence.

Mr. Bridgenorth looked up, smiled a little, but shook his head.

"What did he say, Sir, if I may be so bold as to ask?" continued Job.

"His words were few enough, and he was so reserved and short, that as I said before, I can only give you the impression they conveyed to me. I told him, of course, who I was, and for what I was sent. He looked pleased, I thought, — at least his face (sad enough when I went in, I assure ye) brightened a little; but he said he had nothing to say, no defence to make. I asked him if he was guilty, then; and by way of opening his heart I said I understood he had had provocation enough, inasmuch as I heard that the girl was very lovely, and had jilted him to fall desperately in love with that handsome young Carsons (poor fellow!). But James Wilson did not speak one way or another. I then went to particulars. I asked him if the gun was his, as his mother had declared. He had not heard of her admission, it was evident, from his quick way of looking up, and the glance of his eye; but when he saw I was observing him, he hung down his head again, and merely said she was right; it was his gun."

"Well!" said Job, impatiently, as Mr. Bridgenorth paused.

"Nay! I have little more to tell you," continued that gentleman. "I asked him to inform me, in all confidence, how it came to be found there. He was silent for a time, and then refused. Not only refused to answer that question, but candidly told me he would not say another word on the subject, and, thanking me for my trouble and interest in his behalf, he all but dismissed me. Ungracious enough on the whole, was it not, Mr. Legh? And yet, I assure ye, I am twenty times more inclined to think him innocent than before I had the interview."

"I wish Mary Barton would come," said Job, anxiously. "She and Will are a long time about it."

"Ay, that 's our only chance, I believe," answered Mr. Bridgenorth, who was writing again. "I sent Johnson off before twelve to serve him with his subpœna, and to say I wanted to speak with him; he 'll be here soon, I have no doubt."

There was a pause. Mr. Bridgenorth looked up again and spoke.

"Mr. Duncombe promised to be here to speak to his character. I sent him a subpœna on Saturday night. Though after all, juries go very little by such general and vague testimony as that to character. It is very right that they should not often; but in this instance unfortunate for us, as we must rest our case on the *alibi.*"

The pen went again, scratch, scratch over the paper.

Job grew very fidgety. He sat on the edge of his chair, the more readily to start up when Will and Mary should appear. He listened intently to every noise and every step on the stair.

Once he heard a man's footstep, and his old heart gave a leap of delight. But it was only Mr. Bridgenorth's clerk, bringing him a list of those cases in which the grand jury had found true bills. He glanced it over and pushed it to Job, merely saying,

"Of course we expected this," and went on with his writing.

There was a true bill against James Wilson. Of course. And yet Job felt now doubly anxious and sad. It seemed the beginning of the end. He had got, by imperceptible degrees, to think Jem innocent. Little by little this persuasion had come upon him.

Mary (tossing about in the little boat on the broad river) did not come, nor did Will.

Job grew very restless. He longed to go and watch for them out of the window, but feared to interrupt Mr. Bridgenorth. At length his desire to look out was irresistible, and he got up and walked carefully and gently across the room, his boots creaking at every cautious step. The gloom which had overspread the sky, and the influence of which had been felt by Mary on the open water, was yet more perceptible in the dark, dull street. Job grew more and more fidgety. He was obliged to walk about the room, for he could not keep still; and he did so, regardless of Mr. Bridgenorth's impatient little motions and noises, as the slow, stealthy, creaking movements were heard, backwards and forwards, behind his chair.

He really liked Job, and was interested for Jem, else his nervousness would have overcome his sympathy long before it did. But he could hold out no longer against the monotonous, grating sound; so at last he threw down his pen, locked his portfolio, and taking up his hat and gloves, told Job he must go to the courts.

"But Will Wilson is not come," said Job, in dismay. "Just wait while I run to his lodgings. I would have done it before, but I thought they'd be here every minute, and I were afraid of missing them. I 'll be back in no time."

"No, my good fellow, I really must go. Besides, I begin to think Johnson must have made a mistake, and have fixed with this William Wilson to meet me at the courts. If you like to wait for him here, pray make use of my room; but I 've a notion I shall find him there: in which case, I 'll send him to your lodgings; shall I? You know where to find me. I shall be here again by eight o'clock, and with the evidence of this witness that 's to prove the *alibi*, I 'll have the brief drawn out, and in the hands of counsel to-night."

So saying, he shook hands with Job, and went his way. The

old man considered for a minute as he lingered at the door, and then bent his steps towards Mrs. Jones's, where he knew (from reference to queer, odd, heterogeneous memoranda, in an ancient black-leather pocket-book) that Will lodged, and where he doubted not he should hear both of him and of Mary.

He went there, and gathered what intelligence he could out of Mrs. Jones's slow replies.

He asked if a young woman had been there that morning, and if she had seen Will Wilson. "No!"

"Why not?"

"Why, bless you, 'cause he had sailed some hours before she came asking for him."

There was a dead silence, broken only by the even, heavy sound of Mrs. Jones's ironing.

"Where is the young woman now?" asked Job.

"Somewhere down at the docks," she thought. "Charley would know, if he was in, but he wasn't. He was in mischief, somewhere or other, she had no doubt. Boys always were. He would break his neck some day, she knew;" so saying, she quietly spat upon her fresh iron, to test its head, and then went on with her business.

Job could have boxed her, he was in such a state of irritation. But he did not, and he had his reward. Charley came in, whistling with an air of indifference, assumed to carry off his knowledge of the lateness of the hour to which he had lingered about the docks.

"Here 's an old man come to know where the young woman is, who went out with thee this morning," said his mother, after she had bestowed on him a little motherly scolding.

"Where she is now, I don't know. I saw her last sailing down the river after the *John Cropper*. I 'm afeard she won't reach her; wind changed, and she would be under weigh, and over the bar in no time. She would have been back by now."

It took Job some little time to understand this, from the confused use of the feminine pronoun. Then he inquired how he could best find Mary.

"I 'll run down again to the pier," said the boy, "I'll warrant I 'll find her."

"Thou shalt do no such a thing," said his mother, setting her back against the door. The lad made a comical face at Job, which met with no responsive look from the old man, whose sympathies were naturally in favour of the parent; although he would thankfully have availed himself of Charley's offer; for he was weary, and anxious to return to poor Mrs. Wilson, who would be wondering what had become of him.

"How can I best find her? Who did she go with, lad?"

But Charley was sullen at his mother's exercise of authority before a stranger, and at that stranger's grave looks when he meant to have made him laugh.

"They were river boatmen; — that 's all I know," said he.

"But what was the name of their boat?" persevered Job.

"I never took no notice — the Anne, or William, — or some of them common names, I'll be bound."

"What pier did she start from?" asked Job, despairingly.

"Oh, as for that matter, it were the stairs on the Prince's Pier she started from; but she 'll not come back to the same, for the American steamer came up with the tide, and anchored close to it, blocking up the way for all the smaller craft. It 's a rough evening too, to be out on," he maliciously added.

"Well, God's will be done! I did hope we could have saved the lad," said Job, sorrowfully; "but I 'm gettin very doubtful again. I 'm uneasy about Mary, too, — very. She 's a stranger in Liverpool."

"Se she told me," said Charley. "There 's traps about for young women at every corner. It 's a pity she 's no one to meet her when she lands."

"As for that," replied Job, "I don't see how any one could meet her when we can't tell where she would come to. I must trust to her coming right. She 's getten spirit and sense. She 'll most likely be for coming here again. Indeed, I don't know what else she can do, for she knows no other place in Liverpool. Missus, if she comes, will you give your son leave to bring her to No. 8, Back Garden Court, where there 's friends waiting for her? I 'll give him sixpence for his trouble."

Mrs. Jones, pleased with the reference to her, gladly promised. And even Charley, indignant as he was at first at the idea of his motions being under the control of his mother, was mollified at the prospect of the sixpence, and at the probability of getting nearer to the heart of the mystery.

But Mary never came.

CHAPTER XXX.

"Oh! sad is the night-time,
  The night-time of sorrow,
When through the deep gloom, we catch but the boom
  Of the waves that may whelm us to-morrow."

Job found Mrs. Wilson pacing about in a restless way; not speaking to the woman at whose house she was staying, but occasionally heaving such deep oppressive sighs, as quite startled those around her.

"Well!" said she, turning sharp round in her tottering walk up and down, as Job came in.

"Well, speak!" repeated she, before he could make up his mind what to say; for, to tell the truth, he was studying for some kind-hearted lie which might soothe her for a time. But now the real state of the case came blurting forth in answer to her impatient questioning.

"Will 's not to the fore. But he 'll may be turn up yet, time enough."

She looked at him steadily for a minute, as if almost doubting if such despair could be in store for her as his words seemed to imply. Then she slowly shook her head, and said, more quietly than might have been expected from her previous excited manner.

"Don't go for to say that! Thou dost not think it. Thou 'rt well-nigh hopeless, like me. I seed all along my lad would be hung for what he never did. And better he were, and were shut* of this weary world where there 's neither justice nor mercy left."

She looked up with tranced eyes as if praying, and then sat down.

"Nay, now thou 'rt off at a gallop," said Job. "Will has sailed this morning for sure, but that brave wench, Mary Barton, is after him, and will bring him back, I 'll be bound, if she can

* "Shut," quit.

but get speech on him. She 's not back yet. Come, come, hold up thy head. It will all end right."

"It will all end right," echoed she; "but not as thou tak'st it. Jem will be hung, and will go to his father and the little lads; where the Lord God wipes away all tears, and where the Lord Jesus speaks kindly to the little ones, who look about for the mothers they left upon earth. Eh, Job, yon 's a blessed land, and I long to go to it, and yet I fret because Jem is hastening there. I would not fret if he and I could lie down to-night to sleep our last sleep; not a bit would I fret if folk would but know him to be innocent — as I do."

"They 'll know it sooner or later, and repent sore if they 've hanged him for what he never did," replied Job.

"Ay, that they will. Poor souls! May God have mercy on them when they find out their mistake."

Presently Job grew tired of sittng waiting, and got up, and hung about the door and window, like some animal wanting to go out. It was pitch dark, for the moon had not yet risen.

"You just go to bed," said he, to the widow, "You 'll want your strength for to-morrow. Jem will be sadly off, if he sees you so cut up as you look to-night. I 'll step down again and find Mary. She 'll be back by this time. I 'll come and tell you every thing, never fear. But, now, you go to bed."

"Thou 'rt a kind friend, Job Legh, and I 'll go, as thou wishest me. But, oh! mind thou com'st straight off to me, and bring Mary as soon as thou 'st lit on her." She spoke low, but very calmly.

"Ay, ay!" replied Job, slipping out of the house.

He went first to Mr. Bridgenorth's, where it had struck him that Will and Mary might be all this time waiting for him.

They were not there, however. Mr. Bridgenorth had just come in, and Job went breathlessly up-stairs to consult with him as to the state of the case.

"It 's a bad job," said the lawyer, looking very grave, while he arranged his papers. "Johnson told me how it was; the woman that Wilson lodged with told him. I doubt it 's but a wild goose-chase of the girl Barton. Our case must rest on the uncertainty of circumstantial evidence, and the goodness of the prisoner's previous character. A very vague and weak defence. However, I 've engaged Mr. Clinton, as counsel, and he'll make the best of it. And now my good fellow, I must wish you good-night, and turn you out of doors. As it is, I shall have to sit up into the small hours. Did you see my clerk, as you came up-stairs? You did. Then may I trouble you to ask him to step up immediately."

After this Job could not stay, and, making his humble bow, he left the room.

Then he went to Mrs. Jones's. She was in, but Charley had slipped off again. There was no holding that boy. Nothing kept him but lock and key, and they did not always; for, once, she had him locked up in the garret, and he had got off through the skylight. Perhaps, now he was gone to see after the young woman down at the docks. He never wanted an excuse to be there.

Unasked, Job took a chair, resolved to await Charley's re-appearance.

Mrs. Jones ironed and folded her clothes, talking all the time of Charley and her husband, who was a sailor in some ship bound for India, and who, in leaving her their boy, had evidently left her rather more than she could manage. She moaned and croaked over sailors, and sea-port towns, and stormy weather, and sleepless nights, and trousers all over tar and pitch, long after Job had left off attending to her, and was only trying to hearken to every step, and every voice in the street

At last Charley came in, but he came alone.

"Yon Mary Barton has getten into some scrape or another," said he, addressing himself to Job. "She's not to be heard of at any of the piers; and Bourne says it were a boat from the Cheshire side as she went aboard of. So there 's no hearing of her till to-morrow morning."

"To-morrow morning she 'll have to be in court, at nine o'clock, to bear witness on a trial," said Job, sorrowfully.

"So she said; at least somewhat of the kind," said Charley, looking desirous to hear more. But Job was silent.

He could not think of any thing further that could be done; so he rose up, and, thanking Mrs. Jones for the shelter she had given him, he went out into the street; and there he stood still, to ponder over probabilities and chances.

After some little time he slowly turned towards the lodging where he had left Mrs. Wilson. There was nothing else to be done; but he loitered on the way, fervently hoping that her weariness and her woes might have sent her to sleep before his return, that he might be spared her questionings.

He went very gently into the house-place where the sleepy landlady awaited his coming, and his bringing the girl, who, she had been told, was to share the old woman's bed.

But in her sleepy blindness she knocked things so about in lighting the candle (she could see to have a nap by fire-light, she said), that the voice of Mrs. Wilson was heard from the little back-room, where she was to pass the night.

"Who 's there?"

Job gave no answer, and kept down his breath, that she might think herself mistaken. The landlady, having no such care, dropped the snuffers with a sharp metallic sound, and then, by her endless apologies, convinced the listening woman that Job had returned.

"Job! Job Legh!" she cried out, nervously.

"Eh, dear!" said Job, to himself, going reluctantly to her bed-room door. "I wonder if one little lie would be a sin as things stand. It would happen give her sleep, and she won't have sleep for many and a many a night (not to call sleep), if things goes wrong to-morrow. I 'll chance it, any way."

"Job! art thou there?" asked she again, with a trembling impatience that told in every tone of her voice.

"Ay! sure! I thought thou 'd ha' been asleep by this time."

"Asleep! How could I sleep till I knowed if Will were found?"

"Now for it," muttered Job, to himself. Then in a louder voice, "Never fear! he 's found, and safe, ready for to-morrow."

"And he 'll prove that thing for my poor lad, will he? He 'll bear witness that Jem were with him? Oh, Job, speak! tell me all!"

"In for a penny, in for a pound,' thought Job. "Happen one prayer will do for the sum total. Any rate, I must go on now. — Ay, ay," shouted he, through the door. "He can prove all; and Jem will come off as clear as a new-born babe."

He could hear Mrs. Wilson's rustling movements, and in an instant guessed she was on her knees, for he heard her trembling voice uplifted in thanksgiving, and praise to God, stopped at times by sobs of gladness and relief.

And when he heard this, his heart misgave him; for the thought of the awful enlightening, the terrible revulsion of feeling that awaited her in the morning. He saw the short-sightedness of falsehood; but what could he do now?

While he listened, she ended her grateful prayers.

"And Mary? Thou 'st found her at Mrs. Jones's, Job?" said she, continuing her inquiries.

He gave a great sigh.

"Yes she was there, safe enough, second time of going. — God forgive me!" muttered he, "who 'd ha' thought of my turning out such an arrant liar in my old days."

"Bless the wench! Is she here? Why does not she come to bed? I 'm sure she 's need."

Job coughed away his remains of conscience, and made answer,

"She was a bit weary, and o'er done with her sail; and Mrs. Jones axed her to stay there all night. It was nigh at hand to the courts, where she will have to be in the morning."

"It comes easy enough after a while," groaned out Job. "The father of lies helps one, I suppose, for now my speech comes as natural as truth. She 's done questioning now, that 's one good thing. I'll be off, before Satan and she are at me again."

He went to the house-place, where the landlady stood, wearily waiting. Her husband was in bed, and asleep long ago.

But Job had not yet made up his mind what to do. He could not go to sleep, with all his anxieties, if he were put into the best bed in Liverpool.

"Thou 'lt let me sit up in this arm-chair," said he at length, to the woman, who stood, expecting his departure.

He was an old friend, so she let him do as he wished. But, indeed, she was too sleepy to have opposed him. She was too glad to be released, and go to bed.

CHAPTER XXXI.

"To think
That all this long interminable night,
Which I have passed in thinking on two words —
'Guilty' — 'Not Guilty!' — like one happy moment
O'er many a head hath flown unheeded by;
O'er happy sleepers dreaming in their bliss
Of bright to-morrows — or far happier still,
With deep breath buried in forgetfulness.
O all the dismallest images of death
Did swim before my eyes!" WILSON.

AND now, where was Mary?

How Job's heart would have been relieved of one of its cares if he could have seen her: for he was in a miserable state of anxiety about her; and many and many a time through that long night, he scolded her and himself; her for her obstinacy, and himself for his weakness in yielding to her obstinacy, when she insisted on being the one to follow and find out Will.

She did not pass that night in bed, any more than Job; but she was under a respectable roof, and among kind, though rough people.

She had offered no resistance to the old boatman, when he had clutched her arm, in order to insure her following him, as he threaded the crowded dock-ways, and dived up strange by-streets. She came on meekly after him, scarcely thinking in her stupor where she was going, and glad (in a dead, heavy way) that some one was deciding things for her.

He led her to an old-fashioned house, almost as small as house could be, which had been built long ago, before all the other part of the street, and had a country-town look about it in the middle of that bustling back street. He pulled her into the house-place; and relieved to a certain degree of his fear of losing her on the way, he exclaimed,

"There!" giving a great slap of one hand on her back.

The room was light and bright, and roused Mary (perhaps the slap on her back might help a little, too), and she felt the awkwardness of accounting for her presence to a little bustling old woman who had been moving about the fire-place on her entrance. The boatman took it very quietly, never deigning to give any explanation, but sitting down in his own particular chair, and chewing tobacco, while he looked at Mary with the most satisfied air imaginable, half triumphantly, as if she were the captive of his bow and spear, and half defying, as if daring her to escape.

The old woman, his wife, stood still, poker in hand, waiting to be told who it was that her husband had brought home so unceremoniously; but, as she looked in amazement the girl's cheek flushed, and then blanched to a dead whiteness; a film came over her eyes, and catching at the dresser for support in that hot whirling room, she fell in a heap on the floor.

Both man and wife came quickly to her assistance. They raised her up, still insensible, and he supported her on one knee, while his wife pattered away for some cold fresh water. She threw it straight over Mary; but though it caused a great sob, the eyes still remained closed, and the face as pale as ashes.

"Who is she, Ben?" asked the woman, as she rubbed her unresisting, powerless hands.

"How should I know?" answered her husband, gruffly.

"Well-a-well" (in a soothing tone, such as you use to irritated children), and as if half to herself, "I only thought you might, you know, as you brought her home. Poor thing! we must not ask ought about her, but that she needs help. I wish I 'd my salts at home, but I lent 'em to Mrs. Burton, last Sunday in church, for she could not keep awake through the sermon. Dear-a-me, how white she is!"

"Here! you hold her up a bit," said her husband.

She did as he desired, still crooning to herself, not caring for his short, sharp interruptions as she went on; and, indeed, to her old, loving heart, his crossest words fell like pearls and diamonds, for he had been the husband of her youth; and even he, rough and crabbed as he was, was secretly soothed by the sound of her voice, although not for worlds, if he could have helped it, would he have shown any of the love that was hidden beneath his rough outside.

"What 's the old fellow after?" said she, bending over Mary, so as to accommodate the drooping head. "Taking my pen, as I 've had for better nor five year. Bless us, and save us! he 's burning it! Ay, I see now, he 's his wits about him; burnt feathers is always good for a faint. But they don't bring her round, poor wench! Now what 's he after next? Well! he is a bright one, my old man! That I never thought of that, to be sure!" exclaimed she, as he produced a square bottle of smuggled spirits, labelled "Golden Wasser," from a corner cupboard in their little room.

"That 'll do!" said she, as the dose he poured into Mary's open mouth, made her start and cough. "Bless the man! It 's just like him to be so tender and thoughtful!"

"Not a bit!" snarled he, as he was relieved by Mary's returning colour, and opened eyes, and wondering, sensible gaze, "Not a bit! I never was such a fool afore."

His wife helped Mary to rise, and placed her in a chair.

"All 's right, now, young woman?" asked the boatman, anxiously.

"Yes, Sir, and thank you. I 'm sure, Sir, I don't know rightly how to thank you," faltered Mary, softly forth.

"Be hanged to you and your thanks." And he shook himself, took his pipe, and went out without deigning another word; leaving his wife, sorely puzzled as to the character and history of the stranger within her doors.

Mary watched the boatman leave the house, and then, turning her sorrowful eyes to the face of her hostess, she attempted feebly to rise, with the intention of going away, — where she knew not.

"Nay! nay! whoe'er thou be'st, thou 'rt not fit to go out into the street. Perhaps" (sinking her voice a little) "thou 'rt a bad one; I almost misdoubt thee, thou 'rt so pretty. Well-a-well! it 's the bad ones as have the broken hearts, sure enough; good folk never get utterly cast down, they 've always getten hope in the Lord; it 's the sinful as bear the bitter, bitter grief in their crushed hearts, poor souls; it 's them we ought, most of all, to pity and to help. She shanna leave the house to-night, choose who she is, — worst woman in Liverpool, she shanna. I wished I knew where th' old man picked her up, that I do."

Mary had listened feebly to this soliloquy, and now tried to satisfy her hostess, in weak, broken sentences.

"I 'm not a bad one, missis, indeed. Your master took me out to sea after a ship as had sailed. There was a man in it as might save a life at the trial to-morrow. The captain would not let him come, but he says he 'll come back in the pilot-boat." She fell to sobbing at the thought of her waning hopes, and the old woman tried to comfort her, beginning with her accustomed,

"Well-a-well! and he 'll come back, I'm sure. I know he will; so keep up your heart. Don't fret about it. He 's sure to be back."

"Oh! I 'm afraid! I 'm sore afraid he won't," cried Mary, consoled, nevertheless, by the woman's assertions, all groundless as she knew them to be.

Still talking half to herself, and half to Mary, the old wowan prepared tea, and urged her visitor to eat and refresh herself. But Mary shook her head at the proffered food, and only drank a cup of tea with thirsty eagerness. For the spirits had thrown her into a burning heat, and rendered each impression received through her senses of the most painful distinctness and intensity while her head ached in a terrible manner.

She disliked speaking, her power over her words seemed so utterly gone. She used quite different expressions to those she intended. So she kept silent, while Mrs. Sturgis (for that was the name of her hostess) talked away, and put her tea-things by, and moved about incessantly, in a manner that increased the dizziness in Mary's head. She felt as if she ought to take leave for the night, and go. But where?

Presently the old man came back; crosser and gruffer than when he went away. He kicked aside the dry shoes his wife had prepared for him, and snarled at all she said. Mary attributed this to his finding her still there, and gathered up her strength for an effort to leave the house. But she was mistaken. By-and-bye, he said (looking right into the fire, as if addressing it) "Wind 's right against them!"

"Ay, ay, and is it so?" said his wife, who knowing him well, knew that his surliness proceeded from some repressed sympathy. "Well-a-well, wind changes often at night. Time enough before morning. I 'd bet a penny it has changed sin' thou looked."

She looked out of her little window at a weather-cock near, glittering in the moonlight; and as she was a sailor's wife, she instantly recognised the unfavourable point at which the indicator seemed stationary, and giving a heavy sigh, turned into the room, and began to beat about in her own mind for some other mode of comfort.

"There 's no one else who can prove what you want at the trial to-morrow, is there?" asked she.

"No one!" answered Mary.

"And you 've no clue to the one as is really guilty, if t'other is not?"

Mary did not answer, but trembled all over.

Sturgis saw it.

"Don't bother her with thy questions," said he, to his wife. "She mun go to bed, for she 's all in a shiver with the sea air. I 'll see after the wind, hang it, and the weather-cock, too. Tide will help 'em when it turns."

Mary went up-stairs murmuring thanks and blessings on those who took the stranger in. Mrs. Sturgis led her into a little room redolent of the sea, and foreign lands. There was a small bed for one son, bound for China; and a hammock slung above for another, who was now tossing in the Baltic. The sheets looked made out of sail-cloth, but were fresh and clean in spite of their brownness.

Against the wall were wafered two rough drawings of vessels with their names written underneath, on which the mother's eyes caught, and gazed until they filled with tears. But she brushed the drops away with the back of her hand; and in a cheerful tone, went on to assure Mary the bed was well aired.

"I cannot sleep, thank you. I will sit here, if you please," said Mary, sinking down on the window-seat.

"Come, now," said Mrs. Sturgis, "my master told me to see you to bed, and I mun. What 's the use of watching? A watched pot never boils, and I see you are after watching that weather-cock. Why now, I try never to look at it, else I could do nought else. My heart many a time goes sick when the wind rises, but I turn away and work away, and try never to think on the wind, but on what I ha' getten to do."

"Let me stay up a little," pleaded Mary, as her hostess seemed so resolute about seeing her to bed. Her looks won her suit.

"Well, I suppose I mun. I shall catch it down stairs, I know. He 'll be in a fidget till you 're getten to bed, I know; so you mun be quiet if you are so bent upon staying up."

And quietly, noiselessly, Mary watched the unchanging weather-cock through the night. She sat on the little window-seat, her hand holding back the curtain which shaded the room from the bright moonlight without; her head resting its weariness against the corner of the window-frame; her eyes burning, and stiff with the intensity of her gaze.

The ruddy morning stole up the horizon, casting a crimson glow into the watcher's room.

It was the morning of the day of trial!

CHAPTER XXXII.

"Thou stand'st here arraign'd,
That with presumption impious and accurs'd,
Thou hast usurp'd God's high prerogative,
Making thy fellow mortal's life and death
Wait on thy moody and diseased passions;
That with a violent and untimely steel
Hath set abroach the blood, that should have ebbed
In calm and natural current: to sum all
In one wild name — a name the pale air freezes at,
And every cheek of man sinks in with horror —
Thou art a cold and midnight murderer." MILMAN'S 'FAZIO.'

OF all the restless people who found that night's hours agonising from excess of anxiety, the poor father of the murdered man was perhaps the most restless. He had slept but little since the blow had fallen; his waking hours had been too full of agitated thought, which seemed to haunt and pursue him through his unquiet slumbers.

And this night of all others was the most sleepless. He turned over and over again in his mind the wonder if every thing had been done that could be done, to insure the conviction of Jem Wilson. He almost regretted the haste with which he had urged forward the proceedings, and yet until he had obtained vengeance, he felt as if there were no peace on earth for him (I don't know that he exactly used the term vengeance in his thoughts; he spoke of justice, and probably thought of his desired end as such); no peace, either bodily or mental, for he moved up and down his bedroom with the restless incessant tramp of a wild beast in a cage, and if he compelled his aching limbs to cease for an instant, the twitchings which ensued almost amounted to convulsions, and he re-commenced his walk as the lesser evil, and the more bearable fatigue.

With daylight, increased power of action came; and he drove off to arouse his attorney, and worry him with further directions and inquiries; and when that was ended, he sat, watch in hand, until the courts should be opened, and the trial begin.

What were all the living, — wife or daughters, — what were they in comparison with the dead, — the murdered son who lay unburied still, in compliance with his father's earnest wish, and almost vowed purpose of having the slayer of his child sentenced to death, before he committed the body to the rest of the grave?

At nine o'clock they all met at their awful place of *rendezvous*.

The judge, the jury, the avenger of blood, the prisoner, the witnesses — all were gathered together within one building. And besides these were many others, personally interested in some part of the proceedings, in which, however, they took no part; Job Legh, Ben Sturgis, and several others were there, amongst whom was Charley Jones.

Job Legh had carefully avoided any questioning from Mrs. Wilson that morning. Indeed he had not been much in her company, for he had risen up early to go out once more to make inquiry for Mary; and when he could hear nothing of her, he had desperately resolved not to undeceive Mrs. Wilson, as sorrow never came too late; and if the blow were inevitable, it would be better to leave her in ignorance of the impending evil as long as possible. She took her place in the witness-room, worn and dispirited, but not anxious.

As Job struggled through the crowd into the body of the court, Mr. Bridgenorth's clerk beckoned to him.

"Here 's a letter for you from our client!"

Job sickened as he took it. He did not know why, but he dreaded a confession of guilt, which would be an overthrow of all hope.

The letter ran as follows:

"Dear Friend, — I thank you heartily for your goodness in finding me a lawyer, but lawyers can do no good to me, whatever they may do to other people. But I am not the less obliged to you, dear friend. I foresee things will go against me — and no wonder. If I was a jury-man I should say the man was guilty as had as much evidence brought against him as may be brought against me to-morrow. So it 's no blame to them if they do. But, Job Legh, I think I need not tell you I am as guiltless in this matter as the babe unborn, although it is not in my power to prove it. If I did not believe that you thought me innocent, I could not write as I do now to tell you my wishes. You 'll not forget they are the words of a man shortly to die. Dear friend, you must take care of my mother. Not in the money way, for she will have enough for her and Aunt Alice; but you must let her talk to you of me; and show her that (whatever others may do) you think I died innocent. I don't reckon she 'll stay long behind when we are all gone. Be tender with her, Job, for my sake; and if she is a bit fractious at times, remember what she has gone through. I know mother will never doubt me, God bless her.

"There is one other whom I fear I have loved too dearly; and yet, the loving her has made the happiness of my life. She will think I have murdered her lover: she will think I have caused the grief she must be feeling. And she must go on thinking so. It is hard upon me to say this; but she *must*. It will be best for her, and that 's all I ought to think on. But, dear Job, you are a hearty fellow for your time of life, and may live a many years to come; and perhaps you could tell her, when you felt sure you were drawing near your end, that I solemnly told you (as I do now) that I was innocent of this thing. You must not tell her for many years to come; but I cannot well bear to think on her living through a long life, and hating the thought of me as the murderer of him she loved, and dying with that hatred to me in her heart. It would hurt me sore in the other world to see the look of it in her face, as it would be, till she was told. I must not let myself think on how she must be viewing me now.

"So God bless you Job Legh; and no more from,

"Yours to command,

"James Wilson."

Job turned the letter over and over when he had read it; sighed deeply; and then wrapping it carefully up in a bit of newspaper he had about him, he put it in his waistcoat pocket, and went off to the door of the witness-room to ask if Mary Barton was there.

As the door opened he saw her sitting within, against a table on which her folded arms were resting, and her head was hidden within them. It was an attitude of hopelessness, and would have served to strike Job dumb in sickness of heart, even without the sound of Mrs. Wilson's voice in passionate sobbing, and sore lamentations, which told him as well as words could do (for she was not within view of the door, and he did not care to go in), that she was at any rate partially undeceived as to the hopes he had given her last night.

Sorrowfully did Job return into the body of the court; neither Mrs. Wilson nor Mary having seen him as he had stood at the witness-room door.

As soon as he could bring his distracted thoughts to bear upon the present scene, he perceived that the trial of James Wilson for the murder of Henry Carsons was just commencing. The clerk was gabbling over the indictment, and in a minute or two there was the accustomed question, "How say you, Guilty, or Not Guilty?"

Although but one answer was expected, — was customary in all cases, — there was a pause of dead silence, an interval of solemnity even in this hackneyed part of the proceeding; while the prisoner at the bar stood with compressed lips, looking at the judge with his outward eyes, but with far other and different scenes presented to his mental vision; a sort of rapid recapitulation of his life, — remembrances of his childhood, — his father (so proud of him, his first-born child), — his sweet little playfellow, Mary, — his hopes, his love, — his despair, yet still, yet ever and ever, his love, — the blank, wide world it had been without her love, — his mother, — his childless mother, — but not long to be so, — not long to be away from all she loved, — nor during that time to be oppressed with doubt as to his innocence, sure and secure of her darling's heart; — he started from his instant's pause, and said in a low firm voice,

"Not guilty, my lord."

The circumstances of the murder, the discovery of the body, the causes of suspicion against Jem, were as well known to most of the audience as they are to you, so there was some little buzz of conversation going on among the people while the leading counsel for the prosecution made his very effective speech.

"That 's Mr. Carsons, the father, sitting behind Serjeant Wilkinson!"

"What a noble-looking old man he is! so stern and inflexible, with such classical features! Does he not remind you of some of the busts of Jupiter?"

"I am more interested by watching the prisoner. Criminals always interest me. I try to trace in the features common to humanity some expression of the crimes by which they have distinguished themselves from their kind. I have seen a good number of murderers in my day, but I have seldom seen one with such marks of Cain on his countenance as the man at the bar."

"Well, I am no physiognomist, but I don't think his face strikes me as bad. It certainly is gloomy and depressed, and not unnaturally so, considering his situation."

"Only look at his low, resolute brow, his downcast eye, his white compressed lips. He never looks up, — just watch him."

"His forehead is not so low if he had that mass of black hair removed, and is very square, which some people say is a good sign. If others are to be influenced by such trifles as you are, it would have been much better if the prison barber had cut his hair a little previous to the trial; and as for down-cast-eye, and compressed lip, it is all part and parcel of his inward agitation just now; nothing to do with character, my good fellow."

Poor Jem! His raven hair (his mother's pride, and so often fondly caressed by her fingers), was that, too, to have its influence against him?

The witnesses were called. At first they consisted principally of policemen; who, being much accustomed to giving evidence, knew what were the material points they were called on to prove, and did not lose the time of the court in listening to any thing unnecessary.

"Clear as day against the prisoner," whispered one attorney's clerk to another.

"Black as night, you mean," replied his friend; and they both smiled.

"Jane Wilson! who's she? some relation, I suppose, from the name."

"The mother,—she that is to prove the gun-part of the case."

"Oh, ay — I remember! Rather hard on her, too, I think."

Then both were silent, as one of the officers of the court ushered Mrs. Wilson into the witness-box. I have often called her "the old woman," and "an old woman," because, in truth, her appearance was so much beyond her years, which could not be many above fifty. But partly owing to her accident in early life, which left a stamp of pain upon her face, partly owing to her anxious temper, partly to her sorrows, and partly to her limping gait, she always gave me the idea of age. But now she might have seemed more than seventy; her lines were so set and deep, her features so sharpened, and her walk so feeble. She was trying to check her sobs into composure, and (unconsciously) was striving to behave as she thought would best please her poor boy, whom she knew she had often grieved by her uncontrolled impatience. He had buried his face in his arms, which rested on the front of the dock (an attitude he retained during the greater part of his trial, and which prejudiced many against him).

The counsel began the examination.

"Your name is Jane Wilson, I believe?"

"Yes, Sir."

"The mother of the prisoner at the bar?"

"Yes, Sir," with quivering voice, ready to break out into weeping, but earning respect by the strong effort at self-control, prompted, as I have said before, by her earnest wish to please her son by her behaviour.

The barrister now proceeded to the important part of the examination, tending to prove that the gun found on the scene of the murder was the prisoner's. She had committed herself so fully to the policeman, that she could not well retract; so without much delay in bringing the question round to the desired point, the gun was produced in court, and the inquiry made —

"That gun belongs to your son, does it not?"

She clenched the sides of the witness-box in her efforts to make her parched tongue utter words. At last she moaned forth,

"Oh! Jem, Jem! what mun I say?"

Every one bent forward to hear the prisoner's answer; although, in fact, it was of little importance to the issue of the trial. He lifted up his head; and with a face brimming full of pity for his mother, yet resolved into endurance, said,

"Tell the truth, mother!"

And so she did, with the fidelity of a little child. Every one felt that she did; and the little colloquy between mother and son, did them some slight service in the opinion of the audience. But the awful judge sat unmoved; and the jurymen changed not a muscle of their countenances; while the counsel for the prosecution went triumphantly through this part of the case, including the fact of Jem's absence from home on the night of the murder, and bringing every admission to bear right against the prisoner.

It was over. She was told to go down. But she could no longer compel her mother's heart to keep silence, and suddenly turning towards the judge (with whom she imagined the verdict to rest), she thus addressed him with her choking voice.

"And now, Sir, I've telled you the truth, and the whole truth, as *he* bid me; but don't ye let what I have said go for to hang him; oh, my lord judge, take my word for it, he's as innocent as the child as has yet to be born. For sure, I, who am his mother, and have nursed him on my knee, and been gladdened by the sight of him every day since, ought to know him better than yon pack of fellows" (indicating the jury, while she strove against her heart to render her words distinct and clear for her dear son's sake) "who, I'll go bail, never saw him before this morning in all their born days. My lord judge, he's so good I often wondered what harm there was in him; many is the time when I've been fretted (for I'm frabbit enough at times), when I've scoldt myself, and said, 'You ungrateful thing, the Lord God has given you Jem, and isn't that blessing enough for you.' But He has seen fit to punish me. If Jem is — if Jem is — taken from me, I shall be a childless woman;

and very poor, having nought left to love on earth, and I cannot say 'His will be done.' I cannot, my lord judge, oh, I cannot."

While sobbing out these words she was led away by the officers of the court, but tenderly, and reverently, with the respect which great sorrow commands.

The stream of evidence went on and on, gathering fresh force from every witness who was examined, and threatening to overwhelm poor Jem. Already they had proved that the gun was his, that he had been heard not many days before the commission of the deed to threaten the deceased; indeed, that the police had, at that time, been obliged to interfere, to prevent some probable act of violence. It only remained to bring forward a sufficient motive for the threat and the murder. The clue to this had been furnished by the policeman, who had overheard Jem's angry language to Mr. Carsons; and his report in the first instance had occasioned the subpœna to Mary.

And now she was to be called on to bear witness. The court was by this time almost as full as it could hold; but fresh attempts were being made to squeeze in at all the entrances, for many were anxious to see and hear this part of the trial.

Old Mr. Carsons felt an additional beat at his heart at the thought of seeing the fatal Helen, the cause of all — a kind of interest and yet repugnance, for was not she beloved by the dead; nay, perhaps in her way, loving and mourning for the same being that he himself was so bitterly grieving over? And yet he felt as if he abhorred her and her rumoured loveliness, as if she were the curse against him; and he grew jealous of the love with which she had inspired his son, and would fain have deprived her of even her natural right of sorrowing over her lover's untimely end: for you see it was a fixed idea in the minds of all, that the handsome, bright, gay, rich, young gentleman must have been beloved in preference to the serious, almost stern-looking smith, who had to toil for his daily bread.

Hitherto the effect of the trial had equalled Mr. Carsons' most sanguine hopes, and a severe look of satisfaction came over the face of the avenger, — over that countenance whence the smile had departed, never more to return.

All eyes were directed to the door through which the witnesses entered. Even Jem looked up to catch one glimpse, before he hid his face from her look of aversion. The officer had gone to fetch her.

She was in exactly the same attitude as when Job Legh had seen her two hours before through the half-open door. Not a finger had moved. The officer summoned her, but she did not stir. She was so still he thought she had fallen asleep, and he stepped forward and touched her. She started up in an instant, and followed him with a kind of rushing rapid motion into the court, into the witness-box.

And amid all that sea of faces, misty and swimming before her eyes, she saw but two clear bright spots, distinct and fixed: the judge, who might have to condemn; and the prisoner, who might have to die.

The mellow sun-light streamed down that high window on her head, and fell on the rich treasure of her golden hair, stuffed away in masses under her little bonnet-cap; and in those warm beams the motes kept dancing up and down. The wind had changed — had changed almost as soon as she had given up her watching; the wind had changed, and she heeded it not.

Many who were looking for mere flesh and blood beauty, mere colouring, were disappointed; for her face was deadly white, and almost set in its expression, while a mournful bewildered soul looked out of the depths of those soft, deep, gray eyes. But, others recognised a higher and a stranger kind of beauty; one that would keep its hold on the memory for many after years.

I was not there myself; but one who was, told me that her look, and indeed her whole face, was more like the well-known engraving from Guido's picture of "Beatrice Cenci" than any thing else he could give me an idea of. He added, that her countenance haunted him, like the remembrance of some wild sad melody, heard in childhood; that it would perpetually recur with its mute imploring agony.

With all the court reeling before her (always save and except those awful two), she heard a voice speak, and answered the simple inquiry (something about her name) mechanically, as if in a dream. So she went on for two or three more questions, with a strange wonder in her brain, as the reality of the terrible circumstances in which she was placed.

Suddenly she was roused, she knew not how or by what. She was conscious that all was real, that hundreds were looking at her, that true-sounding words were being extracted from her; that that figure, so bowed down, with the face concealed with both hands, was really Jem. Her face flashed scarlet, and then, paler than before. But in dread of herself, with the tremendous secret imprisoned within her, she exerted every power she had to keep in the full understanding of what was going on, of what she was asked, and of what she answered. With all her faculties preternaturally alive and sensitive, she heard the next question from the pert young barrister, who was delighted to have the examination of this witness.

"And pray, may I ask, which was the favoured lover? You say you knew both these young men. Which was the favoured lover? Which did you prefer?"

And who was he, the questioner, that he should dare so lightly to ask of her heart's secrets? That he should dare to ask her to tell, before that multitude assembled there, what woman usually whispers with blushes and tears, and many hesitations, to one ear alone?

So, for an instant, a look of indignation contracted Mary's brow, as she steadily met the eyes of the impertinent counsellor. But, in that instant, she saw the hands removed from a face beyond, behind; and a countenance revealed of such intense love and woe, — such a deprecating dread of her answer; and suddenly her resolution was taken. The present was every thing; the future, that vast shroud, it was maddening to think upon; but *now* she might own her fault, but *now* she might even own her love. Now, when the beloved stood thus, abhorred of men, there would be no feminine shame to stand between her and her avowal. So she also turned towards the judge, partly to mark that her answer was not given to the monkeyfied man who questioned her, and likewise that her face might be averted from, and her eyes not gaze upon, the form that contracted with the dread of the words he anticipated.

"He asks me which of them two I liked the best. Perhaps I liked Mr. Harry Carsons once — I don't know — I've forgotten; but I loved James Wilson, that 's now on trial, above what tongue can tell — above all else on earth put together; and I love him now better than ever, though he has never known a word of it till this minute. For, you see, Sir, mother died before I was thirteen, before I could know right from wrong about some things; and I was giddy and vain, and ready to listen to any praise of my good looks; and this poor young Mr. Carsons fell in with me, and told me he loved me; and I was foolish enough to think he meant me marriage: a mother is a pitiful loss to a girl, Sir; and so I used to fancy I could like to be a lady, and rich, and never know want any more. I never found out how dearly I loved another till one day, when James Wilson asked me to marry him, and I was very hard and sharp in my answer (for, indeed, Sir, I 'd a deal to bear just then), and he took me at my word and left me; and from that day to this I 've never spoken a word to him, or set eyes on him; though I 'd fain have done so, to try and show him we had both been too hasty; for he had not been gone out of my sight above a minute before I knew I loved — far above my life," said she, dropping her voice as she came to this second confession of the strength of her attachment. "But, if the gentleman asks me which I loved the best, I make answer, I was flattered by Mr. Carsons, and pleased with his flattery; but James Wilson I —."

She covered her face with her hands, to hide the burning scarlet blushes, which even dyed her fingers.

There was a little pause; still, though her speech might inspire pity for the prisoner, it only strengthened the supposition of his guilt. Presently the counsellor went on with his examination.

"But you have seen young Mr. Carsons since your rejection of the prisoner?"

"Yes, often."

"You have spoken to him, I conclude, at these times."

"Only once to call speaking."

"And what was the substance of your conversation? Did you tell him you found you preferred his rival?"

"No, Sir. I don't think as I've done wrong in saying, now as things stand, what my feelings are; but I never would be so bold as to tell one young man I cared for another. I never named Jem's name to Mr. Carsons. Never."

"Then what did you say when you had this final conversation with Mr. Carsons? You can give me the substance of it, if you don't remember the words."

"I'll try, Sir; but I'm not very clear. I told him I could not love him, and wished to have nothing more to do with him. He did his best to over-persuade me, but I kept steady, and at last I ran off."

"And you never spoke to him again?"

"Never!"

"Now, young woman, remember you are upon your oath. Did you ever tell the prisoner at the bar of Mr. Henry Carsons' attentions to you? of your acquaintance, in short? Did you ever try to excite his jealousy by boasting of a lover so far above you in station?"

"Never. I never did," said she, in so firm and distinct a manner as to leave no doubt.

"Were you aware that he knew of Mr. Henry Carsons' regard for you? Remember you are on your oath!"

"Never; Sir. I was not aware until I heard of the quarrel between them, and what Jem had said to the policeman, and that was after the murder. To this day I can't make out who told Jem. Oh, Sir, may not I go down?"

For she felt the sense, the composure, the very bodily strength which she had compelled to her aid for a time, suddenly giving way, and was conscious that she was losing all command over herself. There was no occasion to detain her longer; she had done her part. She might go down. The evidence was still stronger against the prisoner; but now he stood erect and firm, with self-respect in his attitude, and a look of determination on his face, which almost made it appear noble. Yet he seemed lost in thought.

Job Legh had all this time been trying to soothe and comfort Mrs. Wilson, who would first be in the court, in order to see her darling, and then, when her sobs became irrepressible, had to be led out into the open air, and sat there weeping, on the steps of the court-house. Who would have taken charge of Mary, on her release from the witness-box I do not know, if Mrs. Sturgis, the boatman's wife, had not been there, brought by her interest in Mary, towards whom she now pressed, in order to urge her to leave the scene of the trial.

"No! no!" said Mary, to this proposition. "I must be here, I must watch that they don't hang him, you know I must."

"Oh! they 'll not hang him! never fear! Besides the wind has changed, and that 's in his favour. Come away. You 're so hot, and first white and then red; I'm sure you 're ill. Just come away."

"Oh! I don't know about any thing but that I must stay," replied Mary, in a strange hurried manner, catching hold of some rails as if she feared some bodily force would be employed to remove her. So Mrs. Sturgis just waited patiently by her, every now and then peeping among the congregation of heads in the body of the court, to see if her husband were still there. And there he always was to be seen, looking and listening with all his might. His wife felt easy that he would not be wanting her at home until the trial was ended.

Mary never let go her clutched hold on the rails. She wanted them to steady her, in that heaving, whirling court. She thought the feeling of something hard compressed within her hand would help her to listen, for it was such pain, such weary pain in her head, to strive to attend to what was being said. They were all at sea, sailing away on billowy waves, and every one speaking at once, and no one heeding her father, who was calling on them to be silent, and listen to him. Then again, for a brief second, the court stood still, and she could see the judge, sitting up there like an idol, with his trappings, so rigid and stiff; and Jem, opposite, looking at her, as if to say, am I to die for what you know your —. Then she checked herself, and by a great struggle brought herself round to an instant's sanity. But the round of thought never stood still; and off she went again; and every time her power of struggling against the growing delirium grew fainter and fainter. She muttered low to herself, but no one heard her except her neighbour, Mrs. Sturgis; all were too closely attending to the case for the prosecution, which was now being wound up.

The counsel for the prisoner had avoided much cross-examination, reserving to himself the right of calling the witnesses forward again; for he had received so little, and such vague instructions, and understood that so much depended on the evidence of one who was not forthcoming, that in fact he had little hope of establishing any thing like a show of a defence, and contented himself with watching the case, and lying in wait for any legal objections that might offer themselves. He lay back on the seat, occasionally taking a pinch of snuff, in a manner intended to be contemptuous; now and then elevating his eyebrows, and sometimes exchanging a little note with Mr. Bridgenorth behind him. The attorney had far more interest in the case than the barrister, to which he was perhaps excited by his poor old friend Job Legh; who had edged and wedged himself through the crowd close to Mr. Bridgenorth's elbow, sent thither by Ben Sturgis, to whom he had been "introduced" by Charley Jones, and who had accounted for Mary's disappearance on the preceding day, and spoken of their chase, their fears, their hopes.

All this was told in a few words to Mr. Bridgenorth — so few, that they gave him but a confused idea, that time was of value; and this he named to his counsel, who now rose to speak for the defence.

Job Legh looked about for Mary, now he had gained, and given, some idea of the position of things. At last he saw her, standing by a decent-looking woman, looking flushed and anxious, and moving her lips incessantly, as if eagerly talking; her eyes never resting on any object, but wandering about as if in search of something. Job thought it was for him she was seeking, and he struggled to get round to her. When he had succeeded, she took no notice of him, although he spoke to her, but still kept looking round and round in the same wild, restless manner. He tried to hear the low quick mutterings of her voice; he caught the repetition of the same words over and over again.

"I must not go mad. I must not, indeed. They say people tell the truth when they 're mad; but I don't. I was always a liar. I was, indeed; but I 'm not mad. I must not go mad. I must not, indeed."

Suddenly she seemed to become aware how earnestly Job was

listening (with mournful attention) to her words, and turning sharp round upon him, with upbraiding, for his eaves-dropping, on her lips, she caught sight of something, — or some one, — who, even in that state, had power to arrest her attention, and throwing up her arms with wild energy, she shrieked aloud,

"Oh, Jem! Jem! you 're saved; and I *am* mad —" and was instantly seized with convulsions. With much commiseration she was taken out of court, while the attention of many was diverted from her, by the fierce energy with which a sailor forced his way over rails and seats, against turnkeys and policemen. The officers of the court opposed this forcible manner of entrance, but they could hardly induce the offender to adopt any quieter way of attaining his object, and telling his tale in the witness-box, the legitimate place. For Will had dwelt so impatiently on the danger in which his absence would place his cousin, that even yet, he seemed to fear that he might see the prisoner carried off, and hung, before he could pour out the narrative which would exculpate him. As for Job Legh, his feelings were all but uncontrollable; as you may judge, by the indifference with which he saw Mary borne, stiff and convulsed, out of the court, in the charge of the kind Mrs. Sturgis, who, you will remember, was an utter stranger to him.

"She 'll keep! I 'll not trouble myself about her," said he to himself, as he wrote with trembling hands a little note of information to Mr. Bridgenorth, who had conjectured, when Will had first disturbed the awful tranquillity of the life-and-death court, that the witness had arrived (better late than never) on whose evidence rested all the slight chance yet remaining to Jem Wilson of escaping death. During the commotion in the court, among all the cries and commands, the dismay and the directions, consequent upon Will's entrance, and poor Mary's fearful attack of illness, Mr. Bridgenorth had kept his lawyer-like presence of mind; and long before Job Legh's almost illegible note was poked at him, he had recapitulated the facts on which Will had to give evidence, and the manner in which he had been pursued, after his ship had taken her leave of the land.

The barrister, who defended Jem, took new heart when he was put in possession of these striking points to be adduced, not so much out of earnestness to save the prisoner, of whose innocence he was still doubtful, as because he saw the opportunities for the display of forensic eloquence which were presented by the facts; "a gallant tar brought back from the pathless ocean by a girl's noble daring," "the dangers of too hastily judging from circumstantial evidence," &c., &c.; while the counsellor for the prosecution prepared himself by folding his arms, elevating his eyebrows, and putting his lips in the form in which they might best whistle down the wind such evidence as might be produced by a suborned witness, who dared to perjure himself. For, of course, it is etiquette to suppose that such evidence as may be given against the opinion which lawyers are paid to uphold, is anything but based on truth; and "perjury" "conspiracy," and "peril of your immortal soul," are light expressions to throw at the heads of those who may prove (not the speaker, there would then be some excuse for the hasty words of personal anger, but) the hirer of the speaker to be wrong, or mistaken.

But when once Will had attained his end, and felt that his tale, or part of a tale, would be heard by judge and jury; when once he saw Jem standing safe and well before him (even though he saw him pale and careworn at the felon's bar); his courage took the shape of presence of mind, and he awaited the examination with a calm, unflinching intelligence, which dictated the clearest and most pertinent answers. He told the story you know so well. How his leave of absence being nearly expired, he had resolved to fulfil his promise, and go to see an uncle residing in the Isle of Man; how his money (sailor-like) was all expended in Manchester, and how, consequently, it had been necessary for him to walk to Liverpool, which he had accordingly done on the very night of the murder, accompanied as far as Hollins Green by his friend and cousin, the prisoner at the bar. He was clear and distinct in every corroborative circumstance, and gave a short account of the singular way in which he had been recalled from his outward-bound voyage, and the terrible anxiety he had felt, as the pilot-boat had struggled home against the wind. The jury felt that their opinion (so nearly decided half an hour ago) was shaken and disturbed in a very uncomfortable and perplexing way, and were almost grateful to the counsel for the prosecution, when he got up, with a brow of thunder, to demolish the evidence, which was so bewildering when taken in connexion with every thing previously adduced. But if such, without looking to the consequences, was the first impulsive feeling of some among the jury, how shall I ascribe the vehemence of passion which possessed the mind of poor Mr. Carsons, as he saw the effect of the young sailor's statement. It never shook his belief in Jem's guilt in the least, that attempt at an alibi; his hatred, his longing for vengeance, having once defined an object to itself, could no more bear to be frustrated and disappointed, than the beast of prey can submit to have his victim taken from his hungry jaws. No more likeness to the calm stern power of Jupiter was there in that white eager face, almost distorted by its fell anxiety of expression.

The counsel to whom etiquette assigned the cross-examination of Will, caught the look on Mr. Carsons' face, and in his desire to further the intense wish there manifested, he over-shot his mark even in his first insulting question:

"And now, my man, you 've told the court a very good and very convincing story; no reasonable man ought to doubt the unstained innocence of your relation at the bar. Still there is one circumstance you have forgotten to name; and I feel that without it your evidence is rather incomplete. Will you have the kindness to inform the gentlemen of the jury what has been your charge for repeating this very plausible story? How much good coin of her majesty's realm have you received, or are you to receive, for walking up from the docks, or some less creditable place, and uttering the tale you have just now repeated, — very much to the credit of your instructor, I must say? Remember, Sir you are upon oath."

It took Will a minute to extract the meaning from the garb of unaccustomed words in which it was invested, and during this time he looked a little confused. But the instant the truth flashed upon him he fixed his bright clear eyes, flaming with indignation, upon the counsellor, whose look fell at last before that stern unflinching gaze. Then, and not till then, Will made answer.

"Will you tell the judge and jury how much money you 've been paid for your impudence towards one who has told God's blessed truth, and who would scorn to tell a lie, or blackguard any one, for the biggest fee as ever lawyer got for doing dirty work. Will you tell, Sir? — But I 'm ready, my lord judge, to take my oath as many times as your lordship or the jury would like, to testify to things having happened just as I said. There 's O'Brien, the pilot, in court now. Would somebody with a wig on please to ask him how much he can say for me?"

It was a good idea, and caught at by the counsel for the defence. O'Brien gave just such testimony as was required to clear Will from all suspicion. He had witnessed the pursuit, he had heard the conversation which took place between the boat and the ship; he had given Will a homeward passage in his boat. And the character of an accredited pilot, appointed by Trinity House, was known to be above suspicion.

Mr. Carsons sank back on his seat in sickening despair. He knew enough of courts to be aware of the extreme unwillingness of juries to convict, even where the evidence is most clear, when the penalty of such conviction is death. At the period of the trial most condemnatory to the prisoner, he had repeated this fact to himself, in order to damp his too certain expectation of a conviction. Now it needed not repetition, for it forced itself upon his consciousness, and he seemed to *know*, even before the jury retired to consult, that by some trick, some negligence, some miserable hocus-pocus, the murderer of his child, his darling, his Absalom, who had never rebelled, — the slayer of his unburied boy would slip through the fangs of justice, and walk free and unscathed over that earth where his son would never more be seen.

It was even so. The prisoner hid his face once more to shield the expression of an emotion he could not control, from the notice of the over-curious; Job Legh ceased his eager talking to Mr. Bridgenorth; Charley looked grave and earnest; for the jury filed one by one back into their box, and the question was asked to which such an awful answer might be given.

The verdict they had come to was unsatisfactory to themselves at last; neither being convinced of his innocence, nor yet quite willing to believe him guilty in the teeth of the alibi. But the punishment that awaited him, if guilty, was so terrible, and so unnatural a sentence for man to pronounce on man, that the knowledge of it had weighed down the scale on the side of innocence, and "Not Guilty" was the verdict that thrilled through the breathless court.

One moment of silence, and then the murmurs rose, as the verdict was discussed by all with lowered voice. Jem stood motionless, his head bowed; poor fellow, he was stunned with the rapid career of events during the last few hours.

He had assumed his place at the bar with little or no expectation of an acquittal; and with scarcely any desire for life, in the complication of occurrences tending to strengthen the idea of Mary's more than indifference to him; she had loved another, and in her mind Jem believed that he himself must be regarded as the murderer of him she loved. And suddenly, athwart this gloom which made Life seem such a blank expanse of desolation, there flashed the exquisite delight of hearing Mary's avowal of love, making the future all glorious, if a future in this world he might hope to have. He could not dwell on any thing but her words, telling of her passionate love; all else was indistinct, nor could he strive to make it otherwise. She loved him.

And Life, now full of tender images, suddenly bright with all exquisite promises, hung on a breath, the slenderest gossamer chance. He tried to think that the knowledge of her love would soothe him even in his dying hours; but the phantoms of what life with her might be, would obtrude, and made him almost gasp and reel under the uncertainty he was enduring. Will's appearance had only added to the intensity of this suspense.

The full meaning of the verdict could not at once penetrate his brain. He stood dizzy and motionless. Some one pulled his coat. He turned, and saw Job Legh, the tears stealing down his brown furrowed cheeks, while he tried in vain to command voice enough to speak. He kept shaking Jem by the hand as the best, and necessary expression of his feeling.

"Here, make yourself scarce! I should think you 'd be glad to get out of that!" exclaimed the jailor, as he brought up another livid prisoner, from out whose eyes came the anxiety which he would not allow any other feature to display.

Job Legh pressed out of court, and Jem followed, unreasoningly.

The crowd made way, and kept their garments tight about them, as Jem passed, for about him there still hung the taint of the murderer.

He was in the open air, and free once more! Although many looked on him with suspicion, faithful friends closed round him; his arm was unresistingly pumped up and down by his cousin and Job; when one was tired, the other took up the wholesome exercise, while Ben Sturgis was working off his interest in the scene by scolding Charley for walking on his head round and round Mary's sweetheart, for a sweetheart he was now satisfactorily ascertained to be, in spite of her assertion to the contrary. And all this time Jem himself felt bewildered and dazzled; he would have given any thing for an hour's uninterrupted thought on the occurrences of the past week, and the new visions raised up during the morning; aye, even though that tranquil hour were to be passed in the hermitage of his quiet prison cell. The first question sobbed out by his choking voice, oppressed with emotion, was,

"Where is she?"

They led him to the room where his mother sat. They had told her of her son's acquittal, and now she was laughing, and crying, and talking, and giving way to all those feelings which she had restrained with such effort during the last few days. They brought her son to her, and she threw herself upon his neck, weeping there. He returned her embrace, but looked around, beyond. Excepting his mother there was no one in the room, but the friends who had entered with him.

"Eh, lad!" she said, when she found voice to speak. "See what it is to have behaved thysel! I could put in a good word for thee, and the jury could na go and hang thee in the face of th' character I gave thee. Was na it a good thing they did na keep me from Liverpool? But I would come; I knew I could do thee good, bless thee, my lad. But thou 'rt very white, and all of a tremble."

He kissed her again and again, but looking round as if searching for some one he could not find, the first words he uttered were still,

"Where is she?"

CHAPTER XXXIII.

"Fear no more the heat o' th' sun,
Nor the furious winter's rages;
Thou thy worldly task hast done,
Home art gone and ta'en thy wages." CYMBELINE.

"While day and night can bring delight,
Or nature aught of pleasure give;
While joys above my mind can move
For thee, and thee alone I live:

"When that grim foe of joy below
Comes in between to make us part,
The iron hand that breaks our band,
It breaks my bliss — it breaks my heart." BURNS.

SHE was where no words of peace, no soothing hopeful tidings could reach her; in the ghastly spectral world of delirium. Hour after hour, day after day, she started up with passionate cries on her father to save Jem; or rose wildly, imploring the winds and waves, the pitiless winds and waves, to have mercy; and over and over again she exhausted her feverish fitful strength in these agonised entreaties, and fell back powerless, uttering only the wailing moans of despair. They told her Jem was safe, they brought him before her eyes; but sight and hearing were no longer channels of information to that poor distracted brain, nor could human voice penetrate to her understanding.

Jem alone gathered the full meaning of some of her strange sentences, and perceived that by some means or other, she, like himself, had divined the truth of her father being the murderer.

Long ago (reckoning time by events and thoughts, and not by clock or dial-plate), Jem had felt certain that Mary's father was Harry Carsons' murderer; and although the motive was in some measure a mystery, yet a whole train of circumstances (the principal of which was that John Barton had borrowed the fatal gun only two days before) had left no doubt in Jem's mind. Sometimes he thought that John had discovered, and thus bloodily resented, the attentions which Mr. Carsons had paid to his daughter; at others, he believed the motive to exist in the bitter feuds between the masters and their work-people, in which Barton was known to take so keen an interest. But if he had felt himself pledged to preserve this secret, even when his own life was the probable penalty, and he believed he should fall execrated by

Mary as the guilty destroyer of her lover, how much more was he bound now to labour to prevent any word of hers from inculpating her father, now that she was his own; now that she had braved so much to rescue him; and now that her poor brain had lost all guiding and controlling power over her words.

All that night long Jem wandered up and down the narrow precincts of Ben Sturgis's house. In the little bed-room where Mrs. Sturgis alternately tended Mary, and wept over the violence of her illness, he listened to her ravings; each sentence of which had its own peculiar meaning and reference, intelligible to his mind, till her words rose to the wild pitch of agony, that no one could alleviate, and he could bear it no longer, and stole, sick, and miserable down stairs, where Ben Sturgis thought it his duty to snore away in an arm-chair instead of his bed, under the idea that he should thus be more ready for active service, such as fetching the doctor to revisit his patient.

Before it was fairly light, Jem (wide awake, and listening with an earnest attention he could not deaden, however painful its results proved) heard a gentle subdued knock at the house door; it was no business of his, to be sure to open it, but as Ben slept on, he thought he would see who the early visitor might be, and ascertain if there was any occasion for disturbing either host or hostess. It was Job Legh who stood there, distinct against the outer light of the street.

"How is she? Eh! poor soul! is that her! no need to ask! How strange her voice sounds! Screech! screech! and she so low, sweet-spoken, when she 's well! Thou must keep up heart, old boy, and not look so dismal, thysel."

"I can't help it, Job; it 's past a man's bearing to hear such a one as she is, going on as she is doing; even if I did not care for her, it would cut me sore to see one so young, and—I can't speak of it, Job, as a man should do," said Jem, his sobs choking him.

"Let me in, will you?" said Job, pushing past him, for all this time Jem had stood holding the door, unwilling to admit Job where he might hear so much that would be suggestive to one acquainted with the parties that Mary named.

"I 'd more than one reason for coming betimes. I wanted to hear how yon poor wench was;—that stood first. Late last night I got a letter from Margaret, very anxious-like. The doctor says the old lady yonder can't last many days longer, and it seems so lonesome for her to die with no one but Margaret and Mrs. Davenport about her. So I thought I 'd just come and stay with Mary Barton, and see as she 's well done to, and you and your mother and Will go and take leave of old Alice."

Jem's countenance, sad at best just now, fell lower and lower. But Job went on with his speech.

"She still wanders, Margaret says, and thinks she 's with her mother at home; but for all that, she should have some kith and kin near her to close her eyes, to my thinking."

"Could not you and Will take mother home? I 'd follow when—" Jem faltered out thus far, when Job interrupted,

"Lad! if thou knew what thy mother has suffered for thee, thou 'd not speak of leaving her just when she 's got thee from the grave as it were. Why, this very night she roused me up, and 'Job,' says she, 'I ask your pardon for wakening you, but tell me, am I awake or dreaming. Is Jem proved innocent? Oh, Job Legh! God send I 've not been only dreaming it!" For thou see'st she can't rightly understand why thou 'rt with Mary, and not with her. Ay, ay! I know why; but a mother only gives up her son's heart inch by inch to his wife, and then she gives it up with a grudge. No, Jem! thou must go with thy mother just now, if ever thou hopest for God's blessing. She 's a widow, and has none but thee. Never fear for Mary! She 's young and will struggle through. They are decent people, these folk she is with, and I 'll watch o'er her, as though she was my own poor girl, that lies cold enough in London-town. I grant ye, it 's hard enough for her to be left among strangers. To my mind John Barton would be more in the way of his duty, looking after his daughter, than delegating it up and down the country, looking after every one's business but his own."

A new idea and a new fear came into Jem's mind. What if Mary should implicate her father?

"She raves terribly," said he. "All night long she 's been speaking of her father, and mixing up thoughts of him with the trial she saw yesterday. I should not wonder if she 'll speak of him as being in court next thing."

"I should na wonder, either," answered Job. "Folk in her way say many and many a strange thing; and th' best way is never to mind them. Now you take your mother home, Jem, and stay by her till old Alice is gone, and trust me for seeing after Mary."

Jem felt how right Job was, and could not resist what he knew to be his duty, but I cannot tell you how heavy and sick at heart he was as he stood at the door to take a last, fond, lingering look at Mary; he saw her sitting up in bed, her golden hair, dimmed with her one day's illness, floating behind her, her head bound round with wetted cloths, her features all agitated, even to distortion, with the pangs of her anxiety.

Her lover's eyes filled with tears. He could not hope. The elasticity of his heart had been crushed out of him by early sorrows; and now, especially, the dark side of every thing seemed to be presented to him. What if she died, just when he knew the treasure, the untold treasure he possessed in her love! What if (worse than death) she remained a poor gibbering maniac all her life long (and mad people do live to be old sometimes, even under all the pressure of their burden), terror-distracted as she was now; and no one able to comfort her!

"Jem!" said Job, partly guessing the other's feelings by his own. "Jem!" repeated he, arresting his attention before he spoke. Jem turned round, the little motion causing the tears to overflow and trickle down his cheeks. "Thou must trust in God, and leave her in His hands." He spoke hushed, and low; but the words sunk all the more into Jem's heart, and gave him strength to tear himself away.

He found his mother (notwithstanding that she had but just regained her child through Mary's instrumentality) half inclined to resent his having passed the night in anxious devotion to the poor invalid. She dwelt on the duties of children to their parents (above all others), till Jem could hardly believe the relative positions they had held only yesterday, when she was struggling with and controlling every instinct of her nature, only because *he* wished it. However, the recollection of that yesterday, with its hair's breadth between him and a felon's death, and the love that had lightened the dark shadow, made him bear with the meekness and patience of a true-hearted man all the worrying little acerbities of to-day; and he had no small merit in so doing; for in him, as in his mother, the re-action after intense excitement had produced its usual effect in increased irritability of the nervous system.

They found Alice alive, and without pain. And that was all. A child of a few weeks old would have had more bodily strength; a child of a very few months old, more consciousness of what was passing before her. But even in this state she diffused an atmosphere of peace around her. True, Will, at first, wept passionate tears at the sight of her, who had been as a mother to him, so standing on the confines of life. But even now, as always, loud passionate feeling could not long endure in the calm of her presence. The firm faith which her mind had no longer power to grasp, had left its trail of glory; for by no other word can I call the bright happy look which illumined the old earthworn face. Her talk, it is true, bore no more that constant earnest reference to God and his holy word which it had done in health, and there were no death-bed words of exhortation from the lips of one so habitually pious. For still she imagined herself once again in the happy, happy realms of childhood; and again dwelling in the lovely northern haunts where she had so often longed to be. Though earthly sight was gone away, she beheld again the scenes she had loved from long years ago! she saw them without a change to dim the old radiant hues. The long dead were with her, fresh and blooming as in those bygone days. And death came to her as a welcome blessing, like as evening comes to the weary child Her work here was finished, and faithfully done.

What better sentence can an emperor wish to have said over his bier? In second childhood (that blessing clouded by a name), she said her "Nunc Dimittis," — the sweetest canticle to the holy.

"Mother, good night! Dear mother! bless me once more! I'm very tired, and would fain go to sleep." She never spoke again on this side Heaven.

She died the day after their return from Liverpool. From that time, Jem became aware that his mother was jealously watching for some word or sign which should betoken his wish to return to Mary. And yet go to Liverpool he must and would, as soon as the funeral was over, if but for a simple glimpse of his darling. For Job had never written; indeed, any necessity for his so doing had never entered his head. If Mary died, he would announce it personally; if she recovered, he meant to bring her home with him. Writing was to him little more than an auxiliary to natural history; a way of ticketing specimens, not of expressing thoughts.

The consequence of this want of intelligence as to Mary's state was, that Jem was constantly anticipating that every person and every scrap of paper was to convey to him the news of her death. He could not endure this state long; but he resolved not to disturb the house by announcing to his mother his proposed intention of returning to Liverpool, until the dead had been carried forth.

On Sunday afternoon, they laid her low with many tears. Will wept as one who would not be comforted.

The old childish feeling came over him, the feeling of loneliness at being left among strangers.

By and bye, Margaret timidly stole near him, as if waiting to console; and soon his passion sank down to grief, and grief gave way to melancholy, and though he felt as though he never could be joyful again, he was all the while unconsciously approaching nearer to the full happiness of calling Margaret his own, and a golden thread was interwoven even now with the darkness of his sorrow. Yet it was on his arm that Jane Wilson leant on her return homewards. Jem took charge of Margaret.

"Margaret, I 'm bound for Liverpool by the first train tomorrow; I must set your grandfather at liberty."

"I 'm sure he likes nothing better than watching over poor Mary; he loves her nearly as well as me. But let me go! I have been so full of poor Alice, I 've never thought of it before; I can't do so much as many a one, but Mary will like to have a woman about her that she knows. I 'm sorry I waited to be reminded, Jem!" replied Margaret, with some little self-reproach.

But Margaret's proposition did not at all agree with her companion's wishes. He found he had better speak out, and put his intention at once to the right motive; the subterfuge about setting Job Legh at liberty had done him harm instead of good.

"To tell truth, Margaret, it 's I that must go, and that for my own sake, not your grandfather's. I can rest neither by night nor day for thinking on Mary. Whether she lives or dies I look on her as my wife before God, as surely and solemnly as if we were married. So being, I have the greatest right to look after her, and I cannot yield it even to — "

"Her father," said Margaret, finishing his interrupted sentence. "It seems strange that a girl like her should be thrown on the bare world to struggle through so bad an illness. No one seems to know where John Barton is, else I thought of getting Morris to write him a letter telling him about Mary. I wish he was home, that I do!"

Jem could not echo this wish.

"Mary 's not bad off for friends where she is," said he. "I call them friends, though a week ago we none of us knew there were such folks in the world. But being anxious and sorrowful about the same thing makes people friends quicker than any thing, I think. She 's like a mother to Mary in her ways; and he bears a good character, as far as I could learn just in that hurry. We 're drawing near home, and I 've not said my say, Margaret. I want you to look after mother a bit. She 'll not like my going, and I 've got to break it to her yet. If she takes it very badly, I 'll come back to-morrow night; but if she 's not against it very much, I mean to stay till it 's settled about Mary, one way or the other. Will, you know, will be there, Margaret, to help a bit in doing for mother."

Will's being there made the only objection Margaret saw to this plan. She disliked the idea of seeming to throw herself in his way, and yet she did not like to say any thing of this feeling to Jem, who had all along seemed perfectly unconscious of any love-affair, besides his own, in progress.

So Margaret gave a reluctant consent.

"If you can just step up to our house to-night, Jem, I 'll put up a few things as may be useful to Mary, and then you can say when you 'll likely be back. If you come home to-morrow night, and Will 's there, perhaps I need not step up?"

"Yes, Margaret, do! I shan't leave easy unless you go some time in the day to see mother. I 'll come to-night, though; and now good-bye. Stay! do you think you could just coax poor Will to walk a bit home with you, that I might speak to mother by myself?"

No! that Margaret could not do. That was expecting too great a sacrifice of bashful feeling.

But the object was accomplished by Will's going up-stairs immediately on their return to the house, to indulge his mournful thoughts alone. As soon as Jem and his mother were left by themselves, he began on the subject uppermost in his mind.

"Mother!"

She put her handkerchief from her eyes, and turned quickly round so as to face him where he stood, thinking what best to say. The little action annoyed him, and he rushed at once into the subject.

"Mother! I am going back to Liverpool to-morrow morning to see how Mary Barton is."

"And what 's Mary Barton to thee, that thou shouldst be running after her in that-a-way?"

"If she lives, she shall be my wedded wife. If she dies — mother, I can't speak of what I shall feel if she dies." His voice was choked in his throat.

For an instant his mother was interested by his words; and then came back the old jealousy of being supplanted in the affections of that son, who had been, as it were, newly born to her, by the escape he had so lately experienced from danger. So she hardened her heart against entertaining any feeling of sympathy; and turned away from the face, which recalled the earnest look of his childhood, when he had come to her in some trouble, sure of help and comfort.

And coldly she spoke, in those which tones Jem knew and dreaded, even before the meaning they expressed was fully shaped. "Thou 'rt old enough to please thysel. Old mothers are cast aside, and what they 've borne forgotten as soon as a pretty face comes across. I might have thought of that last Tuesday, when

I felt as if thou wert all my own, and the judge were some wild animal trying to rend thee from me. I spoke up for thee then; but it 's all forgotten now, I suppose."

"Mother! you know all this while, *you know* I can never forget any kindness you've ever done for me; and they've been many. Why should you think I 've only room for one love in my heart? I can love you as dearly as ever, and Mary too, as much as man ever loved woman."

He awaited a reply. None was vouchsafed.

"Mother, answer me!" said he, at last.

"What mun I answer? You asked me no question."

"Well! I ask you this now. To-morrow morning I go to Liverpool to see her, who is as my wife. Dear mother! will you bless me on my errand? If it please God she recovers, will you take her to you as you would a daughter?"

She could neither refuse, nor assent.

"Why need you go?" said she querulously, at length. "You'll be getting in some mischief or another again. Can't you stop at home quiet with me?"

Jem got up, and walked about the room in despairing impatience. She would not understand his feelings. At last he stopped right before the place where she was sitting, with an air of injured meekness on her face.

"Mother! I often think what a good man father was! I 've often heard you tell of your courting days; and of the accident that befell you, and how ill you were. How long is it ago?"

"Near upon five-and-twenty years," said she, with a sigh.

"You little thought when you were so ill you should live to have such a fine strapping son as I am, did you now?"

She smiled a little, and looked up at him, which was just what he wanted.

"Thou 'rt not so fine a man as thy father was, by a deal!" said she, looking at him with much fondness, notwithstanding her depreciatory words.

He took another turn or two up and down the room. He wanted to bend the subject round to his own case.

"Those were happy days when father was alive!"

"You may say so, lad! Such days as will never come again to me, at any rate." She sighed sorrowfully.

"Mother!" said he, at last, stopping short, and taking her hand in his with tender affection, "you'd like me to be as happy a man as my father was before me, would not you? You'd like me to have some one to make me as happy as you made father? Now, would not you, dear mother?"

"I did not make him as happy as I might ha' done," murmured she, in a low, sad voice of self-reproach. "Th' accident gave a jar to my temper it's never got the better of; and now he's gone, where he can never know how I grieve for having frabbed him as I did."

"Nay, mother, we don't know that!" said Jem, with gentle soothing. "Any how, you and father got along with as few rubs as most people. But for *his* sake, dear mother, don't say me nay, now that I come to you to ask your blessing before setting out to see her, who is to be my wife, if ever woman is; for *his* sake, if not for mine, love her who I shall bring home to be to me all you were to him: and mother! I do not ask for a truer, or a tenderer heart than yours is, in the long run."

The hard look left her face; though her eyes were still averted from Jem's gaze, it was more because they were brimming over with tears, called forth by his words, than because any angry feeling yet remained. And when his manly voice died away in low pleadings, she lifted up her hands, and bent down her son's head below the level of her own; and then she solemnly uttered a blessing.

"God bless thee, Jem, my own dear lad. And may He bless Mary Barton for thy sake."

Jem's heart leaped up, and from this time hope took the place of fear in his anticipations with regard to Mary.

"Mother! you show your own true self to Mary, and she'll love you as dearly as I do."

So with some few smiles, and some few tears, and much earnest talking, the evening wore away.

"I must be off to see Margaret. Why, it's near ten o'clock! Could you have thought it?" Now don't you stop up for me, mother. You and Will go to bed, for you 've both need of it. I shall be home in an hour."

Margaret had felt the evening long and lonely; and was all but giving up the thoughts of Jem's coming that night, when she heard his step at the door.

He told her of his progress with his mother; he told her his hopes, and was silent on the subject of his fears.

"To think how sorrow and joy are mixed up together. You'll date your start in life as Mary's acknowledged lover from poor Alice Wilson's burial day. Well! the dead are soon forgotten!"

"Dear Margaret! —But you 're worn out with your long evening waiting for me. I don't wonder. But never you, nor any one else, think because God sees fit to call up new interests, perhaps right out of the grave, that therefore the dead are forgotten. Margaret, you yourself can remember our looks, and fancy what we 're like."

"Yes! but what has that to do with remembering Alice?"

"Why, just this. You 're not always trying to think on our faces, and making a labour of remembering; but often, I 'll be bound, when you're sinking off to sleep, or when you 're very quiet and still, the faces you knew so well when you could see, come smiling before you with loving looks. Or you remember them, without striving after it, and without thinking it 's your duty to keep recalling them. And so it is with them that are hidden from our sight. If they 've been worthy to be heartily loved while alive, they'll not be forgotten when dead; it's against nature. And we need no more be upbraiding ourselves for letting in God's rays of light upon our sorrow, and no more be fearful of forgetting them, because their memory is not always haunting and taking up our minds, than you need to trouble yourself about remembering your grandfather's face, or what the stars were like, — you can't forget if you would, what it 's such a pleasure to think about. Don't fear my forgetting Aunt Alice."

"I 'm not, Jem; not now, at least; only you seemed so full about Mary."

"I 've kept it down so long, remember. How glad Aunt Alice

would have been to know that I might hope to have her for my wife! that 's to say if God spares her!"

"She would not have known it, even if you could have told her this last fortnight, — ever since you went away she 's been thinking always that she was a little child at her mother's apron-string. She must have been a happy little thing; it was such a pleasure to her to think about those early days, when she lay old and gray on her death-bed."

"I never knew any one seem more happy all her life long."

"Ay! and how gentle and easy her death was! she thought her mother was near her."

They fell into calm thought about those last peaceful happy hours.

It struck eleven. Jem started up.

"I should have been gone long age. Give me the bundle. You 'll not forget my mother. Good night, Margaret."

She let him out and bolted the door behind him. He stood on the steps to adjust some fastening about the bundle. The court, the street, was deeply still. Long ago all had retired to rest on that quiet Sabbath evening. The stars shone down on the silent deserted streets, and the clear soft moonlight fell in bright masses, leaving the steps on which Jem stood in shadow.

A foot-fall was heard along the pavement, slow and heavy was the sound. Before Jem had ended his little piece of business, a form had glided into sight; a wan, feeble figure, bearing with evident and painful labour, a jug of water from the neighbouring pump. It went before Jem, turned up the court at the corner of which he was standing, passed into the broad, calm light; and there, with bowed head, sinking and shrunk body, Jem recognised John Barton.

No haunting ghost could have had less of the energy of life in its involuntary motions than he, who, nevertheless, went on with the same measured clock-work tread until the door of his own house was reached. And then he disappeared, and the latch fell feebly to, and made a faint and wavering sound, breaking the solemn silence of the night. Then all again was still.

For a minute or two Jem stood motionless, stunned by the thoughts which the sight of Mary's father had called up.

Margaret did not know he was at home: had he stolen like a thief by dead of night into his own dwelling? Depressed as Jem had often and long seen him, this night there was something different about him still; beaten down by some inward storm, he seemed to grovel along, all self-respect lost and gone.

Must he be told of Mary's state? Jem felt he must not; and this for many reasons. He could not be informed of her illness without many other particulars being communicated at the same time, of which it were better he should be kept in ignorance; indeed, of which Mary herself could alone give the full explanation. No suspicion that he was the criminal seemed hitherto to have been excited in the mind of any one. Added to these reasons was Jem's extreme unwillingness to face him, with the belief in his breast that he and none other, had done the fearful deed.

It was true that he was Mary's father, and as such had every right to be told of all concerning her; but supposing he were, and that he followed the impulse so natural to a father, and wished to go to her, what might be the consequences? Among the mingled feelings she had revealed in her delirium, aye, mingled even with the most tender expressions of love for her father, was a sort of horror of him; a dread of him as a blood-shedder, which seemed to separate him into two persons, — one, the father who had dandled her on his knee, and loved her all her life long; the other, the assassin, the cause of all her trouble and woe.

If he presented himself before her while this idea of his character was uppermost, who might tell the consequence?

Jem could not, and would not, expose her to any such fearful chance: and to tell the truth, I believe he looked upon her as more his own, to guard from all shadow of injury with most loving care, than as belonging to any one else in this world, though girt with the reverend name of Father, and guiltless of aught that might have lessened such reverence.

If you think this account of mine confused, of the half-feelings, half-reasons, which passed through Jem's mind, as he stood gazing on the empty space, where that crushed form had so lately been seen, — if you are perplexed to disentangle the real motives, I do assure you it was from just such an involved set of thoughts that Jem drew the resolution to act as if he had not seen that phantom likeness of John Barton; himself, yet not himself.

CHAPTER XXXIV.

"*Dixwell.* Forgiveness! Oh, forgiveness, and a grave!
Mary. God knows thy heart, my father! and I shudder
To think what thou perchance hast acted.
Dixwell. Oh!
Mary. No common load of woe is thine, my father."

Elliot's 'Kerhonah.'

Mary still hovered between life and death when Jem arrived at the house where she lay; and the doctors were as yet unwilling to compromise their wisdom by allowing too much hope to be entertained. But the state of things, if not less anxious, was less distressing than when Jem had quitted her. She lay now in a stupor, which was partly disease, and partly exhaustion after the previous excitement.

And now Jem found the difficulty which every one who has watched by a sick bed knows full well; and which is perhaps more insurmountable to men than it is to women, — the difficulty of being patient, and trying not to expect any visible change for long, long hours of sad monotony.

But after awhile the reward came. The laboured breathing became lower and softer, the heavy look of oppressive pain melted away from the face, and a languor that was almost peace took the place of suffering. She slept a natural sleep; and they stole about on tip-toe, and spoke low, and softly, and hardly dared to breathe, however much they longed to sigh out their thankful relief.

She opened her eyes. Her mind was in the tender state of a lately-born infant's. She was pleased with the gay but not dazzling colours of the paper; soothed by the subdued light; and quite sufficiently amused by looking at all the objects in the room — the drawing of the ships, the festoons of the curtain, the bright flowers on the painted backs of the chairs—to care for any stronger excitement. She wondered at the ball of glass, containing various coloured sands from the Isle of Wight, or some other place, which hung suspended from the middle of the little valance over the window. But she did not care to exert himself to ask any questions, although she saw Mrs. Sturgis standing at the bed-side with some tea, ready to drop it into her mouth by spoonfuls.

She did not see the face of honest joy, of earnest thankfulness, — the clasped hands, — the beaming eyes, — the trembling eagerness of gesture, of one who had long awaited her wakening, and who now stood behind the curtains watching through some little chink her every faint motion; or if she had caught a glimpse of that loving, peeping face, she was in too exhausted a state to have taken much notice, or have long retained the impression that he she loved so well was hanging about her, and blessing God for every conscious look which stole over her countenance.

She fell softly into slumber, without a word having been spoken by any one during that half hour of inexpressible joy. And again the stillness was enforced by sign and whispered word, but with eyes that beamed out their bright thoughts of hope. Jem sat by the side of the bed, holding back the little curtain, and gazing as if he could never gave his fill at the pale wasted face so marbled and so chiselled in its wan outline.

She wakened once more; her soft eyes opened, and met his over-bending look. She smiled gently, as a baby does when it sees its mother tending its little cot: and continued its innocent, infantine gaze into his face, as if the sight gave her much unconscious pleasure. But by-and-bye a different expression came into her sweet eyes; a look of memory and intelligence; her white flesh flushed the brightest rosy red, and with feeble motion she tried to hide her head in the pillow.

It required all Jem's self-control to do what he knew and felt to be necessary, to call Mrs. Sturgis, who was quietly dozing by the fire-side; and that done, he felt almost obliged to leave the room to keep down the happy agitation which would gush out in every feature, every gesture, and every tone.

From that time forward, Mary's progress towards health was rapid.

There was every reason, but one, in favour of her speedy removal home. All Jem's duties lay in Manchester. It was his mother's dwelling-place, and there his plans for life had been to be worked out; plans, which the suspicion and imprisonment he had fallen into, had thrown for a time into a chaos, which his presence was required to arrange into form. For he might find, in spite of a jury's verdict, that too strong a taint was on his character for him ever to labour in Manchester again. He remembered the manner in which some one suspected of having been a convict was shunned by masters and men, when he had accidentally met with work in their foundry; the recollection smote him now, how he himself had thought that it did not become an honest upright man to associate with one who had been a prisoner. He could not choose but think on that poor humble being, with his downcast conscious look; hunted out of the workshop, where he had sought to earn an honest livelihood, by the looks, and half-spoken words, and the black silence of repugnance (worse than words to bear), that met him on all sides.

Jem felt that his own character had been attainted; and that to many it might still appear suspicious. He knew that he could convince the world, by a future as blameless as his past had been, that he was innocent. But at the same time he saw that he must have patience, and nerve himself for some trials; and the sooner these were undergone, the sooner he was aware of the place he held in men's estimation, the better. He longed to have presented himself once more at the foundry; and then the reality would drive away the pictures that would (unbidden) come, of a shunned man, eyed askance by all, and driven forth to shape out some new career.

I said every reason "but one" inclined Jem to hasten Mary's return as soon as she was sufficiently convalescent. That one was the meeting which awaited her at home.

Turn it over as Jem would, he could not decide what was the best course to pursue. He could compel himself to any line of conduct that his reason and his sense of right told him to be desirable; but they did not tell him it was desirable to speak to Mary, in her tender state of mind and body, of her father. How much would be implied by the mere mention of his name! Speak it as calmly, and as indifferently as he might, he could not avoid expressing some consciousness of the terrible knowledge she possessed.

She, for her part, was softer and gentler than she had even been in her gentlest mood; since her illness, her motions, her glances, her voice were all tender in their languor. It seemed almost a trouble to her to break the silence with the low sounds of her own sweet voice, and her words fell sparingly on Jem's greedy, listening ear.

Her face was, however, so full of love and confidence, that Jem felt no uneasiness at the state of silent abstraction into which she often fell. If she did but love him, all would yet go right; and it was better not to press for confidence on that one subject which must be painful to both.

There came a fine, bright, balmy day. And Mary tottered once more out into the open air, leaning on Jem's arm, and close to his beating heart. And Mrs. Sturgis watched them from her door, with a blessing on her lips, as they went slowly up the street.

They came in sight of the river. Mary shuddered.

"Oh, Jem! take me home. Yon river seems all made of glittering, heaving, dazzling metal, just as it did when I began to be ill."

Jem led her homewards. She drooped her head as searching for something on the ground.

"Jem!" He was all attention. She paused for an instant. "When may I go home? To Manchester, I mean. I am so weary of this place; and I would fain be at home."

She spoke in a feeble voice; not at all impatiently, as the written words would seem to intimate, but in a mournful way, as if anticipating sorrow even in the very fulfilment of her wishes.

"Darling! we will go whenever you wish; whenever you feel strong enough. I asked Job to tell Margaret to get all in readiness for you to go there at first. She 'll tend you and nurse you. You must not go home. Job proffered for you to go there."

"Ah! but I must go home, Jem. I 'll try and not fail now in what 's right. There are things we must not speak on" (lowering her voice), but "you 'll be really kind if you 'll not speak against my going home. Let us say no more about it, dear Jem. I must go home, and I must go alone."

"Not alone, Mary!"

"Yes, alone! I cannot tell you why I ask it. And if you guess, I know you well enough to be sure you 'll understand why I ask you never to speak on that again to me, till I begin. Promise, dear Jem, promise!"

He promised; to gratify that beseeching face he promised. And then he repented, and felt as if he had done ill. Then again he felt as if she were the best judge, and knowing all (perhaps more than even he did), might be forming plans which his interference would mar.

One thing was certain! it was a miserable thing to have this awful forbidden ground of discourse; to guess at each other's thoughts, when eyes were averted, and cheeks blanched, and words stood still, arrested in their flow by some casual allusion.

At last a day, fine enough for Mary to travel on, arrived. She had wished to go, but now her courage failed her. How could she have said she was weary of that quiet house, where even Ben Sturgis' grumblings only made a kind of harmonious bass in the concord between him and his wife, so thoroughly did they know each other with the knowledge of many years! How could she have longed to quit that little peaceful room where she had experienced such loving tendence! Even the very check bed-curtains became dear to her, under the idea of seeing them no more. If it was so with inanimate objects, if they had such power of exciting regret, what were her feelings with regard to the kind old couple, who had taken the stranger in, and cared for her, and nursed her, as though she had been a daughter! Each wilful sentence spoken in the half unconscious irritation of feebleness came now with avenging self-reproach to her memory, as she hung about Mrs. Sturgis, with many tears, which served instead of words to express her gratitude and love.

Ben bustled about with the square bottle of Golden Wasser in one of his hands, and a small tumbler in the other; he went to Mary, Jem, and his wife in succession, pouring out a glass for each, and bidding them drink it to keep their spirits up: but as each severally refused; he drank it himself; and passed on to offer the same hospitality to another with the like refusal, and the like result.

When he had swallowed the last of the three draughts, he condescended to give his reasons for having done so.

"I cannot abide waste. What 's poured out mun be drunk. That 's my maxim." So saying, he replaced the bottle in the cupboard.

It was he, who in a firm commanding voice at last told Jem and Mary to be off, or they would be too late. Mrs. Sturgis had kept up till then; but as they left her house, she could no longer restrain her tears, and cried aloud in spite of her husband's upbraiding.

"Perhaps they 'll be too late for the train!" exclaimed she, with a degree of hope, as the clock struck two.

"What! and come back again! No! no! that would never do. We 've done our part, and cried our cry; it 's no use going over the same ground again. I should ha' to give 'em more out of yon bottle when next parting time came, and them three glasses they had made a hole in the stuff, I can tell you. Time Jack was back from Hamburgh with some more."

When they reached Manchester, Mary looked very white, and the expression of her face was almost stern. She was in fact summoning up her resolution to meet her father if he were at home. Jem had never named his midnight glimpse of John Barton to human being; but Mary had a sort of presentiment, that wander where he would, he would seek his home at last. But in what mood she dreaded to think. For the knowledge of her father's capability of guilt seemed to have opened a dark gulf in her character, into the depths of which she trembled to look. At one moment she would fain have claimed protection against the life she must lead, for some time at least, alone with a murderer! She thought of his gloom, before his mind was haunted by the memory of so terrible a crime; his moody irritable ways. She imagined the evenings as of old: she, toiling at some work, long after houses were shut, and folks abed; he, more savage than he had ever been before with the inward gnawing of his remorse. At such times she could have cried aloud with terror, at the scenes her fancy conjured up.

But her filial duty, nay, her love and gratitude for many deeds of kindness done to her as a little child, conquered all fear. She would endure all imaginable terrors, although of daily occurrence. And she would patiently bear all wayward violence of temper; more than patiently would she bear it — pitifully, as one who knew of some awful curse awaiting the blood-shedder. She would watch over him tenderly, as the Innocent should watch over the Guilty; awaiting the gracious seasons, wherein to pour oil and balm into the bitter wounds.

With the untroubled peace which the resolve to endure to the end gives, she approached the house that from habit she still called home, but which possessed the holiness of home no longer.

"Jem!" said she, as they stood at the entrance to the court, close by Job Legh's door, "You must go in there and wait half-an-hour. Not less. If, in that time I don't come back, you go your ways to your mother. Give her my dear love. I will send by Margaret when I want to see you." She sighed heavily.

"Mary! Mary! I cannot leave you. You speak as coldly as if we were to be nought to each other. And my heart's bound up in you. I know why you bid me keep away, but —"

She put her hand on his arm, as he spoke in a loud agitated tone; she looked into his face with upbraiding love in her eyes, and then she said, while her lips quivered, and he felt her whole frame trembling:

"Dear Jem! I often could have told you more of love, if I had not once spoken out so free. Remember that time, Jem, if ever you think me cold. Then, the love that 's in my heart would out in words; but now, though I 'm silent on the pain I'm feeling in quitting you, the love is in my heart all the same. But this is not the time to speak on such things. If I do not do what I feel to be right now, I may blame myself all my life long! Jem, you promised —"

And so saying she left him. She went quicker than she would otherwise have passed over those few yards of ground, for fear he should still try to accompany her. Her hand was on the latch, and in a breath the door was opened.

There sat her father, still and motionless — not even turning his head to see who had entered; but perhaps he recognised the foot-step, — the trick of action.

He sat by the fire; the grate I should say, for fire there was none. Some dull gray ashes, negligently left, long days ago, coldly choked up the bars. He had taken the accustomed seat from mere force of habit, which ruled his automaton-body. For all energy, both physical and mental, seemed to have retreated inwards to some of the great citadels of life, there to do battle against the Destroyer, Conscience.

His hands were crossed, his fingers interlaced; usually a position implying some degree of resolution, or strength; but in him it was so faintly maintained, that it appeared more the result of chance; an attitude requiring some application of outward force to alter, — and a blow with a straw seemed as though it would be sufficient.

And as for his face, it was sunk and worn, — like a skull, with yet a suffering expression that skulls have not! Your heart would have ached to have seen the man, however hardly you might have judged his crime.

But crime and all was forgotten by his daughter, as she saw his abashed look, his smitten helplessness. All along she had felt it difficult (as I may have said before) to reconcile the two ideas, of her father and a blood-shedder. But now it was impossible. He was her father! her own dear father! and in his sufferings, whatever their cause, more dearly loved than ever before. His crime was a thing apart, never more to be considered by her.

Aud tenderly did she treat him, and fondly did she serve him in every way that heart could devise, or hand execute.

She had some money about her, the price of her strange services as a witness; and when the lingering dusk grew on she stole out to effect some purchases necessary for her father's comfort.

For how body and soul had been kept together, even as much as they were, during the days he had dwelt alone, no one can say. The house was bare as when Mary had left it, of coal, or of candle, of food, or of blessing in any shape.

She came quickly home; but as she passed Job Legh's door, she stopped. Doubtless Jem had long since gone; and doubtless, too, he had given Margaret some good reason for not intruding upon her friend for this night at least, otherwise Mary would have seen her before now.

But to-morrow, — would she not come in to-morrow? And who so quick as blind Margaret in noticing tones, and sighs, and even silence?

She did not give herself time for further thought, her desire to be once more with her father was too pressing; but she opened the door, before she well knew what to say.

"It 's Mary Barton! I know her by her breathing! Grandfather, it 's Mary Barton!"

Margaret's joy at meeting her, the open demonstration of her love, affected Mary much; she could not keep from crying, and sat down weak and agitated on the first chair she could find.

"Ay, ay, Mary! thou 'rt looking a bit different to when I saw thee last. Thou 'lt give Jem and me good characters for sick nurses, I trust. If all trades fail, I 'll turn to that. Jem's place is for life, I reckon. Nay, never redden so, lass. You and he know each other's minds by this time!"

Margaret held her hand, and gently smiled into her face.

Job Legh took the candle up, and began a leisurely inspection.

"Thou hast gotten a bit of pink in thy cheeks, — not much; but when last I see thee, thy lips were as white as a sheet. Thy nose is sharpish at th' end; thou 'rt more like thy father than ever thou wert before. Lord! child, what 's the matter? Art thou going to faint?"

For Mary had sickened at the mention of that name; yet she felt that now or never was the time to speak.

"Father 's come home!" she said, "but he 's very poorly; I never saw him as he is now, before. I asked Jem not to come near him for fear it might fidget him."

She spoke hastily, and (to her own idea) in an unnatural manner. But they did not seem to notice it, nor to take the hint she had thrown out of company being unacceptable; for Job Legh directly put down some insect, which he was impaling on a corking-pin, and exclaimed,

"Thy father come home! Why, Jem never said a word of it!

And ailing too! I'll go in, and cheer him with a bit of talk. I never knew any good come of delegating it."

"Oh, Job! father cannot stand—father is too ill. Don't come; not but that you're very kind and good; but to-night—indeed," said she, at last, in despair, seeing Job still persevere in putting away his things; "you must not come till I send or come for you. Father's in that strange way, I can't answer for it if he sees strangers. Please don't come. I'll come and tell you every day how he goes on. I must be off now to see after him. Dear Job! kind Job! don't be angry with me. If you knew all you'd pity me."

For Job was muttering away in high dudgeon, and even Margaret's tone was altered as she wished Mary good night. Just then she could ill brook coldness from any one, and least of all bear the idea of being considered ungrateful by so kind and zealous a friend as Job had been; so she turned round suddenly, even when her hand was on the latch of the door, and ran back, and threw her arms about his neck, and kissed him first, and then Margaret. And then, the tears fast-falling down her cheeks, but no word spoken, she hastily left the house, and went back to her home.

There was no change in her father's position, or in his spectral look. He had answered her questions (but few in number, for so many subjects were unapproachable) by monosyllables, and in a weak, high, childish voice; but he had not lifted his eyes; he could not meet his daughter's look. And she, when she spoke, or as she moved about, avoided letting her eyes rest upon him. She wished to be her usual self; but while every thing was done with a consciousness of purpose, she felt it was impossible.

In this manner things went on for some days. At night he feebly clambered up stairs to bed; and during those long dark hours Mary heard those groans of agony, which never escaped his lips by day; when they were compressed in silence over his inward woe.

Many a time she sat up listening, and wondering if it would ease his miserable heart if she went to him, and told him she knew all, and loved and pitied him more than words could tell.

By day the monotonous hours wore on in the same heavy,

hushed manner as on that first dreary afternoon. He ate, — but without that relish; and food seemed no longer to nourish him, for each morning bis face had caught more of the ghastly foreshadowing of Death.

The neighbours kept strangely aloof. Of late years John Barton had had a repellant power about him, felt by all, except to the few who had either known him in his better and happier days, or those to whom he had given his sympathy and his confidence. People did not care to enter the doors of one, whose very depth of thoughtfulness rendered him moody and stern. And now they contented themselves with a kind inquiry when they saw Mary in her goings-out or in her comings-in. With her oppressing knowledge, she imagined their reserved conduct stranger than it was in reality. She missed Job and Margaret too; who, in all former times of sorrow or anxiety since their acquaintance first began, had been ready with their sympathy.

But most of all she missed the delicious luxury she had lately enjoyed in having Jem's tender love at hand every hour of the day, to ward off every wind of heaven, and every disturbing thought.

She knew he was often hovering about the house; though the knowledge seemed to come more by intuition, than by any positive sight or sound for the first day or two. On the third day, she met him at Job Legh's.

They received her with every effort of cordiality; but still there was a cobweb-veil of separation between them, to which Mary was morbidly acute. While in Jem's voice, and eyes, and manner, there was every evidence of most passionate, most admiring, and most trusting love. The trust was shown by his respectful silence on that one point of reserve on which she had interdicted conversation.

He left Job Legh's house when she did. They lingered on the step; he holding her hand between both of his, as loth to let her go, he questioned her as to when he should see her again.

"Mother does so want to see you," whispered he. "Can you come to see her to-morrow, or when?"

"I cannot tell," replied she, softly. "Not yet. Wait awhile;

perhaps only a little while. Dear Jem, I must go to him, — dearest Jem."

The next day, the fourth from Mary's return home, as she was sitting near the window, sadly dreaming over some work, she caught a glimpse of the last person she wished to see — of Sally Leadbitter!

She was evidently coming to their house; another moment, and she tapped at the door. John Barton gave an anxious, uneasy side-glance. Mary knew that if she delayed answering the knock, Sally would not scruple to enter; so as hastily as if the visit had been desired, she opened the door, and stood there with the latch in her hand, barring up all entrance, and as much as possible obstructing all curious glances into the interior.

"Well, Mary Barton! You 're home at last! I heard you 'd getten home; so I thought I'd just step over and hear the news."

She was bent on coming in, and saw Mary's preventive design. So she stood on tip-toe, looking over Mary's shoulders into the room where she suspected a lover to be lurking; but instead, she saw only the figure of the stern gloomy father she had always been in the habit of avoiding; and she dropped down again, content to carry on the conversation where Mary chose, and as Mary chose, in whispers.

"So the old governor is back again, eh? And what does he say to all your fine doings at Liverpool, and before? — you and I know where. You can't hide it now, Mary, for it 's all in print."

Mary gave a low moan, — and then implored Sally to change the subject; for unpleasant as it always was, it was doubly unpleasant in the manner in which she was treating it. If they had been alone, Mary would have borne it patiently, — or she thought, — but now she felt almost certain her father was listening; there was a subdued breathing, a slight bracing-up of the listless attitude. But there was no arresting Sally's curiosity to hear all she could respecting the adventures Mary had experienced. She, in common with the rest of Miss Simmonds' young ladies, was almost jealous of the fame that Mary had obtained; to herself, such miserable notoriety.

"Nay! there 's no use shunning talking it over. Why! it was in the *Guardian*, — and the *Courier*, — and some one told Jane

Hodson it was even copied into a London paper. "You 've set up heroine on your own account, Mary Barton. How did you like standing witness? Ar'n't them lawyers impudent things? staring at one so. I 'll be bound you wished you 'd taken my offer, and borrowed my black watered scarf! Now didn't you, Mary? Speak truth!"

"To tell truth, I never thought about it, then, Sally. How could I?" asked she, reproachfully.

"Oh — I forgot. You were all for that stupid James Wilson. Well! if I 've ever the luck to go witness on a trial, see if I don't pick up a better beau than the prisoner. I 'll aim at a lawyer's clerk, but I 'll not take less than a turnkey."

Cast down as Mary was, she could hardly keep from smiling at the idea, so wildly incongruous with the scene she had really undergone, of looking out for admirers during a trial for murder.

"I 'd no thought to be looking out for beaux, I can assure you, Sally. — But don't let us talk any more about it, I can't bear to think on it. How is Miss Simmonds? and everybody?"

"Oh, very well; and by the way she gave me a bit of a message for you. You may come back to work if you 'll behave yourself, she says. I told you she'd be glad to have you back, after all this piece of business, by way of tempting people to come to her shop. They'd come from Salford to have a peep at you, for six months at least."

"Don't talk so; I cannot come, I can never face Miss Simmonds again. And even if I could," she stopped, and blushed.

"Aye! I know what you are thinking on. But that will not be this some time, as he 's turned off from the foundry, — you 'd better think twice afore refusing Miss Simmonds' offer."

"Turned off from the foundry? Jem?" cried Mary.

"To be sure! didn't you know it? Decent men were not going to work with a — no! I suppose I mustn't say it, seeing you went to such trouble to get up an *alibi;* not that I should think much the worse of a spirited young fellow for falling foul of a rival, — they always do at the theatre."

But Mary's thoughts were with Jem. How good he had been never to name his dismissal to her. How much he had had to endure for her sake!

"Tell me all about it," she gasped out.

"Why, you see they 've always swords quite handy at them plays," began Sally; but Mary, with an impatient shake of her head, interrupted,

"About Jem, — about Jem, I want to know."

"Oh! I don't pretend to know more than is in every one's mouth: he 's turned away from the foundry, because folks don't think you 've cleared him outright of the murder; though perhaps the jury were loth to hang him. Old Mr. Carsons is savage against judge and jury, and lawyers and all, as I heard."

"I must go to him, I must go to him," repeated Mary, in a hurried manner.

"He 'll tell you all I 've said is true, and not a word of lie," replied Sally. "So I 'll not give your answer to Miss Simmonds, but leave you to think twice about it. Good afternoon!"

Mary shut the door, and turned into the house.

Her father sat in the same at titude; the old unchanging attitude. Only his head was more bowed towards the ground.

She put on her bonnet to go to Ancoats; for see, and question, and comfort, and worship Jem, she must.

As she hung about her father for an instant before leaving him, he spoke — voluntarily spoke for the first time since her return: but his head was drooping so low she could not hear what he said, so she stooped down; and after a moment's pause, he repeated the words,

"Tell Jem Wilson to come here at eight o'clock to-night."

Could he have overheard her conversation with Sally Leadbitter? They had whispered low, she thought. Pondering on this, and many other things, she reached Ancoats.

CHAPTER XXXV.

"Oh, had he lived,
Replied Rusilla, never penitence
Had equalled his! full well I knew his heart,
Vehement in all things. He would on himself
Have wreaked such penance as had reached the height
Of fleshy suffering, — yea, which being told,
With its portentous rigour should have made
The memory of his fault, o'erpowered and lost
In shuddering pity and astonishment,
Fade like a feeble horror." SOUTHEY'S 'RODERICK.'

As Mary was turning into the street where the Wilson's

lived, Jem overtook her. He came upon her suddenly, and she started.

"You 're going to see mother?" he asked, tenderly, placing her arm within his, and slackening his pace.

"Yes, and you too. Oh, Jem, is it true? tell me."

She felt rightly that he would guess the meaning of her only half expressed inquiry. He hesitated a moment before he answered her.

"Darling, it is; it 's no use hiding it — if you mean that. I 'm no longer to work at Duncombe's foundry. It 's no time (to my mind) to have secrets from each other, though I did not name it yesterday, thinking you might fret. I shall soon get work again, never fear."

"But why did they turn you off, when the jury had said you were innocent?"

"I was not just to say turned off, though I don't think I could have well staid on. A good number of the men managed to let out they should not like to work under me again; there were some few who knew me well enough to feel I could not have done it, but more were doubtful; and one spoke to young Mr. Duncombe, hinting at what they thought."

"Oh, Jem! what a shame!" said Mary, with mournful indignation.

"Nay, darling! I 'm not for blaming them. Poor fellows like them have nought to stand upon and be proud of but their character, and its fitting they should take care of that, and keep that free from soil and taint."

"But you, — what could they get but good from you? They might have known you by this time."

"So some do; the overlooker, I 'm sure, would know I 'm innocent. Indeed, he said as much to-day; and he said he had had some talk with old Mr. Duncombe, and they thought it might be better if I left Manchester for a bit; they 'd recommend me to some other place."

But Mary could only shake her head in a mournful way, and repeat her words,

"They might have known thee better, Jem."

Jem pressed the little hand he held between his own work-hardened ones. After a minute or two, he asked,

"Mary, art thou much bound to Manchester? Would it grieve thee sore to quit the old smoke-jack?"

"With thee?" she asked, in a quiet, glancing way.

"Ay, lass! Trust me, I 'll never ask thee to leave Manchester while I 'm in it. Because I have heard fine things of Canada; and our overlooker has a cousin in the foundry line there. — Thou knowest where Canada is, Mary?"

"Not rightly — not now, at any rate; — but with thee, Jem," her voice sunk to a soft, low whisper, "anywhere —"

What was the use of a geographical description.

"But father!" said Mary, suddenly breaking that delicious silence with the one sharp discord in her present life.

She looked up at her lover's grave face; and then the message her father had sent flashed across her memory.

"Oh, Jem, did I tell you? — Father sent word he wished to speak with you. I was to bid you come to him at eight to-night. What can he want, Jem?"

"I cannot tell," replied he. "At any rate I 'll go. It 's no use troubling ourselves to guess," he continued, after a pause for a few minutes, during which they slowly and silently paced up and down the by-street, into which he had led her when their conversation began. "Come and see mother, and then I 'll take thee home, Mary. Thou wert all in a tremble when first I came up to thee; thou 'rt not fit to be trusted home by thyself," said he, with fond exaggeration of her helpnessness.

Yet a little more lover's loitering; a few more words, in themselves nothing — to you nothing — but to those two, what tender passionate language can I use to express the feelings which thrilled through that young man and maiden, as they listened to the syllables made dear and lovely through life by that hour's low-whispered talk.

It struck the half hour past seven.

"Come and speak to mother; she knows you 're to be her daughter, Mary. darling."

So they went in. Jane Wilson was rather chafed at her son's delay in returning home, for as yet, he had managed to keep her in ignorance of his dismissal from the foundry: and it was her way to prepare some little pleasure, some little comfort for those she loved; and if they, unwittingly, did not appear at the proper time to enjoy her preparation, she worked herself up into a state of fretfulness which found vent in upbraidings as soon as ever the objects of her care appeared, thereby marring the peace which should ever be the atmosphere of a home, however humble; and causing a feeling almost amounting to loathing to arise at the sight of the "stalled ox," which, though an effect and proof of careful love, has been the cause of so much disturbance.

Mrs. Wilson had first sighed, and then grumbled to herself, over the increasing toughness of the potatoe-cakes she had made for her son's tea.

The door opened, and he came in; his face brightening into proud smiles, Mary Barton hanging on his arm, blushing and dimpling, with eye-lids veiling the happy light of her eyes, — there was around the young couple a radiant atmosphere — a glory of happiness.

Could his mother mar it? Could she break into it with her Martha-like cares? Only for one moment did she remember her sense of injury, — her wasted trouble, — and then, her whole woman's heart heaving with motherly love and sympathy, she opened her arms, and received Mary into them, as shedding tears of agitated joy, she murmured in her ear,

"Bless thee, Mary, bless thee! Only make him happy, and God bless thee for ever!"

It took some of Jem's self-command to separate those whom he so much loved, and who were beginning, for his sake, to love one another so dearly. But the time for his meeting John Barton drew on: and it was a long way to his house.

As they walked briskly thither, they hardly spoke; though many thoughts were in their minds.

The sun had not long set, but the first faint shade of twilight was over all; and when they opened the door, Jem could hardly perceive the objects within by the waning light of day, and the flickering fire-blaze.

But Mary saw all at a glance.

Her eye, accustomed to what was usual in the aspect of the

room, saw instantly what was unusual, — saw, and understood it all.

Her father was standing behind his habitual chair; holding by the back of it as if for support. And opposite to him there stood Mr. Carsons; the dark out-line of his stern figure looming large against the light of the fire in that little room.

Behind her father sat Job Legh, his head in his hands, and resting his elbows on the little family table, — listening evidently; but as evidently deeply affected by what he heard.

There seemed to be some pause in the conversation. Mary and Jem stood at the half-open door, not daring to stir; hardly to breathe.

"And have I heard you aright?" began Mr. Carsons, with his deep quivering voice. "Man! have I heard you aright? Was it you, then, that killed my boy? my only son?" — (he said these last few words almost as if appealing for pity, and then he changed his tone to one more vehement and fierce.) 'Don't dare to think that I shall be merciful, and spare you, because you have come forward to accuse yourself. I tell you I will not spare you the least pang the law can inflict, — you, who did not show pity on my boy, shall have none from me."

"I did not ask for any," said John Barton, in a low voice.

"Ask, or not ask, what care I? You shall be hanged — hanged — man!" said he, advancing his face, and repeating the word with slow grinding emphasis, as if to infuse some of the bitterness of his soul into it.

John Barton gasped; but not with fear. It was only that he felt it terrible to have inspired such hatred, as was concentrated into every word, every gesture of Mr. Carsons'.

"As for being hanged, Sir, I know it 's all right and proper. I dare say it 's bad enough; but I tell you what, Sir," speaking with an outburst, "if you 'd hanged me the day after I 'd done the deed, I would have gone down on my knees and blessed you. Death! Lord, what is it to Life? To such a Life as I 've been leading this fortnight past. Life at best is no great thing; but such a Life as I have dragged through since that night," he shuddered at the thought. "Why, Sir, I 've been on the point of killing myself this many a time to get away from my own thoughts. I didn't! and I'll tell you why. I didn't know but that I should be more haunted than ever with the recollection of my sin. Oh! God above only can tell the agony with which I've repented me of it, and part perhaps because I feared He would think I were impatient of the misery He sent as punishment — far, far worse misery than any hanging, Sir;" he ceased from excess of emotion.

Then he began again.

"Sin' that day (it may be very wicked, Sir, but it's the truth) I've kept thinking and thinking if I were but in that world where they say God is, He would, may be, teach me right from wrong, even if it were with many stripes. I've been sore puzzled here. I would go through Hell-fire if I could but get free from sin at last, it's such an awful thing. As for hanging, that's just nought at all."

His exhaustion compelled him to sit down. Mary rushed to him. It seemed as if till then he had been unaware of her presence.

"Ay, ay, wench!" said he, feebly, "is it thee? Where's Jem Wilson?"

Jem came forward. John Barton spoke again, with many a break, and gasping pause,

"Lad! thou hast borne a deal for me. It's the meanest thing I ever did to leave thee to bear the brunt. Thou, who wert as innocent of any knowledge of it as the babe unborn. I'll not bless thee for it. Blessing from such as me would not bring thee any good. Thou'lt love Mary, though she is my child."

He ceased, and there was a pause for a few seconds.

Then Mr. Carsons turned to go. When his hand was on the latch of the door, he hesitated for an instant.

"You can have no doubt for what purpose I go. Straight to the police-office, to send men to take care of you, wretched man, and your accomplice. To-morrow morning your tale shall be repeated to those who can commit you to gaol, and before long you shall have the opportunity of trying how desirable hanging is."

"Oh, Sir!" said Mary, springing forward, and catching

hold of Mr. Carsons' arm, "my father is dying. Look at him, Sir. If you want Death for Death, you have it. Don't take him away from me these last hours. He must go alone through Death, but let me be with him as long as I can. Oh, Sir! if you have any mercy in you, leave him here to die."

John himself stood up, stiff and rigid, and replied,

"Mary, wench! I owe him summit. I will go die, where, and as he wishes me. Thou hast said true, I am standing side by side with Death; and it matters little where I spend the bit of time left of Life. That time I must pass wrestling with my soul for a character to take into the other world. I'll go where you see fit, Sir. He 's innocent," faintly indicating Jem, as he fell back in his chair.

"Never fear! They cannot touch him," said Job Legh, in a low voice.

But as Mr. Carsons was on the point of leaving the house with no sign of relenting about him, he was again stopped by John Barton, who had risen once more from his chair, and stood supporting himself on Jem, while he spoke.

"Sir, one word! My hairs are gray with suffering, and yours with years —"

"And have I had no suffering?" asked Mr. Carsons, as if appealing for sympathy, even to the murderer of his child.

And the murderer of his child answered to the appeal, and groaned in spirit over the anguish he had caused.

"Have I had no inward suffering to blanch these hairs? Have not I toiled and struggled even to these years with hopes in my heart that all centered in my boy? I did not speak of them, but were they not there? I seemed hard and cold; and so I might be to others, but not to him! who shall ever imagine the love I bore to him? Even he never dreamed how my heart leapt up at the sound of his footstep, and how precious he was to his poor old father. — And he is gone — killed — out of the hearing of all loving words — out of my sight for ever. He was my sunshine, and now it is night! Oh, my God! comfort me, comfort me!" cried the old man, aloud.

The eyes of John Barton grew dim with tears. Rich and poor, masters and men, were then brothers in the deep suffering of the heart; for was not this the very anguish he had felt for little Tom, in years so long gone by that they seemed like another life!

The mourner before him was no longer the employer; a being of another race, eternally placed in antagonistic attitude; going through the world glittering like gold, with a stony heart within, which knew no sorrow but through the accidents of Trade; no longer the enemy, the oppressor, but a very poor, and desolate old man.

The sympathy for suffering, formerly so prevalent a feeling with him, again filled John Barton's heart, and almost impelled him to speak (as best he could) some earnest, tender words to the stern man, shaking in his agony.

But who was he, that he should utter sympathy, or consolation? The cause of all this woe.

Oh blasting thought! Oh miserable remembrance! He had forfeited all right to bind up his brother's wounds.

Stunned by the thought, he sank upon the seat, almost crushed with the knowledge of the consequences of his own action; for he had no more imagined to himself the blighted home, and the miserable parents, than does the soldier, who discharges his musket, picture to himself the desolation of the wife, and the pitiful cries of the helpless little ones, who are in an instant to be made widowed, and fatherless.

To intimidate a class of men, known only to those below them as desirous to obtain the greatest quantity of work for the lowest wages, — at most to remove an overbearing partner from an obnoxious firm, who stood in the way of those who struggled as well as they were able to obtain their rights, — this was the light in which John Barton had viewed his deed; and even so viewing it, after the excitement had passed away, the Avenger, the sure Avenger, had found him out.

But now he knew that he had killed a man, and a brother, — now he knew that no good thing could come out of this evil, even to the sufferers whose cause he had so blindly espoused.

He lay across the table, broken-hearted. Every fresh quivering sob of Mr. Carsons' stabbed him to his soul.

He felt execrated by all; and as if he could never lay bare the perverted reasonings which had made the performance of undoubted sin appear a duty. The longing to plead some faint excuse grew stronger and stronger. He feebly raised his head, and looking at Job Legh, he whispered out,

"I did not know what I was doing, Job Legh, God knows I didn't! Oh, Sir!" said he wildly, almost throwing himself at Mr. Carsons' feet, "say you forgive me the anguish I now see I have caused you. I care not for pain, or death, you know I don't; but oh, man! forgive me the trespass I have done!"

"Forgive us our trespasses as we forgive them that trespass against us," said Job solemnly and low, as if in prayer: as if the words were suggested by those John Barton had used.

Mr. Carsons took his hands away from his face. I would rather see death than the ghastly gloom which darkened that countenance.

"Let my trespasses be unforgiven, so that I may have vengeance for my son's murder."

There are blasphemous actions as well as blasphemous words: all unloving, cruel deeds are acted blasphemy.

Mr. Carsons left the house. And John Barton lay on the ground as one dead.

They lifted him up, and almost hoping that that deep trance might be to him the end of all earthly things, they bore him to his bed.

For a time they listened with divided attention to his faint breathings; for in each hasty hurried step that echoed in the street outside, they thought they heard the approach of the officers of justice.

When Mr. Carsons left the house he was dizzy with agitation; the hot blood went careering through his frame. He could not see the deep blue of the night-heavens for the fierce pulses which throbbed in his head. And partly to steady and calm himself, he leaned against a railing, and looked up into those calm majestic depths with all their thousand stars.

And by-and-bye his own voice returned upon him, as if the last words he had spoken were being uttered through all that infinite space; but in their echoes there was a tone of unutterable sorrow.

"Let my trespasses be unforgiven, so that I may have vengeance for my son's murder."

He tried to shake off the spiritual impression made by this imagination. He was feverish and ill, — and no wonder.

So he turned to go homewards; not, as he had threatened, to the police-office. After all (he told himself), that would do in the morning. No fear of the man's escaping, unless he escaped to the Grave.

So he tried to banish the phantom voices and shapes which came unbidden to his brain, and to recall his balance of mind by walking calmly and slowly, and noticing every thing which struck his senses.

It was a warm soft evening in spring, and there were many persons in the streets. Among others, a nurse with a little girl in her charge, conveying her home from some children's gaiety; a dance most likely, for the lovely little creature was daintily decked out in soft, snowy muslin; and her fairy feet tripped along by her nurse's side, as if to the measure of some tune she had lately kept time to.

Suddenly up behind her there came a rough, rude errand-boy, nine or ten years of age; a giant he looked by the fairy-child, as she fluttered along. I don't know how it was, but in some awkward way he knocked the poor little girl down upon the hard pavement as he brushed rudely past, not much caring whom he hurt, so that he got along.

The child arose sobbing with pain; and not without cause, for blood was dropping down from the face, but a minute before so fair and bright — dropping down on the pretty frock, making those scarlet marks so terrible to little children.

The nurse, a powerful woman, had seized the boy, just as Mr. Carsons (who had seen the whole transaction) came up.

"You naughty little rascal! I'll give you to a policeman, that I will! Do you see how you've hurt the little girl? Do you?" accompanying every sentence with a violent jerk of passionate anger.

The lad looked hard, and defying; but withal terrified at the threat of the policeman, those ogres of our streets to all unlucky urchins. The nurse saw it, and began to drag him along, with a view of making what she called "a wholesome impression."

His terror increased, and with it his irritation; when the little sweet face, choking away its sobs, pulled down nurse's head, and said,

"Please, dear nurse, I'm not much hurt; it was very silly to cry, you know. He did not mean to do it. *He did not know what he was doing*, did you, little boy? Nurse won't call a policeman, so don't be frightened." And she put up her little mouth to be kissed by her injurer, just as she had been taught to do at home to "make peace."

"That lad will mind, and be more gentle for the time to come, I'll be bound, thanks to that little lady," said a passer-by, half to himself, and half to Mr. Carsons, whom he had observed to notice the scene.

The latter took no apparent heed of the remark, but passed on. But the child's pleading reminded him of the low, broken voice he had so lately heard, penitently and humbly urging the same extenuation of his great guilt.

"I did not know what I was doing."

He had some association with those words; he had heard, or read of that plea somewhere before. Where was it?

Could it be —?

He would look when he got home. So when he entered his house he went straight and silently up-stairs to his library, and took down the great large handsome Bible, all grand and golden, with its leaves adhering together from the bookbinder's press, so little had it been used.

On the first page (which fell open to Mr. Carsons' view) were written the names of his children, and his own.

"Henry John, son of the above John, and Elizabeth Carsons.
Born, Sept. 29th, 1815."

To make the entry complete, his death should now be added. But the page became hidden by the gathering mist of tears.

Thought upon thought, and recollection upon recollection came crowding in, from the remembrance of the proud day when he had purchased the costly book, in order to write down the birth of the little babe of a day old.

He laid his head down on the open page, and let the tears fall slowly on the spotless leaves.

His son's murderer was discovered; had confessed his guilt; and yet (strange to say) he could not hate him with the vehemence of hatred he had felt, when he had imagined him a young man, full of lusty life, defying all laws, human and divine. In spite of his desire to retain the revengeful feeling he considered as a duty to his dead son, something of pity would steal in for the poor, wasted skeleton of a man, the smitten creature, who had told him of his sin, and implored his pardon that night.

In the days of his childhood and youth, Mr. Carsons had been accustomed to poverty; but it was honest decent poverty; not the grinding squalid misery he had remarked in every part of John Barton's house, and which contrasted strangely with the pompous sumptuousness of the room in which he now sate. Unaccustomed wonder filled his mind at the reflection of the different lots of the brethren of mankind.

Then he roused himself from his reverie, and turned to the object of his search — the Gospel, where he half expected to find the tender pleading. "They know not what they do."

It was mirk midnight by this time, and the house was still and quiet. There was nothing to interrupt the old man in his unwonted study.

Years ago, the Gospel had been his task-book in learning to read. So many years ago, that he had become familiar with the events before he could comprehend the Spirit that made the Life.

He fell to the narrative now afresh, with all the interest of a little child. He began at the beginning, and read on almost greedily, understanding for the first time the full meaning of the story. He came to the end; the awful End. And there were the haunting words of pleading.

He shut the book, and thought deeply.

All night long, the Arch-angel combated with the Demon.

All night long, others watched by the bed of Death. John Barton had revived to fitful intelligence. He spoke at times with even something of his former energy; and in the racy Lancashire dialect he had always used when speaking freely.

"You see I 've so often been hankering after the right way;

and it 's a hard one for a poor man to find. At least it 's been so to me. No one learned me, and no one telled me. When I was a little chap they taught me to read, and then they never gave me books; only I heard say the Bible was a good book. So when I grew thoughtful, and puzzled, I took to it. But you 'd never believe black was black, or night was night, when you saw all about you acting as if black was white, and night was day. It 's not much I can say for myself in t' other world. God forgive me; but I can say this, I would fain have gone after the Bible rules if I 'd seen folk credit it; they all spoke up for it, and went and did clean contrary. In those days I would ha' gone about wi' my Bible, like a little child, my finger in th' place, and asking the meaning of this or that text, and no one told me. Then I took out two or three texts as clear as glass and I tried to do what they bid me do. But I don't know how it was; masters and men, all alike cared no more for minding those texts, than I did for th' Lord Mayor of London; so I grew to think it must be a sham put upon poor ignorant folk, women, and such-like.

"It was not long I tried to live Gospel-wise, but it was liker heaven than any other bit of earth has been. I 'd old Alice to strengthen me; but every one else said 'Stand up for thy rights, or thou 'lt never get 'em;' and wife, and children never spoke, but their helplessness cried aloud, and I was driven to do as others did, — and then Tom died. You know all about that — I 'm getting scant o' breath, and blind-like."

Then again he spoke, after some minutes of hushed silence.

"All along it came natural to love folk, though now I am what I am. I think one time I could e'en have loved the masters if they 'd ha' letten me; that was in my Gospel-days, afore my child died o' hunger. I was tore in two often-times, between my sorrow for poor suffering folk, and my trying to love them as caused their sufferings (to my mind).

"At last I gave it up in despair, trying to make folks' actions square wi' th' Bible; and I thought I 'd no longer labour at following th' Bible mysel. I 've said all this afore, may be. But from that time I 've dropped down, down, — down."

After that he only spoke in broken sentences.

"I did not think he 'd been such an old man, — Oh! that he

had but forgiven me," — and then came earnest, passionate, broken words of prayer.

Job Legh had gone home like one struck down with the unexpected shock. Mary and Jem together waited the approach of death; but as the final struggle drew on, and morning dawned, Jem suggested some alleviation to the gasping breath, to purchase which he left the house in search of a druggist's shop, which should be open at that early hour.

During his absence, Barton grew worse; he had fallen across the bed, and his breathing seemed almost stopped; in vain did Mary strive to raise him, her sorrow and exhaustion had rendered her too weak.

So, on hearing some one enter the house-place below, she cried out for Jem to come to her assistance.

A step, which was not Jem's, came up the stairs.

Mr. Carsons stood in the door-way. In one instant he comprehended the case.

He raised up the powerless frame; and the departing soul looked out of the eyes with gratitude. He held the dying man propped in his arms. John Barton folded his hands, as if in prayer.

"Pray for us," said Mary, sinking on her knees, and forgetting in that solemn hour all that had divided her father and Mr. Carsons.

No other words would suggest themselves than some of those he had read only a few hours before.

"God be merciful to us sinners. — Forgive us our trespasses as we forgive them that trespass against us."

And when the words were said, John Barton lay a corpse in Mr. Carsons' arms.

So ended the tragedy of a poor man's life.

Mary knew nothing more for many minutes. When she recovered consciousness, she found herself supported by Jem on the "settle" in the house-place. Job and Mr. Carsons were there, talking together lowly and solemnly. Then Mr. Carsons bade farewell and left the house; and Job said aloud, but as if speaking to himself,

"God has heard that man's prayer. He has comforted him."

CHAPTER XXXVI.

"The first dark day of nothingness,
The last of danger and distress." BYRON.

ALTHOUGH Mary had hardly been conscious of her thoughts, and it had been more like a secret instinct informing her soul, than the result of any process of reasoning, she had felt for some time (ever since her return from Liverpool, in fact), that for her father there was but one thing to be desired and anticipated, and that was death!

She had seen that Conscience had given the mortal wound to his earthly frame; she did not dare to question of the infinite mercy of God, what the Future Life would be to him.

Though at first desolate and stunned by the blow which had fallen on herself, she was resigned and submissive as soon as she recovered strength enough to ponder and consider a little; and you may be sure that no tenderness or love was wanting on Jem's part, and no consideration and sympathy on that of Job and Margaret, to soothe and comfort the girl who now stood alone in the world as far as blood-relations were concerned.

She did not ask or care to know what arrangements they were making in whispered tones with regard to the funeral. She put herself into their hands with the trust of a little child; glad to be undisturbed in the reveries and remembrances which filled her eyes with tears, and caused them to fall quietly down her pale cheeks.

It was the longest day she had ever known in her life; every change and every occupation was taken away from her: but perhaps the length of quiet time thus afforded was really good, although its duration weighed upon her; for by this means she contemplated her situation in every light, and fully understood that the morning's event had left her an orphan; and thus she was spared the pangs caused to us by the occurrence of death in the evening, just before we should naturally, in the usual course of events, lie down to slumber. For in such case, worn out by anxiety, and it may be by much watching, our very excess of grief rocks itself to sleep, before we have had time to realise its cause; and we waken, with a start of agony like a fresh stab, to the consciousness of the one awful vacancy, which shall never, while the world endures, be filled again.

The day brought its burden of duty to Mrs. Wilson. She felt bound by regard, as well as by etiquette, to go and see her future daughter-in-law. And by an old association of ideas (perhaps of death with church-yards, and churches with Sunday), she thought it necessary to put on her best, and latterly unused clothes, the airing of which on a little clothes-horse before the fire seemed to give her a not unpleasing occupation.

When Jem returned home late in the evening succeeding John Barton's death, weary and oppressed with the occurrences and excitements of the day, he found his mother busy about her mourning, and much inclined to talk. Although he longed for quiet, he could not avoid sitting down and answering her questions.

"Well, Jem! he 's gone at last, is he?"

"Yes. How did you hear, mother?"

"Oh, Job came over here, and telled me, on his way to the undertaker's. Did he make a fine end?"

It struck Jem that she had not heard of the confession which had been made by John Barton on his death-bed; he remembered Job Legh's discretion, and he determined that if it could be avoided his mother should never hear of it. Many of the difficulties to be anticipated in preserving the secret would be obviated, if he could induce his mother to fall into the plan he had named to Mary of emigrating to Canada. The reasons which rendered this secrecy desirable related to the domestic happiness he hoped for. With his mother's irritable temper he could hardly expect that all allusion to the crime of John Barton would be for ever restrained from passing her lips, and he knew the deep trial which such references would be to Mary. Accordingly he resolved as soon as possible in the morning to go to Job, and beseech his silence; he trusted that secrecy in that quarter, even if the knowledge had been extended to Margaret, might be easily secured.

But what would be Mr. Carson's course? Were there any means by which he might be persuaded to spare John Barton's memory?

He was roused up from this train of thought by his mother's more irritated tone of voice.

"Jem!" she was saying, "thou might'st just as well never be at a death-bed again, if thou cannot bring off more news about it; here have I been by mysel all day (except when oud Job came in), but thinks I, when Jem comes he 'll be sure to be good company, seeing he was in the house at the very time of the death; and here thou art, without a word to throw at a dog, much less thy mother: it 's no use thy going to a death-bed if thou cannot carry away any of the sayings!"

"He did not make any, mother," replied Jem.

"Well to be sure! So fond as he used to be of holding forth, to miss such a fine opportunity that will never come again! Did he die easy?"

"He was very restless all night long," said Jem, reluctantly returning to the thoughts of that time.

"And in course thou plucked the pillow away? Thou didst not! Well! with thy bringing up, and thy learning, thou might'st have known that were the only help in such a case. There were pigeons' feathers in the pillow, depend on't. To think of two grown-up folk like you and Mary, not knowing death could never come easy to a person lying on a pillow with pigeons' feathers in!"

Jem was glad to escape from all this talking to the solitude and quiet of his own room, where he could lie and think uninterruptedly of what had happened and remained to be done.

The first thing was to seek an interview with Mr. Duncombe, his former master. Accordingly, early the next morning Jem set off on his walk to the works, where for so many years his days had been spent; where for so long a time his thoughts had been thought, his hopes and fears experienced. It was not a cheering feeling to remember that henceforward he was to be severed from all these familiar places; nor were his spirits enlivened by the evident feelings of the majority of those who had been his fellow-workmen. As he stood in the entrance to the foundry, awaiting Mr. Duncombe's leisure, many of those employed in the works passed him on their return from breakfast; and, with one or two exceptions, without any acknowledgment of former acquaintance beyond a distant nod at the utmost.

"It is hard," said Jem to himself, with a bitter and indignant feeling rising in his throat, "that let a man's life have been what it may, folk are so ready to credit the first word against him. I could live it down if I stayed in England; but then what would not Mary have to bear? Sooner or later the truth would out; and then she would be a show to folk for many a day as John Barton's daughter. Well! God does not judge as hardly as man, that 's one comfort for all of us!"

Mr. Duncombe did not believe in Jem's guilt, in spite of the silence in which he again this day heard the imputation of it; but he agreed that under the circumstances it was better he should leave the country.

"We have been written to by government, as I think I told you before, to recommend an intelligent man, well acquainted with mechanics, as instrument maker to the Agricultural College they are establishing at Toronto, in Canada. It is a comfortable appointment, — house, — land, — and a good per-centage on the instruments made. I will show you the particulars if I can lay my hand on the letter, which I believe I must have left at home."

"Thank you, Sir. No need for seeing the letter to say I'll accept it. I must leave Manchester; and I 'd as lief quit England at once when I 'm about it."

"Of course government give you your passage; indeed I believe an allowance would be made for a family if you had one; but you are not a married man, I believe?"

"No, Sir, but —" Jem hung back from a confession with the awkwardness of a girl.

"But —" said Mr. Duncombe, smiling, "you would like to be a married man before you go, I suppose; eh, Wilson?"

"If you please, Sir. And there 's my mother, too. I hope she 'll go with us. But I can pay her passage; no need to trouble government."

"Nay, nay! I 'll write to-day and recommend you. And say that you have a family of two. They 'll never ask if the family goes upwards or downwards. I shall see you again before you sail, I hope, Wilson; though I believe they 'll not allow you long to wait. Come to my house next time; you 'll find it pleasanter, I daresay. These men are so wrong-headed. Keep up your heart!"

Jem felt that it was a relief to have this point settled; and that he need no longer weigh reasons for and against his emigration.

And with his path growing clearer and clearer before him the longer he contemplated it, he went to see Mary, and if he judged it fit, to tell her what he had decided upon. Margaret was sitting with her.

"Grandfather wants to see you!" said she, to Jem, on his entrance.

"And I want to see him," replied Jem, suddenly remembering his last night's determination to enjoin secrecy on Job Legh.

So he hardly stayed to kiss poor Mary's sweet woe-begone face, but tore himself away from his darling to go to the old man, who awaited him impatiently.

"I 've getten a note from Mr. Carsons," exclaimed Job, the moment he saw Jem; "and man-alive, he wants to see thee and me! For sure, there 's no more mischief up, is there?" said he, looking at Jem with an expression of wonder. But if any suspicion mingled for an instant with the thoughts that crossed Job's mind, it was immediately dispelled by Jem's honest, fearless, open countenance.

"I can't guess what he 's wanting, poor old chap!" answered he. "May be there 's some point he 's not yet satisfied on; may be — but it 's no use guessing; let 's be off."

"It wouldn't be better for thee to be scarce a bit, would it, and leave me to go and find out what 's up? He has, perhaps, getten some crotchet into his head thou 'rt an accomplice, and is laying a trap for thee."

"I 'm not afeard!" said Jem; "I 've done nought wrong, and know nought wrong, about yon poor dead lad; though I 'll own I had evil thoughts once on a time. Folk can't mistake long if once they 'll search into the truth. I 'll go and give the old gentleman all the satisfaction in my power, now it can injure no one. I 'd my reasons for wanting to see him besides, and it all falls in right enough for me."

Job was a little re-assured by Jem's boldness; but still, if the truth must be told, he wished the young man would follow his advice, and leave him to sound Mr. Carsons' intentions.

Meanwhile Jane Wilson had donned her Sunday suit of black,

and set off on her errand of condolence. She felt nervous and uneasy at the idea of the moral sayings and texts which she fancied were expected from visitors on occasions like the present; and prepared many a good set speech as she walked towards the house of mourning.

As she gently opened the door, Mary sitting idly by the fire, caught a glimpse of her, — of Jem's mother, — of the early friend of her dead parents, — of the kind minister to many a little want in days of childhood, — and rose and came and fell about her neck, with many a sob and moan, saying,

"Oh, he 's gone — he 's dead — all gone — all dead, and I am left alone!"

"Poor wench! poor, poor wench!" said Jane Wilson, tenderly kissing her. "Thou 'rt not alone, so donnot take on so. I 'll say nought of Him who 's above, for thou knowest He is ever the orphan's friend; but think on Jem! nay, Mary, dear, think on me! I 'm but a frabbit woman at times, but I 've a heart within me through all my temper, and thou shalt be as a daughter henceforward, — as mine own ewe-lamb. Jem shall not love thee better in his way, than I will in mine; and thou 'lt bear with my turns, Mary, knowing that in my soul God sees the love that shall ever be thine, if thou 'lt take me for thy mother, and speak no more of being alone."

Mrs. Wilson was weeping herself long before she had ended this speech, which was so different to all she had planned to say, and from all the formal piety she had laid in store for the visit; for this was heart's-piety, and needed no garnish of texts to make it true religion, pure and undefiled.

They sat together on the same chair, their arms encircling each other; they wept for the same dead; they had the same hope, and trust, and overflowing love in the living.

From that time forward, hardly a passing cloud dimmed the happy confidence of their intercourse; even by Jem would his mother's temper sooner be irritated than by Mary; before the latter she repressed her occasional nervous ill-humour till the habit of indulging it was perceptibly decreased.

Years afterwards in conversation with Jem, he was startled by a chance expression which dropped from his mother's lips;

it implied a knowledge of John Barton's crime. It was many a long day since they had seen any Manchester people who could have revealed the secret (if indeed it was known in Manchester, against which Jem had guarded in every possible way). And he was led to inquire first as to the extent, and then as to the source of her knowledge. It was Mary herself who had told all.

For on the morning to which this chapter principally relates, as Mary sat weeping, and as Mrs. Wilson comforted her by every tenderest word and caress, she revealed to the dismayed, and astonished Jane, the sting of her deep sorrow; the crime which stained her dead father's memory.

She was quite unconscious that Jem had keep it secret from his mother; she had imagined it bruited abroad as the suspicion against her lover had been; so word after word (dropped from her lips in the supposition that Mrs. Wilson knew all) had told the tale, and revealed the cause of her deep anguish; deeper than is ever caused by Death alone.

On large occasions like the present, Mrs. Wilson's innate generosity came out. Her weak and ailing frame imparted its irritation to her conduct in small things, and daily trifles; but she had deep and noble sympathy with great sorrows, and even at the time that Mary spoke she allowed no expression of surprise or horror to escape her lips. She gave way to no curiosity as to the untold details; she was as secret and trustworthy as her son himself; and if in years to come her anger was occasionally excited against Mary, and she, on rare occasions, yielded to ill-temper against her daughter-in-law, she would upbraid her for extravagance, or stinginess, or over-dressing, or under-dressing, or too much mirth, or too much gloom, but never, never in her most uncontrolled moments, did she allude to any one of the circumstances relating to Mary's flirtation with Harry Carsons, or his murderer; and always when she spoke of John Barton, named him with the respect due to his conduct before the last, miserable, guilty month of his life.

Therefore it came like a blow to Jem, when, after years had passed away, he gathered his mother's knowledge of the whole affair. From the day when he learnt (not without remorse) what hidden depths of self-restraint she had in her soul, his manner to her, always tender and respectful, became reverential; and it was more than ever a loving strife between him and Mary, which should most contribute towards the happiness of the declining years of their mother.

But I am speaking of the events which have occurred only lately, while I have yet many things to tell you that happened six or seven years ago.

CHAPTER XXXVII.

"The rich man dines, while the poor man pines,
And eats his heart away;
'They teach us lies,' he sternly cries,
Would *brothers* do as they?'"
'THE DREAM.'

MR. CARSONS stood at one of the breathing-moments of life. The object of the toils, the fears, and the wishes of his past years, was suddenly hidden from his sight, — vanished into the deep mystery which circumscribes existence. Nay, even the vengeance which he had taken away from before his eyes, as by the hand of God.

Events like these would have startled the most thoughtless into reflection, much more such a man as Mr. Carsons, whose mind, if not enlarged, was energetic; indeed, whose very energy, having been hitherto the cause of the employment of his powers in only one direction, had prevented him from becoming largely and philosophically comprehensive in his views.

But now the foundations of his past life were razed to the ground, and the place they had once occupied was sown with salt, to be rebuilt no more for ever. It was like the change from this Life to that other hidden one; when so many of the motives which have actuated all our earthly existence, will have become more fleeting than the shadows of a dream. With a wrench of his soul from the past, so much of which was as nothing, and worse than nothing to him now, Mr. Carsons took some hours, after he had witnessed the death of his son's murderer, to consider his situation.

But suddenly, while he was deliberating, and searching for motives which should be effective to compel him to exertion and action once more; while he contemplated the desire after riches, social distinction, a name among the merchant-princes amidst whom he moved, and saw these false substances fade away into the shadows they truly are, and one by one disappear into the grave of his son, — suddenly, I say, the thought arose within him that more yet remained to be learned about the circumstances and feelings which had prompted John Barton's crime; and when once this mournful curiosity was excited, it seemed to gather strength in every moment that its gratification was delayed. Accordingly he sent a message to summon Job Legh and Jem Wilson, from whom he promised himself some elucidation of what was as yet unexplained; while he himself set forth to call on Mr. Bridgenorth, whom he knew to have been Jem's attorney, with a glimmering suspicion intruding on his mind, which he strove to repel, that Jem might have had some share in his son's death.

He had returned before his summoned visitors arrived; and had time enough to recur to the evening on which John Barton had made his confession. He remembered with mortification how he had forgotten his proud reserve, and his habitual concealment of his feelings, and had laid bare his agony of grief in the presence of these two men who were coming to see him by his desire; and he entrenched himself behind stiff barriers of self-control, through which he hoped no appearance of emotion would force its way in the conversation he anticipated.

Nevertheless, when the servant announced that two men were there by appointment to speak to him, and he had desired that they might be shown into the library where he sat, any watcher might have perceived by the trembling hands, and shaking head, not only how much he was aged by the occurrences of the last few weeks, but also how much he was agitated at the thought of the impending interview.

But he so far succeeded in commanding himself at first, as to appear to Jem Wilson and Job Legh one of the hardest and most haughty men they had ever spoken to, and to forfeit all the interest which he had previously excited in their minds by his unreserved display of deep and genuine feeling.

When he had desired them to be seated, he shaded his face with his hand for an instant before speaking.

"I have been calling on Mr. Bridgenorth this morning," said he, at last; "as I expected, he can give me but little satisfaction on some points respecting the occurrence on the 18th of last month, which I desire to have cleared up. Perhaps you two can tell me what I want to know. As intimate friends of Barton's you probably know, or can conjecture a good deal. Have no scruple as to speaking the truth. What you say in this room shall never be named again by me. Besides, you are aware that the law allows no one to be tried twice for the same offence."

He stopped for a minute, for the mere act of speaking was fatiguing to him after the excitement of the last few days.

Job Legh took the opportunity of speaking.

"I 'm not going to be affronted either for myself or Jem at what you 've just now been saying about the truth. You don't know us, and there 's an end on't; only it 's as well for folk to think others good and true until they 're proved contrary. Ask what you like, Sir, I 'll answer for it we 'll either tell truth or hold our tongues."

"I beg your pardon," said Mr. Carsons, slightly bowing his head. "What I wished to know was," referring to a slip of paper he held in his hand, and shaking so much he could hardly adjust his glasses to his eyes, "whether you, Wilson, can explain how Barton came possessed of your gun. I believe you refused this explanation to Mr. Bridgenorth."

"I did, Sir! If I had said what I knew then, I saw it would criminate Barton, and so I refused telling aught. To you, Sir, now I will tell every thing and any thing; only it is but little. The gun was my father's before it was mine, and long ago he and John Barton had a fancy for shooting at the gallery; and they used always to take this gun, and brag that though it was old-fashioned it was sure."

Jem saw with self-upbraiding pain how Mr. Carsons winced at these last words, but at each irrepressible and involuntary evidence of feeling, the hearts of the two men warmed towards him. Jem went on speaking.

"One day in the week — I think it was on the Wednesday, — yes, it was — it was on St. Patrick's day, I met John just coming out of our house, as I were going to my dinner. Mother was out, and he 'd found no one in. He said he 'd come to borrow the old gun, and that he 'd have made bold, and taken it, but it was not to be seen. Mother was afraid of it, so after father's death (for while he were alive, she seemed to think he could manage it) I had carried it to my own room. I went up and fetched it for John, who stood outside the door all the time."

"What did he say he wanted it for?" asked Mr. Carsons, hastily.

"I don't think he spoke when I gave it him. At first he muttered something about the shooting-gallery, and I never doubted but that it was for practice there, as I knew he had done years before."

Mr. Carsons had strung up his frame to an attitude of upright attention while Jem was speaking; now the tension relaxed, and he sank back in his chair, weak and powerless.

He rose up again, however, as Jem went on, anxious to give every particular which could satisfy the bereaved father.

"I never knew for what he wanted the gun till I was taken up, — I do not know yet why he wanted it. No one would have had me get out of the scrape by implicating an old friend, — my father's old friend, and the father of the girl I loved. So I refused to tell Mr. Bridgenorth aught about it, and would not have named it now to any one but you."

Jem's face became very red at the allusion he made to Mary, but his honest, fearless eyes had met Mr. Carsons' penetrating gaze unflinchingly, and had carried conviction of his innocence and truthfulness; Mr. Carsons felt certain that he had heard all that Jem could tell. Accordingly he turned to Job Legh.

"You were in the room the whole time while Barton was speaking to me, I think?"

"Yes, Sir," answered Job.

"You 'll excuse my asking plain and direct questions; the information I am gaining is really a relief to my mind, I don't know how, but it is, — will you tell me if you had any idea of Barton's guilt in this matter before?"

"None whatever, so help me God!" said Job, solemnly. "To tell truth (and axing your forgiveness, Jem), I had never got quite shut of the notion, that Jem here had done it. At times I was as clear of his innocence as I was of my own; and whenever I took to reasoning about it, I saw he could not have been the man that did it. Still I never thought of Barton."

"And yet by his confession he must have been absent at the time," said Mr. Carsons, referring to his slip of paper.

"Ay, and for many a day after, — I can't rightly say how long. But still, you see, one 's often blind to many a thing that lies right under one's nose, till it 's pointed out. And till I heard what John Barton had to say yon night, I could not have seen what reason he had for doing it; while in the case of Jem, any one who looked at Mary Barton might have seen a cause for jealousy clear enough."

"Then you believe that Barton had no knowledge of my son's unfortunate, —" he looked at Jem, "of his attentions to Mary Barton. This young man, Wilson, has heard of them, you see."

"The person who told me, said clearly she neither had, nor would tell Mary's father," interposed Jem. "I don't believe he 'd ever heard of it; he weren't a man to keep still in such a matter, if he had."

"Besides," said Job, "the reason he gave on his death-bed, so to speak, was enough; 'specially to those who knew him."

"You mean his feelings regarding the treatment of the workmen by the masters; you think he acted from motives of revenge, in consequence of the part my son had taken in putting down the strike?"

"Well, Sir," replied Job, "it 's hard to say: John Barton was not a man to take counsel with people; nor did he make many words about his doings. So I can only judge from his way of thinking and talking in general, never having heard him breathe a syllable concerning this matter in particular. You see he were sadly put about to make great riches and great poverty square with Christ's Gospel" — Job paused, in order to try and express what was clear enough in his own mind, as to the effect produced on John Barton by the great and mocking contrasts presented by the varieties of human condition. Before he could find suitable words to explain his meaning, Mr. Carsons spoke.

"You mean he was an Owenite; all for equality, and community of goods, and that kind of absurdity."

"No, no! John Barton was no fool. No need to tell him that were all men equal to-night, some would get the start by rising an hour earlier to-morrow. Nor yet did he care for goods, nor wealth; no man less, so that he could get daily bread for him and his; but what hurt him sore, and rankled in him as long as I knew him (and, Sir, it rankles in many a poor man's heart far more than the want of any creature-comforts, and puts a sting into starvation itself), was that those who wore finer clothes, and eat better food, and had more money in their pockets, kept him at arm's length, and cared not whether his heart was sorry or glad; whether he lived or died, — whether he was bound for heaven or hell. It seemed hard to him that a heap of gold should part him and his brother so far asunder. For he was a loving man before he grew mad with seeing such as he was slighted, as if Christ himself had not been poor. At one time, I 've heard him say, he felt kindly towards every man, rich or poor, because he thought they were all men alike. But latterly he grew aggravated with the sorrows and suffering that he saw, and which he thought the masters might help if they would."

"That 's the notion you've all of you got," said Mr. Carsons. "Now, how in the world can we help it? We cannot regulate the demand for labour. No man or set of men can do it. It depends on events which God alone can control. When there is no market for our goods, we suffer just as much as you can do."

"Not as much, I 'm sure, Sir; though I 'm not given to Political Economy, I know that much. I'm wanting in learning, I'm aware; but I can use my eyes. I never see the masters getting thin and haggard for want of food; I hardly ever see them making much change in their way of living, though I don't doubt they 've got to do it in bad times. But it 's in things for show they cut short; while for such as me, it 's in things for life we 've to stint. For sure, Sir, you 'll own it 's come to a hard pass when a man would give aught in the world for work to keep his children from starving, and can't get a bit, if he 's ever so willing to labour. I 'm not up to talking as John Barton would have done, but that 's clear to me at any rate."

"My good man, just listen to me. Two men live in a solitude: one produces loaves of bread, the other coats, — or what you will. Now, would it not be hard if the bread-producer were forced to give bread for the coats, whether he wanted them or not, in order to furnish employment to the other: that is the simple form of the case; you've only to multiply the numbers. There will come times of great changes in the occupation of thousands, when improvements in manufactures and machinery are made. — It 's all nonsense talking, — it must be so!"

Job Legh pondered a few moments.

"It 's true it was a sore time for the hand-loom weavers when power-looms came in: them new-fangled things make a man's life like a lottery; and yet I 'll never misdoubt that power-looms, and railways, and all such-like inventions, are the gifts of God. I have lived long enough, too, to see that it is a part of His plan to send suffering to bring out a higher good; but surely it's also part of His plan that so much of the burden of the suffering as can be, should be lightened by those whom it is His pleasure to make happy, and content in their own circumstances. Of course it would take a deal more thought and wisdom than me, or any other man has, to settle out of hand how this should be done. But I 'm clear about this, when God gives a blessing to be enjoyed, He gives it with a duty to be done; and the duty of the happy is to help the suffering to bear their woe."

"Still facts have proved, and are daily proving, how much better it is for every man to be independent of help, and self-reliant," said Mr. Carsons, thoughtfully.

"You can never work facts as you would fixed quantities, and say, given two facts, and the product is so and so. God has given men feelings and passions which cannot be worked into the problem, because they are for ever changing and uncertain. God has also made some weak; not in any one way, but in all. One is weak in body, another in mind, another in steadiness of purpose, a fourth can't tell right from wrong, and so on; or if he can tell the right, he wants strength to hold by it. Now to my thinking, them that is strong in any of God's gifts, is meant to help the weak, — be hanged to the facts! I ask your pardon, Sir; I can't rightly explain the meaning that is in me. I 'm like a tap as won't run, but keeps letting it out drop by drop, so that you've no notion of the force of what 's within."

Job looked and felt very sorrowful at the want of power in his words, while the feeling within him was so strong and clear.

"What you say is very true, no doubt," replied Mr. Carsons; "but how would you bring it to bear upon the masters' conduct, — on my particular case?" added he, gravely.

"I 'm not learned enough to argue. Thoughts come into my head that I 'm sure are as true as Gospel, though may be they don't follow each other like the Q. E. D. of a Proposition. The masters has it on their own conscience, — you have it on yours, Sir, to answer for to God whether you 've done, and are doing all in your power to lighten the evils, that seem always to hang on the trades by which you make your fortunes. It 's no business of mine, thank God. John Barton took the question in hand, and his answer to it was NO! Then he grew bitter and angry, and mad; and in his madness he did a great sin, and wrought a great woe; and repented him with tears of blood, and will go through his penance humbly and meekly in t'other place, I 'll be bound. I never seed such bitter repentance as his that last night."

There was a silence of many minutes. Mr. Carsons had covered his face, and seemed utterly forgetful of their presence; and yet they did not like to disturb him by rising to leave the room.

At last he said, without meeting their sympathetic eyes,

"Thank you both for coming, — and for speaking candidly to me. I fear, Legh, neither you nor I have convinced each other, as to the power, or want of power in the masters, to remedy the evils the men complain of."

"I 'm loth to vex you, Sir, just now; but it was not the want of power I was talking on; what we all feel sharpest is the want of inclination to try and help the evils which comes like blights at times over the manufacturing places, while we see the masters can stop work, and not suffer. If we saw the masters try for our sakes to find a remedy, — even if they were long about it, — even if they could find no help, and at the end of all could only say, "Poor fellows, our hearts are sore for ye; we 've done all we could, and can't find a cure,' — we 'd bear up like men through bad times. No one knows till they have tried, what power of bearing lies in them, if once they believe that men are caring for their sorrows and will help if they can. If fellow-creatures can give nought but tears, and brave words, we take our trials straight from God, and we know enough of His love to put ourselves blind into his hands. You say, our talk has done no good. I say it has. I see the view you take of things from the place where you stand. I can remember that, when the time comes for judging you, I sha'n't think any longer, does he act right on my views of a thing, but does he act right on his own. It has done me good in that way. I 'm an old man, and may never see you again; but I 'll pray for you, and think on you and your trials, both of your great wealth, and of your son's cruel death, many and many a day to come; and I 'll ask God to bless both to you now and for evermore. Amen. Farewell!"

Jem had maintained a manly and dignified reserve ever since he had made his open statement of all he knew. Now both the men rose, and bowed low, looking at Mr. Carsons with the deep human interest they could not fail to take in one who had endured and forgiven a deep injury; and who struggled hard, as it was evident he did, to bear up like a man under his affliction.

He bowed low in return to them. Then he suddenly came forward and shook them by the hand; and thus, without a word more, they parted.

There are stages in the contemplation and endurance of great sorrow, which endow men with the same earnestness and clearness of thought that in some of old took the form of Prophecy. To those who have large capability of loving and suffering, united with great power of firm endurance, there comes a time in their woe, when they are lifted out of the contemplation of their individual case into a searching inquiry into the nature of their calamity, and the remedy (if remedy there be) which may prevent its recurrence to others as well as to themselves.

Hence the beautiful, noble efforts which are from time to time brought to light, as being continuously made by those who have once hung on the cross of agony, in order that others may not suffer as they have done; one of the grandest ends which sorrow can accomplish; the sufferer wrestling with God's messenger until a blessing is left behind, not for one alone but for generations.

It took time before the stern nature.of Mr. Carsons was compelled to the recognition of this secret of comfort, and that same sternness prevented his reaping any benefit in public estimation from the actions he performed; for the character is more easily changed, than the habits and manners originally formed by that character, and to his dying day Mr. Carsons was considered hard and cold by those who only casually saw him, or superficially knew him. But those who were admitted into his confidence were aware, that the wish that lay nearest to his heart was that none might suffer from the cause from which he had suffered; that a perfect understanding, and complete confidence and love, might exist between masters and men; that the truth might be recognised that the interests of one were the interests of all, and as such, required the consideration and deliberation of all; that hence it was most desirable to have educated workers, capable of judging, not mere machines of ignorant men; and to have them bound to their employers by the ties of respect and affection, not by mere money bargains alone; in short, to acknowledge the Spirit of Christ as the regulating law between both parties.

Many of the improvements now in practice in the system of employment in Manchester, owe their origin to short earnest sentences spoken by Mr. Carsons. Many and many yet to be carried into execution, take their birth from that stern, thoughtful mind, which submitted to be taught by suffering.

CHAPTER XXXVIII.

"Touch us gently, gentle Time!
We 've not proud or soaring wings,
Our ambition, our content,
Lies in simple things;
Humble voyagers are we
O'er life's dim unsounded sea;
Touch us gently, gentle Time!"

BARRY CORNWALL.

NOT many days after John Barton's funeral was over, all was arranged respecting Jem's appointment at Toronto; and the time was fixed for his sailing. It was to take place almost immediately: yet much remained to be done; many domestic preparations were to be made; and one great obstacle, anticipated by both Jem and Mary, to be removed. This was the opposition they expected from Mrs. Wilson, to whom the plan had never yet been named.

They were most anxious that their home should continue ever to be hers, yet they feared that her dislike to a new country might be an insuperable objection to this. At last Jem took advantage of an evening of unusual placidity, as he sat alone with his mother just before going to bed, to broach the subject; and to his surprise she acceded willingly to his proposition of her accompanying himself and his wife.

"To be sure 'Merrica is a long way to flit to; beyond London a good bit I reckon; and quite in foreign parts; but I 've never had no opinion of England, ever since they could be such fools as to take up a quiet chap like thee, and clap thee in prison. Where you go, I 'll go. Perhaps in them Indian countries they'll know a well-behaved lad when they see him; ne'er speak a word more lad, I 'll go."

Their path became daily more smooth, and easy; the present was clear and practicable, the future was hopeful; they had leisure of mind enough to turn to the past.

"Jem!" said Mary to him, one evening as they sat in the twilight, talking together in low happy voices till Margaret should come to keep Mary company through the night, "Jem! you 've never yet told me how you came to know about my naughty ways with poor young Mr. Carsons." She blushed for shame at the remembrance of her folly, and hid her head on his shoulder while he made answer.

"Darling, I 'm almost loth to tell you; your aunt Esther told me."

"Ah, I remember! but how did she know? I was so put about that night I did not think of asking her. Where did you see her? I 've forgotten where she lives."

Mary said all this in so open and innocent a manner, that Jem felt sure she knew not the truth respecting Esther, and he half hesitated to tell her. At length he replied,

"Where did you see Esther lately? When? Tell me, love, for you 've never named it before, and I can't make it out."

"Oh! it was that horrible night, which is like a dream." And she told him of Esther's midnight visit, concluding with, "We must go and see her before we leave, though I don't rightly know where to find her."

"Dearest Mary, —"

"What, Jem!" exclaimed she, alarmed by his hesitation.

"Your poor Aunt Esther has no home: — she 's one of them miserable creatures that walk the streets." And he in his turn told of his encounter with Esther, with so many details that Mary was forced to be convinced, although her heart rebelled against the belief.

"Jem, lad!" said she, vehemently, "we must find her out, we must hunt her up!" she rose as if she was going on the search there and then.

"What could we do, darling?" asked he, fondly restraining her.

"Do! Why! what could we *not* do, if we could but find her? She 's none so happy in her ways, think ye, but what she 'd turn from them, if any one would lend her a helping hand. Don't hold me, Jem; this is just the time for such as her to be out, and who knows but what I might find her, close at hand."

"Stay, Mary, for a minute; I 'll go out now and search for her if you wish, though it 's but a wild chase. You must not go. It would be better to ask the police to-morrow. But if I should find her, how can I make her come with me? Once before she refused, and said she could not break off her drinking ways, come what might."

"You never will persuade her if you fear and doubt," said Mary, in tears. "Hope yourself, and trust to the good that must be in her. Speak to that, — she has it in her yet, — oh, bring her home, and we will love her so, we 'll make her good."

"Yes!" said Jem, catching Mary's sanguine spirit; "she shall go to America with us; and we 'll help her to get rid of her sins. I 'll go now, my precious darling, and if I can't find her, it 's but trying the police to-morrow. Take care of your own sweet self, Mary," said he, fondly kissing her before he went out.

It was not to be. Jem wandered far and wide that night, but never met Esther. The next day he applied to the police; and at last they recognised under his description of her, a woman known to them under the name of the "Butterfly," from the gaiety of her dress a year or two ago. By their help he traced out one of their haunts, a low lodging-house behind Peter Street. He and his companion, a kind-hearted policeman, were admitted, suspiciously enough, by the landlady, who ushered them into a large garret where twenty or thirty people of all ages and both sexes lay and dozed away the day, choosing the evening and night for their trades of beggary, thieving, or prostitution.

"I know the butterfly was here," said she, looking round. "She came in, the night before last, and said she had not a penny to get a place for shelter; and that if she was far away in the country she could steal aside and die in a copse, or a clough, like the wild animals; but here the police would let no one alone in the streets, and she wanted a spot to die in, in peace. It 's a queer sort of peace we have here, but that night the room was uncommon empty, and I 'm not a hard-hearted woman (I wish I were, I could ha' made a' good thing out of it afore this if I were harder), so I sent her up, — but she 's not here now, I think."

"Was she very bad?" asked Jem.

"Ay! nought but skin and bone, with a cough to tear her in two."

They made some inquiries, and found that in the restlessness of approaching death, she had longed to be once more in the open air, and had gone forth, — where, no one seemed to be able to tell.

Leaving many messages for her, and directions that he was to be sent for if either the policeman or the landlady obtained any clue to her where-abouts, Jem bent his steps towards Mary's house; for he had not seen her all that long day of search. He told her of his proceedings and want of success; and both were saddened at the recital, and sat silent for some time.

After a while they began talking over their plans. In a day or two, Mary was to give up house, and go and live for a week or so with Job Legh, until the time of her marriage, which would take place immediately before sailing; they talked themselves back into silence and delicious reverie. Mary sat by Jem, his arm round her waist, her head on his shoulder; and thought over the scenes which had passed in that home, she was so soon to leave for ever.

Suddenly she felt Jem start, and started too without knowing why; she tried to see his countenance, but the shades of evening had deepened so much she could read no expression there. It was turned to the window; she looked and saw a white face pressed against the panes on the outside, gazing intently into the dusky chamber.

While they watched, as if fascinated by the appearance, and unable to think or stir, a film came over the bright, feverish, glittering eyes outside, and the form sank down to the ground without a struggle of instinctive resistance.

"It is Esther!" exclaimed they, both at once. They rushed outside; and, fallen into what appeared simply a heap of white or light-coloured clothes, fainting or dead, lay the poor crushed Butterfly — the once innocent Esther.

She had come (as a wounded deer drags its heavy limbs once more to the green coolness of the lair in which it was born, there to die) to see the place familiar to her innocence, yet once again before her death. Whether she was indeed alive or dead, they knew not now.

Job came in with Margaret, for it was bed-time. He said Esther's pulse beat a little yet. They carried her up-stairs and laid her on Mary's bed, not daring to undress her, lest any motion should frighten the trembling life away; but it was all in vain.

Towards midnight, she opened wide her eyes and looked around on the once familiar room: Job Legh knelt by the bed, praying aloud and fervently for her, but he stopped as he saw her roused look. She sat up in bed with a sudden convulsive motion.

"Has it been a dream, then?" asked she, wildly. Then with a habit, which came like instinct even in that awful dying hour, her hand sought for a locket which hung concealed in her bosom, and, finding that, she knew all was true which had befallen her since last she lay an innocent girl on that bed.

She fell back, and spoke word never more. She held the locket containing her child's hair still in her hand, and once or twice she kissed it with a long soft kiss. She cried feebly and sadly as long as she had any strength to cry, and then she died.

They laid her in one grave with John Barton. And there they lie without name, or initial, or date. Only this verse is inscribed upon the stone which covers the remains of these two wanderers.

Psalm ciii. v. 9. — "For he will not always chide, neither will he keep his anger for ever."

I see a long low wooden house, with room enough, and to spare. The old primeval trees are felled and gone for many a mile around; one alone remains to over-shadow the gable-end of the cottage. There is a garden around the dwelling, and far beyond that stretches an orchard. The glory of an Indian summer is over all, making the heart leap at the sight of its gorgeous beauty.

At the door of the house, looking towards the town, stands Mary, watching for the return of her husband from his daily work; and while she watches, she listens, smiling;

"Clap hands, daddy comes,
With his pocket full of plums,
And a cake for Johnnie."

Then comes a crow of delight from Johnnie. Then his grandmother carries him to the door, and glories in seeing him resist his mother's blandishments to cling to her.

"English letters! 'T was that made me so late!"

"Oh, Jem, Jem! don't hold them so tight! What do they say?"

"Why, some goods news. Come, give a guess what it is?"

"Oh, tell me! I cannot guess," said Mary.

"Then you give it up, do you? What do you say, mother?"

Jane Wilson thought a moment.

"Will and Margaret are married?" asked she.

"Not exactly,— but very near. The old woman has twice the spirit of the young one. Come, Mary, give a guess!"

He covered his little boy's eyes with his hands for an instant, significantly, till the baby pushed them down, saying in his imperfect way,

"Tan't see."

"There now! Johnnie can see. Do you guess, Mary?"

"They 've done something to Margaret to give her back her sight!" exclaimed she.

"They have. She has been couched, and can see as well as ever. She and Will are to be married on the twenty-fifth of this month, and he's bringing her out here next voyage; and Job Legh talks of coming too,—not to see you, Mary,—nor you, mother,—nor you, my little hero" (kissing him), "but to try and pick up a few specimens of Canadian insects, Will says. All the compliment is to the earwigs, you see, mother!"

"Dear Job Legh!" said Mary, softly and seriously.

THE END.